D1441330

BLUE BUCKET

☼☼☼

SUZANNE GRANT

Published in the United States

Author: Suzanne Grant

ISBN-13: 978-0-984015405

Version 1.0

This is a work of fiction. All characters in this novel were created by the author and are purely fictitious. If you think you are portrayed on these pages, please be assured that you are not.

suzannegrant.com

*To my antiquing gal pals—Marcia, Julie, Tina, and Delisa—and
Mike and Debbie who lit the spark and fueled the flame.*

A seed is planted to flourish and blossom. In my case, my father nourished it when he spoke of the lost Blue Bucket mine. He sparked my curiosity, and I delved deeper, searching back through time for answers. Thanks to wonders of the internet, materials in the Grant County Historical Museum, and the book *Terrible Trail: The Meek Cutoff, 1845*, coauthored by Keith Clark and Lowell Tiller, I spun my own mystery around one of Oregon's historical mysteries. I hope you enjoy reading it as much as I enjoyed writing it.

PROLOGUE

It was that damn sherry. For years, it'd been her companion, a friend with whom to share those endless, empty moments before sleep shut out the loneliness. And now it had turned on her. If she didn't reach help soon, she'd be dead.

She sucked in air and heard the rasp, like steel wool on rusty iron. Her throat was closing fast. "My desk," she gasped, eyeing the plastic tube in the outstretched hand, craving what it contained. Surely, she'd get it now.

Instead, a death grip encircled her arm and propelled her forward. She tripped on the hem of her nightgown and stumbled, only to be hauled up and dragged from the bedroom to the stairs. Steeling herself, she drew in another ragged breath and struggled to get her limp feet under her. It was hopeless. The iron arm clamped beneath her armpits towed her down the steps, her feet flopping painfully against the hardwood.

By the time she was dropped into her oak office chair, she was a rag doll—heavy and soft and numb. Fog clouded her thoughts. She fought for one more breath, then pushed through the haze to tug the top drawer open and slip her hand inside, searching for the ampoule, her only hope for survival.

"This is your last chance. It better be in there." The voice was vile, offensive, the ultimate betrayal. It was proof that you can never truly trust anyone.

She ignored it. Putting energy into talk was a luxury she couldn't afford. Besides, she'd already divulged enough.

Her hands stilled, too heavy to move. Velvety blackness oozed forward, beckoning her.

Her eyes drifted up to the painting of the covered wagons. The vibrant blue oxen yolk seemed to reach out. Finally, after all of these years of searching, she was a few mere breaths from unraveling the secret. And her life was ending. Like Olivia.

Then, from somewhere, it came to her. Just like that, the pieces slid silently into place.

As her head sank down onto the desktop, she felt a smile touch her lips. She'd done it; she knew where to find the key.

And now that secret would go to her grave with her, too.

Chapter 1

A specter's blazing eyes reached out to me through the predawn murkiness. I froze. Blood pooled heavy in my feet. Icy raindrops stung my face and hands, triggering prickly tendrils. Fatigue blurred coherent thought. Ensnared, I squinted into the twin shafts of light.

"Cripes, Kit! It's only a car," I muttered testily.

Flames of righteous indignation ignited within me—angry and festering—my mind flashing grievances: the sleepless night of plowing through neglected paperwork. The empty coffee canister. The unlit parking lot. The weather lady's delusional assurance of clear skies. And now my sweatshirt clung like chilled plastic to my back and a profusion of bulging bags inched down the fingers of my weakening left arm. One quick move and I'd kiss my night's work goodbye.

"Over my dead body," I hissed, then cringed at my choice of words. The idiot must see me, a frazzled teacher trapped in his rapidly approaching headlights.

My hand tightened around the grande skinny mocha clutched in it, my one reward for getting to work at this ungodly hour. Heat seared my palm. I winced but stood my ground and watched the threatening beams draw dangerously near.

The inconsiderate jerk; he was probably texting.

The roar of an engine and squeal of tires screamed through the murmur of pelting rain. My treasured mocha slipped to explode on the wet pavement. Scalding heat exploded on my calf, and my leg jerked, fighting the searing denim plastered against it. Bags slid from my fingers. My foot shot down to propel me onto the gritty, muddy pavement, where I landed with a jarring thud that left me numb. I swore I felt the sear of rotating tires against the soles of my Nikes—rubber against rubber—as they sped past, showering me with icy water. Bitter anger burned in my throat as I cautiously lifted my head to watch the taillights recede into the gloomy spring morning.

Good grief! At this rate, I'd be lucky to survive the day.

☼☼☼

"Please tell me you finally duked it out with S&M and she looks ten times worse than you," Patty begged, concern gradually replacing shock on her face. She was, of course, referring to our highly overrated principal, Doreen Sanders-Masters, queen bee of the elementary school in which we both taught. There was no love lost between Doreen and me, and Patty, being my closest friend, was privy to the long list of injustices that sent all respect for our boss spiraling in a never-ending stream down the toilet. In my current state, Queen Doreen would be wise to steer clear of me.

Swallowing an unflattering remark concerning our flawed leader's unethical qualities, I cringed with the pain radiating from my left knee and limped down the otherwise empty hall towards Patty. We were both wearing Friday garb—denim, baggy faded sweatshirts, and scuffed Nikes. The school mascot, an obese bumblebee, was plastered across the upper portion of her sweatshirt, resembling a set of mismatched breasts. Fortunately, my soiled sweatshirt was turned inside-out; no one would be eyeing my disparate bosom today.

I leaned against the wall to rest my aching leg while Patty's dark eyes studied me, questioning. "My God, Kit, you look like one of those messes Eleanor leaves at my front door."

My eyes dropped to scrutinize my mud-splotched jeans and shoes, a bit vexed by her remark. Now I'd spend the day worrying that I resembled one of her cat's discarded carcasses.

"Are you okay?" she prodded.

Evidently, more okay than I appeared to be. Thanks to depleted first aid supplies, a giant wad of masking tape-secured Kleenex peeked through a gaping hole over my left knee. No doubt, I looked equally as bad from the neck up. The raw abrasion on my cheek still stung.

Hoping that my hair had calmed down, I ran a hand over the unruly mess. Thankfully, an industrial-strength rubber band still corralled the coiled mass of springy spirals.

"I'm getting there," I assured her, a barely tempered fire simmering below my surface calm. "I was nearly run down in the parking lot this morning."

Patty stared at me, open-mouthed, well-tweezed brows arched high into frosted-to-mask-the-gray bangs. "By a car?"

I nodded, a painful lump quivering in my throat. Her intent gaze held mine. "An accident . . . or intentional?"

"An accident," I gasped. Still, tiny needles of unrest poked at the periphery of my mind, refusing to be squelched by my assertion. "Why would someone want to hurt me?"

"I can think of two *someones* right here in this building," she assured me.

I shifted onto my sore leg, cringed, and glanced away, only to lock eyes with one of those *someones,* his choppy bulldog strides eating up the distance between us. On my bum leg, it was too late to escape.

"Can this morning get any worse?" I muttered.

Patty frowned.

"Walker," I mouthed as he closed in from behind her, professionally pressed oxford shirt tucked neatly over his jiggling belly and into faded designer jeans. A severe crease streaked down each leg to touch faux gator cowboy boots. Not a hair on his gelled comb-over had dared to budge. Smug and arrogant, his weasel eyes were glued on me.

"Another building maintenance meeting," Patty smirked.

It was common knowledge that Dr. Ronald Walker, resident idiot and building vice principal, held as his latest conquest our day custodian Gina Bloom. For the past three months, the two of them had been doing more behind closed doors than discussing products to eradicate the urine stench that lurked outside the student restrooms.

Suddenly awash in a haze of repulsive cologne, I fought the urge to gag and tried not to stare at the shirttail peeking out his partially zipped fly.

"Surely, you ladies have something more stimulating to do than stand here and gossip?" he demanded, hands placed strategically on his narrow hips.

"So is that what you've been up to in Gina's office this morning, Ronny, stimulation?" Patty taunted.

Crimson crept from the gold chain around his neck upward until his face brought to mind a pot of simmering red-hot chili. Steaming and speechless, he glared at us.

Patty didn't let up. "Be assured that hall duty can be very stimulating. Unless you want to witness it first hand, you'd better scoot on into your office before the bell rings. Oh, and you might want to check your plumbing while you're in there."

Walker's eyes shifted down to his telltale fly, then bounced off Patty's before he made his escape, the clipped cadence of his boots on the polished floors echoing through the long hallway.

Patty shook her head. "I can't figure out if he's still obsessed with you or not."

I studied Patty. "Well, I can't figure out how you get away with that. And he definitely dislikes me. Rejection and embarrassment aren't things he handles well. He'll get his revenge."

It was an off-the-cuff remark that sent frigid shivers skittering across my shoulders. Walker rarely arrived at school before the students were safely tucked into their classrooms, and my scuffed and torn appearance hadn't seemed to surprise him. Was his dalliance with Gina the only reason he was here early on this particular morning?

"Ronny and I go way back, far enough that I don't take any crap from him," Patty declared. "And far enough that I know he's all bark, no bite." She reached out to touch my arm. "On the other hand, S&M goes for the jugular."

I shifted uncomfortably. Was Patty right? No doubt about it; Doreen was a narcissistic bitch who'd trample family and friends to get what she wanted. But Walker? Patty had known Ronny Walker before he'd become Dr. Walker. I'd only met him in August of the previous school year when I'd landed a teaching position at Hazelnut Grove Primary School. Fortunately, Walker had interviewed and hired me. Unfortunately, he'd spent the next nine months stalking me with a determination that would've put Terminator to shame.

As soon as my contract was renewed, I'd had a little heart-to-heart with Doreen, who'd informed me that Dr. Walker was a highly respected professional and that perhaps I should quit "coming on" to him. Queen Bee had made it clear: there was no place in her hive for a troublemaker. She was furious when Patty and the teachers' union had come to my rescue, but a warning from them had finally convinced Walker to keep his hands and his amorous intentions to himself.

Still, might Walker feel a need to harm me—maybe just frighten me—as retribution? Surely, not. I shoved my paranoid thoughts aside and eyed the petite redhead strutting at a brisk clip towards us, a contagious smile on her flushed face, a beige envelope waving in her hand.

"Kit, thank goodness I caught you," chirped Louise, our over-worked office manager. The staccato click of her three-inch plum heels ceased. Her smile melted. "What happened to you?"

I checked my watch; six minutes before the stampede of eager students would create pandemonium. "Short story: I took a dive onto the muddy pavement to escape a lunatic driver in the parking lot this morning."

She handed the envelope to me, her face emanating concern. "Are you all right?"

I nodded and mumbled, "Yeah," then reached for the official-looking document.

What would bring Louise away from her desk to deliver it to me in person? Memories of my lost mocha—a jolt of caffeine to take the edge off—haunted me.

No stamp decorated the envelope. The return address listed the name of a law firm, *Frye and Lewis*. My full name—Kitturah Ann

O'Maley—was scrawled across the middle. While disquieting thoughts bounced around in my head, my stomach did nosedives. A summons of some kind? Was I being accused of something awful? I looked to Louise for an explanation.

Her upper lip curled in disgust. "A very obnoxious man bulldozed his way into my office late yesterday. He was looking for you, Kit. Ronny'd told me you left early, so I told the guy to skedaddle. He wouldn't budge; said he had to deliver the letter to you by the end of the day."

A nervous tick had prodded her left eyebrow to twitch. "Jerk!" she snapped. "As if I hand out home addresses willy-nilly to just anyone." She paused to compose herself, then added, "After I informed him of the legal issues surrounding confidentiality and promised on the graves of various ancestors and deceased pets to give it to you first thing this morning, he finally gave me the letter. Ronny wanted to drop it by your house last night but. . . ."

"Well, open it," Patty demanded.

Chunks of foreboding churned in my gut. I studied Louise. "Did you have to sign for it?"

She nodded, scowling, her eyes flicking her office.

I sighed. How bad could it be? I ripped open the envelope and unfolded the enclosed letter, then glanced at Patty and Louise. Their eyes were scanning back and forth over the upside-down lines. My eyes dropped to join theirs, a race to read the entire letter before they did. As I read, puzzlement replaced apprehension.

The message was brief and to the point: on the following Friday, one week from today, my presence was requested at the reading of the will of Levina Ann Johnson.

"Who's Levina Johnson?" Patty asked.

I shook my head. "I haven't a clue."

"Well, think of it as a day off work," Louise advised. "All you have to do is listen to some attorney spout off for a few minutes. Then you can spend the rest of the day shopping. Let me know if you want company. I'm always up for a trip to Nordies and a leisurely lunch that isn't interrupted to hand out baggies of ice." She patted my arm reassuringly and headed back to her office. "And fill out an accident report," she threw over her shoulder.

I shrugged resignedly and looked to Patty. Her brows were furled, her lips working. Finally, a quirky smile lit up her face. "Say, didn't you tell me you were born here in Oregon? Maybe this Levina is connected to you from way back then, a long lost relative worth millions. You'll be able to leave S&M and Ronny and all of their crap behind and travel to your heart's content. I'll even make the sacrifice and haul your luggage around for you."

"Sorry, dear." I shook my head. "I don't have any relatives.

None. Not even a nasty eccentric hidden away in the closet. My mother died thirty-two years ago when I was two. After that, it was just my father and me. And he avoided Oregon like the plague. Claimed there was nothing left for us here, that our past was best left buried."

"Well, I'm fresh out of ideas. You think you'll go?"

"I am intrigued," I admitted.

Patty eyed the rattling front doors where students were jockeying to be the first to charge down the halls to their classrooms. "You could call the law office," she suggested.

"Yeah . . . but when?" I sighed, frustrated with a daily schedule that forced maintenance of a behemoth bladder and didn't afford a five-minute private phone conversation.

A deafening buzz vibrated the air around us. Patty snarled, then planted herself in the middle of the hall, palms facing forward in an attempt to slow the mob storming through the doors. Soon the breakfast crowd would swarm from the opposite direction. Miraculously, we always survived the melee without an injury.

"Friday school days should be banned," I uttered, lost in thought, barely aware of hurrying bodies pummeling me.

Clearly upset by memories from his past, my father had always skirted my relentless questions concerning my birthplace. I'd moved to the Portland area with hope of finding answers to some of those questions. Now nearly two years had passed while I wrestled with the trepidation with which he'd gifted me. So far, no doors had opened.

I stared at the letter. Was it the key to my past I'd always dreamed of finding?

CHAPTER 2

Raindrops pelted me like spitballs. I hunched further into my umbrella and stared at the water bouncing off the wet sidewalks, cascading into overflowing street gutters. A gust of bodies pushed their way past from left and right, and I peeked from under my umbrella to watch for a *walk* signal just as a TriMet bus sped past and threw up an icy spray. Several disgruntled remarks from the sea of drenched overcoats and dripping umbrellas followed its passing.

My heart raced madly as I gazed across the street at the building I sought. It rose high into the gray-shrouded Portland sky, a fortress of glass and steel. I swallowed hard, fighting to control the anxious twitters that had my insides churning. Soon I would find out why I was invited to the reading of the will of a woman I'd never met. Fervor and fear waged a heated battle within me. Why was I here?

During the past week, I'd done my homework, a lesson in frustration and futility. All the law office would disclose to me was that I was listed as a person who was needed at the reading of Levina Johnson's will. An internet search disclosed that Levina had died of natural causes the week before I'd received my summons. A brother and sister and several other relatives, none of whom were familiar to me, survived her.

I'd learned that Levina's hometown, Aurora, was a historic district touted as the *Antique Capital of Oregon*. Since I'd never been there and wouldn't know an antique if it plopped into my lap, that information didn't initiate any *ah-hahs*. Settled by Germans in the 1850's, the town was nestled midst endless miles of Willamette Valley farmland about forty miles south of Portland. More dead-ends.

There were several Levina-related blurbs on the internet concerning garden club, historical society, town council, and Red Hat functions. No help there. I'd even perused my father's correspondence and records. No mention of anyone named Johnson. Basically, I'd drawn a big blank. As I saw it, my only option was to take the afternoon off from work to attend this meeting in the heart of a downtown Portland downpour.

The signal flashed white, and the throng surged forward, me

along with it. My pulse quickened with each step; my head pounded with apprehension.

Visions of my father flashed before me, a father who was now dead, a victim of melanoma in his mid fifties. *He* was my family. Orphaned at the age of twelve, he'd passed his adolescence in a series of foster homes and in and out of Oregon's juvenile rehabilitation system. It was my mother who'd saved him—or so he'd always claimed. That was all he'd say about my mother, other than the fact that she was killed in an automobile accident one summer afternoon when I was two years old, the day my life, as I knew it, began.

I had no photo albums filled with baby pictures and adoring parents, doting grandparents or playmate cousins. No little plastic rattles or locks of silken baby hair. Not even a wedding photo to put a face to the woman who'd once cradled me in her arms. In my father's words: "There's nothing left for us back there, Kitty. It's all gone." It was the angst in his eyes when he muttered those words that hinted at more. Was it really gone or just too painful for him to discuss?

"If you plan to stand there much longer, please step to the side, so we can get past." The voice was deep and smooth as well-aged bourbon with a pinch of Southern heritage and a fistful of irritation. My arm shot up, the umbrella with it, and a frigid shower of raindrops startled me out of my reverie. In front of me was a pair of glass doors. Cripes! How long had I been standing there? Heat radiated in my cheeks as I stepped aside to allow the rude man to pass by and into the building.

I glimpsed him as he shuffled past—willow-thin and hunched with age, rain streaming off his felt hat and tan overcoat—and stared. The voice didn't match the man.

Prepared to apologize for making him stand in the relentless downpour, I caught movement at the corner of my eye and watched a younger man trail the older gentleman. Tall and ramrod straight in a drenched Gore Tex jacket, worn jeans, and leather hiking boots, he had to be the owner of the arrogant voice. A dripping ponytail clung to his broad back. He leaned close to the elderly man, then put a hand on his arm to steer him around a corner.

Dreary gray dampness pressed in on me, suffocating, exacerbating the pounding in my head. I reached up to confirm that my unruly curls were still firmly confined in a somewhat tidy bun at the base of my neck before I pushed open the door.

The law offices of *Frye and Lewis* were on the fifth floor. The reception area was sleek and nondescript in varying shades of beige, with black accents and enough large potted fronds to cut the austerity. With her brown skin and black hair, the receptionist was a chameleon. Her snug skirt and high-heeled boots were black, an affirmation that I'd made the correct choice with my black slacks and sweater. I trailed her swinging hips down a narrow hall and gulped when she stopped and motioned for me to precede her.

My heart threatened to pound through my chest as I pushed the door open and stepped into the room. Six startled faces turned to gape at me. The urge to retrace my footsteps was strong, but the chameleon blocked my exit.

"This is Ms. O'Maley," she announced.

As if on cue, jaws dropped and eyes popped. My face was aflame, not a good thing when one is fair-skinned. Instinctively, my eyes skimmed the other occupants, who were seated loosely around a rectangular conference table, and came to rest on the two men who'd preceded me into the building. Still dripping, the younger man towered over his elder, a scowl marring his chiseled features. The only people who appeared to be unperturbed by my presence were the older gentleman and a man in an expensive-looking charcoal suit who sat at the head of the table. The former looked glum and the latter rose from his chair.

"I'm Pete Lewis," he said, offering his hand, "Levina's attorney." He had a reassuring smile and an unremarkable face that was most likely older than it looked.

"Kit O'Maley," I responded with surprising poise considering the roomful of strangers who were ogling me. I focused on Pete.

He turned to the chameleon. "Is this everyone?"

"Jack isn't here yet," she informed him.

Pete frowned. "We'll start without him. When he shows up, he can join us."

He cupped my elbow and steered me toward a chair, where he took my raincoat to add to the already loaded coat tree that slouched in the corner. I swore I heard the tree groan with the added weight of yet another waterlogged coat to its branches; then again, the complaint might've come from one of the three unsmiling faces across from me.

Ever so slowly, I set my umbrella and purse on the floor, my head spinning with trepidation. No doubt about it, I'd never laid eyes on any of these people before. But they seemed to know who I was.

While Pete slipped on a pair of wire-rimmed glasses and shuffled through a stack of papers, I gave myself a quick mental pep talk. Confrontation, even staring down dirty looks, wasn't one of my fortes. I braced myself and raised my eyes to meet the glares emanating from across the table.

A white-haired woman wearing enough bling to decorate the holiday tree in Pioneer Square sat directly across from me. Though small in stature and fine-boned, she sat tall, as if someone had glued a steel rod down her spine. Her dark eyes pierced mine with what could only be hostility . . . and something else. Fear perhaps?

On her left sat her clone—same features and but in a much younger, more wired version, her hair still lustrously blonde. A strikingly handsome, though somewhat tattered, man finished out the unfriendly trio. There was enough of a resemblance between him and the two women that I was confident they were related through genetics rather than marriage. With my nearly black hair, green eyes, and height, I was certain I hadn't even a shoestring connection to their gene pool, nor did I desire one; they looked downright mean.

To my right were the two men I'd trailed into the building. I could feel them studying me, but fastened my gaze on Pete, my quivering hands clenched in my lap.

At last, Pete removed his glasses and looked up. "As you're aware, we're here to read the last will and testament of Levina Ann Johnson. So rather than keep you all waiting, we'll go ahead and get started."

He glanced around the table, then worried his lower lip a bit. "Maybe we should start with introductions." He looked to his left. "Bernice, why don't you start?"

Bernice looked like she'd rather drink a bottle of battery acid. She flashed Pete a nasty look, pursed her lips and announced haughtily, "Bernice Oates, Levy's sister."

"Janet Bass. Aunt Levy was my aunt," uttered the blonde woman shakily. Bernice placed her hand over Janet's and squeezed it. Evidently, Janet was having a rough day.

"Roy Oates. Ditto," said the handsome man before he stuffed a stick of gum into his mouth.

Cousins or siblings? It was difficult to tell. Roy oozed an easy self-confidence that Janet lacked.

"Bart Graves." It was the voice I'd heard while standing in the rain, more cultured and minus the sharp edge. "Levina and I were . . . close."

Close? With a seventy-year-old woman? How wealthy was this Levina lady? I leaned forward to shoot a fleeting glance down the table to where Bart sat, long, slender fingers folded on the table in front of him and dark hair and goatee emitting an arrogant, sinister air. His cold gaze met mine, and I shrank back into my chair to hide behind the man next to me.

"I'm Milton Hein. Levina was my neighbor. My sweetheart," he said, a catch in his husky voice. "I'm gonna miss her."

With Milton's words, a tidal wave of emotions crested within me. I, too, had lost the love of my life. The fact that it was two years ago and that I'd lost him to another woman was irrelevant; it still hurt like hell. Tears stung my eyes, and I fought the urge to put my arm around Milton and tell him that he would be okay—never the same again, but the engulfing pain would eventually fade into a dull, empty ache.

"Ms. O'Maley?"

It was Pete. My brain was mushy peas. What could I say: *Kit O'Maley. No idea who in the hell Levy was.* I steeled myself, my vision blurred. "Kit O'Maley," I mumbled.

"And?" Pete prompted.

"And nothing." My mouth felt like it was stuffed with cotton balls, but I was becoming annoyed with the whole situation. "I don't know why I'm here. I assume there's a reason you invited me?"

Pete blinked. "Uh . . . yes. You're one of the. . . ."

"Sorry I'm late. Rain's a royal bitch out there," claimed a gravelly voice from behind me. I followed the lead of those around me and turned to see who'd joined us.

He stood tall, over six feet, and sported a healthy head of snowy hair and a bushy mustache. His complexion was ruddy and gnarled. When his bloodshot eyes landed on me, shock registered in them. That shock morphed into a disgruntled frown. Life came to an uncomfortable halt in the room while he glowered at me.

"Good lord, Jack! Would you quit standing there like a gawking idiot and take a seat so we can get this over with," demanded Bernice irritably.

Jack took a couple of steps and leaned down, engulfing me in whiskey fumes. "You're like your mother," he mumbled before he shuffled to the other end of the table.

Bitter bile rose in my throat—whether from the second-hand alcohol or Jack's words I wasn't sure—and I struggled to keep it there. My mother! Jack had known my mother?

A hand on my arm offered comfort. Hesitantly, I met Milton's concerned eyes.

"Levina didn't talk with you, did she?" he asked.

Blinking at the sting of tears, I shook my head.

"She planned to. Guess she didn't get to it. She had too much on her plate what with the antiques and the garden club and . . . her research. She was healthy as a young ox. Probably thought she had all the time in the world to see to you."

"See to me?" I asked shakily. "Why?"

"Good lord, Pete! Would you get this thing going so we can get out of here before rush hour."

It was Bernice again. The woman was a tyrant. I glared at her and relished the look of surprise on her face. "Perhaps you can answer my question then?" I challenged.

She huffed several times, then barked, "Levy was your aunt, your mother's sister. I'm your aunt, too. And Jack's your uncle. Roy and Janet are my children." She brushed me aside to turn her claws on Pete. "Can we *please* get started now?" It was more a command than a request.

The room spun around me as if I were on a carousel looking out at the blurred faces of those who were watching. Fearful that I was going to be sick in front of these unpleasant strangers, I dropped my eyes to my lap and breathed deeply, trying to still the waves pounding in my head. Somewhere in the background, Pete's voice droned on.

For as long as I could remember, I'd dreamed of this day. Only it wasn't supposed to be like this. Where were the love and joy, the hugs and kisses? My father's words echoed through my mind: "Wishes can turn on you, Kitty."

Although these people claimed to be my blood relation, they weren't welcoming me into their lives. In fact, it was clear that they wanted me out of their lives. Why?

"Ms. O'Maley?"

Somewhere in the fog, someone called my name. I looked up at Pete.

"Are you okay?" he asked, his face full of concern.

Was I okay? If I told him that I wanted to go back to living in the dark, full of hope and dreams, would he let me walk out of here and then forget about me? My presence here couldn't be of any importance, a long lost niece Levina had never met. I managed to nod.

"Rather than read the entire will, Bernice has asked me to summarize it, and the others are in agreement. Do you have a problem with that?"

I shook my head. The sooner I got out of here, the better.

"Okay. Well, let's see then." Pete fidgeted with his papers before he skimmed several pages and continued. "Levina had me write up this will last month. It was. . . ."

"That's bullshit, Pete," Bernice snapped. "You wrote Levy's will years ago. I have a copy of it at home. Jack has one, too, don't you, Jack?" Bernice was leaning forward, nearly in Pete's face. Her eyes were smoking. Roy didn't look any too happy, either. Janet was visibly trembling.

"Sure do," Jack slurred. My eyes traveled down the table to where Jack sat slumped back in his chair, his eyes glazed and droopy.

Pete cleared his throat and plodded on. "Unless you have one that is more recent than April 6, 2006, this *is* her last will and testament and it *will* hold up in court."

"I don't know what you're trying to pull here, Pete, but there's no way on God's green earth that Levy asked you to rewrite her will and didn't tell me about it," Bernice fumed.

Roy's perturbed sigh funneled across the table. "Let's hear what Pete has to say before we make accusations, Mother," he said, looking more like his sister, jaws madly masticating gum, fingers drumming on the table.

Bernice shot her son a look that would deflate Donald Trump, but she did keep her mouth shut. Roy was too busy glaring at me to notice.

"Well, all right then." Pete gulped. With Bernice in his face, her eyes throwing daggers at him, it was no wonder he was hesitant to continue. "I'll start with her bequeaths."

He pushed at his glasses and perused the page in front of him before his eyes traveled to the far end of the table. "Jack, Levina willed you your great-grandfather's tools. They're in a carpenter's chest in the basement of her house."

"Well, thank goodness she didn't sell them," Bernice chimed. "Those tools go way back in our family."

I looked down the table to see how Jack was taking the news that he'd inherited the family tools. He was scowling. "That's it?" he muttered gruffly.

"Appears to be," Pete told him.

"Hardly worth the effort it took to get here. Not sure what the hell I'm supposed to do with a bunch of old beat up tools," Jack grumbled, pushing himself unsteadily to his feet.

"Sit down, Jack," Bernice demanded tersely.

Jack eyed her blearily, then sank back into his chair.

Pete cleared his voice. "Milton, Levina left you the 1936 Cord. She wants you to know that her spirit will be with you when you take it out for a drive."

Poor Milton. He pulled a white handkerchief from his pocket and dabbed at the tears trickling down his cheeks. A burning lump lodged in my throat. I focused on Pete, reliving the pain of lost love, and willed Bernice to keep her big mouth shut.

"Bart, Levina wanted you to have several of those rare Civil War books you've been eyeing. I'll give you a list of the titles."

"That was thoughtful of her," was Bart's response

"Thoughtful of her? It goes way beyond that. Those books are worth a shit load of money and you know it," Roy challenged, shifting his glare from me to Bart.

I peeked around Milton. Bart appeared unfazed, his eyes meeting Roy's evenly. "Their value isn't monetary," he replied. "Levina knew I'd appreciate them."

Roy came up out of his chair and stabbed an index finger at Bart. "If you know what's good for you, you'll leave those books right where they are. They belong to *my* family. You might've fooled her but you don't fool me. Hanging around a bunch of old folks, so you can con them out of what they have. We all know why you befriended Aunt Levy."

I studied Bart. Was he now befriending Milton to get what he could from him? Just how much of a sleaze was he?

Whatever the case, he seemed unaffected by Roy's tirade. "I'm assuming they're still locked in the bookcase in her office?" he asked Pete.

If they were fighting over a bunch of old books that couldn't be worth more than a few bucks, I wondered what would happen when we got to the good stuff. I looked to Pete, my heart beating wildly. Was I on his hit list?

Pete nodded to Bart before he glanced warily at Roy, who was back in his seat, fretfully chewing and cracking his knuckles. Finally, he eyed Janet. She grabbed her mother's hand and gnawed agitatedly on her lower lip.

"Janet, Levina wanted you to have her antique dolls. They're in the smaller upstairs bedroom in her house. You'll get a list of the contents of the collection."

Janet seemed to be waiting for Pete to continue. At last she scowled and squeaked shakily, "Is that all?"

"Yes," Pete informed her, nodding.

"That's not right. I get the house and store," Janet shrieked. "Aunt Levy promised."

Bernice slid her arm around Janet and patted her shoulder. "Don't you worry; we'll get to the bottom of this." Her focus slid to Pete. "I *know* what Levy wanted and it's not this. If she had you draw up a new will, she was under duress. Not thinking straight. Obsessed by those old Blue Bucket rumors that had no credence whatsoever. Just like Olivia. This *is not* right." She ended her speech with a wounding glower aimed at me.

No way was I going to take the blame for her dysfunctional family. I met her twin daggers and didn't give an inch, surprised by my nerve. Something about Bernice brought out the warrior in me. Perhaps it was in deference to my mother, who must've had to endure hell with this beastly sister plaguing her childhood.

"Levina had full mental capacity when we discussed her wishes and she asked me to draw up this new will. If you feel you need to contest it, go ahead, but it'll save you money and a whole lot of headaches if you just accept it." Pete took a deep breath and glanced at me. "Levina had her reasons for making the changes. Some things came to. . . ."

"And they were all based on a misplaced guilty conscience," Bernice interrupted. "Olivia was headstrong and impulsive. She lived in her own little dream world. What happened to her was because of her own doings, not anyone else's."

My heart pounded at the mention of my mother. This was more information about her than I'd gotten from thirty years of begging to my father. Bernice's description of her wasn't very flattering. What did my mother's death have to do with what was going on here today? I searched faces for answers. All eyes were riveted on the exchange between Pete and Bernice.

"So what did Levy leave me in this *new* will?" Bernice challenged.

If looks could speak, Pete's would say that he'd give his gold Rolex for the opportunity to fade unobtrusively from the room. I tensed.

Pete rubbed his forehead and scanned the papers on his desk. He coughed, then met Bernice's fiery gaze. "She left you the emerald necklace, your mother's ruby ring, and the diamond and sapphire brooch."

"That's it?" Bernice yelped incredulously, leaning forward, mouth hanging open.

Pete nodded. "You'll find them in the safe."

"And Roy?" she asked, her eyes spitting venom.

"Roy gets his grandfather's watch and the sterling vesta and desk set. Levina kept them in her office."

Roy bounced in his chair, his dark eyes popping before they dropped to his trembling hands. He breathed deeply and harrumphed, then sank back, eyes fretful and arms crossed over his chest, jaws hammering.

"And the rest of it: the store? The house? The money?" Bernice demanded.

Pete glanced my way and seemed to waver, then breathed deeply and announced, "Everything else is to go to her niece Kitturah Ann O'Maley, daughter of David and Olivia O'Maley."

The store, the house, the money? Everything? Numbed with shock, fighting nausea and dizziness, I glanced around the table at the unbridled rage rife in most of the faces. These people detested me.

All I could think was *Oh, God, what have my wishes gotten me into?*

"And what if *she* dies?" Bernice spat, her voice raw with fury.

His face now a pasty white, Pete stared at her in disbelief. "Well . . . then her estate is to be divided evenly between you and your offspring and Jack."

I closed my eyes against the evil permeating the room. Cripes! These people didn't just detest me; they wanted me dead.

CHAPTER 3

Yellow crime scene tape stretched along the white picket fence that marked the periphery of the tidy yard, blocking anyone from getting near the impressive honey-colored house cloistered beneath two massive maples. The inviting front porch and flowery tole-painted welcome sign were a tease. To further discourage wayward thoughts of trespassing, two black and white police cruisers sat in the driveway to the right of the house.

"This is getting too weird," I said to Patty, transfixed by the scene before me. Since discovering that I not only had family but that they would happily disinherit me—maybe even figure out a way to get rid of me—I'd been an emotional mess. My stomach churned, my mind wandered in troubling circles, and my limbs twitched as if I'd chugged a dozen espressos. This new development wasn't helping.

"Are you sure this is the right address?" Patty asked from the passenger seat of my Santa Fe, her eyes studying me through rhinestone-studded sunglasses.

My eyes dropped to the slip of paper I held in my hand. The number matched the one on the floral plaque beside the front door. "This is Levina's house."

"Maybe your new kinfolk ransacked it."

"Maybe." I thought back to the meeting the previous day. "After the attorney popped their bubbles, Bernice and her troops stormed out in a flurry of glowers and threats. The other two men were on their heels. Milton—bless his heart—paused long enough to invite me over for a glass of his homemade gooseberry sherry once I get moved in."

Patty's lips puckered into what resembled a pair of dried prunes. "Gooseberry, huh? Once you taste it, you might not be blessing him quite so freely. What about the other guy?"

"He treated me as if I was an unsavory crumb he could flick aside." I shivered with the memory of the hostility in his glowering black eyes. "He's big and dark and hairy, a real mountain man. Probably lives in a cave up in the Coast Range. Whatever the case, I doubt I'll ever see him again."

I squinted at the front of the house, searching for clues to what was going on inside, then let my gaze wander the green lawn and colorful bushes. For weeks, the spring weather had been an endless series of cold, dreary downpours. Today was pull-out-the-stops gorgeous. Even the rhododendron and azalea blossoms were smiling.

Too bad my mood didn't match the cheery flora. Patty had dragged me on this mission. "Just to check things out," she'd prodded. "If you know what you're dealing with, you won't feel so blindsided. And you'll figure out what to do next."

Ah yes, that was the big question: what was I going to do with this newfound, supposed windfall? And this newfound family? Unfortunately, I *could* picture them breaking into Levina's house to pilfer what they could before I arrived.

"What do you do when the family you've always dreamed of suddenly materializes?" I wondered aloud. "Only they're worse than any worse case scenario imaginable."

Patty sighed and eyed me. Oh, great! She had her lecture face on. "No family is perfect, Kit. They'll take some getting used to."

Shifting uncomfortably under her scrutiny, I considered my four genetic links. "Depending on how close a friend he is to whiskey, Jack might be okay. But Bernice and her brats will never warm up to me."

"Which has its perks: they won't be hanging around your house," she pointed out.

"If I take the house," I muttered.

I could feel her eyes piercing me, tiny darts trying to puncture my reasoning. "My God, Kit! Don't tell me you're thinking about giving it all to those bozos?"

So now they were bozos.

"This is not about those four screwballs. Your aunt chose to leave this house and store and whatever money she had to you. Don't you dare feel guilty about accepting what's rightfully yours." Irritation was evident in her voice.

I examined the ominous structure secured behind yellow plastic ribbon. The mere thought of owning it and the responsibility of managing a business were worse than any stomach flu I'd ever endured. Was it merely too much, too fast, or a petrifying fear of the unknown?

"I'm not a house person," I explained. "Since we didn't stay in any one place longer than a year or two, my father and I always lived in apartments."

"It's a house, Kit, not a commitment."

Shudders shot through me in the warmth of the car. "It *is* a commitment," I argued. "Besides, it'd take over an hour both ways to drive to work."

"So tell Ronny and S&M where to shove it and walk out of there. Try your hand at selling antiques. You might find you're ready to settle down and stay in one place."

What had Patty put in her coffee this morning? "I don't know diddly about antiques. And I won't give up teaching; it's my life," I argued.

She sighed, clearly exasperated. "Kit, isn't it time for you to have a life? I've seen those photo albums you've spent eons of hours scrap booking. They're full of buildings and scenery—places. Not homes. Not people."

An image of my father flashed before me, a haunting sadness shrouding his features even when he smiled. He was the one constant in my life. It was when he retreated further into himself and I sensed his growing unrest that I'd pack our meager belongings. My father couldn't handle attachments.

"I knew we'd be moving on," I reasoned. "Why get close to someone you'll soon be leaving behind?"

"Like me?" she probed, her voice husky.

Yes, like you, I realized. Only I had gotten close to Patty. A heavy ache swelled in my chest.

"I know you don't want to hear this," Patty said, "And I probably have no business saying it, but I don't want to see you toss away the one opportunity you might have to. . . ."

It wasn't like Patty to lose her train of thought. I turned to see what had drawn her attention. A man in faded jeans and a black tee-shirt had exited the house. Vague memories twitched. His head swiveled and my heart rate kicked up a notch. Surely, that wasn't a ponytail?

I blinked hard. "Cripes!" I muttered. "What's *he* doing here?"

"Mountain man?" Patty asked.

He was closing in on us. "In the flesh," I mumbled, wondering if he would stop to make a curt comment or just curl his lip in disgust and proceed on his way.

"You didn't tell me he was a hunk."

A hunk? Was she joking? Her eyes were fixed on the man who was now stepping over the crime scene tape. He looked up and met my stare, a glint of recognition flashing across his chiseled features before his black brows slashed into a frown. A slight dip of his head in what, under hostile conditions, might be construed a greeting and he was on his way to the gray house next door.

Irked by his rudeness, I searched for something to distract Patty from further conversation concerning the *hunk*. "That must be where Milton lives," I finally offered.

She squinted at the gray house. "Why's that?"

Ah, success. "Well, because Milton said he's Levina's

neighbor, and he and that guy seemed to be friends."

"Speaking of *that guy*, you need to clean your contacts, girl."

I ground my teeth. With a persistence that was unstoppable, Patty pushed men at me. And I was currently off men. I'd already met and lost the love of my life. Until hell froze over, I wouldn't be putting myself out on that brittle limb again. Besides, I wasn't clinging to some desperate mid thirties timeline. If I wanted to take a man break, so be it.

"Patty, he's a jerk. A big, brawny, arrogant, rude jerk," I stormed. "He's probably worried about his precious books, afraid he won't get them. Besides, my guess is he prefers older women—much older."

Patty shook her head. "I don't want to pry, so if you'd rather I shut up and mind my own business, please tell me. Not that I will, of course."

A smile touched my lips.

Her grin told me she cared. "So tell me; what *do* you want, Kit."

"Not a man," I stated emphatically.

"Then what? There must be something you want from this whole experience."

That was easy. It was something I'd hungered for since I was a small child. "I want to know my mother," I told her. "Who was she? What color were her eyes? Did she like caramels and capers like me? Was she as fond of baking as I am? Did I inherit my Amazon height and this horrendous hair from her? And I want to be a part of something—to belong."

Those old feelings pulsed through me, a driving need to know and understand. I struggled to compose myself, to calm my pounding heart.

"Well, there you go," Patty reasoned. "Your mother's history is here, not back in Hazelnut Grove Primary School and not in that cookie cutter apartment you live in."

I studied Levina's imposing home. I wanted to believe Patty's words, but some ever-vigilant part of me reminded me to keep a grip on reality. Was I willing to give up my teaching and a paycheck for something with no guarantees? I might end up alone, except for my loony relatives, with a money-guzzling house and no funds to maintain it.

A sudden knocking sound on the window behind Patty sent my already frazzled nerves into spasms. Patty flinched and spun around. An elderly woman peeked in at us, her youthful bright eyes at odds with the deep wrinkles ingrained in her pale face. Flashy pink earrings dangled from her earlobes, and white hair padded her forehead, bringing to mind the Chia pet I'd nurtured as a child.

Fighting it all the way, I climbed out of the car and walked to the other side. Patty was already towering over the tiny woman who wore a sweat suit so pink it would put a flamingo to shame.

Aware that I was several inches taller than Patty, I slouched. No need to overwhelm the poor lady. "I'm Kit O'Maley," I said, extending a hand. "This is my friend Patty."

Her hand was easily lost in mine, soft and fragile as parchment. Sharp eyes narrowed with interest. "So you're Levina's long lost niece, eh?" Without breaking stride, she shook Patty's hand. "Can't tell you how much you've got things riled up around here. Serves them right, too. All they ever gave Levina was a lot of grief. Guess she showed them, huh? It's most likely one of them that did it."

"I beg your pardon," I asked, unclear of exactly who did what.

"Oh, I'm sorry. I'm Sophie Williams. I live in that white house, the one that's not for sale." She pointed a slightly bowed index finger at a small house across the street from us. The door was a vibrant hot pink, as were the profusion of rhododendrons and plastic flamingos dotting the yard and the wicker furniture that sat on the front porch. I shuddered as visions of strawberries and cream danced in my head; I was deathly allergic to strawberries.

"Mind you, Levina and I were close enough to share secrets," Sophie informed us. "You seem like a nice girl. Thank goodness she left her stuff to you instead of that bitchy Bernice and her brood. They treated Levina like she was white trash. Like she owed them the world, especially Bernice and that psycho daughter of hers. The two of them have a spending addiction, you know. Go through money like they have to get rid of the old to make room for the new. The whole lot of them were always after Levina to fork over dough to get their farm or some piece of crap out of hock, especially Roy. Way I hear it, he foots the bills for the whole worthless clan."

Sophie paused to catch her breath and I jumped in. "Do you know what's going on here?"

Undeterred, she blinked several times, then continued. "Roy's got his good points. At least, *he* spent time with Levina. Dropped by for a visit. Checked on the house and store when she was gone. Took her to dinner now and then. Even invited me to join them a couple of times. Course, he always let Levina pick up the tab. Creepy, though, how he'd hang out in her house when she wasn't around. Knowing who his mother is, there has to be something not quite right with him, too.

"Then there's Jack. Mind you, I'm not one to spread gossip. But I don't call it gossip if it's the honest to God truth. And it's clear as my pear jelly that Jack imbibes, if you get my drift. Can't even remember the last time I saw him that he wasn't slurring his words and reeking of liquor. Heard he spends a lot of time at the casino in Grand Ronde, too. Too bad; he's a hotty when he's sober."

Patty was ogling Sophie, her eyebrows arched high over her rhinestoned rims. I listened with half an ear, interested in news of my kinfolk yet anxious to learn why crime scene tape enclosed my new prospective property.

"Janet's husband was a nice guy. Don't know how he got mixed up with her, what with her mental problems and all. Finally got smart and divorced her. They have a son and he seems okay. When he was younger, he spent some time with Levina."

Janet had a son? Perhaps the kid hadn't inherited the loony gene. I was about to interrupt and question Sophie about him when a middle-aged man in a blue uniform stepped out the front door of the house. Light flashed from the silver badge pinned to his shirt. A blast of adrenalin shot my already over-stimulated system into hyper-drive.

Sophie must've noticed him, too, because there were two seconds of silence before she charged on. "That's just Cal, the police chief. He can be a pain in the patooty, but you'll get along fine with him. He'll ask you some questions. That's standard procedure. He'll want to talk with me, too, and mind you, I have plenty to tell him what with people snooping around here at all hours of the night and. . . ."

I jerked around to question Sophie just as Patty asked, "People snooping around here? What do you mean?"

The chief had spotted us and was fast approaching. He looked troubled, his bushy eyebrows furled and his mustache twitching. Sophie scampered around the car towards him at a surprisingly brisk pace. Patty and I locked eyes, shrugged and fell in behind her.

"What'd I tell you, Cal," Sophie screeched, waving her crooked finger at him. "I told you there was something fishy goin' on, didn't I? And you wouldn't listen to me. No, sirrreee. You think I'm dementiatic, don't you? Well, I'm not one to rub it in a person's face, mind you, but I was right, wasn't I?" Sophie's finger nearly tapped the chief's nose.

He scowled at her, chewing on the hair hanging over his upper lip, then stepped aside and held out his hand to Patty. "Cal Preston, Chief of Police."

Patty shook his hand. "Patty Lowens," she said in a strangely syrupy voice. I easily envisioned an intent gleam in her eyes.

I checked him out, too. Not bad but much closer to Patty's age than mine and only a couple of inches taller than me. He was slim, wiry, as if he were all sinewy muscle under his uniform. Flecks of gray gleamed in his closely clipped brown hair, and his face wore the wrinkles of too much stress and time in the sun. When he turned to me, his handshake was firm, confident.

"Kit O'Maley," I said. "I'm Levina's niece. She left this house to me."

Interest sparked in his sapphire eyes, his gaze intensifying as he studied me. Not one to take on a challenge, I instinctively took a step back to put some distance between his inquisitive eyes and my jittery nerves.

"You didn't waste much time gettin' out here to claim it. When did you get the key, yesterday?" he asked gruffly.

I nodded uncertainly. What was he implying? Obviously, he knew about the reading of the will. Was he a friend of the family, ticked off because they'd lost their prospective inheritance?

Gathering words, I watched a van creep down the street, its driver gawking at us, before I spoke. "And things aren't looking very promising. What's going on here?"

"Suspicious goings-on, that's what," Sophie chimed in. "So are you finally through making excuses and ready to do your job, Cal?" Her hands were on her narrow pink-clad hips, chin set, eyes threatening. For her size, she was one intimidating woman.

This time it was the chief who took a step back. "Tell you what, Sophie, why don't *you* just stand here quietly and let *me* do my job?" His threatening frown slid back to me.

"Now, Ms. . . . O'Maley is it?"

Our eyes locked. I nodded.

"Levina left the store and the house to you, right?"

I nodded again.

"And why is that?"

"Why is what?"

"Why did she leave them to you?"

Good question, I thought. *If you find out, please fill me in.* "I don't know," I said.

"You don't know?" he asked, his manner unsettlingly derisive.

Why was it any of his business? And why was I standing here shivering in my shoes, allowing him to treat me like this? "No, I *don't* know," I told him. "Before yesterday, I didn't know who Levina was or that she even existed. I have no idea why she left her belongings to me. And to be quite truthful, I wish she hadn't. I don't need the headache."

"You never met Levina?" he asked sardonically.

Dazed, I shook my head. Did he think I was lying?

"Never spoke with her or exchanged mail?"

Tongue-tied, I fought unsuccessfully to still the agitation building inside me. "No, I didn't know I had any family, Levina included."

Chief Preston studied me, his teeth gnawing on his mustache.

What was he thinking? The three of us—Patty, Sophie and I—stood silently and watched him.

"You and I are gonna need to have a little chat, and when we do, I'll need to know where you were on the evenin' of April twenty-sixth," the chief said.

"What?" I blurted. Things were closing in around me, strangling me. I couldn't breathe. "Why?" I managed to whisper.

A few seconds turned into an eternity. While I struggled to stay upright, the world swaying and fading around me, Chief Preston eyes drilled holes into mine.

At last, he spoke. "Turns out Sophie here was right. Levina didn't die from natural causes. She was murdered."

Chapter 4

"**A**nd that's how in only two days time, I became the prime suspect in a murder investigation," I told my fellow fourth grade teacher and close friend Grace.

We were nibbling on low cal lunches. Behind the staff room door, bedlam reigned. Even with smooth jazz playing on the donated boom box and the murmur of voices from the spattering of lunchers at the other tables, excited children's voices filtered through the walls.

Grace swallowed the spinach salad she'd been chewing, a look of disbelief on her strikingly attractive face. "That's amazing," she said. "So when are you going to talk with him?" *Him* being, of course, Cal Preston, Aurora's deranged police chief.

"He said he'd call me to set a time." Struggling to contain my agitation, I took a bite of fat free, caper-laced cottage cheese and rolled it slowly around in my mouth to savor the salty bite. Quite honestly, I wasn't any too anxious to meet up with Chief Preston again.

"What does Patty think you should do?"

"Wait and see what happens. Thank God she was there to get me away from that place. I never want to see it again."

My thoughts reached back to Saturday. Was it really only two days ago? After Chief Preston had followed his less than subtle interrogation by mentioning the words *Levina* and *murdered* in the same sentence, I'd snapped and said things I now regretted saying. But I hadn't asked to be pulled into this mess. And though the chief clearly thought I was guilty, there was no way that I had anything to do with my Aunt Levina's death.

Still, I probably shouldn't have called him an ignorant jerk. Nor a redneck idiot. Nor told him that he couldn't solve a crime if the answer was flashing in florescent neon letters right in front of his accusing eyes, even if Sophie was standing there yelling, "You go, girl!"

My face warmed at the memory. After the events of the last three days, it was clearly time to bid adieu to my inheritance and my newfound kinfolk, who so obviously detested me, and get my life back on track.

"Geez, you think sick leave can be used to cover jail time?" Grace asked, eyeing the chicken cube skewered on her fork. She was the epitome NEA dedicated teacher: pencil stored strategically above her right ear, lime green sticky notes protruding from her blouse pocket, and dry erase pen marks streaking her fingers. Thick, dark hair that had flowed freely to her shoulders when she'd arrived that morning was now caught up in a topknot, strands sticking out from it rather like an ostrich plume. Grace was a single mother with a set of very rambunctious twin six-year-olds. I doubted that her life ever slowed down.

Overwhelmed by it all, I set my spoon on the table and rubbed my forehead, a lame attempt to lessen the pain throbbing beneath the skin. "My biggest fear is that he'll show up at my classroom door with a warrant and arrest me in front of my students," I confessed.

Grace gave me an empathetic look. "I'm so sorry, Kit. If I can do anything to help, please tell me. You know, like if you need a character witness or someone to organize a carwash to raise bail money. Whatever." She frowned, her eyes focused behind me, as if she were considering how else she might be of help.

Suddenly, her face lit up. "If they do come to arrest you, send your kids to my room before they put the handcuffs on. Surely, they'll let you do that?"

"Did I hear someone mention handcuffs?" It was Walker, vice principal and office lackey, approaching from behind me. Ugh! As if on cue, the nauseatingly spicy fragrance of his aftershave tickled my nose, and I sneezed.

Grace curled one of her full lips. "This is a private conversation, Ronny," she said, toying with what remained of her salad. "Take my word on it; you don't want to play handcuffs with me."

"Funny. I don't remember ever asking you to play anything, Grace," Walker taunted.

Grace smiled up at Walker smugly. "And I thank God daily for that."

"We could share insults all day but *I* have work to do," he said gruffly.

Hair follicles on the back of my head prickled. Cripes! Was this visit about me?

"Kit, we need you. It's about one of your students," his demanding voice confirmed.

I huffed and rolled my eyes at Grace. There went my contract-guaranteed, duty-free lunchtime. The throbbing in my temples kicked up a couple of notches while I shoved my half-eaten lunch back into my canvas bag.

"We'll be in Doreen's office." With that, he left us sniffling in a cologne haze.

"What an ass!" Grace whispered.

"Mega ass," I muttered, grinding my teeth, exasperated. "If Frank's in trouble again, I'm going to revolt and set up my own time out place for him." Frank was forever experiencing problems on the playground, and it was no wonder. He'd much rather sit in the office during recess, snacking out of the staff's candy stash and listening to gossip.

Grace pressed the lid onto her plastic container and stuffed it into a peeling Ninja Turtles lunchbox. "Hang in there. If you're not back by twelve-thirty, I'll watch your kids."

I paused to flash Grace a smile. "Thanks. And thank you for listening," I told her before I hurried towards the office.

Doreen's door was closed, the blinds pulled. I drew several deep breaths and told myself to remain calm. My reactions to stress lately had me concerned. If I called Walker or Queen Doreen an ignorant jerk or an idiot, I'd be out the door and into the unemployment line no matter who was cheering me on from behind closed doors.

Steeling myself, I opened the door. Cottage cheese curds rose in my throat when I saw who was seated at the round table with Doreen and Walker, a self-satisfied smirk plastered across his devious face. It was Jared Dawson, the bane of my existence, a child who spent hours devising mean things to do simply because he knew he could get away with them. Though I knew it was in vain, I gave him my *you are in deep trouble* teacher look before I slid into an empty chair and waited patiently for news of Jared's latest aggression.

Doreen eyeballed me for several moments before she spoke. "It seems that Jared brought a knife to school in his backpack today."

A knife! Oh, God. Jared wouldn't just bring a knife to school. He'd have to do something nasty with that knife. I sat quietly, my heart hammering, waiting for her to continue. She didn't. I looked to Walker. He was cleaning his fingernails with a mangled paperclip. I swallowed hard to keep the cottage cheese below gag level.

"Did you take the knife out of your backpack?" I asked Jared.

"Yeah," he said proudly, smiling, gloating in my powerlessness.

"And what did you do with it?"

"Told Frank I was gonna slit his throat if he didn't give me the basketball." He glared at me defiantly, clearly a dare.

Sparks of anger ignited within me, sparring with fear and guilt. No wonder Frank avoided recess.

"Jared understands that he made some poor choices," Doreen said in her most placating principal voice. "We'll keep the knife, but he can return to class with you. The children will probably be talking about it, so we thought you should know about it up front."

I closed my eyes and pinched the bridge of my nose, battling for control. At last, I looked at Jared. "Please step outside and wait in a chair in the office."

He eyed each of us belligerently, shrugged and swaggered from the room.

"May I see the knife," I asked, praying that it was a tiny, two-inch plastic knife with one very small, very dull blade.

Doreen's pencil-thin eyebrows rose, and she chewed at the top coat of lipstick on her burgundy lips. Would she refuse? Jaw set, I stiffened my back and leaned forward—a standoff. Finally, she huffed and turned to retrieve the knife from her desk drawer.

A loud gasp escaped before I could swallow it. The narrow silver blade she held in her hand looked deadly, a solid five inches of steel.

I silently prayed for divine intervention. Could I walk away from this and retain any integrity whatsoever? I looked to Walker. He was polishing a boot with a sweater sleeve. I looked at Doreen, her eyes narrowed and threatening, clearly warning me to back off.

"I'll take care of the call to the police," I said, surprised at how composed I sounded since my insides were swirling and rolling as if I'd just climbed off a death-defying carnival ride. "Until his parents can pick him up, Jared will be in the office." I stood quickly, an instinctive effort to get out of there before Doreen gathered munitions.

"Sit down!" she barked.

I plopped down, my limbs so weak they ached, prepared to fight. Our eyes locked.

"We *don't* need to involve the police in this!" Doreen ordered.

Something snapped inside me. "We have a policy here. Perhaps *you* remember it since *you* helped to formulate it. It's called *zero tolerance*," I paused to glare at Doreen's flushed face. She was speechless. It had to be a first.

Invigorated, I caught my breath, then continued. "Jared broke some rules. He brought a knife to school and threatened another child in *my* class with it. He needs to start living with the consequences of his behavior. I don't care who his parents are. I don't care how much money they have. And I don't care if his mother *is* head of our site council and the school district superintendent's sister. I'm reporting this to the police."

I stood, nodded firmly at Doreen, glanced briefly at Walker—who was now taping lint from his sweater—and marched from the room.

"And I'm doing it right now!" I threw over my shoulder before I closed the door.

"Cripes, Kit, way to commit career suicide," I muttered to myself as I met Louise's questioning gaze. As if I hadn't enough problems, I'd now planted myself on the firing line where Doreen, a clique of influential parents, Superintendent Adams, and only God knew who else, strategic weapons loaded, would soon be taking potshots at me.

☼☼☼

Patty peeked inside my classroom door. "How are you holding up?" she whispered.

I put my hand over the telephone mouthpiece, shrugged, and smiled feebly. It wouldn't take much to turn me into a sobbing mass of self-pity. That would have to wait until later, when I was safely ensconced inside my tiny apartment.

She frowned. "We need to talk, but I'm already late for a math committee meeting. Ice cream at five?"

I nodded.

"My treat," she added as she shut the door.

An hour later, I was still at my desk, ear to the phone. I rotated my neck on my shoulders, stretching out the kinks, while my eyes perused the classroom. Desks and tables were cleared and clean. Bookcases were neat and orderly. Dry erase boards sparkled. Instead of talking on the telephone, I should be finalizing the next day's lessons. But I was determined to contact each of my student's parents concerning today's knife incident, to assure them that their children were safe in my classroom. I had one call left to make.

My fingers punched in the number as Walker sauntered into the room, cool as a mint julep, every hair gelled in place. Reflexively, I dropped the phone and reached up to pat my unruly curls. "Shit," I breathed, mentally fabricating an excuse to get Walker out the door.

He scanned the room, smiled his squirmy smile, and shuffled forward to perch on the corner of a desk directly in front of me. "Kitty, Kitty, Kitty," he drawled, shaking his head. "You've really done it this time. Doreen is furious. And she's getting flack from above."

Though my nostrils burned with the urge to sneeze, I fought it. "So sad for the *two* of you," I drawled back.

A ruby blush stained his cheeks. "Jared was suspended. Doreen's been talking with a police officer for over an hour. He might want to talk with you, too." He paused as if to gather his thoughts. "You know, we're a community here. As a member of our staff, we *all* need to support each other."

Doreen's words, for sure. The two of them wouldn't know how to support a case of head lice. Tiny beads of perspiration glistened on his forehead; I let him sweat.

"There's really no need for you to mention that Doreen asked you to not involve the police," he finally muttered, his eyes darting around the room.

"You're telling me to lie to the police?"

He paused, his mouth slack, eyes fidgety. "Well . . . no. Just don't bring it up."

On any other day, I would've laughed. "Thanks to you, I know to cover my butt. I made two phone calls. The first was to the police. The second was to my union. When I spoke with them, I didn't intentionally omit anything. And I don't plan to."

That had him wiggling. He stood and paced, then stopped to point a trembling finger at me. "Well, you just remember it was Doreen who said it, not me!"

"And by sitting quietly and letting her do that, you're somehow absolved of all responsibility?"

"I would've handled it," he whined. "You didn't give me a chance."

"Too bad you didn't mention that in Doreen's office." Weary of dealing with Walker's self-absorption, I rubbed my aching temples. Please leave. I have work to do."

He stepped toward me. I froze. "Kit, my feelings for you haven't changed. Doreen's determined to get rid of you, and I won't be able to stop her. I. . . ."

The phone buzzed. I grabbed it. "This is Kit O'Maley," I said, eyes on Walker.

"Hi, Kit," chirped Louise. "There's a cute cop here who wants to talk with you."

"Cute, huh? Maybe my day is finally looking up. I'll be right down." I silently thanked Louise for rescuing me as I dropped the phone. "The officer wants to talk with me now," I informed Walker before I headed for the door and strode at a fast clip towards the office, Walker trailing in my dust.

Louise was alone in the office. She pecked on her Dell midst photos of her five grandchildren and a bouquet of purple tulips. "They're in the conference room," she said, her fingers not missing a beat.

Doreen's office door was shut, her blinds closed. "You don't want to go there," Louise muttered. Years of dealing with children and their parents had gifted her with a psychic ability that was unnerving. "Besides, Patty's with cute cop, and the way they're eyeing one another, they'll soon be all over each other. You don't want to walk in on that."

I smiled. Leave it to Louise to provide levity in what she knew was a difficult situation. I ambled toward the conference room, then paused to draw strength.

When I opened the door, Patty stopped speaking, her mouth gaping. I looked across the table. Suddenly lightheaded, I seemed to have misplaced my legs. Fear gripped my throat, throttling me. Somehow, I managed to slip into a chair.

Was I going to be arrested right here in Hazelnut Grove's conference room? After the stand I'd taken today, it hardly seemed fair. I glared at Patty. "Traitor," I muttered. Then I glared at Chief Preston.

Patty chuckled. "I'll make it up in ice cream." She stood and walked to the door. "Bye, Cal," she said in a syrupy voice as she closed the door.

Seconds later, the chief dragged his eyes from that door. During those seconds, I studied him and labored to regain my equilibrium. Admittedly, he was kind of cute with his unruly hair and eyes the color of the sky on a clear day. Those eyes settled on me and I squirmed, knowing it only made me look guilty.

"I'm sorry I was a little unpleasant on Saturday," I said tentatively.

He frowned skeptically. "A *little* unpleasant?"

"I had a rough couple of days."

"Your friend Patty filled me in," he admitted, watching me squirm. Finally, he sighed. "Considerin' the circumstances, I suppose I would've done the same thing."

Relief spread through me like warm honey. Maybe I'd misconstrued the reason for his visit. Bolstered by hope, I broached my fear. "Are you going to arrest me?"

The corners of his mouth twitched, ruffling the mustache that draped it. "No, not this time. Just promise me that the next time you fly off the handle, you'll do it when Sophie's not around. That woman's got a mouth on her that won't quit."

I frowned, confused, and sat forward, forearms on the table. "Levina . . . you don't think I did it then . . . you know. . . .?" My fretful stomach swirled.

He slowly shook his head. "I had a conversation with Pete Lewis, Levina's attorney. He's convinced you were caught completely off guard at the readin' of Levina's will. That you didn't know any of the family even existed. Milton confirmed that. Still, for the record, I'd like to know what you were up to that night."

My mind slid back to the night of Levina's murder, Wednesday, my evening to respond to my students' reading journals. "I was at home," I mumbled.

"Anyone see you?"

I shrugged uneasily. "I doubt it."

He hesitated, then smiled a warm smile. "Well, then it's probably a good thing you're not high up on my list of suspects . . . for now, anyway."

Air spewed from my mouth in a long sigh. Suddenly bone weary, I relaxed back into the chair and gazed out the window. Both Walker's and Doreen's cars were still in their reserved parking spaces, the closest to the front door. Still, things were definitely looking up, enough that I considered forgiving Patty for her crush on Aurora's police chief.

I turned back to him, formulating questions of my own. "So, Chief Preston, Sophie told you that she saw someone hanging around Levina's house, right?"

He nodded, a perturbed look settling on his features. "Please call me Cal. And yeah, Sophie called the office to report it. We checked it out but didn't see anything suspicious. Probably should've taken it more seriously but Sophie has an active imagination. If we don't get a phone call from her every so often, one of us drives by to see if she's still kickin'."

"Did she get a good look at who it was?"

Chief Preston—Cal—furled his brows and worked his mustache when he was thinking. He was doing it now. "Both times it was late at night, so the only light was from the one streetlight on the corner. She said he was lookin' in the front windows and then went to the back of the house." He sighed and settled back into his chair, intertwining his sinewy fingers across the silver belt buckle that covered a good chunk of his flat belly. "Might've been someone just checkin' on things."

"So it was a man?"

He shrugged.

I waited. Surely, he wasn't going to clam up now. I leaned forward, narrowing my eyes, hoping I looked adamant. "Had someone been inside the house?"

Another shrug. He was working his mustache again, his perturbed eyes probing mine. I forced myself not to look away. At last, he huffed and spoke. "Levina'd put in a security system. After her death, the code was changed. If anyone had tried to get in there, they'd have set off the alarm."

Now we were getting somewhere. "So the night she . . . uh . . . died, was she inside the house?" *The house I'm supposed to live in,* I silently added.

"Yeah."

My stomach clenched. How many other people had died inside that house?

Cal appeared to be lost in thought, his head nodding like Bobber, the ceramic turtle that had once sat on my father's desk. I took a few moments to gather my thoughts. "So how did someone get inside without the alarm going off *that* night?"

He blinked hard, as if to refocus. "The next mornin' the alarm was turned off. Accordin' to the security company, Levina set it at nine-thirteen, probably when she went to bed. The code was punched in around four-thirty in the mornin'."

The conference room door flew open, startling us both. Adrenalin surged through my veins. Clearly, murder wasn't something I was comfortable discussing.

Louise stood in the doorway, clutching her bulging purse and a purple vinyl lunch bag. Her eyes danced back and forth between Cal and me. "Sorry; I didn't mean to startle you." She turned to me. "I'm leaving. Would you mind locking up?"

I nodded, my pulse subsiding. "Of course. Enjoy your evening."

"You, too." She turned to leave, then glanced back. "I need that accident report I put in your mailbox, Kit."

"I'll fill it out tonight," I promised as the door shut. Louise's workday ended at four-thirty. Even if I left this conversation now, I'd be lucky to meet Patty by five. A brow arched in query, Cal appeared to be attuned to my dilemma. I sighed and settled back into my chair. I needed some answers. "What happened to Levina?" I asked.

"I suppose you could say she was poisoned," Cal muttered.

"*Poisoned?*" I'd pictured weapons—guns and knives and silk scarves wrapped around unsuspecting throats. Poison was such a sneaky, cowardly way to kill someone.

"Yeah." He nodded his head in his slow, steady manner. "We chalked her death up to a heart attack or a stroke. She was downstairs in her office, wearin' her nightgown, sittin' in her chair and slumped over onto her desk. Looked like she'd been readin' through some papers and passed away peacefully.

"Except for some small bruises, I couldn't come up with a good reason to look further." A troubled expression settled onto his features. "But Milton kept buggin' me about Levina's bifocals and the sherry glass. Convinced me to have her body exhumed. Sure enough, they found she died from cardiac arrest, but caused by anaphylactic shock."

"Her bifocals and sherry glass?" What did they have to do with anaphylactic shock?

"Yeah, they were both sittin' on the nightstand beside her bed. She'd have needed those glasses to do any up close work. We found strawberry traces in the empty glass. Turns out Levina was deathly allergic to strawberries. And both Sophie and Milton swear she always drank her sherry in bed right before she fell asleep, to help her relax."

Strawberries! My throat constricted, and I forced myself to breathe slowly, shallow and even. A miniscule drop of strawberry juice would leave me struggling to draw air into my lungs. I carried an EpiPen in my purse at all times, my only hope of survival should I happen to ingest anything tainted by a strawberry.

A newborn connection to the aunt I'd never known sprouted inside me. If nothing else, we shared a common gene, one that left both of us vulnerable to conniving, cowardly degenerates. How could I possibly turn my back on her now? I swallowed my horror and pressed forward. "So what was she doing downstairs in her office without her glasses? And how did she get down there if she was already dead?"

Cal smiled. "Good questions. Wish I knew the answers."

I shivered, wondering about those answers. Were there clues hidden inside that house? "When can I get into the house?" I asked, not certain that I wanted to get into it.

"It'll be awhile yet. I'll give you a call when we're through processin' it."

So that was that. We both sat in uncomfortable silence, the air growing heavy between us. "Well, I better get going," I said, pushing myself up.

Cal leaned forward, alert. "I was wonderin' about a couple of things."

I sank slowly back into the chair, studying him, anxious.

"When you were at the attorney's office, did anything seem . . . off?"

Well, yes. Now that you mention it, everything seemed off I wanted to say. "What do you mean?" I asked.

His brows and mustache went into thinking mode. "Milton and Bart were there along with the family members. Did any of their actions seem strange to you?"

"That's difficult to say since I don't actually know any of them." I paused to consider what he was seeking, my mind searching for disparity in a discrepant setting.

When I spoke, it was hesitatingly, thinking aloud. "Except for Milton, they were all obviously displeased with my presence. I gather from Sophie that Bernice is always a bitch and Jack likes his liquor, so I suppose their behavior makes sense. Janet, Bernice's daughter, is the person who didn't quite jive. She seemed really nervous and upset, and I don't think it was because of me. She thought she was inheriting the house and store."

"How about Bernice's son?"

Ah, Cousin Roy with his too perfect good looks and his fiery temper. "Levina left Bart several old books, and Roy tore into him and accused him of taking advantage of Levina. And he looked pretty frantic when he found out what he was getting. Other than that, he didn't say much."

"How about you?" Cal asked, scowling. "The secretary mentioned an accident. Has anything unusual happened to you lately, other than what took place at the attorney's office?"

Did Cal think my life was in danger? Was that why he'd come here? I struggled with my overactive nerves and told myself to focus, to think back over the last few weeks. Except for today's conflict with Walker and Doreen and the incident in the parking lot, nothing out of the ordinary had happened.

I shrugged, an attempt to make light of his question. After all, even Louise had called my parking lot dive an accident. "A little over a week ago, I was nearly hit by a car in the school parking lot."

His gaze grew intense. "Did you get a good look at the car . . . or the driver?"

"No," I answered tentatively. "It was early morning, dark and gloomy and pouring rain. The headlights blinded me. Then I jumped out of the way and the car was gone before I got a good look at it."

"The driver didn't see you?" His head dipped and he frowned skeptically.

I shrugged again. "I don't know." The conversation was unsettling, heading to a place I didn't want to go. I'd been so caught up in the invitation to the reading of Levina's will and the aftermath that I hadn't given the incident much thought. Now that I did, I realized that, even with the murky light and heavy rain, it would've been hard to miss me standing right there in the middle of the road.

Why hadn't the driver stopped the car? A wave of dizziness shook me. I clutched my churning stomach.

Cal studied me, still frowning, clearly concerned.

"You think he saw me?" I whispered.

His head nodded slowly, speculatively. "Most likely," he muttered.

✧✧✧

I was late—I didn't like to be late—when I pulled into the parking space in front of Baskin and Robbins. Grace glanced my way, smiled, and wiggled several fingers. She and Patty sat at a small round table directly outside the front window, the one we'd dubbed our *fat fix* table, looking carefree and relaxed. Patty's eyes were hidden behind a pair of over-sized sunglasses, one of her latest finds at the local flea markets she often frequented.

Aware of the contrast between my anxious, unsettled

emotions and their calm, laid-back appearance, I closed my eyes and attempted to breathe away the day's upsets. No need to ruin a perfectly nice evening with my two favorite people and a zillion luscious calories.

When I joined them, Grace and Patty eyed me closely. I forced a smile. "All I can think about is my fix, so you'd better stay out of my way," I warned them.

"We'd never get between a woman and her ice cream. After the day you've had, we'll even bring it to you," Patty said as she rose to her feet and flexed her back. Though I tried, it was difficult to tell what was going on behind the dark lenses hiding her eyes.

"Yeah, sit down and put your feet up," Grace added, pushing a third chair out from the table with her Croc-clad foot. "I can't wait to hear about how you, our new staff superhero, took down the great S&M."

What could I say? I didn't want to be a superhero. I didn't want to be privy to intimate details in the murder of an aunt I'd never met. And I certainly didn't want to be the intended victim of a botched hit-and-run. I wanted my mundane, predictable life back.

"My God, Kit, sit down before you pass out," Patty ordered.

Nix the lighthearted visit with two close friends. With a resigned sigh, I sank down into the ornate iron chair.

Patty grabbed her purse from under the table. "It was inevitable, you know," she added as she rummaged inside the bulging bag. "Doreen's had her evil eye on you since the day Walker cast his two lustful eyes your way. It was only a matter of time before the two of you came to blows. You had no choice; you could've lost your teaching license." She stopped talking to search the wallet she'd pulled from her purse.

"I know," I admitted. "I just wish it hadn't happened when the rest of my life is falling apart." I ground my teeth at the pathetic whine in my voice.

Patty's discerning ears had heard it, too. "Things could be worse. At least, you have options," she reminded me. "Come on, Grace. Let's get her medicated. Then we'll talk."

Grace pushed herself to her feet and followed Patty.

Taking advantage of the few moments to myself, I tried to view my latest troubles through the eyes of an observer. Even from a distance, the situation was an irreparable disaster. I'd defied Queen Doreen, and in the process, I'd ticked off the school district superintendent. His nephew was now in deep trouble. Since I was in the right, they couldn't get rid of me over this incident, but they *would* make my job a daily lesson in misery and undoubtedly, would latch onto any misstep as an excuse to terminate my employment. With that on my résumé, I'd never teach again.

Overwhelmed by a weak, shaky feeling, I rested my elbows on the table and rubbed my aching temples. Standing up for what was right was supposed to make one feel proud, not defeated and scared shitless. I'd lost control of my life. Would I be able to get it back or had I made a fatal error?

Lost in thought, I flinched when a mountain of ice cream dripping rivulets of gooey, golden caramel appeared in front of me. The buttery fragrance was already gluing inches to my waistline. I glanced up at my two friends with their single scoops and smiled. "Do I look that bad?"

"Worse," Patty said, sliding into her chair. "Eat up. Then you'll be on a sugar high when what you've done finally hits you."

"I've already been walloped," I told her as I spooned a glob of ice cream into my mouth. The cold sweetness melted across my tongue, and I closed my eyes to savor its creamy texture. Prolonging the decadent experience as long as I could, I finally lifted my lids and gazed at Patty and Grace. "I'm in big trouble, aren't I?"

The two women eyed each other briefly, then nodded their heads in unison before they held their ice cream out to me. "Here's to the choices we make. May they always be the right ones . . . even if they land us in the doggy doo-doo," Patty said.

I raised my container and touched it to theirs. "To doggy doo-doo," I said. "May it please not be as bad as it smells."

Grace smiled, her beautiful face lighting up. "Actually, some dogs eat doo-doo so it must not be all that bad."

"Thank you for sharing that repulsive fact, Grace," Patty muttered before she spooned a sliver of chocolate ice cream into her mouth.

A flush crept into Grace's cheeks. "Well Geez, we're supposed to be cheering her up, not making her miserable."

I felt Patty's intense scrutiny emanating from behind her dark glasses and scooped another dollop of fat and sugar into my mouth, determined to enjoy every single calorie.

"She's already miserable," Patty announced. "And sugar-coating it isn't going to solve her problems or help her make some important decisions,"

"Decisions?" I asked, unsure of exactly to which decisions she was referring.

"Yes, decisions." Patty sighed. "If you stay in that school now, your teaching career is history. They'll fabricate something to get rid of you. It won't be pretty, Kit."

"I know," I admitted, then stabbed my spoon into the melting mound, my appetite gone.

Grace stared at Patty, an incredulous look on her face. "Couldn't you've at least given her time to eat her ice cream before you became Ms. Blunt?" She turned to me, all sad eyes and worry lines. "I'm sorry, Kit."

I forced a smile. "Patty's right. Walker as much as told me I'm out of there. If I turn in my resignation, at least I won't have a termination of employment on my records. I suppose that's my best hope to save my career."

"Not necessarily," Patty declared. "You can always ask for a year-long leave of absence. Since the school board gives them to everyone who requests them, they'd have to grant you one, too.

"Or you can move into your aunt's house for the summer, on a trial basis. You only have to give the school district four weeks notice. That would give you until the first of August to decide about your job and your other choice."

"What other choice?" Grace asked.

"A life in Aurora, living in her aunt's house and managing an antique business," Patty announced with a definite nod of her head and a persuasive smile.

Grace gazed at me, a look of wonder on her face. "Wow! You're so lucky, Kit. What I wouldn't give to have something like that drop into my lap."

The expression on my face had to be even more incredulous than Grace's. Was she nuts? "Grace, we're talking about a very old house in a little hick town out in the sticks—a house which, by the way, was the scene of a recent murder—and a store crammed full of junk I know absolutely nothing about. And all of it's linked to a group of people who want me dead." I stared at both of them in disbelief. "That's not a *choice*."

Patty pushed her sunglasses onto the top of her head, baring an intense gaze that made me squirm. "Well, it's the best one you have right now, Kit, so you'd better make peace with it. And in my opinion, you're damn lucky to have it," she stated rather bluntly.

Usually, I appreciated Patty's candor, but today it stung, a deep down feeling of betrayal. "It's a good thing you're my friend," I told her. "First you cozy up to Cal, who you knew was going to arrest me, and now this."

She seemed taken aback. "So now it's . . . *Cal*?" she asked, her eyebrows arching.

I'd never before known practical Patty to latch onto a man she barely knew. "Don't worry," I assured her. "He's as gooey-eyed over you as you are over him." Then it suddenly hit me. "Is that why you want me to move there, so you can be near him?"

A contented smile blossomed on her face. "Sorry, girlfriend. Whether you're there or not, I plan to pursue what promises to be a very interesting relationship with a very intriguing—and I might add *hot*—man."

"Who's Cal?" Grace chimed in, a puzzled frown distorting her perfect features.

"Chief Preston," I muttered absently, still sorting through my exchange with Patty.

"Oh, him." Grace still looked confused. "Did he arrest you?"

Sometimes Grace's train of thought wandered to places I couldn't follow. How had she sprouted this notion? Then I realized that I'd planted it. "No, he's changed his mind . . . for now, anyway. But Patty didn't know that when she decided to be so friendly to him."

"Actually, I was *so* friendly to him because I wanted to tell him a few things, like the fact that you didn't know your aunt even existed on the night she was murdered," Patty pointed out. "But I'm sure he told you that. So why are you miffed?"

Actually, I wasn't miffed. In fact, as of this afternoon, I was rather fond of Cal. Patty was right; he was hot . . . for a guy who must be in his fifties. "I'm sorry," I said. "Cal's a nice man, and if you and he feel a connection, then I say, 'go for it.'"

I studied my two best friends—the best friends I'd ever had—and saw the concern on their faces. "I'm having a tough time right now, but I shouldn't take it out on the two of you," I admitted over the painful egg lodged in my throat. To prevent a meltdown, I grabbed my discarded bowl and ran the spoon through the gooey mess. "And I'm not going to let a caramel sundae go to waste, especially since the two of you so lovingly bought it for me."

The spoonful of sweet cream was a self-indulgence, one on which I could usually rely to melt away unsettling thoughts and take me to a place of calm contentment.

Today that was not the case. Today I slurped melting ice cream with my two best friends and couldn't shake an image of me standing on the stage of *Let's Make a Deal* before three closed curtains. Behind one curtain was a wretched year with Doreen S&M and her sidekick Walker—a fate that filled me with dread. Behind a second curtain was a new teaching position in a new location, probably outside the country, where the *good old boy* network hadn't eradicated my chances of being hired.

But was what the third curtain concealed any better: a new life, one weighted down by uncertainty, animosity, and a lifestyle as foreign to me as an Australian walk-about?

When Monty Hall asked, "Which curtain do you choose?" would I pick the right one?

CHAPTER 5

"Time to head to the buses," I announced to twenty-seven dewy-eyed fourth graders. I was dewy-eyed myself—actually more like barely containing a geyser of tears.

It was the last day of school, a time for goodbyes, more than I wanted to contemplate. I gazed out at the jumble of young bodies as they hefted over-loaded backpacks onto drooping shoulders and eyed each other forlornly. My glance caught Frank's, my office nester. It was amazing what having Jared Dawson out of the classroom, and school—he was now terrorizing students in one of the Portland area's more prestigious private schools—had done for Frank. Turns out, Frank was a whiz at recess once he felt safe on the playground.

I wallowed in the guilt for several long, uncomfortable moments. In hindsight, I should've been more vigilant and taken action sooner. Next time would be different.

"If there is a next time," I whispered over the giant goose egg lodged in my throat.

"Did you say something, Ms. O'Maley?"

I blinked back the impending tear storm and gazed down at Maria, always first in line. "Just thinking out loud," I informed her. She gave me a look that said it was what one might expect from someone my age.

I clicked off the lights. A hush fell over the classroom. "Remember, we all agreed that we will have an exciting and fun summer," I said. I perused their oh-so-familiar faces and nearly lost it before I turned and waved them forward.

"On to new adventures," I threw over my shoulder in a strangled voice as we trekked out the door and headed for the buses.

New adventures? Here I was encouraging my students to reach out and embrace theirs, yet I was only dreading mine. I thought back to the harrowing conversation I'd had with Grace and Patty over ice cream several weeks before. I'd spent countless hours debating the pros and cons of what I should do next. It was Patty who'd pressed me into a promise to move into Levina's house, just to check it out, until the first of August—thank you, Patty! As she had repeatedly pointed out, that would give me time to consider *all* of my options.

Patty was now approaching the front doors through the primary hall, leading her first graders and an entourage of proud parents. She caught my eye, and a look of concern settled on her features. A tear escaped to trickle down my cheek and I brushed at it.

God forbid, what if I decided to stay in Aurora and didn't return to Hazelnut Grove? Or was forced to search for a teaching job elsewhere? I might never again see these familiar faces.

"Get a grip," I told myself, reassuring Patty with a quivery smile.

That smile froze on my lips as I plowed through the mass of bodies milling outside the front doors. Hot, stale air pushed in around me, clinging like sticky candy. We'd done our goodbyes and hugs, so all that was left was to see them off. Barely holding my feelings in check, I waved and wished them well as they disappeared with parents or climbed onto yellow buses. Then there was only me, swathed in a veil of sadness. It pulled at my insides and drained my spirit, leaving me empty and hollow.

Other than my father, school had been the one constant in my life. No matter where we went or how often we moved, there was always a teacher and a classroom full of children there for me to join. The gift I was given by the educational system is one I wanted to share with others. And after graduating from college, I had, until my father was diagnosed with cancer and I'd turned my focus from teaching to him. Three years later he'd died a quiet death at home. For the first time in my life, I was alone.

It'd taken me a full year to pull myself back together, to look forward instead of backward. Somewhere in those months, a seed had been planted: maybe I wasn't alone. Maybe I did have family. I'd taken a giant step when I'd sought a teaching job in Oregon.

Now here I was at Hazelnut Grove, a semi seasoned teacher, finally ready to stay in one school and make a difference in children's lives. And despite lousy leadership, I was doing that. That is, until I'd blown it.

A clammy hand landed on my bare shoulder. "Hey, you want to come over this evening? I promised the boys we'd celebrate summer with a barbecue. They'll want hot dogs, but I can throw on some chicken for us," Grace asked as she slid in beside me.

The buses gunned their motors, shooting diesel fumes at us. Kids were hanging out of the windows, waving their arms and yelling. It was tradition. I smiled my frozen smile and waved back as they paraded out of the parking lot. "That would be nice," I replied.

"Great. I asked Patty, too, but she's going out with her hot cop. Geez, I've never seen her so *gaga* over a guy before. What am I gonna do this summer? Patty'll be shacked up with him, and you'll be miles away selling antiques."

"Yeah, well, we'll see if I actually sell any," I muttered.

"Geez, Kit, are you okay?" Through my watery eyes, her striking features were distorted. Still, her concern was evident.

I nodded and glanced back to watch the last bus rumble off, trailing a haze of sooty exhaust. "It's just hitting me that I might not be back here next year," I admitted as we turned to make our way into the school.

She slowed her pace and drifted to the side of the walkway to let other staff members stride past. "Hey, a lot of things can happen over the summer," she assured me. "I hear S&M is in serious trouble over how she handled Jared's knife incident. Maybe she's the one who won't be here next year." She paused as if to consider something, then added, "Course, Superintendent Adams isn't very happy with you either."

"And I'm not happy with myself. I should've done something about Jared long before I did."

She shrugged. "Well, look what happened when you did. Doreen's been practically living in your classroom—no doubt, she's documenting every little mistake you make. And how many times has she called you into her office before and after school to chew you out for some minor infraction one of your students made?"

Grace's words were not helping. During the past three weeks, Doreen *had* been on my back. She'd examined my lesson plans and observed my teaching, then critiqued them to the point of being ridiculous, all under the guise of *evaluation*. She'd sent Walker my way just to annoy me. Even Superintendent Adams had shown up at the school, an event so rare that within minutes of his arrival, the halls were buzzing. The fact that mine was the only classroom he'd entered hadn't gone unnoticed.

"And there's not an extra duty or extra committee or extra whatever that she hasn't assigned you to. She'll probably even make you clean up after the staff luncheon today."

"Kit, Doreen's office. Now," demanded a familiar male voice.

Walker? I glanced around and sighted him lounging in the office doorway. "Please, not the *queen* today," I muttered to Grace. "Can't it wait?" I yelled to Walker.

"Now." His eyes were fidgety. His fists were clenching. What was going on?

"Don't worry; I'll help you clean up the lunch mess," Grace assured me.

I sighed and stiffened my backbone, then swallowed any chance of even one tear escaping. "I think this is about something else," I told her before I passed by Walker and trudged to the royal chamber, surprised to find the door wide open.

Doreen glanced up from a pile of paperwork. A perturbed look flitted across her features, then disappeared.

Why, I wondered. She'd never before gone out of her way to mask her dislike of me. She was always immaculately attired, every hair in place, nails neatly polished and accessories to match her expensive outfits. Today she was a disheveled, frazzled mess.

"You wanted to see me?" I prodded.

Good grief! Was she attempting a smile? "Close the door and sit down . . . please."

Please? With shaky fingers, I shut the door and slid into a chair.

Now she was studying me intently, teeth gnawing on her lips. Her gaze slid out the window when she spoke. "I know you don't like me, that you think I'm an ineffectual leader."

It was my turn to dispute her words; I didn't.

She turned back to me, a frown slowly furling her brows. "And I'm sure you also know that I don't like you. You have Dr. Walker to thank for your position here. If it weren't for him, you'd be gone. You're a trouble-maker, and as I've told you before, there's no place for trouble-makers on my staff."

In truth, I'd gone out of my way to avoid trouble. Nonetheless, I kept my mouth shut.

She huffed and shook her head. "Still, I thought even you would draw the line somewhere. Going to the teachers' union about those silly accusations you invented about Ronny was one thing. But calling the Teachers' Standards and Practices Commission concerning that minor incident with Jared was totally uncalled for."

Huh? Had I heard right? Adrenaline flooded my veins as I considered Doreen's allegation. I hadn't called TSPC. So who had? Patty? My position here was already fried; Patty's wasn't. No way was she going down with me.

Hoping I looked appropriately guilty, I gazed silently at Doreen.

She shook her head disgustedly. "No apologies, huh? The investigator will be contacting you to schedule an interview." She paused to mangle her lower lip, most likely strategizing. "You know, I was planning to deal with Jared in an appropriate manner after I'd discussed his behavior with Superintendent Adams. Then you overreacted. *You* made me look bad."

It was my turn to huff. "I see no need to rehash this. You know what really happened, as do I. And so does Dr. Walker."

"Dr. Walker's memory of the incident is similar to mine."

Of course, it was. So why was she worried about what I might say to the investigator? I grabbed my somersaulting stomach and fought to meet her glare.

"You defied me and made it impossible for me to do my job. If you think back, you'll realize that I'd planned to notify the police," she declared. "Later."

Was she offering me an out? Or was it a threat? It felt like an insult.

"No, you didn't," I informed her before I stood and strode from her office.

CHAPTER 6

Sophie scurried across the scarred asphalt towards us, a flurry of pastel pink, a saran-wrapped plate clutched in one hand and a small jar in the other. From the driver's seat, my eyes met Patty's shielded ones, her brows arched high above leopard print sunglass frames.

"Welcome to small town, U.S.A.," she drawled.

I studied Sophie in her gauzy, flowing sundress and pink sandals, then took in my own attire: frayed cut-off jeans, a stained McTeacher's Night tee-shirt, and lilac flip-flops. Still skittish about this move to Aurora, I chewed on a mangled thumbnail, patted my churning stomach, and wished I'd skipped my third cup of coffee. How bad could it be, anyway? And if it was, come August, I'd be out of here.

"How did she know I was coming?" I wondered aloud.

"Hey, you're in the boonies. From this point forward, if you want to keep something a secret, don't share it with anyone."

"I'm assuming that includes you, too. Did you tell Cal?"

"I might have mentioned it to him," she admitted sheepishly, her tight smile settling somewhere behind me.

I whirled around and couldn't help but smile myself. Today Sophie had obviously taken the time to do full makeup and coordinating jewelry. A mass of sparkling pink chunks clung to her neck; two smaller versions bejeweled her earlobes.

Hot air engulfed me when I climbed out of the air-conditioned vehicle. Ten o'clock in the morning and it was already a sauna. If Levina's house wasn't air conditioned, I wouldn't make it to the end of the day, let alone to August.

"Good morning, Sophie," I said, eyeing the pastries beneath the saran wrap.

"Good morning," Patty echoed from beside me.

"Mornin', ladies," Sophie chimed. "I almost gave up on you. Milton told me you were coming. Cal told him. He came by yesterday to make sure they got all of their crime scene stuff out of your house. Cal's like that, you know—thoughtful of others. Not married either, if you get my drift. If he was a few years older, I'd. . . ."

It appeared we wouldn't be privy to what Sophie would do

had Cal been well into his golden years. With the crunch of gravel, we all swiveled to watch a Toyota van pull in behind my Santa Fe. It was loaded to the sunroof with Grace, her twin sons, and my paraphernalia.

"You have kids?" Sophie squawked. She was eyeing me suspiciously, scowling.

I shook my head. "No."

As soon as the van stopped, the boys shot out and ground to a stop before us, eyeing Sophie curiously. "I like your trees," Davy said to me, his blue eyes sparkling.

"I'm goin' tree climbing," Danny announced, poised for take off.

"No!" Both boys looked up at their frazzled mother, who placed a hand around each of their shoulders. "Just stay with me for now. Later you can play in the backyard." Grace shook her head and sighed. "I'm sorry I lost you. Danny had to go to the bathroom."

"No problem. We just got here," I told her.

She turned to ogle my new home. "Oh, Kit, it's beautiful. And what a perfect little town. Have you seen all of those wonderful antique shops? I can't wait until I get a chance to browse through them." Her eyes landed on Sophie. "I'm Grace," she said pleasantly. "These are my sons Danny and Davy. They're twins."

Sophie lifted her troubled eyes momentarily from the two young boys. "Sophie. I live across the street in that white house," she muttered.

"Why don't we go inside and have a look around," I said, hoping to get us moving. The heat and humidity had my clothes sticking to me in uncomfortable places, and I wasn't sure how long the standoff between Sophie and the boys would last.

"Pink's a *baby* color!" Davy blurted.

Sophie's eyes, narrow slits of aggravation, zeroed in on him.

"Sophie, perhaps you can show us the way," I added quickly.

"Yippee!" Danny yelled and took off at a run for the front gate. Clearly torn between his silent battle with Sophie and his need to be in on the action, Davy hesitated several seconds before he streaked off after his brother.

"I'd better stick with them," Grace murmured before she strode off, too.

"It's nice and quiet around here," Sophie uttered tersely. "No kids."

"Can I help you carry that, Sophie?" Patty offered.

"I've got it," Sophie responded. "I'm a lot stronger than I look. I work out every day with Jane Fonda, you know. Bought the video at the First Saturday Flea Market for two bits. Levina used to work out with me, but I guess that won't be happening now, will it?"

She eyed me speculatively as we rounded the car. "You could join me. I'd get you into shape. There are a few eligible men around here, you know, and you gotta be prepared. When you take your clothes off, there's no hiding the bulges."

Over the top of Sophie's kinky white curls, Patty's shaded eyes met mine, her lips twitching. I dropped behind to check for unsightly bulges. What I saw wasn't all that bad: mostly flat stomach, muscular but slender legs, breasts that I tried hard to minimize beneath loose-fitting tops. Of course, compared to Sophie's petite frame, I was a Beluga whale.

"A Beluga whale out of water," I muttered as I surveyed this place that would be my home for the next few weeks. The sweet fragrance of roses pressed in around me, mingling with the scent of freshly mown grass. Dappled shade from the two maples painted the yard in splotches of sunlight. Here and there a rainbow of bright blossoms raised their cheery faces to the sun. And Sophie's voice filtered from the front porch, somehow comforting.

An overwhelming sense of peace settled over me. I sighed deeply, then stepped forward to meet whatever lay beyond that closed door.

By the time I inserted the key into the lock, Sophie had moved on to a sermon concerning the merits of silk underwear versus cotton. Though I only got in on the tail end of the lecture, there was no doubt that my lingerie drawer was not up to her high standards. God help me!

I pushed the door open to a wall of stale, musty air. Thankfully, the alarm didn't scream. In front of me stretched a narrow hallway, its walls plastered with ornately framed paintings. To my right was a formal dining room, and to my left was what looked like an office, most likely the room in which Levina had been found slumped over onto her desk—dead. A cold shiver passed through me. Had she spent the last moments of her life there? Or had that happened upstairs in her bedroom?

"The living area is down the hall," Sophie said, pushing past me to lead us to the back of the house.

Overwhelmed, I followed her. Every space was crammed with something that looked older than dirt. Cabinets stuffed with glass, silver, china, and books hugged the walls. Patterned rugs covered the hardwood floors. Pictures and heavily carved furniture filled the in-between spaces.

"My God!" Patty murmured in my ear. "You're going to live in a museum."

"Don't touch anything," Grace ordered from behind Patty. I could well imagine her apprehension. For a mother of six-year-old boys, this place was a living nightmare.

We entered a large area that was more open and bright—and modern, thank goodness—though it was still jam-packed with everything imaginable. To the right, lay a spacious kitchen and eating area, and to the left was a sitting area dominated by a majestic mantle. Carved from a beautiful dark wood, it rose from the floor to reach to the ceiling and framed a fireplace large enough that one could rotisserie a whole cow in it.

"I'm gonna roast marshmallows," Danny announced, running over to stand on the slate hearth. Davy was soon parked beside him.

Grace joined them to stare up at the massive piece of wood. "Not today. We'd all die from heatstroke."

Intrigued by the carvings, I stepped closer to examine them. They appeared to be of pioneers, some traveling in covered wagons or crossing a river on a large raft. Others were of settlers clearing land, building houses, and planting crops. Someone had put a lot of painstaking work into creating this amazing memorial to Oregon's history. It seemed sadly out of place in this small room. I touched the lovely carvings and let my fingers glide over the contours. The wood was cold and smooth as blown glass.

"Kind of gaudy, ain't it?" Sophie said from beside me. "One of Levina's ancestors made it. She was always talking about him. He was one of the original settlers here in Aurora, way back in the mid 1800's when it was called Aurora Colony. It was some kind of commune, cult-type place back then. Praise God it's not now. I wouldn't put up with some religious fanatic ordering me around. Forcing me to be his sex toy."

I stared at her, searching for words. "Uh . . . this house is that old?"

"Yep, the grandest house around at one time. Levina was darned proud of that. Although, according to her, this ancestor of hers didn't fit in all that well with the rest of the cult. Too artistic. Disappeared a lot and wanted to sit around and paint pictures instead of doing his share of the work. One of his pictures is around here somewhere. And he made that clock. Hmmm . . . wonder where it is? Levina kept it right there on that shelf. Chimed loud enough to set off my atrial fib."

Amazing! Not only did I have a family, but that family stretched back at least one hundred-fifty years. And I was standing in what was probably their original home. I gazed around at the furnishings, some of which might be as old as the house. No wonder Bernice and her offspring were so upset. It was a part of their history, too.

The room began to spin, whether from the stale air or too much coming at me I wasn't sure. I stepped purposefully toward a pair of open French doors. Patty stood on the covered back porch talking with an older gentleman—Milton, a wide-brimmed straw hat pulled low over his forehead and a pair of gardening gloves sheathing his hands.

The fresh air helped. "Nice to see you, Milton," I said.

He smiled. "Ms. O'Maley. I was just telling your friend Patty that I hoped to have this done before you got here."

I frowned, puzzled. "Please call me Kit. Have what done?"

Two small bodies streaked past us, taking the steps in long leaps, racing towards a gigantic oak tree that stood towards the back of the lot. Grace stepped gracefully down the steps and pursued them.

Milton's eyes followed the boys, an enchanted smile touching his lips. He gestured with a hand, indicating the yard. "Gardening was one of Levina's passions. After all the work she put into this, I can't let it go. I wanted to have it in tip-top shape for you. Still need to trim the roses." His voice cracked when he added, "Levina's pride and joy."

A painful lump settled in my throat. "What a thoughtful thing to do for both me and Levina, especially since I know absolutely nothing about garden. . . ."

"Milton!" Sophie screeched. "I've been looking for you all morning. I have some freshly baked scones and homemade strawberry jam for you." She turned to me. "I made some for you, too. They're on the kitchen counter."

Strawberry jam! I automatically scratched my arms, which I knew was ridiculous and only the product of my own imagination. "Thank you, Sophie. I'm allergic to strawberries, but I'm sure everyone else will enjoy your treat."

Sophie eyed my red-streaked arms curiously. "So you inherited Levina's affliction, huh? I guess you know it's what killed her? She had medicine for it, mind you, so she must've gone to sleep before what was in her sherry hit her. Or maybe there was someone right there with her, and he wouldn't let her get her medicine. Someone had to be in the house, you know. Otherwise, how did she get downstairs?"

The sun beat down from a cloudless sky, heating the moisture in the air. I should be steaming. Instead, chills skittered up and down my spine, sprouting goose bumps on my bare arms and legs. Did the lady not realize that I had to spend the night in this house—the scene of the disturbing murder she was describing?

In what I was beginning to realize was true Sophie fashion, she kept talking until she'd said all she had to say on the subject. "And it had to be someone who knew her, mind you, someone who knew she was deathly allergic to strawberries . . . just like you are."

☼☼☼

With the promise of a few whiffs of cooler air, afternoon stretched into evening. Still, even sitting in the shade of the back porch, the annoying tickle of perspiration trickled in rivulets down the sides of my face and into the valley between my breasts. Like the air, I was heavy, sodden, and listless.

Patty reclined in the wicker lounge beside mine, a dew-dripping glass clutched to her chest. "We should paint our toenails," she said halfheartedly.

I studied my feet. My left big toe sported several drops of blood where I'd stubbed it earlier in the day, and my toenails were bare and badly in need of loving care. "That'd take way more energy than I have right now," I told Patty. "Besides, I have several days' worth of cleaning and organizing in this cluttered-beyond-belief house and a store that's probably even worse to tackle before I put any effort into my toes.

"And this yard, what am I going to do with it?" My eyes scanned the trimmed shrubs, cascading blossoms, and neatly clipped, lush grass. "It's probably already wilting at the prospect of my gardening ineptitude." I took a sip of frosty daiquiri and relished the icy pang as it slid down my throat.

"Hey, girl, the glass is not half empty here—I mean that figuratively, not literally," she said, holding up what remained of her drink. "You were given a gift. You're smart. You'll learn. Taking care of a yard is a lot like teaching. Just be observant, and take your cues from what's going on around you. The plants will tell you what they need." Her eyes bored into mine, filled with exhaustion and frustration.

Heat rose in my cheeks. The air was too heavy to breathe.

She sighed. "And if they don't, you can always hire a gardener."

Guilt settled in the pit of my stomach, an uneasy tight ball. During the last few weeks, I'd been so wrapped up in my own pity party that I hadn't considered the many merits of the gift I'd been given. Through it all, Patty and Grace had tolerated me while I played the martyr. What they saw as a Godsend, I saw only as an agonizing affliction.

Cripes! It was time for an attitude adjustment. Mine. I gulped a strong slug of slushy rum and lime juice. The surge of ice hit my head, a painful stab that made me wince.

"I'm sorry," Patty murmured.

Rubbing my temple, I met Patty's troubled gaze. "It's not you; it's the ice." I studied her face. Though Patty was forty-nine years old, she could pass for a woman ten years younger. Her abilities to confront life head on and not perseverate on circumstance were surely keys to her fountain of youth. If only some of it would slough onto me.

"One of your many qualities that I truly appreciate is your frankness," I told her. "And you're right. I've been so caught up in all of the reasons I shouldn't make this move that I haven't seen the good things inherent in it. Even I'm fed up with myself."

"You've got to admit that lounging here in this beautiful yard beats the hell out of cuddling together on your playpen-size apartment balcony." She sighed blissfully. "I could be content to sit here the rest of my life, especially if you keep the daiquiris flowing."

In truth, it did feel nice. But Patty didn't have to deal with my tomorrow and all of the tomorrows after that, each of them full of the unknown. In a couple of hours, she'd return to her familiar life and leave me here alone to confront whatever this new life chose to throw my way.

"You know, you're always welcome to one of the spare bedrooms upstairs," I offered. "I'd love to have you here with me."

"Oh, mark my word, I do plan to be here, dear. But not necessarily with you."

"With Cal?"

"Uh-huh—unsightly bulges and all."

I chuckled. If Patty had any bulges, she kept them well hidden.

"You laugh. Your day will come. One can only wonder where all of that excess skin comes from and why it suddenly takes chugging bottles of water and slathering on gallons of expensive skin products to keep from feeling like a wrinkled sheet of parchment." She sighed and started to rise. "And speaking of keeping all of my skin cells well hydrated, I'm ready for a refill. How about you?"

I jumped up before she got her seat off the cushion. "I'll get it. You sit here and rest your aged, arthritic bones."

She sank back into the chair, stretching languidly. "Looking after your elders. At least, you have your priorities straight, girl."

I couldn't help but snicker. "Girl? I'll be thirty-five in December, fast approaching *over the hill* and the dreaded *old maid* label." Though I said it flippantly, a desolate, empty heaviness settled inside me.

"Well, maybe you should do something about that?" Patty offered hesitantly.

I grabbed Patty's empty glass and turned to retreat into the house.

"Kit."

I froze, my free hand clutching the doorknob so tight it hurt.

"I've been alone for more than twenty years," Patty

continued. "Sure, I've dated men and had some fun times doing it. But I've always missed having a special man to share my life with through thick and thin. Finally, I've found someone who has serious possibility. When I'm with Cal, nothing else matters. I feel giddy. My heart beats faster. My middle-aged body does wanton things. I don't want you to miss out on that."

I hadn't missed out on it. I'd had it and lost it. Truth be told, I'd prefer to have never experienced it at all. Then I wouldn't feel this unrelenting loss every time I thought about it.

The memories were with me now: the love of my life parked before me, hand-in-hand with his new bride. Due to the demands of his job and my father's lingering illness, we'd taken separate vacations. Dog-tired from changing Dad's bedding and emptying his bedpans, I'd welcomed my fiancé home. He'd returned with a gorgeous tan and an even more gorgeous wife.

I scratched out the image and spun to face Patty. "Look; you've found Cal and that's great. But just because you have him, doesn't mean that I need someone, too." I stepped into the stuffy house and closed the door firmly behind me, determined to give Patty time to move past my nonexistent love life and on to a new topic.

Still uncomfortable in someone else's kitchen, I emptied the container of daiquiri mixture into the two glasses, then let my eyes wander as I sipped at the slushy drink. Shelves lined with junk that looked like it had been culled from the local dump appeared to be the theme, some of it sporting a good deal of rust. Well, it would find its way back to the dump as soon as I had a chance to clear it out. Then I'd display some of the beautiful dishes that were hidden away in numerous cabinets.

Somewhat revived, I sidled back to the porch. Milton was back, looking dapper in grey slacks and a navy polo, his silver hair gel-slicked into place. He stood on the grass, a mammoth yellow cat cradled in his spindly arms.

"Jiminy Cripes! Does that thing eat people?" I blurted without thinking.

He chuckled. "No, but she'll eat more than her share of the birds and frogs around here if you don't keep her food dish filled."

My nose wrinkled in disgust at visions of the carnage. "Well, by all means, keep it filled then. I don't want any cute little birdies to fall prey to that monster."

"When Milton said 'you,' he was actually referring to *you*," Patty informed me.

"Me?" I stared at her, puzzled.

"That *monster* is yours."

"Mine?" The drinks in my hands slipped, nearly falling. I was *not* an animal person.

Milton's furrowed face looked way too serious. "Yep, she's yours. Comes with the house. I've been taking care of her, but she needs to get settled back into her own home. Her name's Annabelle."

"Annabelle?" Annabelles were supposed to be dainty and harmless, not brutes who killed innocent birds. I eyed the golden-eyed beast, searching frantically for a way out of this new predicament. "Uh . . . you know, Milton . . . now that she's comfortable with you, maybe we shouldn't upset her with another move. I'm sure you'll miss her company."

"You know, she is good company. But I'll sacrifice that for a good night's sleep." He leaned down to set the mass of fur on the porch and stroke its round head. The cat had a look about her, as if life were one big endless bowl of extra heavy whipping cream. Hers.

"Annabelle's outside most of the day, but she's an inside cat at night." Milton sighed and rose somewhat creakily. "Which would be fine if she didn't insist on going outside at exactly four-thirty every morning, probably because that's the time Levina was in the habit of getting out of bed? I like to sleep late. Annabelle's got my schedule all screwed up."

Great! Here I was, bound by my recent promise of an attitude adjustment, facing a summer of four-thirty awakenings by a carnivorous feline. And I was supposed to view *that* in a positive light.

Annabelle and I scrutinized each other. Her drooping eyes spoke of cunning and wisdom. Or was it just my imagination? Surely, cats weren't all that bright. "How long has Annabelle been with you?" I asked.

Milton mulled it over. "Oh, it's been a couple of months now. She showed up on my doorstep the morning of Levina's passing. Once she's done her business, Annabelle wants back inside to eat her breakfast. When she wants food, there's no stopping her. She woke me up, scratching on my back door and yowling. Her claw marks are still there."

I was intrigued. "What time was that?"

"Oh, must've been around six-thirty or seven."

"So she was outside?" My mind was madly stringing pieces together. "But Levina couldn't have let her out."

Milton frowned. "I suppose not." He hesitated, worrying his lips. "But Annabelle's pretty picky about who she takes up with. If she doesn't like you, she lets you know about it. I can't see just anyone putting her out."

Quite truthfully, my knowledge of cats wouldn't fill a sticky note. Still, I'd lay good money on the fact that Annabelle was a creature of habit. "Do you think she'd go outside on her own in the middle of the night?"

He shrugged, his face sad, clearly upset by our conversation.

Still, I wasn't ready to let go. "Do you know what time they found Levina?"

"Well, let's see." He rubbed his chin. "It must've been around one or so. When Annabelle showed up at my house that morning, I figured Levina'd gone somewhere—she did that sometimes—so I didn't think much about it.

"Then when Levina didn't open the store, Cal came by looking for her. Her car was in the driveway. Levina had given me a key so I let him into the house. That's when we found her." Milton ended with a catch in his voice, tears glistening in his eyes.

I felt like a jerk. "You said you stayed up late. Did you hear or see anything?"

"No," he answered in a husky voice. "Cal asked me the same thing. I don't remember anything out of the ordinary. Levina'd been over at my house for dinner. We played Cribbage until around nine. Then I walked her home."

He cocked his head as if he were considering something, then stared hard at me. "I *do* remember that the alarm wasn't set . . . and Annabelle went into the house with Levina. She was standing outside the door there, meowing. We had a chuckle about her singing for her supper." A smile touched his lips. "That's the last time I saw Levina alive. It's how I want to remember her—laughing."

Though questions begged to be asked, I swallowed them. Best to leave Milton with happy memories sparkling in his eyes.

Instead, I locked eyes with Annabelle. What secrets did she harbor in that minute brain of hers? Had she watched from a dark corner while Levina was being. . . . ?

A loud ringing sound clanged through the backyard. I jerked and turned to search for the source of the noise. Unsure, I looked to Patty, then Milton. "The doorbell?"

He nodded, his eyes on the French doors. "Levina spent a lot of time working in her yard, so she hooked it up out here."

Patty pushed herself up out of her chair. "I'll see who's there." She slipped her feet into her sandals and disappeared through the French doors.

Milton chewed on his lower lip and rubbed his hands together. "I need to get back to my house," he said hurriedly. "I'll bring Annabelle's things by later."

"I'll be here." And Annabelle? Would she stay or follow him? "Thank you for all of the work you did in the yard, Milton. I really do appreciate it. It's incredibly beautiful. Once I'm settled, I'd like you to come to dinner. I've been known to put together a fairly decent meal."

A twinkle lit up his eyes. "That'd be nice." Hunched over with age, he turned and shuffled away. Annabelle didn't budge.

I studied her for several long moments, then set the daiquiris on the table and turned to make my way through the house to the front door. Annabelle scooted in through the French doors at my feet and padded down the hall ahead of me, a waddling mound of golden fur, her fluffy tail swishing behind her. Evidently, she was back home.

Patty stood in the entry, a starry-eyed look to her. It didn't take much logic to figure out who was there with her, hidden from view.

"Hi, Cal," I said as I fell in beside Patty.

Cal tore his lovesick eyes from Patty and nodded. "Evenin', Kit."

"Is this a *social* call?" I asked meaningfully. "Or do you want to talk with *me*?"

His blue eyes caressed Patty. "Oh . . . a little of both."

Cripes! This was like reliving the worst parts of my high school years — not one of my favorite times. "So?" I said in an effort to draw his attention away from Patty and back to the matter at hand. "Do you want to sit down?"

"Uh . . . no. I just need to check on a couple of things."

After a lingering glance in Patty's direction, he walked into the office, a room I'd purposefully avoided. I looked to Patty for answers. She raised her eyebrows, shrugged, and followed him. Bracing myself, I followed suit.

The room was crowded, three of its walls nearly covered with file cabinets and shelves jam-packed with books. Cal was sorting through the papers on a large desk. My eyes were drawn to an immense painting that took up a good portion of the wall above the desk. Its subject was ox-drawn covered wagons, an endless line of them. They were making their way across a flat, dry slab of land. Dust clouds billowed from the wooden wagon wheels and blurred the hills in the distance. The picture was bleak—awash in muted earth tones, browns and grays and sage—except for the yoke of the oxen pulling the lead wagon. The artist had painted it a brilliant blue. The only word I could think of to describe it was *bizarre*.

"Have you touched anything in here?" Cal asked.

"No, this is the first time I've been in here." Even now, not alone, prickles of unrest pestered the base of my neck. "This *is* where you found her, right?"

He frowned and nodded. "Yep, right here in this chair. Her head was down on the desk. Meg, down at the coffee shop, said Levina was in there the afternoon before she died. Said she was real excited about somethin' she'd found. But Levina hurried out of there.

Didn't tell Meg what it was. If it was somethin' new, I figured it'd either be on her desk at the store or here. I already checked the store; nothin' there but bills and receipts." His eyes traveled to a nearby computer. "We already checked that."

While he chewed on his mustache, his gaze wandered the room. Finally, he shook his head. "There's a lot of stuff here, too much for me to go through right now. I'd appreciate it if you'd keep your eyes open, and let me know if you see somethin' interesting."

Interesting? This house was brimming with interesting things. What kind of find would it take to excite Levina? "Of course," I assured him. "Anything else?"

His focus returned to Patty. "Uh . . . the alarm system."

Patty and I followed him to a small panel on the wall beside the French doors, where he punched some squeaking buttons. "I'll reset it for you. You'll need to contact the provider in the next few days and get things set up with them. But this will do for now." He pulled a small leather-bound notepad out of his pocket and wrote in it. "This is the code and the instructions," he said, handing a piece of paper to me. "That's the company's phone number at the bottom."

Memories of hot, stale air flooded me. "I can keep the windows open, right?"

"Not a good idea."

I must've looked as distraught as I felt because he didn't even wait for my response. "Kit, someone murdered your aunt right here in this house. Not long after that, you were nearly run down." His bushy mustache was twitching. "Has anything else happened?"

If he was trying to frighten me, it was working. I shivered and clutched my abdomen, worry an unsettling ball in my gut. Patty's arm settled around my shoulders to pull me close beside her. I managed to shake my head.

"Well, let's keep it that way," he said firmly. "At this point, I don't even have a list of suspects. The one thing I do suspect is that it was someone Levina knew, most likely someone close to her. Be cautious. Keep your doors and windows locked. And set this alarm at night and every time you leave this house."

Overwhelmed by the sudden need to dash around the house closing and locking all of the windows, I nodded.

His eyes darkened even more. "I hear you're allergic to strawberries."

My eyes shot to Patty. She shook her head.

Cripes! Patty was right; in a small town, gossip spread faster than air.

"That's the kind of thing you might want to keep to yourself," he informed me.

Thoroughly chastised and sufficiently frightened—I'm sure

that was his intention—I filled my lungs with air and expelled it slowly. "Okay. I get your message."

"Good," he muttered before he turned his attention to Patty. "You ready?"

Evidently, she and Cal had made plans for the evening. Exhaustion, or was it relief, settled over me, seeping into my arms and legs.

Patty looked concerned. "Do you mind?"

Truth be told, I was ready for some alone time. I studied the cat sprawled near my feet and amended that to include an obese feline who was fast becoming a leech. "Of course, not. You two kids get out of here and have some fun."

Patty withdrew her arm from my shoulders. "I need to get my Starbucks mug out of your car."

"I'll walk you out," I said.

Though it was still uncomfortably warm outdoors, the temperature had definitely dropped a couple of degrees. Across the street, Sophie's sprinklers sprayed, and the burr of a lawnmower drifted from somewhere nearby. Bird twitterings filled the air. Behind me, Cal and Patty murmured. Mercifully, I wasn't privy to their conversation.

I glanced at the gray house next door and wondered why Milton always came to my backdoor. I hadn't noticed a gate between our two yards.

"Since your windows will be closed, you'll need the air conditioner," Cal said.

I had to be beaming. "Air conditioner?" I sighed. With cool air flowing from my vents, all would be right with the world.

"The thermostat's in the dining room," he assured me.

A red sedan crept down the street towards us. Patty's gaze followed it, her eyes narrowed to slits. Immediately, the car accelerated and sped by, the driver a blur of pale blonde hair and sunglasses. Cal watched it pass, then pulled out his notepad and scribbled something in it.

"What is it?" I asked.

Patty shrugged. "Oh, probably nothing. But that lady drove by several times while we were unloading the cars this afternoon. She has too much of a rubber neck to be a curious neighbor." She seemed to mull something over. "And I'd swear I've seen her somewhere before."

Knots twisted in my stomach. I turned to Cal. "Did you recognize the car?"

He shook his head. "No. I'll run the license plate tomorrow."

I felt like I was in the middle of a Lifetime original movie—if only it were true. I surveyed my surroundings, an anxious search for a reason to stay.

Annabelle sat dauntingly at the front gate, guarding *our* house. She looked fierce, a presence not to be messed with.

"Let's hope there's action behind that attitude," I muttered, mostly to myself.

CHAPTER 7

Annabelle was dead to this world, sprawled on her broad back on a patch of sun-warmed hardwood, paws in the air. I studied her and sipped lukewarm coffee. If I could retrain kids, surely I could retrain a cat.

True to Milton's words, at exactly four-thirty the past two mornings, I'd been awakened from a deep, dreamy sleep by a shrill mewling noise—Annabelle. After traipsing groggily down the stairs to let her out this morning, I'd ended up in Levina's office in search of something Cal might have overlooked two days ago.

Other than an EpiPen handily stored in the top drawer, which could've saved Levina's life, I hadn't uncovered anything unusual. Instead, I'd organized paperwork and paid several bills. Fortunately, she'd left me a tidy bit of money and several investments that I'd yet to investigate thoroughly. My meager teaching salary wouldn't support Annabelle's eating habits, let alone two households.

A yawn escaped as I leaned back in the sturdy oak chair. I rubbed under my eyeglasses at a gritty eye, then drained the bitter dregs from the mug as my gaze wandered the room, past the laden bookcases to the brass clock on the far wall—only seven-sixteen.

Heavy pounding noises reverberated from the front porch. I froze, heart racing, then tip-toed to the window to peek out. Cripes! What was going on?

One of the ugliest runty dogs I'd ever seen was perched at the top of the steps, tiny tee-pee ears twitching and beady eyes tracking the man who was hauling junk up onto *my* porch—junk that I'd spent the entire previous day discarding!

"What the heck?" I muttered. My blood simmering in my veins, I marched out the front door to plant my feet between two boxes of garbage, fists on my hips. His eyes met mine—two spears of dark hostility—and I flinched. He set his jaw. Not to be outdone, I ground my back teeth together.

Abruptly, an ear-piercing yapping broke my focus, and my eyes snapped over to where the ugly dog bounced up and down like a noisy pogo stick. Annabelle sat a good foot from it, a bored-beyond-belief look to her.

"Stonewall, quiet!" the man barked.

Stonewall squirmed and danced on his tiny paws, his claws clicking on the white boards, but other than a few token whimpers, he followed orders. I turned my glare back to the tall, dark, sweat-dripping man with the ponytail. "What are you doing?" I hissed.

He leaned several ancient pictures against the porch railing. "No, the question is what are *you* doing?"

His jaw was working and he was taking deep breaths. Instinctively, I knew he was way better at this than I. Tenacious feelings of inadequacy rose within me, and I took a deep breath to fortify myself—stoic ice on the outside, quivering puddle inside.

"Do you think you can just waltz in here and discard Levina's possessions—her treasures? It took her a lifetime to collect them. I wonder how long it'll take *you* to dispose of them? At this rate, not long!" His voice was harsh, his eyes lethal.

The man was crazy, unstable, most likely worried I'd trash his lousy old books. "I have no plans to do anything with her treasures *or* your precious books," I informed him. "All I threw out was junk I couldn't even haul to Goodwill."

I grabbed a gray and white speckled pitcher from a box. "Look at it. Some of it's even rusted. And how much cast iron does the average person use today?" I picked up some old spice tins. "Most of these are empty, and their shelf life expired decades ago."

He was staring at me like I'd sprouted horns and a forked tail. "And the pictures?"

Surely, he wasn't serious. "I saved the good ones. Those are just old prints. If I keep them, they'll need to be matted and reframed."

His face turned a crimson color. "Reframed?" he choked.

Good grief! I didn't want him to pass out on my front porch. "Well, look at them. The glass is thick and wavy, and the frames are tacky and covered with little cracks."

His insolent eyes snaked down my body. He slowly shook his head, his mouth hanging open like his panting dog. "Da-amn, lady. Are you for real?"

Which was meant to be the insult it was! "Real enough to tell you to get off of my property. And stay off of it. If you get within ten feet of it again, I'll call Cal . . . er . . . Chief Preston and have you physically removed."

He didn't even blink. "That's not gonna happen."

"Chief Preston is a friend. If I call, he'll come."

His right eyebrow rose a good two inches. "Maybe so. But that's not the problem."

I narrowed my eyes to where he was a distorted blur.

"I live in the gray house next door," he said with a smirk.

"You live with Milton?" Why had Milton not mentioned that?

He harrumphed and gave me a look that said he'd put my IQ at around fifty. "Milton lives in the house behind this one."

I longed for a can of Easy Off and a giant wad of steel wool to scrub the disdain off his face. My recent rotten luck had just slid past bearable with the news that this jerk was my neighbor. A bundle of irritated nerve endings, I searched for something scathing to say.

He beat me to it. "Look, since you're so obviously *ignorant* of antiques, how about if you don't throw anything away unless you first run it by someone who knows the difference between trash and something of value?" His seedy gaze settled on the boxes at my feet. "Of course, I'll be more than happy to take anything you don't want off your hands."

The *ignorant* remark was totally out of line . . . even if it was true. I scanned the items he'd dumped on my porch. Surely, none of it had any value. "So, what is it with you? You slink around the neighborhood every morning snooping in people's garbage?"

He swallowed and clenched his fists. "I was running, and when I passed by your house, I noticed that you'd discarded some items that aren't actually garbage."

Running, huh? I'd been so irritated by his *holier than thou* attitude that I hadn't noticed his attire: baggy nylon shorts, sweat-soaked tee-shirt, and streamlined Adidas, chiseled features begging for a sharp razor. Tattoos? None that I could see.

A splash of pink grabbed my attention, and my eyes slid sideways to fasten on Sophie's mini shorts and pasty bird legs as she scurried towards us. Glittery pink sneakers adorned her feet.

"Bart, you're back," she shrieked, skirting the re-energized dog as she climbed the steps. She eyed the paraphernalia on the porch, a perplexed look on her face, then shifted her attention back to Bart. "Did you have a nice trip?"

Just like that, he was all smiles, etiquette, and southern charm. "Yes, thank you for asking. Charlotte in June wasn't unbearably sultry."

"You'll wish you'd stayed there. It's been a scorcher here." Her face scrunched up into a frown. "Have either of you seen Milton?"

"He's out in the Cord," Bart told her. "I saw him heading south on Highway Ninety-nine when I was running."

Her smile wilted. "If you see him, tell him I'm making him cabbage rolls for dinner. His favorite, you know. With Levina gone, he gets lonely." Leaning forward conspiringly, she whispered, "Good thing I'm currently available."

She waved halfheartedly at a black Lexus as it passed by, then paused and shook her head. "Have they stopped by yet?" she asked me, a disgusted look on her face.

My mind searched furtively and came up blank. "Has *who* stopped by?"

"That bitch Bernice and her loony daughter, that's who. They keep driving by, staring at *your* house as if it's miraculously going to be in their greedy hands."

Stunned, I searched down the street for the vehicle. It had disappeared from view. My stomach did a series of threatening flip-flops. "Driving by? You mean this morning?"

"And yesterday. And the day before that." She shook her crooked finger ominously. "I don't trust any of them. If Levina'd given them half a chance, they'd have robbed her blind. And mind you, they'll do the same to you. Don't you worry, Kit. If they come calling, I'll be right behind them. I won't let you spend one minute alone with those crooks."

"I doubt they'll stop by, Sophie. But thank you for your concern."

"Just be careful. A woman like you living here alone, who knows what might happen?" She gave Bart a lengthy, meaningful look before she scurried home.

Woman like me? What was that supposed to mean?

"About Levina's things," Bart said, interrupting my thoughts. His troubled eyes perused the jumbled mess on the porch. "There's an auction house over on the other side of Highway Ninety-nine. Harv's a fair guy. He'll tell you what has the most value—things you might want to sell in the store. And he can auction the rest for you."

Our eyes met. Maybe he wasn't totally irrational. Maybe some of this stuff was worth something. Unwilling to acquiesce verbally, I nodded.

From four feet away, I felt him relax. "I'll put it in your car for you?"

I shrugged. "I'll do it later."

It would be hard to miss the shifting of his jaw into a hard line.

Prickles of irritation turned to fury. "I'll do it. Good-bye."

His dark brows slashed into a stormy frown. "I'll be over this evening to get my books . . . and any of this stuff you don't want." A disparaging right eyebrow rose. "You know, Levina worked hard for what she had. If she'd known how little respect you'd have for her life's work, I doubt she would've left *any* of it to you."

With that, he turned and jogged away, ignoring the steps completely. "Stonewall!" he barked over his shoulder. Stonewall gave a yip and followed his master, his stunted legs churning.

I closed my eyes and tried to shut out his hurtful words and the prickles of guilt they'd ignited. In truth, it was none of his business what I did with my inheritance. So why was he so set on making it his business?

☼☼☼

Harv was as wide as he was tall, rather like a redneck Santa Claus in his snug, unbelievably soiled overalls. He wiped his dirty hands on a rag that looked to be equally as grimy and peered over the top of his bent wire-rims up at me.

"So you're Levina's niece, huh? Don't look much like her. She was a little scrap of a thing. Had a good eye, though. Let her loose in a pile of junk, and she'd root around and come out with somethin' she'd sell for beaucoup bucks."

A sad look settled on his face. "Yes sirree. I'm gonna miss her. Hear you inherited her house and the store. You inherit her uncanny ability to sniff out treasures, too?"

I pasted a pleasant smile on my face and shook my head. "Unfortunately, no."

"More like your cousin Roy, huh?"

Not sure what he was getting at, I waited. From my viewpoint, Roy and I were as different as cinnamon and cayenne—both spices but worlds apart in flavor.

"He stops by every so often to ask what somethin's worth. Must do a little antiquin' on the side. This your stuff?" he asked, eyeing the boxes I'd dropped just inside the door of the huge, stifling room.

"Yes." I wiped a rivulet of perspiration from my right temple. "My next-door-neighbor suggested that if there's anything of value here, you could sell it for me?"

"Bart, huh?" A knowing, tight-lipped smile creased his plump face. "Yep, I've a good idea how that conversation went." He chuckled, then added, "Bart's an okay guy. Just a touch overboard when it comes to anything old. Must be chewin' at his innards to have you livin' in Levina's house with all her things—a big, strong, attractive gal like you that won't put up with no guff like his Southern gent folderol."

Rendered speechless, I took a healthy swig from my bottle of Calistoga.

In the meantime, Harv managed to creak down onto his knees and begin pawing through boxes. Every so often, he'd hold something out to the sunlight filtering in through the dusty windows and push his glasses into place, one eye closed, to examine it closely. I watched him, noting the idiosyncrasies involved in examining prospective treasures.

With a good deal of effort and several helpful grunts, he finally scooted back up onto his feet, then tugged at the back of his crotch. "Well, little lady,"—merely an expression, I'm sure, since I towered over Harv by several inches—"you'll do better by most of this stuff if you sell it in your store. I won't get you what it's worth."

He pointed at the box of cast iron. "Those are all Griswolds— old as the hills. Can't beat that. That one Dutch oven's worth about seven big ones."

Big ones? "Dollar bills?"

"If you're talkin' hundreds."

Blood drained from my brain. Harv's voice pulsed on.

"The graniteware's pretty much as good as it gets, too. I once saw that there puddin' pan in an antique hole in Colorado. Had a nine hundred dollar price tag on it."

This was *not* good news. I'd been so certain that it was only *junk*. Now I'd never hear the end of it from Mr. Rub-it-in-your-face next door.

"You're as white as a trout's belly. You okay?"

I blinked several times. "I didn't expect these things to be so valuable."

"Like I said, what your aunt lacked in size, she made up for in good taste." With a sweep of his hands, he indicated the pictures stacked against the wall. "Those frames alone are worth a small fortune. The Audubon prints'll bring several grand each. Can't believe Bart hasn't nabbed those Civil War prints. I'm sure the rest are worth a pretty penny, too. Probably best to contact an auction house that deals with old art to get top dollar."

The room seemed so close, hot and stuffy, devoid of air. My skin was clammy, my cotton shorts and blouse damp and sticky. I rubbed at my temples, then faced Harv. "I'm sorry I took up so much of your time. You've been so gracious and helpful. Thank you."

A red glow suffused his cherub cheeks. "Well, I've never been known to turn away a pretty gal." He grinned a surprisingly white-toothed smile and nodded at several boxes. "Actually, you might want to leave those spice tins and the other containers for me to auction off. They're a hassle to mess with in a store. I'll make you some fun money."

I studied his perspiring features. "Sounds good. Do we just shake on it?"

He sniggered. "Nowadays there's some kind of form to fill out every time you take a crap. Damn near need a warehouse to store all the paperwork. If you trust me to count the stuff, it'll only take a couple of minutes. I get twenty percent of whatever it goes for." With that, we headed to the far end of the room, his short legs doing double time to my longer ones.

A stage filled with a hodgepodge of assorted items flanked the far wall. As we drew near, my eyes scanned its contents and landed on a large painting. Curious, I climbed the steps and wove my way through the maze of tables and chairs to get a closer look.

The artist had painted a pastoral setting—sweeping meadow, meandering stream, and puffy clouds. In the foreground, snaking out across the canvas, was a tree branch. On that branch sat a nest filled with three huge eggs. The painting should have evoked images of spring, in lush, verdant colors. Instead, it was painted in drab hues of brown, green, and gray. The one exception was the three eggs; they popped from the canvas, a bizarre bright blue.

"Can't help but wonder what the guy was high on when he painted it, huh?" Harv asked from behind me. "It's your Uncle Jack's."

"Uncle Jack? I don't have. . . ." But I did, whiskey fumes and all. I eyed Harv.

"Brought it in last week. Said it was painted by some long gone ancestor of his. Said he was tired of lookin' at it. 'Depressin' as hell,' is how he put it." Harv gave his head a slow, troubled shake. "Tried to talk him out of it. Told him I wouldn't get him what it's worth. He said it wasn't worth shit hangin' on his wall, and if it brought in enough for a couple of bottles of prime Kentucky bourbon, he'd be satisfied."

Jack was selling the family painting to buy alcohol? And hadn't Sophie mentioned gambling, too? Was he that desperate for money?

If so, what measures would he be willing to take to appease his addictions?

☼☼☼

The shrill ring from a phone startled me. I jerked and nearly dropped a rosebud-adorned plate I was arranging on a shelf. "Whew!" I breathed. If the junky-looking stuff I'd shown Harv was worth a fortune, I didn't even want to contemplate the value of that gorgeous plate. Instead, I grabbed the phone off the hook. This is Kit."

"Hi, Kit. Cal here. I got a name on that license plate from the other evenin'."

My pulse quickened. "And?"

"The car belongs to Janet Bass. Isn't she family?"

A vision formed before me—petite woman, thick mane of blond hair, nerves strung tighter than a fiddle string. "Yeah, she's Bernice's daughter. Sophie said she and her mother have been driving by this house regularly during the last couple of days." Another picture formed in my mind, one from that morning. "Bernice drives a black Lexus."

"They just drive by? Don't stop?" He sounded perturbed.

"Nope." I considered his words and wished I hadn't. "As far as I know, the things Levina left them are here in this house. Maybe they're working up the courage to get them."

"Hmmm," his voiced hummed. "You keeping your doors and windows locked?"

"Just like I promised," I assured him. The thermostat was currently set at a cool sixty-five, cold enough to drive Annabelle to the heat of the back porch.

"Well, keep your eyes open and let me know if anything happens." A clicking sound followed, then the telltale buzz.

"Nice talking with you, too," I muttered, slipping the phone back into place.

So that bitch Bernice and her loony daughter—I saw no reason not to use Sophie's highly suitable adjectives—were spying on me. Roy, too? After my visit with Harv, I now had a better understanding of how enraged my kinfolk must be by the few token items Levina had left them. They had truly lost a fortune.

But was I also flailing away under someone else's microscope? The thought made my skin crawl. Bart was right next-door, and Milton spent a lot of time in my backyard. Sophie was clearly watching my every move. The house next to hers appeared to be empty.

The doorbell's piercing ring interrupted my ruminations. I shook my head to clear my thoughts and settle the erupting jitters in my stomach. What was it Harv had said, something about being surprised that Bart hadn't taken some of Levina's pictures? Well, he wouldn't be leaving this house with anything except his precious books. "Arrogant jerk," I muttered as I ambled to the front door.

My hand on the doorknob, I paused, my heart beating wildly. If he might steal to get what he wanted, might he also commit murder? As I opened the door, Bart's name shot to the top of my suspect list. I stepped back to let him pass by me into the entry, where he stopped to peruse the menagerie of boxes housed in the dining room.

Flames radiated from my cheeks. "Harv wasn't interested in selling it," I explained.

He smiled—actually, it was more a smirk than a smile. Cripes. This visit couldn't be over soon enough. "Do you know where the books are?" I inquired.

Evidently, he did because he stepped into the office. The sturdy desk chair seemed a familiar sanctuary from which I could keep my eyes on him so I settled into it, caressing the smooth, well-rubbed wood on the arms for support.

His eyes lingeringly circled the room, scanning the plethora of items, caressing them. I watched, fascinated that something so static could hold so much allure. Obviously, the guy was lost in his own private nirvana; his perusal passed over me as if I were a speck of dust hidden beneath the layers that coated the room.

At last, his gaze settled on the peculiar painting with the bright blue splotch of color. "I'd like to buy it," he said, his voice soft, husky.

Why would he want that weird picture? "Pardon?" I queried.

He turned to me, his glare piercing me with its intensity. "The painting; I'd like to buy it."

The guy had intimidation down to a fine art. Like a blow-up toy, I deflated deeper into the chair's arms. "I'm not interested in selling it," I muttered.

"You interested in throwing it in the garbage?" he goaded.

Heat blossomed in my cheeks. I forced my lips into a smile. "If I do, I'm sure you'll be the one to rescue it. Then you won't be out any money, will you?"

His jaw locked. "I'll pay you what it's worth."

It was a mute point; a million bucks wouldn't place that unappealing painting in his covetous hands. Still, I couldn't help but wonder what he might do to get it. "I can't place a value on a family heirloom," I informed him.

His right eyebrow shot up. "You know about it then?"

Know what about it? My brain shot into overdrive, weighing the merits of possible responses—to pretend wisdom or admit ignorance. "It depends on what you're referring to."

He hesitated, studying me. "I was referring to the artist."

My pulse quickened. "Well, yes, I do have some knowledge of the artist," I hedged—like that he was some long dead relative of mine and that he must have viewed his world through some grossly distorted lenses. Or perhaps he was off his rocker and has passed the defective gene down through the generations to my aunt and cousins.

I felt him poking about in my head before he spoke. "I thought you weren't on speaking terms with Bernice and her kids. So what tasty tidbits did they divulge to you about Great-great-granddaddy?"

"Great-great-granddaddy?"

The reproving sneer on his face made me wish I'd checked my tongue. "You don't know a damn thing about the painting or the artist, do you?" he challenged.

I was cornered, and he was basking in the knowledge of it. "For your information, I *do* know something about that painting," I informed him, pausing to search frantically for something—anything—to prove my point. "I know there's another one by the same artist . . . err, Great-great-granddaddy, at the auction house. Harv's selling it for my Uncle Jack."

Both eyebrows shot up this time. "Jack's selling his painting? Are you sure?"

His passion-filled eyes held me spellbound. "I saw it with my own eyes," I murmured. "Same drab colors, except for three bright blue eggs that practically reach out and grab you."

He turned away, back to the painting on the wall. Seconds seemed to stretch into minutes. "Have you seen any others?"

I shook my head—a flat-out lie—my mind flitting to a painting currently stashed in storage with the rest of my father's belongings. Then I thought of the intricately carved monstrosity. "The carved mantle," I ventured.

He nodded tentatively. His troubled eyes were on me, but his thoughts seemed far away. "Your great-great-grandfather was an interesting man," he said softly, as if he were telling himself, not me. "He went to his grave too early . . . and with too many secrets."

Several rapid blinks later, he added, "At least, your aunt thought so."

"Levina? What are you talking about?"

Now that he'd captured my curiosity, he seemed hesitant to elaborate. Seconds ticked by. "It's hard to say exactly," he finally said. "Unless she had a couple of glasses of wine in her, Levina was tight-lipped about the whole thing. But she was obviously obsessed by it."

My mind shot back to that afternoon in the attorney's office, searching for words Bernice had uttered in anger. "Obsessed by what?" I asked.

"Your great-great-grandfather—James Wallace—and the Blue Bucket. She was convinced he'd found it."

That was it! Bernice had claimed that both my mother and Levina were obsessed by a blue bucket. The hammering of my heart seemed to fill the room. "You're saying Levina was obsessed because she thought her great-grandfather had found a blue bucket?"

He had a way of tilting his head forward to look at me; it was not an accolade. "Not *a* blue bucket," he enunciated, "*The* Blue Bucket."

I turned to the painting, searching. No blue buckets. Resigned, I eyed him. "Okay. What is *the* Blue Bucket?"

A smug smile touched his lips. "Gold. More accurately, a cache of gold nuggets."

"And my great-great-grandfather found this gold?" Curious trickles of nervous energy shot along my nerve endings.

"Levina thought so. She didn't have any evidence, of course. It was based mostly on stories that had passed down through the generations in your family."

Bernice had alluded to that. Still, if both my mother and Levina were convinced, perhaps there was something to it. "Where was this gold?"

He shrugged and his focus returned to the painting. "No one knows for sure. Somewhere out there in those endless miles of desert and sagebrush. As far as anyone knows, it's still there."

"Is that why you want the painting? You think it's tied to the gold?"

Our eyes met. His seemed dazed, as if he'd returned from a distant place. "If it is, Levina would've figured it out. But no, she was still searching." He rubbed his temples and shrugged. "There's probably nothing to it, anyway. Just a legend family members concocted to explain your great-great-grandfather's unusual behaviors."

"Sophie mentioned that he didn't fit in; why not?"

Bart walked to a wooden stool in the corner and lowered himself onto it. He extended his long legs and crossed them at the ankles. The stool was hidden, giving the appearance that he was perched on a puff of air. Overbearing and, beneath the facial hair, possibly decent looking, he oozed a self-confident intensity that left me feeling vulnerable.

His eyes, narrowed to mere slits, focused on me. "From what Levina told me, I gathered that James Wallace wasn't a good match with the community that was here at that time. For one thing, the colony was founded by a group of German immigrants—religious zealots—and he was a Highland Scot.

"Aurora Colony wasn't your typical frontier settlement. It was more like what we call a commune today. All property and possessions were common to all members of the community, and everyone was expected to labor for the good of all who resided here. Plain living was the expectation."

Was it any wonder his paintings were so conflicting? "How did he end up here?" I probed.

"Your great-great-grandmother; evidently, she was quite a looker—tiny, blonde, and beautiful." He eyeballed me, obviously trying to figure out how my height and coloring had descended from her petite perfection. "She was also German and a devout member of the colony. The James Wallace Levina spoke of was a man who tried to fit in. But he was an artist, a dreamer. While he wanted to create artistically, he was expected to do his share of the labor. He'd leave home and be gone for long periods of time, supposedly searching for the Blue Bucket gold."

Instinctively, I leaned forward, enthralled by this snapshot of my ancestors—living, breathing people with distinct personalities who'd lived on the very land on which I was now residing. "But if he found the gold, he'd have to give it to the colony, right?"

Bart shrugged. "That's why he hid it, or so the story goes. Certain that the colony would soon be breaking up, he stashed the gold somewhere. Then he died suddenly in 1875—a fall from his horse—two years before Aurora Colony disbanded. Unfortunately, he didn't tell anyone where he hid the gold, not even his wife or son. Probably thought they'd turn it over to Dr William Keil, their leader."

I studied him. Dim light from the windows softened his sharp features. "Do you think it's true?"

His eyes shot to the painting and he shrugged. "One thing's certain: James Wallace was on the wagon train. So I suppose he could've been one of the kids who discovered the gold originally."

He'd lost me again. "On the wagon train?"

"Uh-huh." His weight shifted forward on the stool, and he rested his forearms on his thighs. "There are as many stories about the lost Blue Bucket as there are people who've wasted their time looking for it. Your great-great-grandfather came west with his parents on the Meek wagon train in 1845. The train got lost out in the desert, heading west from the Idaho border across the dry central portion of Oregon. They'd gone days without water and finally, as a last resort, sent several young people out to search for water. Levina believed that Wallace was one of the young men in that group.

"Miraculously, they did find water. The story goes that they also found gold—lots of it—but they were so excited by the water that they didn't realize it was real gold until years later when someone took a closer look at the samples they'd kept."

Noticing that I had a death grip on the chair arms, I took a deep breath and tried to relax. "And when Wallace found out it was real gold, he went back to get it?"

Bart's eyes drifted to a large bookcase with glass doors. "That's the story," he mumbled distractedly. "Only, it wasn't that easy."

"What do you mean?" I probed sharply.

His gaze flicked back to me, intense through the evening murkiness. "At that time, there were no roads . . . or even trails. The region is rugged—full of rocky hills and ravines and long flat spaces that go on forever. Much of it looks the same. And it wasn't mapped. The wagon train had covered a lot of area in their search for water. They were lost and they were desperate. Years later, no one remembered where the gold was."

"Then why did Levina think Wallace had found it?"

"During the last few years of his life, he stayed home. He built an extravagant house for his family —the one we're sitting in right now —and pretty much isolated himself from the rest of the colony. That's when he carved the mantle and painted the pictures." His eyes slid back to the painting on the wall; mine followed. "Levina believed he was biding his time until the colony broke apart and he could bring the gold out of hiding."

In some weird way, it all made sense. And Bernice had said that my mother believed it to be true. Still. . . . "So why did they call it the Blue Bucket?"

"Legend has it that several of the wooden buckets on the wagon train were painted an unusual shade of blue. When the kids went out to search for water, they took those buckets with them. That's the name that stuck."

A disquieting thought pestered me: could what Bart had just disclosed to me have something to do with Levina's death? If she believed so strongly in the family legend, perhaps someone else did, too. Someone who wanted that gold. Someone like Bart.

Cripes! Here I was alone with him. My pulse quickened and I clenched the chair arms. "If Levina was so closed-mouthed, how do you know so much about all of this?"

Sparks flickered in his eyes. His jaw tightened into a steely line. In one fluid movement, he rose to his feet and strode to the corner to pull the switch on an ornate floral lamp. Fingers of light reached out into the room, creating unsettling shadows. "Once again, you're talking about something you know absolutely nothing about," he said snootily before he made his way to the bookcase he'd been eyeing.

I flinched at the rancor in his voice. His dislike of me was a heavy fog, shrouding the room in disquiet. I stared at his broad back. He was burly, potent, overshadowing all else in the room with his presence.

A muted rattling sound invaded my thoughts. "I need the key," he muttered testily.

I swiveled the chair to retrieve the jangling mass of keys I'd found in a drawer that morning. Hesitant to turn them over to him, I tentatively made my way to his side. As I worked my way around the ring, trying one key at a time, my damp fingers fumbled. He was too close. Warm breaths tickled the hairs on the back of my neck, sending prickly shivers down my back. Heat radiated from his body into mine, and something else—a coiled tension that threatened to explode.

Desperate to escape, I handed the keys to him and met his fiery gaze. He was mere inches from me, a hovering threat. Frozen in place, the thunder of my heartbeat pounding in my head, I struggled frantically to decipher his thoughts before he acted on them.

Would he reach out to plant an offensive kiss on my lips? Or would he reach out to wrap his strong fingers around my neck and squeeze the life from my body?

Quirking an eyebrow, he turned his attention to the lock on the bookcase.

Air seeped from my body, sucking the strength from my limbs. I dragged myself across the room, then collapsed into the chair, a limp noodle.

Down on his knees now to gain access to the soft light from the lamp, he was absorbed, his movements barely discernible. Every so often he added a book to the growing stack on the floor. Darkness crept into the corners of the room, giving his actions an otherworld ambiance, as if he were on stage and I merely a spectator.

Just like that, it hit me, a boulder landing in the pit of my stomach. This was *his* life, not mine. I was the outsider here—a circle trying to fit into a triangular hole. He probably had in-depth knowledge of every book in that bookcase, yet I didn't even know how old the bookcase was.

A cloud of melancholy settled over me, an empty, hollow feeling deep in my soul. Until this moment, I hadn't realized how much I wanted this new life to work out. Sometime during the last two days, I'd grown attached to my new home and all that it offered. Foolishly, I'd begun to believe that my living here might work. In truth, I didn't belong here; would I ever?

At last he gathered the books into the crook of an arm, and in one fluid movement, he rose to his feet. Our eyes locked, his brooding. "Did you remove some books from the bookcase?" he asked.

I shook my head.

His frown deepened. "I noticed that several volumes are missing. You sure you didn't clean out the bookcase, too?"

Was he accusing me of stealing his stupid books? "I haven't touched that bookcase or anything in it," I muttered.

His eyes slowly scanned the room and halted in a far corner. "The Handel is gone, too. Levina wouldn't have let that go." He turned to me. "You do something with it?"

A painful chill sliced through me. I hadn't a clue what a Handel was. But whatever it was, I hadn't tossed it in the garbage.

"It's a lamp," he uttered curtly.

My eyes darted to the corner. There definitely was no lamp there. I shook my head, then scanned the rest of the room. What else was missing? I vaguely remembered Sophie yammering on about a missing clock.

Bart stepped to the desk and pawed through several neat piles, my morning's work. "Make yourself at home," I uttered, shocked by his rudeness.

He glanced up. "What?"

"This is my desk, not yours."

I wanted to believe that his face turned a tad pinkish. "Levina kept a notebook of all of her business dealings," he explained. "If she bought something or sold something or even gave it away, she recorded it in that book. She kept it right here . . . always." He pointed to an empty compartment. "You remember seeing it?"

"No," I told him. And I was certain of that. I'd sorted through every piece of paper on that desktop. There was no notebook.

"You sure?"

I ground my back teeth together, struggling for composure. "I did not see that notebook. I did not hide it. And I didn't dump it in the garbage," I assured him.

He appeared to be thinking, his fingers caressing his furry chin. "Makes me wonder what else is missing. That notebook would help. Odd that it's gone . . . *now*." He gave me a final searching look, then held out his books to me. "You want to check them?"

I shook my head, willing him to leave.

"Suit yourself," he muttered before he headed for the door.

Bone weary, I relaxed back into the chair and let my eyes roam the office in search of other missing items. Cripes! I didn't have a clue what was supposed to be in this house, so I couldn't even keep Levina's prized possessions safe.

And what if someone was stealing them; would that be a motive for murder?

CHAPTER 8

I squeezed my pint-size SUV into the parking space next to a police cruiser, then soaked up cooled air as Eva Cassidy crooned about the perils of love. "You tell 'em, girl," I mumbled, rubbing at the apprehension that clung to me like drier-charged polyester.

Outside the window, ancient-looking buildings lined the street. Couples strolled on warped sidewalks, lingered at outdoor displays, and gazed into shop windows. Profusions of purple, pink, and white petunias cascaded from halved oak barrels, and a crooked line of droopy saplings provided meager shade from the sun's incessant rays.

Nestled behind a profusion of bushes and vibrant blossoms, *Levy's Loot*, my recently inherited antique shop, beckoned to me. Trepidation sent my eyes to the building next door. *The Coffee Counter—ice cream, pastries, sandwiches* screamed in gold Calligraphy on one of the front windows. If my ignorance became too overwhelming, it was reassuring to know that quality sustenance was only a few steps away.

Suddenly, the very air began to vibrate, and a deafening roar muted Eva. I stilled, my car trembling on its four tires. A series of shrill screams erupted. Gritting my teeth against the pain in my ears, I turned to watch an Amtrak fly by the old depot across the street. When I least expected it, one of those wretched things blasted through town. It was unsettling.

Sighing deeply, I steeled myself. It was time to prove to my irksome next-door neighbor that I *could* handle Levina's possessions responsibly. And not just him. After several days of removing dust that, like powdered sugar on a warm cake donut, clung to everything inside Levina's house, I now harbored a bizarre closeness to her. She'd trusted me with her possessions; I wouldn't betray that trust. I'd taken this on, and now I was determined to press forward in a manner befitting my dead aunt—at least, until the first of August.

If I had it, the missing notebook would certainly be of help. Unfortunately, I hadn't uncovered it, nor any photographs, which didn't mesh with the borderline obsessive packrat tendencies Levina clearly possessed. It was as if someone had rummaged her whole house and confiscated every photo album and framed snapshot in the place.

I sighed again. Undoubtedly, there were many mysteries to solve in that house. Not today; today I was determined to become acquainted with her antique shop. That is, after I checked out the coffee and pastries next door.

When I stepped inside, the aroma of high-end coffee and freshly baked bread saturated me like a decadent mist. I paused, blinking to adjust to the dim coolness of the room. As happened so often lately, I felt as if I'd entered another time. From the ceiling of ornately decorated tin squares high above, several rotating fans dangled. The darkly stained wallboards displayed scars from decades of wear, and checkered yellow and white oilcloth squares covered the few tables that dotted the scuffed wooden floors.

Two couples occupied a table to my right, sipping from ceramic mugs and nibbling on gooey-looking pastries while they chatted. On the wall directly above them was a picture that stopped me in my tracks. Again, the scene was pastoral—a luxuriant grassy carpet stretched across the crest of a hill and down to a river that beckoned below it. Bushy trees and shrubs and splotches of flowers should have made the scene blossom. Instead, they added to its dreariness. The only bright spot in the painting was the brilliant blue river. If not for it, the picture would go unnoticed, fading into the dark wall behind it.

"Sit wherever you want."

The chipper voice pulled me from my reverie to an elaborately decorated counter that bordered the back wall. A stunning blond woman in a revealing halter-top posed behind the counter, a disarming smile lighting up her perfect features. A couple of feet from her sat Cal, his hands cradling a coffee mug, his brows furled into a frown.

"Mornin'," he muttered as I approached them. "Meg, this here's Kit, Levina's niece. Kit, this beautiful young lady is Meg. She owns this place."

I paused, my eyes darting from Meg to Cal. Did he think of Patty as his beautiful *old* lady? I could discern fine lines around Meg's eyes and mouth, telltale signs of a woman in her thirties—too young for Cal.

I forced a grin. "Nice to meet you, Meg."

"You, too," she said. "So you're my new neighbor. Awesome! It'll be so nice to have someone nearer my own age to hang out with. As you've probably noticed, this town is a seniors' haven. I'm convinced you have to flash your AARP card to buy property." A rosy glow accentuated her finely chiseled cheekbones when she turned to Cal. "No offense, Cal. If everyone aged as nicely as you, I wouldn't be complaining."

The evocative smile she gave him could've melted the polar ice cap. It turned his face a vivid shade of red. "Coffee?" she asked, breaking the awkward silence.

I slipped onto a vinyl-covered stool and murmured, "Yes, please; black." Intrigued by the painting, I glanced over my shoulder to have a second look. When I turned back, Meg was studying me, a puzzled expression on her face. A steaming mug sat on the counter, and a rich fragrance swirled enticingly around me.

"You want anything else?" Meg asked.

Calorie-laden pastries beckoned to me from a glass case, and my stomach growled in anticipation. "No, thank you," I blurted before I succumbed.

Meg's focus shifted to the front of the building. "I better check on my guests."

She disappeared around the corner of the bar, and I switched my focus to Cal. He was frowning into his coffee, mustache chewing.

His obvious anxiety was contagious. Suddenly aware that my nails were clicking rhythmically on the coffee mug, I stilled them. "Something bothering you?" I ventured.

Cal huffed and shook his head. "It's your friend . . . Patty."

"Oh," I breathed, sneaking a glance at Meg. A tight knot twisted in my stomach as I pictured Patty's radiant face, up to her frosted locks in love with Cal from their first tumultuous meeting. Was he as fickle as the rest of his species? I took a hefty gulp of coffee and stared into its murkiness. "What about her?"

He cleared his throat. "Well, I was kinda hopin' maybe you could tell me somethin' she likes—perfume, flowers, candy, whatever. I wanted to buy her somethin'. You know, make a good impression," he stammered.

Like sinking into a hot tub at the end of a tough day, relief seeped through me. My eyes sought his. Red suffused his cheeks and spread in blotchy patches down his neck. He surely was a treasure, this man Patty had managed to snare. How could I have doubted him?

"Patty adores orchids," I told him. "Any color will do, but she absolutely loves white orchids. She's allergic to perfume, and although she's a chocolate fanatic, she'd probably strangle you if you gave her some because she'd devour every single bite of it. Then she'd spend weeks exercising every ounce of it off of her perfect body. I'm sure you'd much rather that she spends that time with you."

A strange twinkle sparkled in Cal's blue eyes. "Orchids it is then. Thanks."

"You're welcome," I said before I turned to coffee sipping and mind-wanderings.

Cal seemed content to muse and sip in silence, too. I couldn't help but wonder if his blooming relationship with Patty was causing him to neglect his job.

"Any news on Levina's death," I finally ventured.

He sighed and scratched his temple. "Nope, nothin'."

I matched his sigh and took a fortifying swig of caffeine. "You know, something's been bothering me. Levina's house, and most likely the store, too, is full of very valuable items, and they're still there." *Most of them, anyway,* I added silently as I struggled to pull my thoughts together. "So, unless her murderer planned to inherit all of her stuff, the motive must've been something other than money. Maybe someone just wanted her dead."

"Could be there is somethin' missin'."

I shrugged. He was right. Without her notebook, I had no idea what was supposed to be in that house, nor the store. "Actually, Sophie mentioned a missing clock. And Bart claims that several books aren't in the bookcase and that a lamp Levina prized is gone."

His brows furled, he pulled a small notepad and pen from his shirt pocket and jotted some notes. "Anything else?" he finally asked.

"I really don't know," I admitted. "Bart said Levina had a notebook that she recorded all of her business dealings in, but I can't find it."

He scribbled, then stuffed the pad and pencil back into his pocket. "I'll check into it. In the meantime, keep your eyes open, and let me know if somethin' else comes up missin'."

I eyed my empty mug and considered Cal's words, which brought up another question. "You know, there was an EpiPen in the desk drawer. So far, it's the only one I've found. If Levina was that allergic to strawberries, surely she'd keep medication strategically placed around her house. Did you find any?"

He shook his head. "No, once we knew how she was murdered, we went through every inch of her house. That's one of the things we were lookin' for. That kit in the desk drawer was the only one we found. And it hadn't been used."

"So, what if someone took them from the more obvious places, but they didn't know about the one in her office. Maybe that's why she was down there. She managed to get to the office but wasn't able to open the drawer and get to the kit in time."

He worked his mustache, contemplative. "I suppose you'd know more about that than me, you bein' allergic to strawberries," he said just as Meg rounded the counter.

She froze and stared at me, open-mouthed. "You're allergic to strawberries, too?"

I nodded, perturbed. At this rate, I might as well put a notice in the local newspaper.

"Bummer." She stuffed a wad of money into a monstrous archaic cash register.

Rustling noises from the front of the café drew my attention—Meg's guests returning to their antiquing adventures—and my eyes were drawn to the painting. "Meg?" I probed.

"Yeah." Carafe in hand, she faced me.

"That picture on the wall over there, the one with the bright blue river?"

A curious frown wiped the cheery smile from her face. "Yeah?"

"Do you know anything about it?"

The frown deepened. "Other than that one of your ancestors painted it, not much."

So, it *was* yet another family painting. "Where did you get it?"

She shrugged her tanned shoulders. "As far as I know, it's been in my family since the beginning of time. My ancestor was a neighbor of yours. That's all I know about it . . . except that it totally pisses off your Aunt Bernice that I have it." She filled our empty mugs, then added, "But if you want to know more about it, ask Uncle Milton."

"Milton is your uncle?" I gasped. As a fiery Jalapeno pepper to your basic Bell, I couldn't quite fit Meg's gregarious personality with Milton's more somber one.

"Yep," she cheeped. "My mother's one and only sibling. He resides in the family mansion now. Someday it'll be mine, and we'll be double neighbors. Won't that be a hoot?"

"Uh-huh," I breathed.

"We can sit on your back porch, sip Mojitos, and ogle Bart over the picket fence," she continued. "Maybe he'll even take his shirt off." She paused to fan herself with a plastic-covered menu. "Whew! Can't help but get a bit worked up thinking about that big, hunky body of his strollin' along behind a power mower."

I felt my cheeks grow warm and considered my own menu to fan the glow away.

She was studying me. "So you've met him, huh? He can be a real jerk. But he can also be a pretty decent guy."

"That remains to be seen," I muttered.

She tittered nervously, her gaze drifting off to the painting. "You know, as depressing as that picture is, it kinda cracks me up."

"Why's that?" I asked, grasping onto the change of topic.

"Well, it's supposed to be the Pudding River, you know, the way it was back then, without all of the buildings and roads we have here now. Only you've seen the Pudding River, right? It looks just like its name—thick and dark like chocolate pudding. No way is it the clear blue river in that picture. Wishful thinking, I guess."

I studied the painting, wondering if it might be possible to find the exact spot from which it was painted. What looked to be a stone well was in the foreground."

"Your long dead ancestor painted that smaller picture, too," Meg informed me.

My eyes shifted left to the painting of a woman and a small boy. They posed in wooden chairs in front of a newly planted tree, their faces quiet and composed, almost sad. Both of them were covered from head to toe in black.

"Something tells me Great-great-grandma wasn't the life of the party," I said.

Meg laughed. "They're *my* ancestors, not yours. The boy is Uncle Milton's grandfather. Life wasn't easy back then, especially here in Aurora. Not much to get excited about."

Which triggered a memory: "You know, Meg, Cal told me that Levina was in here the day she died, that she seemed excited."

Meg nodded slowly, her gaze darting to Cal before it settled back on me.

"But you don't know why?" I prodded.

She shook her head, her eyes guarded. "Levina'd come over to chat or show me her latest purchase. I think she'd forget it was me she was talking to."

"Before she moved to Arizona, Meg's mother ran this place. She and Levina were close friends," Cal added from beside me.

My eyes slid over to note the sudden spark of interest in his, then slid back to Meg. "But she was unusually excited about something on that afternoon, right?" I prodded.

"Yeah." Meg rubbed her lips together as if she were searching for answers. "It was around two. I could tell she was really wound up, but also distracted. Then all of a sudden, she got up and left. Didn't pay for her coffee, something she'd never done before.

"I had some customers—a bunch of rowdy teenagers—so I was distracted, too. It was later, when Cal asked me about it, that I got to thinking about how she wasn't herself on that day." She paused, then added, "Actually, she seemed more anxious than excited."

Abruptly, her eyes lit up and her focus shifted to the front of the building. "You know, it just hit me. Levina kept looking toward that front window. I thought the kids were bothering her, but it wasn't them she was looking at; it was the painting."

I turned to study the picture. "Are you sure?"

"Yeah, it was you, the way you kept glancing at it—one of those déjà vu moments. You have that same look on your face, as if you're searching for something in it."

I stood and made my way to the painting to inspect it more closely. It was clear that the artist had talent. He could've left a legacy of tranquil beauty. Instead, he'd created a series of absurd disparities. Why?

As I examined the two paintings, I realized that Meg was right. Instinctively, I was searching for something. Had Levina finally seen what I couldn't? And had that knowledge somehow led to her death that night?

☼☼☼

Secure in my cozy nest at the desk behind the counter, I peeked through a glass display case crammed with sparkling jewelry, small silver objects, and translucent perfume bottles to the profusion of items on the other side. Glassware sparkled from inside cabinets, mingling with colorful pottery and china. Worn books and a hodgepodge of other items rested on crowded shelves. Fragile garments and lacy linens hung from racks.

I rubbed at the growing pain above my right temple, then took a swig of Calistoga, doubt gnawing at me as I envisioned glowing dollar signs breaking free to slowly evaporate into the great beyond. What was I doing here in Levina's pride and joy—*Levy's Loot*?

A loud series of knocks erupted and I choked on the water. "Hello. Anyone in there?" It was a male voice and it sounded determined.

I swiped at the water on the front of my blouse and squinted at the door. A face was framed in the window—Liam Neeson features, fashionably styled auburn hair, searching eyes, glimmering set of pearly whites. I had no idea who he was, but it was midday in the center of town—surely safe—so I shuffled past the array of old stuff to the door.

He towered over me. "Bob Crosley," he announced, his voice resonant, handshake firm, and twin dimples dancing. "I own the depot across the street. I saw you come in here, and as soon as I got a break, I hustled over here to introduce myself."

I stepped through the door to join him in the sweltering heat, my eyes drifting across to where a boxy, yet rambling, nineteenth century train station stretched along a railroad track. Red, white, and blue flags burst from its mellow buttery-yellow siding. If not for the cars parked along the street, it would be as if I'd gone back in time. Was it my imagination or did the air even smell old? "Kit O'Maley, Levina's niece. It's nice to meet you," I murmured.

"Yes, she told me all about you, and I must say you're as

beautiful as your pictures. She said such wonderful things about you. It's too bad you didn't get to meet her." His gaze flicked across the street, then back to me.

I knew I was probably gaping but I couldn't help it. He knew about me? Had seen pictures of me? He seemed pleasant enough—actually, rather nice—but why had Levina shared information with him that she hadn't even shared with her family? "Yes, it seems she was quite a woman," I mumbled, madly scrambling to make sense of his disclosures.

"One-of-a-kind. A real treasure." He looked away, across the street again. When he looked back, his gaze froze on Meg, who'd stepped out of the *Coffee Counter* next door. Her eyes were riveted on the two of us, the oddest expression on her face.

"You knew Levina well?" I probed.

A hood seemed to have dropped over his face. "Uh . . . yes." His eyes darted across the street and he murmured, "Looks like I have customers. I better get back." And he was off, throwing over his shoulder, "Nice to meet you," as he strode away.

"Huh," I grunted as I watched three people walk through the front door of the depot. I glanced next door. Meg's eyes were following Bob. "Something wrong?" I yelled.

She gave me one final hard look before she marched across the street.

"Cripes," I whispered as I made my way back to the desk. What was that all about? Meg had been polite and welcoming that morning—downright bubbly, in fact. What had changed between then and now? And who, exactly, was Bob Crosely?

I wiped perspiration from my face and stared at the air-conditioner humming above me, then unbuttoned several buttons on my cotton blouse and tugged forward on the opening to relish the chilling tingle on my chest and stomach. If Levina had shared secrets with Bob, why had no one mentioned him? And where had she gotten pictures of me?

Thoughts of Levina took me back to my morning conversation with Meg. What had prompted Levina to leave the diner so quickly the day she'd died? It'd been mid afternoon. Several hours later, she'd dined with Milton, yet he hadn't mentioned her amazing discovery or even that she'd seemed overly excited. So what had she been up to before she'd arrived at Milton's house?

My eyes scanned the massive oak desk. Did it hold clues to the answers I was seeking? "Well, you'll never know if you don't get back to work," I scolded myself.

With a deep sigh of resignation, I studied the unstable wall of paper I'd plucked from the desk. I'd been pulling files from the top of the stack and perusing their contents for several hours. It was slow, tedious work, but hopefully I'd leave the store with a better understanding of antique dealings than when I'd entered it.

Fortifying myself, I chugged a slug of Calistoga. Stray tendrils tickled annoyingly against my cheeks. I set the bottle down, loosened my ponytail, and gathered the strands of hair together. The rubber band shot across the room.

"Shit!" I snapped, then hunted frantically for something else strong enough to control my seriously out-of-control locks. My eyes landed on the drawer that ran along the front of the desk, one that would be useful for housing a rubber band. I pulled on it, and it opened an inch, then balked. I tugged harder, and it flexed as if caught on something. I slid my hand beneath the drawer; only a smooth surface.

However, there was a small space between the bottom of the drawer and the desk. I wiggled an index finger through the opening and touched something that had the texture of paper. "What the heck?" I muttered as I pushed the chair aside and crouched to get a closer look. With some maneuvering and serious squinting, I could make out what appeared to be a manila envelope. Had Levina hidden it here for safekeeping?

Overcome by a sudden wave of dizziness, I sank onto my seat and dropped my head forward. A sheen of cold sweat coated my body, and anxious jitters unsettled my stomach.

At last, the vertigo passed, and I was able to retrieve the Leatherman I kept in my purse. I pried out the knife and by running the thin blade beneath the envelope, was able to coach the drawer, with the envelope attached beneath it, slowly forward. I ripped the tape that held the thick envelope in place free, and a parcel fell into my waiting hands.

A loud banging reverberated from the front door. "Cripes. Not again," I whispered, fighting to silence the blood surging through my veins. Was I visible from the front door?

Clutching the envelope to my chest, I peeked through the display case. A face I had grown to dread peered in through the window, his probing eyes locked on me.

Swearing under my breath—a vice I saved for only the direst circumstances—I pushed myself up onto my feet and traipsed to the door, where I settled the envelope securely in my left hand and hid it behind my back. "No need to invite nosy questions from Mr. Snoopy himself," I muttered as I turned the knob.

Bart stood in the blinding sunlight, a fireball of heat and ill will, staring at me as if I'd sprouted a prized set of antlers. "Wow!" he said, a strange fire glowing in his dark eyes. "Your hair!"

Heat surged up my neck and into my cheeks. I fought the urge to reach up and check what most assuredly was a riotous mess and instead shoved my right hand behind my back, too. At least, it couldn't get any worse.

I was wrong. The moment my fingers touched the envelope, his eyes dropped to my chest and settled there. He swallowed so hard that I swore I heard it from three feet away.

Hesitantly, I glanced down. Good grief! I'd forgotten to button up after my foray under the air conditioner. My blouse gaped, exposing more cleavage than Meg had ever dreamed of having and a good portion of my lacy bra.

Reflexively, both hands shot forward, envelope in tow, to cover my exposed skin. Plotting ways to get rid of him, I tentatively raised my eyes. "You wanted something?"

"Uh. . . ." Now his gaze lingered on the envelope. "Yeah," he said, finally looking me in the eye. "Meg said you were here. I thought you might like some help."

He glanced briefly at the envelope again, a frown creasing his forehead. "I'm familiar with how Levina organized and ran things. You must have some questions."

Though his offer seemed sincere, no way was he coming into my store. For all I knew, he'd murdered my predecessor. "Maybe another day," I offered—anything to get rid of him. "Today I'm just sorting through paperwork; tidying up the office space."

"You find Levina's record book?"

I shook my head. "No."

He eyed the envelope. "You find that in there?"

"It and a whole lot of other paperwork, which means I need to get back to work." I forced a smile and grasped the doorknob. He ignored my cue. "Was there something else?"

His right eyebrow arched, he studied me. Several endless moments ticked by while I held my breath and forced myself to meet his stare.

At last, he visibly relaxed. "I'd appreciate a go at your discard pile before it goes in the garbage. And let me know if you want some help." With that, he strode off, descending the steps in one leap. I stuck my head out the door to watch him walk past *The Coffee Counter* and on up the street, his striking physique turning heads.

Air spewed from my mouth. "Jerk," I muttered as I considered the envelope I held in my hand. With trepidation, I unclasped the metal fasteners and pulled out a pile of papers only to stare in fascination at what lay on top—my high school graduation photo. I flipped through the rest of the paperwork. At first glance, it appeared to be about me—a series of pictures, clippings, and letters that would, most likely, be a somewhat accurate rendition of my life. Evidently, Levina had shared some of it with Bob. So why did she hide the information?

Back at the desk, I began a painstaking search through the envelope's contents. An hour later, stretching aching knots from my shoulders, I still questioned why Levina had kept the envelope hidden. It appeared that during my early teens, she'd hired a detective to locate my father and me. There were letters from my father in which he pleaded with her to leave us alone. Clearly, he blamed her family for my mother's death. Why? As far as I knew, my mother had died in an automobile accident.

Somehow, Levina had managed to collect a stack of newspaper articles in which my name was, at least, mentioned. There were also several pictures that portrayed a bumpy ride through my teens, from braces and bottle-thick glasses to straight, white teeth and contact lenses. Most likely, she had finagled those out of my father.

I picked up a picture and studied it, a painful lump throbbing in my throat. In the photo, a radiant smile lit up my face, and long, curly locks swirled freely around it. On that day, the man with his arm draped lovingly around my shoulders had asked me to marry him.

Lance. I'd loved his name. I'd loved his voice. In fact, I'd loved everything about him, even the way he cracked his knuckles when he was angry. We'd met at a high school in Colorado; he was a counselor and I, a long-term sub. It'd started out like my other relationships: casual and don't get too attached since I would soon be moving on.

But Lance had been different. For one thing, I hadn't moved on. The cancer had taken over my father's life. Mine, too. With each day that passed, the pain and fear had grown inside me until it was as consuming as the cancer was inside him. And Lance had been there to counsel me and, eventually, to love me. Or so I'd thought.

A sick feeling settled deep inside me as my mind traveled back to that day. Finally, I'd taken a chance and trusted someone. He'd spit on me. I pictured myself standing there, exhausted and grimy from taking care of my father, who was slowly dying in the next room. And there was my fiancé, his new bride clutched against his side, both of them beaming like a couple of sunbursts streaming through storm clouds. Too bad Levina didn't have a picture of that. I could pull it out every time I got the urge to become involved with another man.

I'd destroyed every picture I had of him. Now I studied the one in front of me.

Odd how my memories of him and the image in the photo didn't quite jibe. Was he really that short? And did he actually wear his hair in that too sleek, coiffed style? How had I not noticed that self-absorbed glint in his eyes or the smile that wasn't really a smile?

My mind replayed his words: "There's just too much of you,

Kit: too much skin. Too much hair. Too much . . . life. Everything about you is so . . . out of control." He'd traded me in for a woman more to his liking—petite, with silky, golden tresses and a quiet, compliant persona. And deep down inside I'd known that he wasn't even sorry he'd treated me so badly; he was just glad to be rid of me.

Well, good riddance! I returned the paperwork and pictures to the envelope and set it aside, then reached for the next document. *Last Will of Levina Ann Johnson* was typed at the top of the first page. It seemed rather strange that she'd hidden a copy of her final will here. Why was she so secretive?

I flipped through several pages, scanning the lines, then paused on my name and the words following it. According to this will, Levina was leaving her house and store to Janet. With Janet's death, they would pass on to me. Dumbfounded, my eyes skimmed quickly through the next few pages, a growing sense of unease settling in. The rest of the will appeared to be pretty much the same as the one Pete had presented in May except that the residue of her estate was to be divided between Bernice and her two children, Jack and me.

I flipped to the last page. This will was dated February 14, 2003, just a few days after my father's death. The letter attached to the back of the document was written on *Frye and Lewis* letterhead and was signed by Pete Lewis. So he'd been involved in this will, too.

It was a conundrum. This will definitely made more sense than her final one. So why had she changed it only a couple of weeks before her death? Why had she made me her primary beneficiary?

CHAPTER 9

The aged face on the wind-up alarm clock glared at me. I glared back and snarled.

Six-thirty! Annabelle was probably on the back porch, howling to the whole neighborhood about the ill-treatment she suffered at my hands.

Her four-thirty risings were a bad curse whose repercussions stretched out before me like my bad hair days—morning after morning of tight-lipped endurance with no hope of reprieve in sight. I pictured myself mid summer—a shuffling, hollow-eyed zombie—and vowed to look into the possibility of installing a sizable kitty door into the backyard.

A vision of Annabelle roaming the dark streets in the wee hours triggered an uncomfortable uneasiness that settled somewhere near my heart. "You've got to be kidding," I muttered. "It's only a cat, and you are *not* becoming attached to it . . . her."

The aroma of coffee drifted up the stairs, beckoning me. I'd set it to brew at five o'clock, an incentive to lure me downstairs to let Annabelle back inside for her breakfast. Luxuriating in caffeine fumes, I quickly reviewed the day that lay before me. My plan was to return to the store early and finish the paperwork I'd begun the day before. By noon, I hoped to be well on my way to familiarizing myself with my merchandise.

A faint knocking sound from below interrupted my planning. Breathing a deep sigh of resignation, I climbed out of bed, then pulled on a cotton robe as I trotted downstairs. Another knock, this time louder, urged me towards the back door. Milton gazed in at me through the glass. When I opened the door, Annabelle raced in, her fluffy tail up and twitching, throwing me an irritated *meow* as she streaked past my bare feet.

"You're all right," Milton breathed, relief relaxing the strain from his face.

"Of course," I assured him, noting the fear in his eyes. "Is something wrong?"

He shook his head slightly and breathed deeply. "It was Annabelle. She was yowling so loud. Usually, you let her back in."

Warmth blossomed in my cheeks. Milton was worried about me. Annabelle's tantrum must've taken him back to that other morning—the morning Levina had been unable to let her back into the house because she was . . . well, dead.

"I'm so sorry, Milton," I told him. "It's Annabelle; she gets me out of bed before sunrise every morning. This morning I was so exhausted that I fell back asleep."

Milton nodded, a sad smile touching his lips. "Annabelle can be demanding. I suppose it'll take awhile for the two of you to adjust to each other."

I nodded, too, hoping the adjusting on Annabelle's part would begin soon. "Can you come in for a cup of coffee?"

He glanced over his shoulder to the back of the yard. "Thank you, but I want to get the roses dead-headed before the heat sets in."

He was *dead-heading* his roses? Sounded gory. I followed his gaze across the dew-covered grass to the colorful profusion of roses that lined my back fence, wondering where Milton had planted his rosebushes. Breathing deeply, I savored the sweet, musky fragrance of the blossoms as they awakened to the new day. It was something to which a person could become accustomed if she weren't careful.

"Thank you for your concern, Milton. I'll try to keep Annabelle from disturbing you," I promised as a plaintive stream of irate meows sounded from behind me.

Milton raised a gloved hand and smiled. "That's all right. I know what an old crank she can be." He chuckled, then added, "Enjoy your day," before he turned away.

Touched by his concern, I watched him mosey across the porch until howls from the kitchen made me scurry towards the demanding cat. "You know, you could stand to do without a few meals," I muttered as I filled her dish with a healthy portion of kibbles. She didn't bother to thank me, just scarfed down the smelly nuggets as if they were the last meal on which her greedy little jaws would chomp. I poured myself a cup of coffee and savored my first sip of the day, always my favorite, before I made my way back upstairs.

A half hour later I descended the stairs, showered and comfortable in a pair of capris and a sleeveless shirt, my hair secured in a tightly woven French braid. With my mind on Meg's sinful-looking pastries, one of which I planned to be munching on in a matter of minutes, I entered the kitchen and froze in my tracks, my heart lodged in my throat.

"Good grief, Meg!" I gasped, once I got my breath back.

Her eyes darted up from what she was reading, and splotches of red crept up her neck onto her cheeks. "I'm sorry. Since we're soon-to-be neighbors, I thought it'd be okay if I came in. I knocked first . . . and Uncle Milton said you were here."

I glanced at the door. Cripes! Did I forget to lock it after my visit with Milton?

"I really am sorry. Levina let me wander in and out of here on my own. I guess I didn't stop to consider that it's your house now, not hers."

She actually did seem contrite. "It's okay . . . really. You just surprised me."

I started to offer her a cup of coffee, then noticed she already had her scarlet-tipped fingers curled around one. Not far from her mug sat a coffee cake topped with golden pecans and dripping gooey caramel. One slice was missing.

"Sorry again. I can't resist my own cooking. It's a *welcome to the neighborhood* gift." She eyed my empty mug. "Sit down. I'll get you a fresh cup. Good coffee, by the way. And I don't say that very often . . . unless it's my own, of course."

"Of course," I mouthed as Meg made her way to *my* coffeemaker. I barely knew the lady and she'd already taken over my kitchen. In fact, she knew right where to find a plate and fork. Evidently, she'd spent a good deal of time here with Levina.

She set a steaming mug of coffee on the table, then loaded a hefty slice of the calorie-laden concoction onto the plate and slid it in front of me. "My specialty. I hope you like it."

How could I not. Cloying caramel and pecans trailed through decadent-looking dough. I forked a bite into my mouth and moaned as it melted across my tongue, sweet and buttery. "Oh, my God," I murmured. "I'll be popping my seams by the end of summer."

Meg laughed. "You can stand to put on a few pounds. Otherwise, I'd have brought you my Yo-veg Loaf—loaded with yogurt and other health nut ingredients but still pretty darn good."

I glanced down, wondering if she and I were seeing the same body; the sight was almost enough to make me push the cake aside. Almost. I took another bite and languished in the burst of warm flavors in my mouth. "Have a seat," I said once I'd swallowed.

"Thanks but I've gotta get to the coffee shop. I just wanted to drop the cake off." Her eyes narrowed, studying me.

Under her intense gaze, I fidgeted. "Is there something wrong?"

She sighed and licked her full lips. "I was thinking about what you asked me, you know, about when Levina was in the shop that day."

I nodded.

"Well, I remembered that she did say something before she walked out. I don't think she was talking to me . . . more to herself it seemed."

I set my fork down. "Yeah?" I prompted, my heart rate kicking up.

"She said something about the key being right there in front of her all the time."

I glanced around the room. A key? Was she speaking literally or figuratively? In this cluttered house, or in the store, the possibilities were too numerous to consider. "What do you think she was talking about?" I probed.

She shrugged. "I turned around to ask her about it, but she was already out the door. Like I said yesterday, she seemed anxious and distracted. And she kept staring at the pictures."

"Was she interested in the pictures before that day?"

A knowing smile curved Meg's mouth, revealing straight, white teeth. "Everything old interested Levina, especially if it involved her family. It was kind of an obsession."

Meg seemed to be back to her genial self today—no more strange behaviors. "You saw me talking with Bob yesterday," I reminded her, "you know, from the train depot."

Her spine stiffened and a frown creased her forehead. "Yeah."

The shrill chime of a doorbell startled me. My heart raced along with my mind as I contemplated who might be standing on my front porch. "I'll be right back," I told her as I pushed myself up from the table.

She held up her hand, palm forward. "Time for me to take off. My purse is over at Uncle Milton's, so I'll go out the back door."

Another loud blast pressed me to hurry. "Thank you for the coffee cake. It's delicious," I called after Meg as I strode towards the front door.

Prudence begged me to flit into the office and peek out the window. Instead, I opened the door only to be shocked senseless for the second time that morning. This time a wave of dizziness threatened to topple me. I grabbed the doorframe for support and closed my eyes briefly, then took several fortifying breaths, resolved to get through the next few minutes of my life, sanity intact.

Bernice's snippy voice cut through the haze. "Frankly, I didn't think you'd be out of bed this early. But Janet insisted." Her prying eyes slid over my cringing frame before she harrumphed and curled her upper lip. "We're here to get *our inheritance*." Her gaze skimmed past me into the house. "Oh, wait a minute. *You* have our inheritance. So we're here to pick up the few items you weren't able to get your scheming little hands on."

She eyed the hand I'd braced against the doorframe. "But then, your hands aren't little, are they? All of the women in *our* family are petite and blonde . . . even your mother."

The mention of my mother stiffened my backbone. I pushed

myself erect and glared down at the tiny woman in her tailored blue linen suit and three-inch heels. As if to defy the sizzling heat, she wore panty hose. The morning light wasn't kind to her, highlighting the deep network of lines time and petulance had carved into her heavily made up face.

Roy and Janet stood ready at her flanks—Roy in a well-worn, two-piece suit with a pleasant smile pasted on his handsome face and Janet looking as if she would collapse into a whimpering heap of blonde fluff if I so much as greeted her. I couldn't help but wonder what had caused her to be strung so tight. Of course, if I spent much time with Bernice, my eyes might be twitching, too.

The four of us stood, staring at each other, my mind numbed by the prospective threat posed by these three strangers—my family.

"Kit! Kit! I brought you that coffee you wanted!"

The three of them pivoted like soldiers on parade, allowing me a peek at Sophie, who was wobbling across the street toward us midst a cloud of pink chiffon. In her right hand, she clutched a small bag. Bless her heart; true to her word, she'd arrived to provide support.

If only she'd taken the time to ditch the peignoir in favor of something a little more discreet.

She bustled up the front walk towards us, the click of plastic heels on her sexy lounge slippers drowning out lazy morning noises. I glanced at my three visitors. For once, Bernice was speechless, her mouth dangling open, eyes bulging.

"Good morning, Bernice. Roy. Janet," Sophie offered in a clipped voice when she came to a stop mere inches from the silent trio. "Quite a coincidence that we all arrived here at the same time." She pushed past Janet and Roy and nudged Bernice aside to stand in front of me, the fact that she'd slathered on lipstick without the support of a mirror obvious. "Here," she said and handed me a half-full bag of ground Seattle's Best Hazelnut Cream.

"Thank you, Sophie. Now I can have my morning coffee," I mumbled, playing along with the charade.

I eyed my three visitors. Roy's mouth was curled in an amused smile. "How're you doing, Sophie?" he asked. "Hope we didn't get you out of bed."

"Fine. And thanks for asking," Sophie chirped, leveling a reproving glare at Bernice.

Bernice studied Sophie and worked her mouth a bit, then turned to me. "Can we get on with this? I have a Republican Women's breakfast, and Roy needs to get to work."

It seemed that I had no choice in the matter. I steeled myself. "Sophie, would you mind taking them into the living area? I'll get their *inheritance* and join you." I handed Sophie the coffee. "Would you put this in the kitchen, please?"

Sophie threw an *I've got it under control* look my way and marched past me to the back of the house. Bernice, Janet, and Roy trailed her, rubbernecking as they walked.

With a resigned sigh, I rubbed at the throbbing in my right temple and made my way to the desk, where I grabbed the document I sought. The letterhead glared at me, a silent reminder of that awful hour I'd endured in the attorney's office. I glared back at it and ordered myself to buck up. Levina left the bulk of her possessions to me, not them. She must've had a darn good reason.

I skimmed the list and made my way to the safe. Since I'd previously practiced the combination, it was open in seconds. I'd had ample time to examine Bernice's three pieces of jewelry and had concluded that they were definitely the *real* thing. The diamond and sapphire brooch was especially stunning. I grabbed the three boxes they lay in, along with a pocket watch and small sterling box that I assumed was a vesta, and slammed the safe shut, then perused the room, praying a sterling desk set would materialize. No such luck. I'd already mentally added it to the *missing* list. "You can do this," I pep-talked myself as I stiffened my spine and trekked to the living area.

Bernice and Janet were huddled together by the mantle, whispering conspiratorially. Roy sat at the kitchen table, shoving a forkful of coffee cake into his mouth. Sophie was nowhere in sight. Shivers unsettled me. "Where's Sophie?" I asked as I dropped the items onto the table next to the packet of Seattle's Best.

Roy eyed the pile broodingly and took a swig of coffee from a steaming mug. "Good coffee," he said sardonically, saluting with the mug. "Sophie's outside talking with Milton. I don't think she's aware that you can see through that pink concoction she's wearing." He stopped as if to consider what he'd said, chuckled, and added, "Then again, maybe she is."

I ignored his jibe about the coffee and instead walked to the door to search for Sophie. Milton was busily snipping on my rosebushes while Sophie stood to his side, her mouth flapping. Roy was right: in the early morning sunlight, Sophie's cover-up was transparent, displaying a clear view of her matchstick-thin legs and arms. Fortunately, she wore some of her silk undies beneath the peignoir.

"How'd you get Meg to bake you a cake?" Roy asked from behind me.

I twirled around. "You know Meg?"

His striking features scrunched up into a shrug. "We go out occasionally."

"How often is occasionally?" I prodded.

He sipped his coffee. "Whenever we're in the mood. Why?

You jealous?"

Heat rose in my cheeks. "No."

"Good thing. We're not kissin' cousins, you know?"

I studied him—his enigmatic dark eyes and perfect nose and chin, the sensual mouth and bad haircut—and I felt absolutely no connection to him.

"Good lord, Roy, are you about done? At this rate, I'm not going to get to the clubhouse in time for breakfast." Bernice's voice had a demanding edge that grated on my nerves.

It didn't seem to faze Roy in the least. "Your jewelry and Great-grandfather's stuff are here on the table," he said matter-of-factly. "We can get Janet's old dolls on the way out." He casually forked a bite of coffee cake into his mouth.

My heart tripped. He hadn't mentioned the missing desk set.

"Well, it's about time," Bernice barked as she marched across the room, Janet shadowing her. "I never could fathom why Levy was given the jewelry. She *never* wore it. Mama knew how much I loved it and still . . . Levy ended up with it."

I scrutinized the expensive-looking pearls adorning her neck and earlobes and the rows of bling decorating her fingers and couldn't help but wonder if Bernice hadn't already been given more than her fair share. Rather than voice my thoughts, I picked up the three boxes and handed them to her.

Her hands slowly caressed each one before she lifted the lid on the top box. A strange fire glowed in her inky eyes. "Mama's ruby ring," she purred as she slid it onto her right index finger and held her hand out to admire the brilliant stones.

Janet's edgy eyes shone, too. "It's beautiful, Mother," she breathed.

"It is, isn't it?" Bernice crowed, fanning her fingers. "I think I'll wear it to my meeting. Wait until the ladies get a look at it. They'll turn green with envy."

Janet's eyes hopped to me, then back to her mother. "It's a good thing Aunt Levy didn't leave it to her. There's no way it'd fit on *her* fingers."

I didn't need her to tell me that; I'd already tried it. Swallowing a retort, I glanced at Roy. He swallowed his last bite of coffee cake.

I'd had my fill of the vicious female duo. Although I really didn't want to leave them here alone, I also couldn't stomach any more of their verbal abuse. "Why don't you help me bring the dolls down, Roy?" I asked, then winced at the catch in my voice.

Roy's eyes met mine, probing. I thought his softened a bit, most likely wishful thinking. "Sure thing," he agreed. He took one last swig of coffee before he pushed himself up and eyeballed

Bernice, irritation flickering in his intense stare. "If you're not gonna sell those pieces, you better be ready to sell off some of your other jewelry. I'm through being your piggy bank," he threw at her before he passed by me.

I paused to take a last look at the two women, who were now drooling over the flashy emerald necklace adorning Bernice's neck. With any luck, she'd wear it to her meeting, too. It was dreadfully out of place accessorizing the summer business suit.

When I caught up with Roy, he was examining the stacks of canvas-covered cases in the smaller back bedroom. There were seven of them, each about the size of a small trunk. "I think that's all of them," I said. "If I find any more, I'll let Janet know."

He glanced up, a cynical expression on his face, his jaw tight. "Don't worry about it. Janet's living at the farm with Mother. With all of her stuff and Mother's, too, the last thing they need around there is more junk to clutter up the place."

"She lives with Bernice?" Age-wise, Janet looked to be somewhere close to forty. Was she too unstable to live alone?

Roy lifted one of the boxes, then set it back down and turned to me. "Yep, she went through bankruptcy and a nasty divorce several years ago." He eyed the boxes resignedly and shrugged off his jacket. "Looks like I'll be late to the office. There's no way these'll fit in Janet's car, and it can't do them any good to sit in my hot car all day."

He pulled a stick of Black Jack gum from his jacket pocket and folded the frayed jacket neatly before laying it carefully across the patchwork quilt on the bed. "Anyway, as I'm sure you noticed, Janet's wires are strung a little tight. Have been since she was a child—one of those family secrets that's not really a secret. Her divorce pushed it along. There wasn't much money left after the creditors took their fair share. When Chase, her son, got a job in Denver, she moved home to live with Mother."

An intent look settled on his face. "They were both counting on Aunt Levy turning this house and the store over to Janet. And we were *all* counting on the money to keep the farm out of hock. When Aunt Levy left it all to you, it totally screwed up our plans. I think we have a right to be pissed."

Somewhere inside me, guilt reared its insidious head to gnaw away at my conscience. Why was he telling me all of this? Did he think I should walk away and leave everything to appease the four of them? "I'm sorry," I said for lack of anything better.

He shrugged. "What they're doing now works out well for both of them. Mother has someone to listen to her grouse, and Janet has someone to watch after her. She wouldn't be able to manage the store and this house, too. And the way the two of them go through money, they'd end up losing it all *and* the family farm. That's not what Aunt Levy wanted."

"So it's a family farm? And you really might lose it?"

"Yeah, it's been in Grandma's family for generations. Both Mother and Uncle Jack are stubborn as hell. Since Dad's death, all they do is argue about how to run the farm and who's gonna do what. Nothing gets done, so it's not generating enough income to even pay the property taxes, let alone all the loans they take out against it. They've counted on me to come up with money to cover them." He paused, a determined set to his jaw. "I hoped it'd be mine someday, but I'll be damned if I'm gonna keep shelling out money now that there's no end in sight." He harrumphed, then spit out, "I'm through."

Our eyes held for several long moments, his hands working at the gum wrapping.

With a sigh, he stuffed the gum into his mouth and shifted his focus to the stack of boxes. "I'd better get these loaded," he muttered unenthusiastically.

"I'll help," I said, lifting one of the boxes. It was lighter than I'd expected.

We made our way down to the lower level and trudged towards the front door. As we passed by the office, movement caught my eye. I glanced into the room, spotted Bernice and Janet leaning over the desk, and froze.

Fresh from my conversation with Roy, I tried to work up some empathy for their plight before I spoke. "Can I help you?" I asked, forcing a conciliatory tone into my voice.

Their heads popped up. "The desk set," Bernice snapped accusingly. "It's supposed to be here and it's not. What'd you do, sell it?"

I swallowed an angry retort, my heart pounding against the box in my arms. "I'm not sure where it is," I told her. Then I added feebly, "Levina had a book where she recorded all of her dealings. Once I find that, I'll know where to look."

Sparks ignited in her inky eyes. "You expect me to believe that? I'm not g. . . ."

"I have the desk set, Mother," Roy said from behind me. "Aunt Levy gave it to me several months ago."

Relief flowed through me, a warm, melting sensation that mingled with unsettling feelings of déjà vu—the strong scent of licorice sent my senses reeling. My father had loved licorice. Evidently, Roy did, too. I detested the stuff.

Bernice narrowed her eyes at Roy. "I haven't seen it in your office."

Roy's sigh fanned my ear, sending chills across my shoulders.

"It's worth too much to be sitting out where someone could take it."

"You better not be covering for her."

"I've got it so just drop it!" he barked. I felt him brush past me and out the door.

Bernice's glare turned to me, her lips pursed. "This isn't over. You might be the stray cat with all the cream now, standing there gloating. But in the end, we'll be the ones gloating, and you'll be standing out on the street . . . with nothing."

The venom in her words wound my insides into painful knots. Most likely, she was right. My whole life I'd never managed to hold onto anything that mattered to me. Why would this be different? Against my better judgment, I was growing attached to this new life. Thoughts of losing it were already a destructive organism eating away at me.

Sickened by a truth I didn't want to confront, I made my way out the front door, Janet's dolls in my arms. A battered green SUV sat in front of the house, its back door flipped up. Roy was striding up the walk toward me, Annabelle prancing at his heels, her tail fanning. "Just stick it in the back," he muttered as he passed by me.

I'd done just that when I heard a welcome voice from behind me. "Wow, Kit. Don't tell me you got an old car to haul all of your old things around?"

"Thank you," I whispered as I turned to watch Patty power walk towards me. She looked hot and fit in a pair of black knee-length leggings and a skin-hugging white tank, jeweled sunglasses shading her eyes.

"Patty," I sighed when she drew nearer. "Just when I'm in dire need of your *can-the-crap* support, you magically appear. It's amazing."

"Not as amazing as the last twelve hours of my life," she announced excitedly, an insinuating twinkle in her eyes.

"Really?" I studied her. She was absolutely beaming. I could think of only one thing that would put that look on her face. "Chief Preston?"

"Uh-huh. And it started with white orchids. Imagine that. Confirmed what I already knew: we're soul mates." She glanced toward the front porch and frowned. Arguing voices were spilling from inside the house, growing progressively louder.

"Bernice and her brats," I informed her. "They've come to get their inheritance."

The concern in her eyes nearly snapped the fragile control I held over my emotions. Through watery eyes, I watched Roy exit my house with a box in his arms, a determined set to his mouth, and a glower marring otherwise perfect features. Bernice and Janet were on his heels. Bernice was on one of her tirades, her shrill voice wailing.

"My God. She's worse than I imagined. What a shrew!"

Roy's face grew stormier as they drew nearer. Then Bernice spotted Patty, and her mouth snapped shut while her eyes slid down and then up Patty's sweaty body.

I felt a smirk creep onto my face as Patty and I moved toward my kinfolk. Bernice was about to meet her match. "Patty, this is Roy, Bernice, and Janet," I said flatly, refusing to label them as my aunt and cousins. "This is my friend Patty."

"Nice to meet you," Roy said formally before he passed around us to the vehicle.

"Nice to meet you, too," Patty responded. She and Bernice's eyes remained locked in silent battle. Janet was gnawing on her lower lip and wringing her hands.

"You live here in this house?" Bernice finally snapped.

Patty shook her head. "No."

"Somewhere near here?"

Patty shook her head again. "No."

"Well, then what are you doing *here* in that getup?" Bernice demanded.

Patty smiled tightly. "Not that it's any of your damn business, but, as you so *rudely* put it, I'm in this *getup* because I spent the night with a friend here in Aurora. And now I'm taking my morning walk, something those of us who care about our health tend to do."

My eyes shot over to her. Wow! The relationship between Cal and her was heating up fast. Her eyes met mine for a millisecond, a knowing look passing between us.

"By the way," Patty continued. "Since we're talking fashion here, I need to put my two cents in concerning that flashy brooch you're wearing. It's a bit over the top, don't you think? I mean, add it to the pearls and the rings and one might think you're . . . flaunting."

A thundercloud descended onto Bernice's face. She clenched her jaw, threw Patty a lethal glare, and stomped to her car—family treasures safely clutched in her hands.

Janet stood rooted to her spot, tense, her eyes blinking, hands clenching. Fearful that she was having a nervous breakdown, I stepped forward to assist her when she suddenly pivoted and called, "Mother, wait." She scampered off just as Roy walked out the front door.

"I know her from somewhere," Patty muttered.

"Bernice?"

Patty frowned in concentration. "No, the screwy one; I know I've met her before. I just can't quite remember where." She rubbed at her forehead. "But I will."

✿✿✿

Patty's eyes were veiled behind dark lenses. Still, I could tell she was troubled as she stared out the car window at Cal's sixties-era ranch-style house and sighed. "Choices: a two-hour drive home in rush-hour traffic with drivers crazed by this heat or a romantic evening with a too intriguing man?" she murmured.

Hmmm? Maybe she was just as exhausted as I after several hours of sorting, dusting, and arranging old stuff at *Levy's Loot*. And that was after she'd taken Bernice down a couple of notches that morning. "What do you want to do?" I asked.

"What I want to do and what I *know* I should do are two different things."

There was a catch in her voice. Patty—my best friend, a tenacious force, a woman I idolized for her independence and total lack of fear—was on the brink of tears. I grabbed her hand and squeezed it. "Cal's crazy about you," I assured her.

She rubbed at the ridge of her nose as if in an effort to staunch the flow. "Well, I think I'm well past the *crazy* phase."

"Oh," slipped from my mouth. I wished I could inhale it back and come up with something so deeply profound that it would alleviate Patty's fears, but there was no escaping the ultimate truth: men are fickle.

"Patty, you're the one who's always preached to me about taking chances in life, about the importance of being a player, not an observer." I stared past her to the massive fir trees towering over Cal's house, then down to the sluggish, murky Pudding River below it. "You're the reason I'm here in Aurora."

She yanked off her sunglasses. "And I wish you could see yourself. You are so much more alive than I've ever seen you before." She swallowed hard. "But you don't have to worry about losing this. If you want it, it's yours."

Deep down inside, pain tugged at my own heart. "I wish that were true. Bernice will do everything within her power to get the house and the store and, especially, the money. Roy said she and Jack might lose their farm, so she's desperate. But until then, I'm going to enjoy this gift Levina gave me." I paused to gather my thoughts. "You've been given a gift, too. Whether it lasts a day or a year, enjoy it while you have it."

She smiled, though somewhat feebly. "You're right. Give up one minute with that delicious man? What was I thinking?" This time her voice sounded more resolute.

She opened the car door. "I'm heading to Seaside for a wedding tomorrow but should be back on Sunday. If Cal seems okay with it, I might spend a few days out here with him. Might even bring

Eleanor with me. She and Annabelle can have a play date."

Eleanor was a force best not reckoned with. Patty had named her in honor of her own personal heroine, Eleanor Roosevelt. The thought of Eleanor and Annabelle in the same town, let alone the same play space, was disconcerting. No doubt, fur would fly.

"I'll have to check that out with Annabelle," I told her. "She doesn't seem like a *play nice* kind of cat."

Patty chuckled and, clutching her bulging handbag, slid out of the car. "Thanks, Kit," she said meaningfully before she turned towards the house.

"Thank *you!*" I yelled after her.

A pang of loneliness sliced through me. I pictured Patty and Cal, a candlelit dinner, their eyes touching in silent communiqué. I pictured them on his back deck, darkness settling in around them while they chatted and sipped chilled wine, fingers entwined. All night long Cal would be there to provide solace and whisper sweet endearments.

I wanted to scream to the world that I deserved that, too. Instead, I told myself to focus on winding my way home through unfamiliar streets.

The late afternoon sun beat down, heavy, shrouding the neighborhood in lethargy. Even the giant oaks and maples appeared listless, as if their thick leafy coats were too much of a burden to bear. Through a picket fence, I spotted three young girls in bright swimming suits, wet hair clinging to their heads like seaweed, sitting in an inflated pool. They were licking popsicles. There was something so intimate about it—the three of them just sitting there licking and chatting, oblivious to the rest of the world and the relentless heat.

A vision of my mother as a small girl tugged at my heart, and I winced. On hot days, had she and her two sisters sat together in the yard of their grandparents' house—the house in which I now lived— licking popsicles and sharing secrets? What if my mother had lived? Would I have been the one sitting there with my two cousins, Janet and Roy? I hadn't developed close relationships with other children when I was younger. At the time, it hadn't seemed important. Suddenly, it was very important.

Tears tingled in my nostrils. "Cripes, Kit. Are you PMSing or what? Get a grip!" I muttered as I pulled to a stop and gazed longingly at the water spraying from my sprinklers. My eyes slid to the porch and did an eye-popping double-take.

Was there really a man reclining on the metal glider on my front porch? My heart kicked into overdrive as I turned off the ignition.

Freshly mown grass announced that Milton had been busy in my yard, but it wasn't him in the glider. This man was too bulky. I examined the rusty, scarred turquoise and white pickup truck parked in front of me. It, too, was unfamiliar.

Then I studied the gray house next door, for once wishing that Bart was there glowering at me. There was no sign of life, not even the four-legged Stonewall type. A glance across the street confirmed that Sophie wasn't rushing over to provide support.

My gaze fastened on the man on the porch—hopefully, he was only sleeping—as I pulled my keys from the ignition, grabbed my purse, and opened my car door as quietly as possible to slip out. It was like stepping into a pizza oven, the heat thick and heavy in my lungs and melting to dampness on my skin. I paused several moments to acclimate and work up courage before I treaded softly to the front gate.

Annabelle materialized from the porch shadows and stretched her legs far out in front of her, working them and arching her back. Then she sidled to the top of the steps and sat, her cunning eyes glued to the spray spitting from the sprinklers in graceful arches.

I eyed the spray, too, then my bare legs and flip-flops, before I inched open the gate and shuffled tentatively toward the porch. Icy droplets pelted my limbs and tickled in rivulets down to my already wet feet. I paused to savor the cold, wet, tingling sensation until a shiver snaked across my shoulders.

The man awakened, rubbing his eyes and breathing deeply, as if trying to suck strength from the sluggish air. A bushy cloud of white hair hid his face, but I recognized his large frame and the slump to his shoulders and pictured Bernice ordering him to get his butt over here and claim his great-grandfather's tools before I hocked them.

Frozen by indecision, I squinted, trying to see through that mop of hair to the man beneath. Just who was my Uncle Jack? Before today, I'd only seen him the one time when he'd appeared to be well on his way to being smashed. Could I trust him?

He looked up. His dark eyes, groggy with sleep, met mine and held, then turned sad. "You *do* look like your mother, you know?" he said, his voice a warm, rich hum.

Something curled in my stomach, a painful longing. "Bernice said my mother was petite and blonde."

His massive shoulders floated through a shrug. "She was. You're a larger, darker version of her." He paused, probing, as if he could see through my clothes and skin to all of the good and bad beneath. "Only you're not *really* like her, are you?"

A giant, burning lump settled in my throat. "What do you mean?" I croaked.

As if by magic, the wet spray retreated, sinking slowly back into the earth, leaving me dripping and covered with zillions of tiny goose bumps. Shivers zipped through my body.

Annabelle trotted to the bottom step, where she lapped at a puddle, eyes closed, her pink tongue flicking in and out like a gorging lizard. I took several hesitant steps to get a closer look at Jack—his red-rimmed eyes and sweat-stained face. He appeared to be sober.

"Olivia was spoiled and headstrong," he said. "She thought the world revolved around her. If she wanted it, she got it. There was no arguing with her. And you? I get the feeling you've had to make do with whatever life threw at you."

His voice was sad when he spoke of my mother, yet his words were not ones that spoke of love. They ignited little sparks within me. I tried to push them aside until later when I would take them out, examine them more closely and perhaps twist them into something more flattering.

Jack sighed so deeply his whole body seemed to lift and fall. "To your mother, life was one big party, and she was the main attraction." His voice cracked, and he paused momentarily, eyes boring into mine. "You seem much more tentative. Not a dreamer."

"A dreamer?"

"Olivia saw everything through her own fairytale eyes. If she hadn't been such a dreamer . . . who knows? She might still be alive today."

"What do you mean?" I asked, a queasy, unsettled feeling sliding around inside me.

He shrugged, resignedly this time. "You'll have to talk with Bernice to get the whole story. I was away serving God and country at the time." His lip twisted cynically, and he hesitated, as if he couldn't continue until those words had dissipated.

"When Grandma Kitty died, she left this house to the four of us—Bernice, Levy, Olivia, and me. Dad and Mom had passed away, and Bernice and her husband were trying to raise their kids and keep the family farm going. Levy and her husband Art lived in Bend. Had a sporting goods store. Sold fishing and hunting gear, camping supplies, stuff like that."

To me, these people were blank faces leading lives as foreign as those of the Hiltons or the Trumps. "Grandma *Kitty*?" I asked, latching onto a scrap of familiarity.

A smile touched his lips as his eyes slowly scanned the yard and porch. "Yep. She and Grandpa Jim lived here. Grandpa Jim's dad built this house."

"James Wallace—the man who painted the pictures?"

"Uh-huh." His eyes narrowed. "Seems he was a dreamer, too."

"A dreamer? You mean because of the gold?"

Now he was really studying me. Reflexively, I patted my hair.

"You know about that, huh?" he asked. A deep frown had turned his eyes to ominous slits. "He spent most of his time out in eastern Oregon searching for the Blue Bucket gold. Passed the dreamer bug on to Grandpa Jim who made sure Olivia got a good dose of it. My dad wouldn't have nothin' to do with it. Called it all a bunch of poppycock. He tried to talk some sense into your mother, but Grandpa Jim had brainwashed her good. She really believed that Great-grandpa found the gold and hid it somewhere here." The look on his face said it all: only a total idiot would think something so ludicrous.

"You mean in this house?" I blurted, intrigued by Jack's revelation. My eyes slowly scanned the two-story building in front of me. If what Jack said was true, my mother had truly believed gold was hidden within these walls.

"Course, no one's ever found even a fleck of it. And you can be sure that, after Olivia died, Levy spent a good deal of time looking for it." An intense look came into his eyes. "You appear to have enough sense not to get pulled into that kind of nonsense."

I couldn't tell if it was a statement or a question so I let it go. "After my mother died? Why did Levina get interested in it then?"

"Bernice'd know more about that then me," he said, shaking his head. "I wasn't here, so I don't know what all went on the day Olivia died. I do know that Bernice and Levy were for selling this house. They wanted the money. Your mom refused to sign the papers. She threw one of her tizzy fits and ended up dead because of it."

A pained look crossed his face. He left me hanging—wanting to know yet not wanting to know. The lump in my throat burned so much I couldn't get words passed it.

Jack must've seen the desperation in my eyes. "Didn't look before she pulled onto the highway, and . . . a hay truck slammed into her," he said softly.

I felt like a hay truck slammed into me, sending body parts flying. Mentally, I tried to pull the pieces back together, to focus on something other than my mother's body being pulverized by a monster truck, buried under a pile of bloody hay bales. As if she sensed my need for comfort, Annabelle rubbed her soft fur against my damp legs.

"I think your mom's spirit climbed into Levy's body that day and took it over," Jack continued, unaware that I was still dealing with his last bombshell. "Just like that, Levy was obsessed with living here in this house and finding the gold. She and Art sold their business and paid Bernice and me for our shares of the property.

"I don't know what happened between Bernice and your dad. When I came home, the two of you were gone. No one knew where you went. If I asked about you, Bernice'd bite my head off. Levy got so upset when your name was brought up that I avoided the subject altogether. After awhile, you pretty much slipped from my mind."

He pushed himself up off the glider, pausing periodically to adjust to his new stance, then lumbered to the top of the steps and leaned his hunched torso against a post. "When I saw you in Pete's office that day, I about lost my lunch," he admitted. "The minute I laid eyes on you, I knew who you were. Olivia was a natural beauty— same as you." His eyes narrowed, examining me closely. "Some of your features are hers . . . and the looks you get on your face. The way you move."

I wanted to believe that my mother and I had something in common, even if it was only a few facial expressions, but the conversation had me feeling empty and exhausted. I took a deep, determined breath. "I suppose you came here to get your tools?"

He nodded.

Curiously, our visit had alleviated any qualms I had of being alone in the house with him. I walked up the steps to the front door and unlocked it. "Come inside," I said.

A shrill whistle blared, pulling me to the back of the house. I punched in the code and the house fell silent. Cool air chilled my damp skin.

Jack, looking uncomfortable, stood in the middle of the room. "Have a seat," I said, indicating the overstuffed couch in the living area. "I'm going to change into some dry clothes, and then we can search for your tools." I took a step, then paused. "Would you like something to drink?"

A panicked look blossomed on his face.

"Water? Soda? Iced tea?"

He licked his lips and shook his head. "No, thank you."

"If you change your mind, help yourself to whatever's in the fridge." As I made my way up the stairs, my mind raced backwards, trying to remember what was in my fridge. Hopefully, no wine or beer.

My reflection in the full-length mirror caught my attention when I entered the bedroom, and I paused to consider Jack's words. "You might be natural, but you're certainly no beauty," I whispered to my reflection before I yanked off wet clothes.

When I returned to the living area, Jack stood at the massive mantle. The tips of his fingers traced slowly over its contours as if he were blind and reading Braille. I approached him tentatively so as not to startle him.

"James Wallace was definitely a talented man," he murmured. "Makes you wonder why he didn't use his talent on something other than this monstrosity and those hideous paintings."

My thoughts exactly. Still, weird though they were, there was something oddly alluring about his work. "I saw your picture . . . the one you left at the auction house," I told him.

Surprise flickered in his eyes. "I always hated the damn thing. But Levy would've hit the ceiling if I got rid of it. Now I don't suppose it matters." His words sounded hollow, empty. "Besides, I need the money more than the painting."

"I found one of those paintings after my dad died, when I cleaned out his storage," I confessed.

He nodded. "Grandma Kitty gave us each one—Bernice, Levy, Olivia, and me. I'm surprised your dad held onto your mother's."

"Me, too." I'd discovered it stacked behind several other pictures. Being in the construction industry, my father's art had consisted of images of buildings, so the painting had been a conundrum, enough of one that I'd kept it. "Maybe he didn't know its significance?"

"He knew," Jack stated matter-of-factly. "You still have it?"

I nodded. "Would you be willing to sell me yours?" The words slipped out before I even considered them. Cripes. Why would I want another one of those bizarre paintings?

Jack's eyes narrowed. "Wouldn't be right to pull it from the auction now. Harv most likely has the program worked up." His voice was gruff, as if he were irritated.

Like caramel and chocolate, auctions and antique shops seemed a good match. "When's the auction?" I asked.

"You don't want to let your imagination get out of control," he warned.

Heat rose in my cheeks. "I took some things to the auction house for Harv to sell. I'd like to see how they do." I almost convinced myself that was the reason I wanted to attend.

He sighed resignedly. "Thursday evening. And now I better hit the road. If I don't get back to the farm soon, Bernice'll be here lookin' for me, and I'll hear about it."

My guess was that he heard from Bernice no matter what he did or didn't do. "You think the tools are in the basement?" Merely mentioning that place made my skin crawl. Up to this point, I'd avoided it. A quick peek had me convinced that it was dark and creepy and reeked of slimy black mold and humongous, hairy spiders.

Jack shook his head, a set to his jaw. "I'm gonna leave them here."

"Oh?"

"Yep. The mantle's here; the tools should be with it. Bernice'll have a royal cow but they're my tools. And I say they stay here where they'll be safe."

"The mantle was made with those tools?"

He studied the carvings, his brows furled. "Most likely. Great-grandpa James died when he was in his forties, and they didn't bury his tools with him. This here mantle represents a lot of Oregon history."

Ever so slowly, his battered index finger snaked across a portion of the mantle. "The Columbia River flowing through the gorge: not a pleasant experience for those who were trying to reach the Willamette Valley in their covered wagons." His voice was soft as velvet, mesmerizing. "And here's Celilo Falls. Before they built a dam and flooded it, the Indians caught salmon there with nets, on platforms hanging out over the water."

His finger moved on, then stopped. "The falls at Oregon City, long before they built a paper mill to stink up the place." He traced a winding river to the next stop. "This here, it's Boone's Ferry. Some descendants of Daniel Boone ran a ferry there, one of the few places you could cross the Willamette River at that time. It's where Wilsonville is today."

Inside me, something amazing transpired. I tingled all over, totally enthralled with Jack's words. He was right. My great-great-grandfather had carved this mantle over a hundred years ago. It wasn't just a bunch of bumps and grooves; it truly was a depiction of what life had once been. Awed by what it signified, I reached out to touch it, too.

Jack's eyes met mine. "Grandpa Jim used to park us here and lecture us about it." He sighed, his eyes distant. "I've forgotten most of what he said."

I examined the numerous carvings on the wood, searching for a long, flat area. "Do you know where Wallace went when he traveled east searching for the gold?"

"I think it was over around Burns . . . or John Day," he said, a sweep of his hand indicating an area of the mantle that was riddled with small hills and steep cliffs."

"Hmmm," I mumbled as I moved to get a closer look. There were miners with picks and mining pans along with several covered wagons and what looked like cattle. Ribbons of water wound through what I'd imagined as somewhat dry country.

"I better get a move on," Jack said from beside me.

I dragged my attention back to him. "Thank you for telling me about my mother."

He nodded before he turned away and shuffled towards the front door.

It would take some time for me to understand what had just transpired. Inexplicably, there'd been some kind of connection between Jack and me. I followed his hunched back and felt a soft, peaceful glow settle inside me.

Surely, my Uncle Jack didn't need money badly enough to kill for it.

✿✿✿

I'd just slid the second cake pan into the oven when the doorbell rang. I jerked and the oven door slammed shut. Ten minutes later and Milton's luscious cake would've been flat as a flapjack. I owed him more than a chocolate layer cake for the work he'd done in my yard, but for now, the cake would have to suffice.

As I strode towards the door, I wiped my sticky hands on the front of my bumblebee sweatshirt and considered who might be waiting there. Patty? Maybe Sophie? Certain that it was one of them, I opened the door with the word *hi* already forming on my lips.

What came out was a garbled, gagging sound.

Walker stood in front of me—magenta polo shirt tucked neatly into plaid Bermuda shorts—displaying a deep tan that could only be described as burnt orange. I sneezed, and my alarmed brain shifted through several gears. Why was *he* standing on my front porch?

"How did you find me?" I spluttered.

He smiled his slick Walker smile. "You left your summer address with Louise."

"Yes. *For Louise.*" Had he gone through her desk?

"I needed to talk with you," he whined, his voice falsetto.

Annoying rivers of sweat dribbled down my stomach. I wanted to scream, to tell him to go away and call me on his cell phone from his car. I searched across the street. No Sophie. I glanced next door. No Bart. Why weren't they around when I needed them?

Annabelle appeared from nowhere—Super Cat to the rescue—and waddled up the steps to roost next to me, her eyes fixed on Walker and her fluffy tail twitching erratically, as if she sensed my distress. As lame as I knew it to be, I drew strength from her presence.

Walker's brows furled and his eyes narrowed at Annabelle.

Annabelle's lips curled back to expose a set of fangs any true vampire would covet. A ferocious stream of snarls erupted from her mouth. I silently cheered her on.

Walker's orange face deepened to red. "Doreen's waiting in the car," he prodded.

Doreen was here, too? Instinctively, my eyes were drawn to his flashy BMW. Sure enough, Doreen was in the passenger seat, her head resting back, eyes closed.

I scanned the porch. We couldn't sit out here and talk, the

two of us sitting side-by-side in the glider, thighs touching. "Come inside," I muttered through clenched teeth as I reluctantly stepped back to give him access. He trod unwaveringly down the hall, curved right into the kitchen, and lowered himself into one of the well-worn wooden chairs that circled the oak table. I dropped into the chair farthest from him.

The room was alive with the fragrance of chocolate. The table's clutter nagged at me: Sophie's coffee donation, dirty dishes, and the remnants of Meg's coffee cake. Morning seemed like a lifetime ago.

Walker's beady eyes ogled the globs of flour and chocolate streaking my bumblebee-emblazoned chest. I rounded my shoulders and placed my elbows on the table, twitters spiraling up from my stomach. He sniffed and his beady eyes rose to meet mine. "Doreen and I need to know your plans for next year," he said.

I felt my jaw drop. Were the two of them plotting my dismissal? "Why?" I choked.

His shrug was too stiff to be spontaneous. "We're interviewing and have some good candidates."

"And why would you think I won't be returning?"

The skin on his neck and face turned motley, as if it were sponge-painted with blobs of crimson over the tube tan. "You've made some questionable choices . . . professionally speaking. It'll be difficult for you to be an effective member of our staff."

The queen's decree, for sure, with Walker as her mouthpiece. I was fuming. "According to my contract, I need to give you four weeks notice should I decide to terminate my employment. I will." I smiled. "But for now, plan on me being back at Hazelnut Grove intent on being an even *more* effective staff member."

"You're not being fair with Doreen, you know," he groused. "She would've involved the police. You flew off half-cocked, and now, because of you, she might lose her job." He paused, his intense gaze riveted on mine. "And you'll probably lose yours, too."

"Is that a threat?" I blurted, incredulous. Was he stupid enough to make one?

Something—alarm maybe—flashed in his eyes. "No." A sleazy smile slid onto his lips. "You need to reign in that wild imagination of yours, Kit. You jump to too many conclusions. Make wild accusations. They just might. . . ."

The blare of the doorbell blasted. Cripes! Today, this place was busier than downtown Portland during the Rose Festival. Irritated, I studied Walker.

The doorbell resounded two more times in rapid succession. I rose to my feet shakily. "I'll be right back," I said. "We're not done with this."

I nearly sprinted down the hall, then yanked the door open. Sophie stood before me, a wilted pink blossom with a purple sticky notepad and a pencil in her hands.

"Oh, good," she said with a relieved sigh. "You're okay. I didn't recognize that swanky car out front and got to worrying about what might be goin' on over here. And me just staring out my window and letting it happen. Then I'd have to testify in court about the dead lady inside it and all, and I wouldn't know the license number. So I hurried over to check out the plates. And since I'm here, I thought I might as well ask if you'd spend the Fourth of July with me at Willamette Park. I was hoping you'd drive?"

Touched, I gave her a quick hug. "Oh, Sophie, thank you. I'd love to spend the Fourth with you . . . and drive."

"Hello, Sophie," Walker said from behind me.

In my arms, Sophie stiffened. "*Ronny*? What are you doing here?"

Sophie knew Walker? Shocked, my hold loosened and I stepped back.

Walker was all goodwill and smiles. "I just dropped by for a short visit with Kit. She teaches at my school."

My brain scurried, struggling to change gears, unable to formulate a retort.

Sophie's mouth twisted. "Hmmm," she hummed, clearly as confused as I.

"I need to get going. It was nice chatting with you, Kit; think about it," Walker said cheerily as he passed by us and down the steps. Before he climbed into his cherry red BMW, he glanced back and gave me a meaningful look—definitely meant to be a warning.

"You know Walker?" I asked dazedly, my eyes now focused on the intimidating woman marching up my walkway. Good grief. What did *she* want?

"Ronny? Millie Swank's nephew?"

"Ronny Walker," I said just as Queen Doreen parked beside Sophie.

Sophie blinked, her eyes raking Doreen from her perfectly fluffed curls to the French pedicure on her toenails. As usual, the queen was well turned out. If only she could squeeze one itty bitty little smile onto her lips to soften her dour air.

"Where's your restroom?" she demanded, her eyes hard and cold, knees pressed shakily together.

I blinked. Not even a greeting? This woman was angry enough to spit shrapnel. And desperate. "Down the hall next to the laundry room," I muttered.

She pushed by me and trotted off down the hall.

Her mouth hanging open, Sophie's questioning gaze turned

from Doreen to me.

"The principal at the school where I teach," I told her, unable to keep the contempt out of my voice. I made myself a mental note to fumigate that bathroom, then shook unseemly thoughts of Doreen aside. "So Ronny Walker, you know him?"

"Yep." Her penciled-on eyebrows rose a couple of inches, pulling the many folds around her eyes taut. "When he was young, he spent time here with Millie. Always sneaking around and snooping in people's yards. I don't know how she put up with him. But he buttered up to her good, and she didn't see him for the bratty little kid he was."

"Is his aunt still alive?" I asked, unraveled by this latest bombshell.

Sophie shook her head. "Oh no, she died awhile back." Her fuchsia-splotched lips scrunched, and she frowned as if she were searching the deep recesses of her mind. "Not last summer but the summer before. June, I think, because Millie loved lilacs. She had so many lilacs in her yard that come May, I couldn't stand to visit her. The whole place smelled like that cheap toilet water stuff they used to sell at the *Five and Dime*. Anyway, it was just past lilac season when Millie died. I couldn't find any lilacs to take to her service, so I took a potted purple hydrangea, instead. Millie liked hydrangeas, too. And purple was her favorite color."

Sophie stilled and sniffed the air, a puzzled frown settling on her features. A cricket took advantage of the silence to begin its chirrup, the sonorous drone of its song familiar and comforting.

"Way I heard it," she continued, "Millie left her house and most of her stuff to Ronny. Course, he sold it all, including the house. Levina handled the estate sale."

I froze, my mind buzzing, numb with the shock that Levina and Walker were acquaintances and what that might signify. The aroma of baking chocolate wafted from the house, drawing my attention momentarily.

"The sale was . . . two years ago?" I stuttered. Instinct screamed that there were too many coincidences here. Two years ago, Walker had interviewed and hired me. Did Levina handle that, too?

CHAPTER 10

Suddenly awake, I stared into the blurry, sun-drenched room. Something was not right. Blood surged through my veins and throbbed in my head like the rhythmic pounding of a bass drum. The dryness in my mouth made cotton seem wet.

I forced my attention to the morning sounds that had become so familiar: birds twittering as they foraged for food outside the window, the distant hum of a power tool, the purr of a car passing by on the street. The blare of a not-too-far-off train whistle intruded into the morning chorale, two short blasts of warning. I eyed the clock.

Annabelle! She'd been sitting on the back porch over three hours now, probably driving Milton crazy.

I bounced out of bed, rushed down the stairs, and sprinted to the back door. No massive fur-ball peeked in through the window, irritation spouting from her eyes and mouth.

My hand reached for the locks, only to find them unlocked. Odd; I could've sworn I'd locked them after letting Annabelle out. I stepped out onto the porch. No Annabelle? "Annabelle!" I called. "Kitty! Kitty! Kitty!"

"She's devouring her breakfast," a deep, masculine voice drawled from behind me.

I jumped about a foot, and my heart landed somewhere near the back of my throat. Somehow, I managed to twirl around.

Bart! Inside my house! Sparks of irritation flared into a full-fledged firestorm. If I squinted just so, I could make him out, grungy in a sleeveless tee-shirt, paint-splotched shorts, and ratty tennis shoes. Minus my contact lenses, his face was a dark, unshaven blur.

"What are you doing here?" I gasped, my heart pounding, nearly choking me.

"Trying to get *your* cat to shut up, so I can work in my yard in peace."

I swallowed over the throbbing mass in my larynx and squinted past him, searching for a blob of golden fur. "How did you get in here?"

"Cal gave me a key, so I could let in whoever needed to get

inside." Though I couldn't see his face clearly, I suspected he was gloating.

"Well . . . why didn't you ring the doorbell?"

"I did, several times. I figured you were gone. And your howling cat had to be fed!"

My job, not his. I marched into the house and held out my hand. "My key," I said as forcefully as I could muster without a single drop of caffeine revving my system.

His brows furled into a brooding frown. "You're welcome," he muttered as he dug the key out of his pocket and dropped it into my waiting palm.

Some too reasonable part of me alleged that I was the one at fault here, not Bart. That I owed him words of appreciation, not censure. I chose to ignore it. I needed coffee!

With a huff, I passed by him, shoved the key inside a drawer, and grabbed two coffee mugs. I filled them both with dark brew from the decanter, the fragrance suffusing the air, enticing. I'd mixed Sophie's bag of Hazelnut Cream with some of my own Kona blend to calm down the hazelnut flavor a bit. I closed my eyes and took a calming sip. Perfect.

Annabelle was absorbed, crunching on her breakfast, no worse for wear after several hours of caterwauling. As I passed by her, my eyes skimmed the lacy edge of my long cotton nightgown. Cripes! I was here with this irritating man, half-dressed! Heat flared in my cheeks. I raised my eyes and took a healthy gulp of coffee to fortify myself.

Then I felt it—the unbearable itching on my arms and chest. I glanced down to see large ruby welts blossom on my smooth white skin. My throat constricted. I fought to pull air into my lungs. The sound of my rasping breath echoed through my head. The mugs slipped from my hands, and pain seared my abdomen and thighs. My eyes dropped, unseeing, swollen shut.

Firm hands pulled the burning heat from me.

My injector! I had to get to one before I passed out. But my mind was murky. Where? Upstairs in my purse. Too far. Levina's— was it still inside the desk drawer?

Think, Kit. Think.

I directed what energy I had left into my lungs, forcing air in through my swollen throat. It was like pulling an elephant through a straw. "Desk; top drawer," I wheezed.

Strong arms lifted me. I floated, my whole being focused on getting air into my lungs. The noise was deafening, frightening—the sound of death.

I landed on softness and lay perfectly still, stiff, my throat completely closed. Sounds reached me—the distant whirr of a lawnmower and, from nearby, Bart. I clung to hope, ordering myself to relax, to conserve the oxygen in my body.

Then oh so softly, clouds drifted in to cradle me. I sank into their serenity.

☼☼☼

Dense fog spiraled around me, comforting in its dreaminess. I floated in it, searching languorously for something. All was peaceful silence, just the mist and me.

A strawberry drifted past enticingly—plump and round and juicy, tiny brown seeds dotting its ruby surface. My hand reached for it, and jolts of alarm sliced through my body.

"No!" I screamed, shattering the silence. The fog vanished and my eyes jerked open. I shot up, panting hard, gasping for air, consumed by fear.

The room was mostly blurred dark corners and shadows, unfamiliar. I sensed movement to my right and warily, glanced in that direction as a large dark figure sank down beside me. A loud click and his face swam in a pool of light. I recoiled. Bart!

My stomach surged in warning. I grabbed it and ran my fingers soothingly over satiny cloth, struggling to get my muddled brain to function. Suddenly alert, my fingers stilled, and I glanced down. What was I wearing? It was silky and snug as a pair of control top panty hose—not something of mine!

Reflexively, my eyes shot back to Bart, and I felt my whole body shrink from him. "How do you feel?" he asked, his voice soft and husky.

Bad, that's how I felt. My stomach churned, threatening to erupt. My head was a time bomb ready to explode. And I didn't know where in the heck I was . . . nor how I'd gotten here.

"Where am I?" I whispered through a surprisingly dry, sore throat.

"Levina's bedroom."

Levina's bedroom? Tentatively, my eyes left his to travel around the bleary, heavily shadowed space that I'd avoided up to this point. As foolish as it might seem, I felt as if a part of Levina still resided here in this room. So why was I here now? With Bart?

He smiled, displaying a row of straight, white teeth. "I carried you here."

Yeah. Right. I studied him. He was serious. "Why?" I asked in a raspy voice.

His brows drew together into a frown. Somehow, it was comforting, more familiar. "You don't remember?"

Remember what? My mind searched back, and I saw myself letting Annabelle outside, then nothing. I shook my head.

"Around eight this morning, I let Annabelle into your house." He spoke slowly, hesitatingly, his eyes intent. "You came downstairs and chewed me out. Then, just like that, you couldn't breathe."

Ever so slowly, I pictured it: Bart standing in my kitchen, admitting that he had a key to *my* house. Annabelle munching on her morning chow. That first jolt of caffeine as it slid down my throat. And then. . . ."

My pulse quickened with the memory. I stared at Bart, speechless.

"You had welts everywhere, so I figured it was an allergic reaction. The doctor said I got the Epinephrine into you just in time."

I remembered that welcoming comfort that had claimed me and swallowed hard. If Bart hadn't been here, I wouldn't be here now. Tears stung my eyes. I blinked hard to force them back. Several escaped to dribble down my cheek, and I swiped them quickly away.

"Thank you," I murmured hoarsely.

I wiped my damp fingers on the silky fabric stretched across my abdomen. "Is this Levina's nightgown?" I asked, more to distract myself than to get an answer.

He nodded, a strange light in his eyes. "You spilled hot coffee on yours."

Cripes! That was right. Hot flames burned in my face.

A leisurely smile transformed his face. "Don't get embarrassed. You're not the first woman I've seen in the buff. I wanted to get you covered before Cal and the doctor got here. Picked the wrong bedroom, I guess." With a deep sigh, he turned toward a small nightstand and reached for the phone.

"Who're you calling?" I croaked.

"Cal. He asked me to phone him when you woke up. The doctor thought it'd be best if you slept awhile. He gave you a sedative. You don't remember that?" He punched several numbers into the phone.

I searched my memory, then shook my head. "Why does Cal need to know I'm awake?"

"He wants to ask you some questions about the coffee," he answered distractedly, shifting his focus to the receiver pressed to his ear.

The coffee? My murky brain cleared, and it hit me like a triple-trailer semi: it was the coffee! After I'd taken a couple of gulps of it, I'd nearly had a fatal allergic reaction.

Someone had snuck strawberries into my coffee. Someone had tried to kill me!

☼☼☼

Sophie hovered over me, a pestering mosquito. If only I could slather on some *Off,* and she would buzz away to annoy some other poor soul.

"Sophie, will you please sit down," I begged as I eyed the bowl of chicken noodle soup she'd set in front of me. My stomach did a couple of flip-flops, and I nearly gagged. Whatever it was the doctor had given me, it and my innards were not getting along.

"Fine. But you need to eat, young lady," she ordered before she plopped down into a chair next to Cal and folded her arms over her chest—a living depiction of determination in pastel pink spandex. "That head of yours is still not screwed on straight."

She was right. I was woozy, and my head was one huge, pulsating mass. I gazed self-consciously around the oak table into the three pairs of eyes that were studying me intently. I felt like a specimen on the examining table.

Bart shook his head, clearly exasperated with Sophie and her flittering. "You don't have to eat. Just answer Cal's questions. Then you can go back to bed."

Sophie's eyes shifted to Bart, twin slits of displeasure.

I dropped the spoon and sipped water, closing my lids as it hit my stomach, bounced, then settled. Thank God. My throat was parched, and the water was soothing as it slid down. I managed two more sips.

My eyes scanned the well-lit kitchen. Milton's neglected cake rested next to the bare spot where my brew station had once resided. Cal had confiscated it as evidence along with Sophie's empty coffee bag, the two mugs that had survived their encounter with the hardwood floor, and my coffee canister. A heavy layer of fingerprint dust was an unwelcome reminder that evil lurks where you least expect it—dark, devious, and resilient.

Fear twisted in my chest. I turned to Cal. "I'm ready."

He nodded. "You'll need to head home now, Sophie."

She gave him a glare that would pierce marble. "No way. I'm not leaving Kit here alone with you vultures. She can barely talk, and you're planning to interrogate her into the wee hours. Well, mind you, it ain't gonna happen. I'm gonna see to it."

Eyes lethal, Cal sighed and stared long and hard at Sophie.

Sophie huffed a couple of times. "Why does Bart get to stay?"

"Kit might say somethin' that will help him remember somethin' important."

Her eyes lit up, and she settled back into her chair, a self-satisfied curve to her lips. "Then I'm staying. I might think of something, too."

Cal's brows became one jagged line of irritation. "I already have a notebook full of things you've thought of. Now go home!"

Sophie stuck her chin out a couple of inches. "How do you know Bart didn't do it? And now you're gonna let him hear everything Kit says, so he can cover his tracks."

My gaze shifted to Bart, who appeared to be unfazed by Sophie's accusation. In truth, it was doubtful that he'd tried to kill me only to change his mind at the last second.

"He saved her life," Cal said, his face only inches from Sophie's.

"And it was my coffee that almost killed her." Sophie wagged a crooked finger near Cal's nose. "Is that what you're thinking? Am I a suspect, Cal? Are you gonna storm my house in the middle of the night, handcuff me, and haul me down to the station? If you are, well, I'd rather get it over with right now."

So Sophie feared it was her coffee that had nearly killed me. "Sophie, I know you didn't try to hurt me," I told her, hoping she could hear the sincerity in my tired voice. "Please go home, so I can get this over with and go to bed? We'll talk tomorrow."

She worked her lips a bit, then stood and glowered at Cal before she turned to me. "Only because *you* asked me." She gave one last harrumph and stalked from the room.

Cal mumbled something concerning Sophie and too many TV cop shows, his mustache twitching erratically. Bart's concerned eyes were fastened on me. A giant golden ball of fur purred contentedly in his lap.

I closed my eyes briefly to work up some enthusiasm. It was hopeless. Like a hundred-pound weight, trepidation dragged me down. All I wanted was to climb into my bed and hide under the covers from the fact that someone wanted *me* dead.

Cal's voice was insistent. "Let's start at the beginning. When did you make your last pot of coffee before this mornin's?"

My thoughts pressed backwards as I stared at the yellow legal pad and pen he held in his hands. It was like swimming through murky water, all shadows and sensations and half-formed images.

"You okay?" he asked.

I attempted a reassuring smile, but it felt stiff and shaky. "It was two evenings ago—Thursday—before I went to bed. I put coffee from the canister and water into the coffeemaker and set it to brew at five the next morning." Though my throat was still sore, my voice was only raspy, as if I'd chain-smoked for fifty years.

"The doors were locked and the alarm set all night?"

I nodded.

"And you drank that coffee?"

I thought back to the previous morning. I'd taken a mug

upstairs with me, the first of several. Meg drank a cup of the coffee . . . and Roy. "Yes," I assured him.

He flashed me a pleased smile. "Okay. So Friday morning?"

Unsettling ripples pulsed through me. Cal's smile would be short-lived. A steady stream of likely suspects had traipsed through my kitchen on Friday.

My gaze turned to Bart. At least, he wasn't one of those suspects. Or was he? Like a bolt of lightning, it hit me: when the security system was off, Bart would've had access to my house and everything inside it, including me. Prickles of alarm tingled under my skin. I rubbed at them and forced my thoughts back to the events of the previous day.

"Milton woke me up around six-thirty," I began and continued from there, listing each person by name and highlighting the gist of the conversation I'd had with each of them.

Cal scribbled furiously, his frown deepening with each person I named. Every so often, he interjected a question. By the time I'd described my surprisingly pleasant visit with Jack, he was chewing his mustache agitatedly while he threw me perturbed looks from across the table.

Finally, my voice raw, I paused to gather my thoughts and sip water.

"Dammit, Kit. This place is a freakin' zoo," Cal said accusingly. "You promised me you'd be careful." He skimmed his notes briefly, then added, "So that's it?"

I shook my head, breathed deeply, and studied the chocolate blotches on my bumblebee sweatshirt. "This guy—Ronald Walker— stopped by for a short visit."

Cal's frown deepened. "Ronny Walker? Millie's nephew?" he asked.

I swallowed hard. "You . . . know him?" I stammered.

"Uh-huh." His eyes probed mine. "What the hell did *he* want?"

"He's the vice principal at the school where I work. We had business to discuss."

Cal leaned closer. "Well, that's quite a coincidence, don't you think?"

I fidgeted and avoided his intense gaze. "Coincidence?"

"Yeah," Cal drawled. "You claim you never even knew Levina existed until after she died. But you're workin' with Ronny, and Ronny sure as hell knew Levina. You don't think that's a bit of a stretch?"

"It's the truth," I murmured, scenarios of what might've transpired between Walker and Levina rolling around in my head. I rubbed at my throbbing temples and tried to make sense of it. It was hopeless.

Cal sighed and settled back into his chair. "Was Ronny alone in the kitchen?"

I pictured the two of us sitting across from each other at this very table. "Only a couple of minutes, while I answered the door," I explained. "Sophie rang the doorbell and I answered it. Dr. Walker practically followed me down the hall."

"But a couple of minutes behind you?"

I nodded. "Yeah."

He narrowed his eyes and studied me long and hard. "Any other visitors?"

Good grief—Doreen! She might hate me even more than Bernice might, and she'd been alone in my house for a good five minutes. "Just Doreen Saunders-Masters, the principal at the school where I teach. She sat in the car while I was visiting with Dr. Walker, but she used my bathroom while I was standing on the porch with Sophie."

His brows furled. "And is there any reason to think she might want you dead?"

I shrugged. Doreen would be spittin' more than shrapnel if Cal showed up at her office to question her about my botched murder. "Yes," I squeaked.

"Wanta tell me about it?"

No, I wanted to forget about it. In fact, I'd avoided a call to the investigator, hoping the whole mess would go away. "We got into a little tiff at work," I informed him.

He huffed, rolled his eyes, and turned a page on his pad. "When was that?"

"Not long after you told me Levina was murdered. I was a bit stressed, and I didn't agree with how Doreen handled a situation with one of my students."

His head dropped forward into a doubting scowl. "And because of that, she's holdin' a death grudge?"

"It's a bit more involved than that," I admitted before I launched into a detailed retelling of my meeting from hell with the queen and her lapdog, then hop scotched to the abstruse briefing with Doreen on the last day of school. "So yes, since my testimony could kill her career, she probably does wish I were dead," I recapped, in case he didn't reach that conclusion on his own.

He'd been writing furiously. Now he glanced up. "You said Ronny was there in her office, too?"

"Yes, but he'll do whatever Doreen tells him to do." As soon as the words were out of my mouth, I wanted to suck them back. Even Walker must have his boundaries.

Evidently, Cal didn't want to go down that path either. He

slapped his pad down, shook his head, and asked, "You think they know you're allergic to strawberries?"

Who didn't? "Of course. The whole staff knows."

Air spewed from his mouth in a long sigh, like when you open the door of your car on a hundred-twenty-degree-day. Then he rubbed at his eyes and forehead for a good thirty seconds. "You got a brew?" he finally asked.

"I'll get it," Bart answered. With great care, he set Annabelle on the floor and walked to the fridge, returning with two cans of Guinness. He handed one to Cal before he sank back into his chair, as dirty and disheveled as he'd been that morning.

I closed my eyes and breathed deeply, savoring the yeasty odor that settled in around the table. It seemed so normal, a world apart from murder. Or even attempted murder. Maybe it was time for me to move on. A burning in my throat made me drop my eyelids. I didn't want to leave. I didn't want to go to prison. And I *really* didn't want to die. I swiped at several renegade tears and told myself to get a grip; I was lucky to be alive.

"Maybe we should finish this tomorrow?"

It was Bart's voice and it set off little agitating alarms. Why was he being so nice?

I set my jaw and met his warm gaze. "I'm fine," I said more forcefully than I felt.

I sensed his withdrawal, then breathed more easily.

Cal took a healthy swig of draught and checked his notes. "So, we're to Friday night. Did you get the coffee ready before you went to bed?"

"Uh-huh. I dumped Sophie's coffee in with my regular coffee in the canister."

"And the next mornin'?"

My eyes automatically flitted to Bart. He'd already told Cal his side of the story. Had he included the part about stripping me naked? If so, come morning, no doubt, I would be the subject of hot, spicy gossip in every shop and kitchen in town?

I flicked my gaze back to Cal. "I let Annabelle out at four-thirty, as usual. I must've fallen back into a deep sleep because the train whistle woke me up at eight. When I ran downstairs, Bart was in my kitchen." I paused to emphasize my next statement. "He'd let himself in with a key you gave him."

Cal had the courtesy to blush, then coughed and continued with his questioning. "You didn't reset the security system when you went back to bed?"

"No, I usually get back up at five to let Annabelle inside."

I swore I heard him growl. "Does anyone else have a key to your house?"

My eyes grazed Bart. "Not now . . . unless you gave someone else a key?"

He shook his head. "So Bart was the only person who could've been inside your house between four-thirty and eight this mornin'?"

I glanced at Bart. "Well, yes. Otherwise, Annabelle would've been inside with me." As irritating as it was, it was my good fortune that Bart had let himself into my house. There was no way I could've reached that EpiPen myself.

I swallowed the storm cloud building inside me and pressed on. "I poured us some coffee and took a couple of sips. That's when my throat closed." My gaze touched Bart's. Was the discarded nightgown our little secret? "If Bart hadn't been here, I'd be dead," I admitted.

"He gave you the shot you needed?"

Holding my breath, I nodded.

"How did he know the medication was in the desk?"

"I told him."

He turned to Bart. "Is that the way you remember it?"

Bart's ominous gaze met mine, contemplative. "Pretty much," he finally said, an evocative smile touching his lips.

I tore my eyes from his. Maybe he did have some redeeming qualities.

After a final perusal of his notes, Cal set them on the table and took a swig of beer. "Well, I guess that's that," he announced.

That's that, like with Levina's murder? I wanted to ask. It seemed to me that Cal had made absolutely no headway towards uncovering her killer. Would mine be the same? Only I was still alive—a sitting duck for whomever wanted me dead.

"Way I see it, every single one of those people traipsin' through your house yesterday could've done it—Bernice or one of her two kids, Jack, Ronny, the principal. And since you didn't lock your back door, Milton and Meg and God knows who else would've had access to your kitchen. Course, Sophie was wanderin' around here, too." He shook his head glumly and chugged his beer while he thought it over. "We'll just have to wait and see what the lab results turn up. In the meantime, talkin' to all of these people is gonna keep me damn busy."

With a huff, he sat forward, his eyes stern. "And I want you to be more careful. Chances are, whoever did it's gonna try again. I don't want to be haulin' another dead body out of here."

CHAPTER 11

The rumble of thunder reverberated through the room, an omen of what was to come. When I'd lived in Arizona, I'd learned to calculate the distance, but it was a piece of trivia I'd misplaced along with faces and names and too many dye-cut memories. My life was littered with rejects—no Sophie or Milton to watch over me, nor Annabelle to disrupt my routine.

"Oh God, Kit," I whispered past the stinging in my throat. "How did you grow so attached to this place in only a few days?"

Bright light flashed through the darkened windows. Just like that, I remembered. "One-thousand-one, one-thousand-two, one-thousand. . . ." I counted slowly before the boom of thunder filled the night air, closer.

It had been just past midnight when the thunder had awakened me from unsettling dreams that had everything to do with the attempt on my life only hours before. Now savoring the comfort, I slurped a spoonful of Sophie's soup and felt its warmth slide down my throat and settle into a warm glow somewhere near the waist of my pajama bottoms.

Outside, thunder growled ferociously and turned my thoughts to Cal. If he was right, someone wanted me dead badly enough to make two attempts to kill me, the first in the school parking lot several weeks ago.

It didn't make sense. Even if one of my new kinfolk coveted Levina's belongings enough to kill her, there would be no reason for them to get rid of me until *after* they knew that I was her new beneficiary. Which left others close to Levina: Bart, Sophie, Milton, or maybe even Meg or Bob. Try as I might, I couldn't think of one reason any of them would want me dead.

Unless, of course, one of them was a psychotic killer. That thought sent a whole new series of zings along my already frazzled nerves.

Lighting crackled in the air and—a veritable lighthouse—lit up the darkness outside the windows. The deafening roar of raindrops pounding against the roof and windowpanes closed in around me, nearly drowning the grumbling thunder.

Annabelle trotted past, her tail twitching madly, shaggy fur standing on end, frizzled by the static in the air. She padded to the French doors to stare out into the darkness. I patted my own hair to make sure it didn't look like I'd stuck my finger in an electric socket.

A ferocious *meow* stilled my hands. Lights flickered and the room went black. Lightning flared, crazy flashes slicing through the night. Thunder rumbled and vibrated as if it were pounding its fists on the house. Tickling sensations crept along my arms.

I clutched at my heart and stared into the black void. Cripes! I had no idea where to look for a candle or a flashlight. Something brushed against my leg, and I reached down to touch the comfort of Annabelle's fur. "Okay, girl; what do we do next?" I murmured.

She croaked several throaty meows seconds before the world outside exploded with a resounding boom that shook the house. Light burst into the room, then dimmed.

"What the heck?" Was someone bombing my house in the middle of a thunderstorm?

Shaking, my teeth clicking rhythmically, I stared at the door, unable to move, half expecting a killer to crash through the glass and bludgeon me to death. Flickering light filtered into the room. Except for the pounding torrent of rain, all was quiet.

Ever so slowly, I crept to the door and hid behind the frame, then peeked outside.

Oh, my God! Was that inferno in *my* backyard?

Disoriented by the pillars of flames swirling high into the dark sky, I fiddled with the security alarm and locks. Finally, the door swung open, and cool, damp air engulfed me. I breathed deeply, the acrid scent of burning wood assaulting my lungs.

Focused on the blaze, I tentatively stepped toward the roaring fire. Raindrops pelted me, soaking my flannel pajamas and plastering them to my body. Water trickled down my face and chest and dripped from my fingers. Through the drops on my eyeglass lenses, the world was distorted—all rounded corners and shimmering shapes. I shivered and pressed forward, my bare feet sinking deep into the thick, wet grass.

"Nothing like a nice bonfire, huh?" a deep voice yelled from behind me.

I whirled, and at that exact moment, air crackled and several streaks of lightning illuminated the sky. Bart stood before me, looking like he was plucked from the cover of one of those bodice-ripper paperbacks—all hard muscle and slick, glistening skin, a pair of athletic shorts riding his hips. The mega-watt flashlight in his hand came to life.

Thunder growled as the area surrounding us lit up like a carnival ride. I turned to the flames. "What happened?"

"A bolt of lightning hit your oak tree," he explained. "Poof!"

He walked forward, and I trailed, wobbly from all of the excitement. The rain was letting up, more drizzle than downpour. Still, it was dousing the flames, revealing dark streaks of burnt wood.

Lightning had torn the huge tree down the middle. Half of it still stood, its skeletal branches now bare and charred. The other half had fallen into Bart's yard, crushing the picket fence beneath it.

A stream of light bobbed up and down from behind the mess, shadowed by a hunched figure in a long yellow poncho. Suddenly, it lurched forward. "That dang blasted well! Someday, I'm gonna dig the damn thing up," Milton grumbled, straightening creakily.

"Well?" I asked.

"The old well is still there," Bart said from beside me. "It's not as tall as it once was, but some of the stone masonry is still there. No need to worry; it's been covered."

Milton joined us, limping slightly. We stood side-by-side, facing the still burning tree, mesmerized by the flames. In the distance, thunder groused angrily.

The wail of a shrill siren—too close—shattered the mood.

"You call the fire station?" Bart asked matter-of-factly.

"Yep," Milton replied. "Probably don't need them."

"Nope. The rain'll dowse it."

I eyed the two men. They were as calm as a couple of cows at a clambake, entranced by the flickering firelight. I felt goose bumps rise on my arms and shivered.

"You might want to put on something warmer," Bart murmured.

"I'm fine," I assured him.

"No need to push it. Your body's recovering from a shock, and you're standing out here in wet clothes," he prodded.

Another siren screamed through the night, this time surely at my front door. "At least, I've got some clothes on," I muttered as I marched off.

The house was dark, the open door into it a gaping hole. Fear twisted inside me. "Get a grip," I told myself. "It's the middle of the night. No one has been lurking outside your house waiting for a lightning bolt to create chaos so he can sneak inside and kill you."

Rowdy noises from the front of the house grew louder and spurred me on—thumping and shuffling and men's brisk voices. I steeled myself and stepped resolutely towards the laundry room, where I grabbed my Columbia jacket, slipped it on over my saturated pajamas, and slid my bare feet into a pair of Wellies before I made my way back outside. At the last minute, I returned to the house to wipe off my glasses and retrieve a key. Cal would be so proud of me; this time I locked the door.

Deep, rumbling laughter drifted across the yard. Three well bundled-up bodies had joined Milton and Bart, forming a semicircle around the glowing embers. As I approached, another in a fuchsia raincoat stepped out from behind the still-standing trunk.

"Dammit, Sophie. Don't you ever do what you're told?" a gruff voice barked.

"You're not my boss, Phil," Sophie snapped back, tugging the hood from her head, "so I don't have to do what you say. Besides, I went through Milton's yard, so I didn't get in your way. I came to see you guys do your stuff, and here you are standing around like warts on a toad. If this is what being a fireman's all about, sign me up?" She looked around, searching, and her eyes landed on me. "There you are. You okay?"

"I'm fine," I said, joining the fireside chat, staring at the glowing logs.

The rain had turned to a fine mist, and the air had a crisp, clean smell to it with just a hint of smoke and roses. I breathed deeply, savoring the freshness. "I'm sorry about the rosebushes, Milton," I told him. "Several of them are squashed."

"I'll trim 'em back, and in a few weeks, they'll be blooming again," he assured me.

"Well, sure as hell, that tree's a goner," a familiar voice chimed in.

I turned to study the man behind the voice—short and round in yellow firemen's gear, his hat pulled low over his forehead. "Harv?" I blurted.

"Last time I looked," he replied. "You've lost a mighty fine oak here, one of the oldest in Aurora. Probably a hundred and fifty years old. Sad to see the old guy go."

"Well, hell. At least, the damn thing went out in a *blaze of glory,*" the man Sophie had called Phil added. He was tall and broad-shouldered, towering over Harv who, next to him, looked more like a kid in a Halloween costume than an honest-to-goodness fireman.

The guys had a chuckle over Phil's remark. Sophie gave me a look that matched what I was thinking: put a bunch of men together, and they throw around colorful language and make no sense at all.

Harv finally cleared his throat. "Well, little lady, the rest of that tree's gonna have to come down, preferably, before it falls down." He pulled his hat off and ran his hand through the few sparse hairs dotting the top of his head. "My sister's grandson Skeeter could probably do it for you. He's a spoiled rotten, lazy-ass kid, but if he gets goin' on a job, he gets it done. I can have him get in touch with you?"

I looked at the charred remains of the ancient oak, and a wave of sadness washed through me. On my watch, Levina's once beautiful tree had become a distorted, broken skeleton of its former self. *Cripes, Kit. It's only a tree,* I told myself. "That would be great, Harv," I told him. "Thank you."

Then I eyed the guy called Phil. "I'm Kit O'Maley," I said. "I live here. Thank you for responding to Milton's call."

"Glad to be of service," he replied, flashing me a crooked smile that spoke of something I couldn't quite decipher. "I'm Phil Green and this here's Jorge Gonzalez."

Jorge looked to be in his early twenties with a lanky build and shy dark eyes. I greeted him and he responded in kind.

Sophie huffed impatiently, crossed her arms over her chest, and eyed the three firemen. With a reproving shake of her head, she glared at Phil and blurted, "Well, aren't you guys gonna get your big hoses out and put on a show for Kit and me? We don't pay you to sit around here and shoot the bull, you know."

Sophie's question set the men off again. They were sniggering and having a grand old time. Sophie planted her hands on her hips and gave them each a fierce look.

"No need to drag our *big* hoses out tonight, Sophie," Phil finally snorted. He turned to me, a twinkle in his eye. "You got a faucet nearby, Kit?"

Unsure where there might be a faucet, I glanced toward the darkened house. A shroud of dread settled over me, a heavy, hopeless feeling that sent spirals of fear twirling deep inside me.

I turned back to the group and wondered if it would be totally out of line if I invited them to stay for a sleepover.

✲✲✲

"No, I didn't ask five men to spend the night with me," I informed Patty and Grace. "It was temping, but I was afraid Fireman Phil would take me up on my offer."

I spread slices of turkey and cheese on a platter and savored the comfort of my two friends' companionship. Grace had called that morning to see if she and the boys could drop by for a visit, and Patty had returned from her niece's wedding in Seaside. Here with them, the events of the last two days seemed more a dream than a living nightmare.

Grace's eyes were wistful. "A big fireman hunk. A night of adventure and passion. Geez, what I wouldn't give for an opportunity like that." She held her hand out in front of her. "Look, I'm trembling at the thought of it."

Patty eyed her incredulously. "My God, Grace, we have to find you a man . . . and soon, before you get desperate and do something foolish. How long's it been?"

"Too long." Grace sighed longingly. "Now that the mail carrier's in his summer shorts, even he's looking good. And he's the spittin' image of my Uncle Oscar, who still wears a killer mullet and fluorescent Hammer pants."

I laughed and opened a container of fruit salad. "Maybe I can set you up with the *hunk*. He's not really my type." I pictured his sparkling eyes and bright smile and wondered if I was totally defective. Any other woman would've clamored to get her hands on fireman Phil.

I grabbed a bag of baked potato chips from the pantry, my mind replaying the previous night's adventures. After Phil had soaked the glowing coals, the party had broken up. Sophie had been miffed about the lack of excitement, but I'd had more than enough. The remainder of my night had been spent in fitful slumber on the living room couch.

Promptly at four-thirty, Annabelle had surfaced from her corner of the sofa, stretched, and begun her caterwauling. After she'd darted out the door, I'd eyed the bare spot on the counter, one part of me screaming for a cup of coffee and another part quaking at the thought of it. Alarmed by the prospect of years of coffee abstinence, I'd headed north in search of Starbucks and groceries. On the way, I'd phoned Patty and invited her to lunch.

Now I studied Patty's raised eyebrows and prayed that she wouldn't go off on another *kit needs a man* diatribe.

Grace narrowed her striking dark eyes and frowned. "Geez, that's tempting, Kit, but maybe I should meet the guy first."

Six-year-old screams suddenly filtered in from the backyard. I eyed the French doors, where fresh air streamed in thanks to the previous night's storm.

Grace exhaled exasperatingly. "What are those little imps up to now?"

I dumped the chips into a bowl. "Stay where you are. I'll look."

The boys had the pails and shovels Patty had brought them. They were digging at the base of the giant oak's charred remains, in the loose dirt created when the roots from the toppled half had been pulled from the ground. It appeared that Stonewall now had free run of my backyard. With the boys' help, he was working madly on a large hole, throwing a spray of dirt up behind him. The front portion of his body was down in the soil out of sight.

I turned back to Grace. "They're fine; just digging in the ground."

"Thanks for checking," Grace said. "I swear it's getting harder and harder to keep up with them." She paused, her gaze sliding around the room. "If this house wasn't so full of breakable things, I'd offer to come and stay with you, Kit. I don't like you being here alone."

"That's nice; thank you. But you don't need to worry. Patty's less than a mile away when she's at Cal's, and Sophie watches over me like a mama hawk," I assured her while I set plates, silverware, and napkins on the table. "Hopefully, in the next few days, Cal'll figure out who spiked my coffee and arrest him . . . or her. Then my biggest problem will be deciding whether to stay here or go back to teaching in September."

A pained expression settled on Grace's face. "Like it's even a choice. Please tell me you won't choose S&M and wimpy Walker over this beautiful house and fairytale town?"

"I'm not sure. If someone's determined to kill me, I can't sit here like a mouse in a trap and let it happen. And Bernice is sure to contest the will." My words replayed in my mind, a reminder that my life here was tenuous. In truth, it might be out of my hands.

"What a shrew!" Patty snapped. She'd been uncharacteristically silent, probably mooning over Cal. "But the one who has me concerned is Ronny. Why did he drive all the way out here to ask you if you're returning to the school next year? He could've phoned." She paused to shake her head, her lips pinched, her brows furled. "Something's up."

"It was probably Doreen's call," I told her. "Walker's her talking puppet. He's making sure I know that he'll corroborate her version of the knife incident."

Patty was studying me with her all-seeing eyes. "Well, next time don't let either of them in your house!" she said emphatically. "I'm worried about you, Kit. Someone's trying to kill you, and you seem somewhat distanced from that fact."

I stared at her. Did she really think I wasn't concerned about my own prospective murder? The reality of it was never out of my thoughts. Still, I couldn't allow fear to consume my life. A couple of hours with trusted friends, a time to relax and let my guard down and not to worry—that's what I needed right now.

Grace frowned at Patty, a perturbed set to her lips. "Geez, Patty. We're here to cheer up poor Kit, not give her the heebie-jeebies."

I pulled my gaze from the intensity of Patty's and struggled to calm the anxious twitters her words had reignited. "You can call the boys in now, Grace. There's a bathroom right next to the laundry room where they can wash up."

Patty and Grace both stood, Grace to call the boys and Patty to help me. "I'm serious," Patty murmured while we transferred food from the counter to the oak table. "Be careful. Keep your doors locked and the security alarm on. And for God's sake, don't invite *anyone* in here when you're alone."

Just who did her warning include? Other than Patty and Grace, could I be assured that I was safe with anyone? "I'll be careful," I promised just as Danny and Davy burst into the kitchen, screaming loud enough that, across the street, Sophie's hackles were surely rising. Stonewall's shrill yaps only added to the confusion.

I glanced up at the boys, their knees and hands caked with mud, faces etched with black soot. The dog bounced up and down at their feet, rhythmically, as if he was driven by a piston, trying to get to what Danny held in his hands—a very real-looking skull with a large glistening silver tooth.

I winced. The bowl slid from my hands, and potato chips flicked my bare feet. My mind took in the whole scene but could make no sense of it.

"Yuck! Where did you get that thing?" Grace asked, her lip curled in disgust.

"We're pirates!" Davy exclaimed. "We're diggin' up treasures."

Ever the calm, cool woman of reason, Patty approached the two proud boys. "Can I take a look at your skull?" she asked, holding her hands out to them.

Danny glared at her and took a step back. "I found it; it's mine."

Davy looked at his brother and narrowed his eyes in warning. "I found it, too."

"Geez, Danny! I don't want you touching that gross thing. Give it to Patty right now," Grace ordered. "And get that dog out of here."

Danny took another step back and cradled the skull closer into his body, his dirt-streaked arms encircling it.

"It's mine, too!" Davy insisted.

Patty knelt. "That's the coolest skull I've ever seen. Can you hold it out so I can see it better and feel it?" she entreated, her manner casual and soothing.

Still frowning, Danny glanced from Patty up to his mother. Grace gave him a stern look, and he huffed and stepped forward, holding the skull out to Patty. Like moss stuck to a tree, Davy followed. Except for his stubby tail, which wagged from side to side like an over-wound metronome, Stonewall stilled.

My pulse pounded as Patty ran her manicured fingers over the chin bone and up to a large, jagged gash in the forehead. She tapped on the rounded top with her index finger and felt the single silver tooth directly beneath the hole where the nose would've been. Her shoulders rose and fell. "I think it's real," she said, her voice quivery.

A shudder ran through my body from my head to my toes. "Boys, where did you find your treasure?" I asked, not wanting to know the answer.

"In our diggin' hole," Davy told us. "And there's more!"

More? My God, what did that mean? My stomach heaved. "Where is your diggin' hole?" I asked, struggling to keep my voice steady.

He pointed toward the back of my yard. "By that spooky ghost-eye tree."

☼☼☼

Cal was in a huff, stomping around my backyard and growling like a grumpy grizzly bear. Hoping to avoid him and keep my mind occupied with something less fearsome than human bones buried beneath my roses, I slapped together sandwiches to fortify the crew that had invaded my Sunday afternoon with their shovels and cameras.

The silver-toothed skull sat on the kitchen table, its vacant eyes haunting me through the Saran Wrap in which it was now encased. At the moment, a dead head, even one decomposed to the point of being skeletal, hit way too close to home.

I topped turkey with slices of provolone while I rehashed the events of the last two hours. Grace had wrestled the boys' treasure from them while Patty put in a call to Cal. He'd arrived, scruffy and not a happy camper. Turns out, it was his day off.

Fortunately, he was thrilled to see Patty, enough to greet her with a thorough kiss and a lot of hands-on activity, which had set the boys to moaning and gagging. Grace had stared at the two lovebirds, speechless, her dark eyes bugged out like a housefly. By the time Cal had finally glanced at the plastic-swathed skull, I was mentally moaning and gagging, too.

Cal had examined the skull and questioned the boys about it before he'd stomped to the porch to glare into my backyard and back at the boys' treasure numerous times, his bushy brows growing more furled with each rotation. Finally, he'd turned his stormy eyes my way and demanded to know what had happened during the night. I'd given him the condensed version—minus the parts about the possible sleepover and my leaving the doors wide open while I wandered out into the dark yard in my pj's to cavort in the rain with Bart.

A high-pitched yipping interrupted my ruminations and drew me back to my sandwich slapping. I blinked, then eyed the homely dog that bounced just inside the French doors. Something was agitating him. I squinted through the glass. A young man in a blue police uniform was stringing yellow crime scene tape between my porch railings and the grass.

"Stonewall, quiet!" I ordered, trying to emulate Bart's demanding bark. Unfortunately, it didn't fool the annoying mutt. "Cripes! Where is your owner today?" I rubbed at a sharp, throbbing pain in my right temple. "Probably out having fun. Well, wait until he gets my doggy daycare bill. We'll see who's having fun then." I sighed and returned my attention to the food Cal had requested for the crime scene gang hard at work in my yard, most of whom had been pulled from their Sunday dinners.

The thump of the front door closing silenced Stonewall's yaps. He streaked down the hall, and several seconds later I was looking into Patty's worried eyes. Stonewall flounced back to the doors, dropped onto his haunches and panted, gazing into the backyard.

Patty shook her head. "Poor Grace. I don't know if those boys will ever settle down.

One-at-a-time, Cal had taken Danny and Davy into my office to talk with them privately. After that, Patty, Grace, and I had watched as he walked them out to the ravaged oak tree, an arm around each of their shoulders. Next to Cal, they'd looked so small and vulnerable that I'd wanted to rush out and intervene. To say that it was all my fault for failing to install a lightning rod on the tree the minute I'd arrived at Levina's house.

"I hope Cal wasn't too hard on them?" I probed. Surely, Patty was objective enough to notice that the love of her life did have his flaws—a lack of patience and equanimity being two of them.

Patty's eyes narrowed. "They loved it. 'Just like on TV,' they kept saying."

"Okay," I said, resigning myself to the fact that what I found downright spooky might be an adventure to a six-year-old. "Hopefully, they won't have nightmares." I picked up a knife and began to slice sandwiches and arrange them on a large platter.

"Don't be so hard on yourself. That skull looks like it's been there since the ice age. You didn't bury that body out there, and you didn't make lightning strike that tree."

It was as if a bolt of lightning struck me. I froze. "Body?" I wheezed.

Patty leaned across the counter, in my face. "My God, you look like someone drained every drop of blood from your body. Get off your feet. And eat something. You lose much more weight and that skeleton out there is gonna look healthier than you. I'll finish here."

Like a frozen video recording, the grisly vision of a half buried, decomposing body flashed through my mind repeatedly. "There's a body buried in my backyard?" I whispered, more an effort to come to terms with it than to get clarification from Patty.

"Put that knife down before you cut your fingers off," Patty ordered.

I glanced down at the razor-sharp blade poised directly over my hand, then set it to the side. The slight movement had a sobering effect. I breathed deeply, exhaling a lengthy whoosh of air, and felt my muscles relax. "I'm okay," I assured Patty, eyeing the carnage on my oak table. "Please tell me they're taking it with them."

Patty smiled weakly. "I would think so. Cal said the boys uncovered most of it. They pulled the head off when Grace called them to lunch."

"Yuck," I murmured, shaking my head to rid it of the grisly image.

My eyes dropped to the sandwiches and I returned to slicing. "Would you mind opening that bag of chips?" I asked Patty. "I spilled the last bag on the floor and Stonewall wolfed them down. The poor dog will probably be sick all night. Serves Bart right for taking off and leaving him to run wild."

Patty reached for the bag I'd set on the counter. "You really don't like that guy, do you?"

"No," I admitted, a twinge of guilt poking inside me with the knowledge that the man of whom I spoke had saved my life. "If he just wasn't so patronizing," I added in an effort to validate my negative feelings. "He treats me like I'm a ten-year-old . . . *idiot*."

Patty smirked. "If you think he's sees you as a ten-year-old, you *are* an idiot."

Choosing to ignore her snide remark, I picked up the loaded platter and strode to the French doors. Stonewall popped up and emitted a barrage of high-pitched yips. I peeked through the glass. Not far away, Annabelle lounged on the grass in a patch of sunlight. A familiar figure loomed over her, his arms crossed over his ruffle-clad chest. He was observing the commotion taking place near the charred log that pierced the clear blue sky.

I eyeballed the over-excited dog at my feet and murmured, "Well, looky there, Stonewall. Your negligent master has finally returned."

But what in the heck was he wearing? I squinted. Sure enough, some kind of pantaloon leggings hugged his muscular legs, and a billowy white blouse-looking garment gaped open, exposing a good-sized portion of his hairy chest. He looked like a half-clothed pirate. Fitting, I suppose, under the circumstances. But . . . bizarre!

I smiled to myself and opened the door. The dog darted out and made a beeline for the far corner of the yard, yapping and wagging his runt of a tail. Bart's head whipped around, his eyes grazing mine before they turned to follow his pet's progress.

"Stonewall, stop!" he roared.

To my consternation, the mutt froze in his tracks, then looked back at his owner. "Stonewall, come!" Bart ordered.

Stonewall's head swiveled back and forth between his dig site and his demanding master. Ever so slowly, his head drooped, and he slunk slowly towards Bart and Annabelle. Bart crouched down and scratched him behind his ears.

"You suppose Cal would dress up like that for me?" Patty murmured from behind me. "Whew! Just the thought of it is bringing on a hot flash."

"You blaming Cal for your hot flashes now?" I ribbed her as I walked out onto the porch to deposit the sandwiches on an ornate wrought iron tabletop.

Patty set the chips and a pitcher of lemonade beside the sandwiches and hand-fanned her face. "Problem is, I can't tell which is making me hot—him or menopause."

For several long moments, we silently observed the activity in the far corner of my yard. Unlike television crime shows, the figures bustling around the expanding pit were an assorted lot, clad in muted shorts and bright polos, faded jeans and logo-splashed tee-shirts. A zebra-striped sundress fanned out around a woman who was crouched near the hole, a measuring stick in one hand and a notepad in the other. Several men strolled about, pausing to visit and examine whatever caught their attention, maybe snap a few pictures. Two were on their knees digging in the soil with what looked like garden trowels. If I hadn't known what they were up to, I'd have assumed they were preparing a barbeque pit to roast a pig or perhaps designing an eye-catcher for one of those yard makeover shows on HGTV.

At the back of the lot, Milton observed from his side of the picket fence, his face shaded by a wide-brimmed straw hat. Poor guy. He probably wished he had Levina and his nice, quiet life back. I waved at him; he waved in return. Interestingly, Sophie hadn't come by to check out the action and take charge.

"I'll get the cups and plates and some condiments and water. Will you try to get Cal's attention?" I asked Patty before I made my way back into the house.

By the time I got the provisions on the table, the motley crew was on the porch. Death didn't seem to put a pallor on their appetites. They demolished the stack of sandwiches and crunched on chips while they joked and ribbed each other, their laughter filling what I'd planned to be a quiet, lazy Sunday afternoon with friends. I managed to paste what I hoped was a sincere smile on my face, introduce myself to my last-minute visitors, and thank them for putting their Sunday activities aside to process what I prayed was a *very* ancient burial site, preferably of someone who had died of natural causes.

"I'm assuming you want these cookies out here," Patty whispered in my ear.

I eyed the box of super-sized chocolate chip cookies, a special treat I'd purchased for Davy and Danny. Had it really been that morning? It seemed ages ago. "Yes, thank you." I paused to glance around, then asked, "Do you know where Cal is?"

"He and Bart are in the kitchen." Patty passed by me, and I retreated through the French doors and followed muddy footprints to Cal and Bart. They sat at the kitchen table, Cal looking like someone had touched his gun without permission and Bart looking like I'd stepped into his own personal male members only club—two centuries back.

I tugged at the hem of my short denim skirt and slid into a chair. Stalling to gather my thoughts, I studied the crevice in the creepy skull's forehead and nervously patted my ponytail. Finally, I met Cal's turbulent eyes. "Surely, you don't blame me for this?"

He chewed his mustache, fingers drumming on the table. "No, but life was sure a hell of a lot quieter around here before you arrived. Now I've got two dead bodies. And I'll have another one if you don't start takin' some precautions—like not leavin' your house in the middle of the night! And if you do, at least lock your damn door!"

My eyes flew over to Bart, the traitor.

"Don't blame Bart," Cal said, leaning forward to nail me with a fierce look. "He's not the one who squealed on you."

I felt like a disobedient child. "I was only out there a couple of minutes. When I came inside to get a jacket, I *did* lock the door."

"All it takes is a couple of *seconds*!" he said heatedly.

His words left me shaky, rubbing my roiling stomach—thank you, Cal.

Something behind me softened his glare. I didn't need to turn around to know who his lovesick eyes were caressing. He sighed. "Listen; if anything happens to you, that woman out there is gonna wring my neck. And between you and me, there're other parts of my body I'd rather she focus on."

"Okay. I will try harder," I promised, my voice a husky whisper, cheeks burning.

Bart was studying Cal. "I think you've made your point," he said before he turned to me. "I'm gonna give you my cell number, and I want you to call me if you even hear a mosquito buzz and it doesn't sound right."

"Thank you . . . just in case something else happens," I murmured, a part of me wondering if I wouldn't be inviting the big, bad wolf into my house with that call.

My body tensed as a door creaked. "They've gone back to digging. Do you want me to bring this stuff inside, Kit?"

Patty's familiar voice soothed me back into my chair. "Sit down and rest. I'll take care of it later," I told her. No doubt, after a snail's pace drive back from the coast that morning and the taxing events of the afternoon, she was as pooped as I.

"Don't mind if I do." She crossed the room and snuggled up close to Cal, her fingertips caressing his forearm. They really did make a cute couple—two baby boomers still willing to embrace romance.

Seeing them together tugged at my heart. I couldn't help but wonder if I'd ever again feel that kind of wholehearted infatuation. "So, who are all of those people out there?" I asked in an effort to move the conversation back to the investigation in my backyard.

Cal pulled his gooey eyes from Patty. "I'm in over my head here. If that body's been dead as long as I think it has, it's gonna need special attention. So I called in the big guns from the State Police Crime Lab in Salem. There're a few county guys there, too."

"Any idea how long it's been there?" Bart asked.

"Stan, from down at the museum, was up here earlier." Cal eyed Patty, gulped and added, "Based on the clothing that's still there, it's male. He placed it around the eighteen-sixties or seventies."

Bart leaned forward. "Huh. So it was buried after Aurora was colonized." He rubbed the bridge of his nose as if in deep thought. "If I remember right, James Wallace, Kit's great-great-grandfather, built this house around 1872. He died in 1875. Maybe they buried him in the backyard. Any sign of a coffin?"

Cal shook his head, eyes glazed, studying Patty's fondling fingers. "Nope. Just the body. Other than that silver tooth, there's nothin' that might help identify him. No watch. No wallet. No rings. Just a few scraps of clothing."

"You might want to talk with Milton," Bart suggested, a slight edge to his voice. "His house was built around the same time as this one, and I think he had ancestors in Aurora back then. And Bernice or Jack—Levina's siblings—might have an idea about who's buried there. Of course, Stan might uncover something in the museum records."

"Yeah," Cal responded in more a sigh than a confirmation.

Bart's perturbed eyes met mine, and something passed between us, a silent understanding. I didn't know which was more disturbing—being a party to Cal and Patty's intimate love play or sharing a personal moment with Bart.

He turned away first. "If you're ever going to figure out who it is, that's probably the route to go," he advised Cal.

Cal's tanned cheeks glowed red. "I'll take care of it," he assured Bart tersely before he gently twined his fingers with Patty's wayward ones, stilling them.

Just like that, everyone seemed to relax a little deeper into their chairs. Even Patty transformed back to her normal, sane self. "Any news on the coffee?" she asked.

"Yep," Cal announced smugly, his blue eyes zeroing in on me. "I got the lab results this mornin'. Seems dried strawberries were mixed in with the coffee in your canister, not with the bag that Sophie brought you."

"In the canister," I reiterated, perplexed. "Why would someone go into the kitchen and search for the coffee container when the bag was sitting right there on the table?"

"Maybe it happened *before* Sophie set the bag there," Patty offered.

I thought back to that morning. Sophie had met us at the front door—Bernice, Janet, Roy, and me—the bag of coffee clutched in her hand. She'd set it on the table. When I walked into the kitchen, she was outside with Milton. Roy was sitting at the table drinking a cup of coffee, very much aware that I hadn't needed Sophie's coffee. Bernice and Janet were standing by the mantle. Any of the three of them could've snuck dried strawberries into my coffee canister.

"Milton and Meg were the only two people here before Sophie brought me her coffee. Why would either of them want Levina dead? Or me?" I wondered aloud.

"Maybe whoever did it wanted to be certain you'd use the coffee with the strawberries," Patty said. "There was always the possibility that Sophie would take her bag back home or that you might put it in the cupboard."

"You had the coffee in the enamelware container, right?" Bart asked me.

I nodded hesitantly. "Enamelware, is that what you call it?"

"Uh-huh. It's *old* and *expensive*." He was studying me intently, probably afraid I would ditch the precious stuff now that it had an unsettling connection to my near death experience. "It had *coffee* written right there on it in large black letters, so it wouldn't be hard to find. Just lift off the lid and pour in the dried strawberries. That's a lot easier than opening and closing a bag."

"By the way, the only prints on the canister were yours, Kit," Cal added.

"I poured out the old coffee and washed it after I moved in," I told them.

Cal chewed on his mustache a bit, then said. "They're still runnin' tests on the strawberries. Maybe there'll be some clues there.

Anything else turn up missin'?"

I shook my head and glanced at Bart.

He rubbed at the fur on his chin thoughtfully, then added his two cents worth: "You know, something that's bothered me since the reading of the will is the way your cousin Roy reacted when he found out Levina left me some of her rare books. It was way over the top. Then some of those books turned up missing."

"You think Roy's a thief because he yelled at you over a few old books?" I challenged somewhat guiltily. I couldn't shake the feeling that Roy had overreacted when Bernice had questioned him about the missing desk set, too. Surely Roy didn't need money badly enough that he'd resorted to stealing his Aunt's possessions?

Bart's black brows furled into a deep *v*. "I'm just saying that it isn't like Roy to blow up like that," he growled. "And he did spend a lot of time here in the house . . . sometimes on his own."

"I'll look into it," Cal muttered, shaking his head, clearly exasperated. "Right now, I'd better get back out there." He patted Patty's arm, rose to his feet, and stretched his back. Before he stepped outside, he eyeballed me. "They'll finish up outside before dark. But until they finish searching the area for more bodies, you need to stay out of your backyard.

Yet again, my world went into a tailspin. "More bodies?" I whispered.

CHAPTER 12

"Shit," I hissed, trickles of irritation sneaking into my determined early morning optimism. A middle-aged man with a poufy crop of salt and pepper hair and a puffy red face, sweat slithering down his pudgy cheeks, glowered at me. Stonewall sat erect in his arms, beady eyes gleaming, pink tongue dangling, power panting like he'd just won the Iditarod.

I muttered a few choice descriptors pertaining to my neighbor Bart, then unlocked the door and faced the obviously irate man. Stonewall greeted me with a cursory yip. His buzz cut fur was damp and smelly. Drool dripped from the sides of his mouth.

"Keep your mutt inside!" the man said curtly, thrusting the sweaty dog at me.

My arms encircled the compact body. Stonewall reached up to run his rough tongue across my chin, then settled into my arms. I drew my eyes from the muddy paw prints on the man's white shirt. "Any idea how long you guys will be?" I asked, referring to the hodgepodge of busy crime fighters who were scrutinizing every inch of my backyard.

He pulled a wrinkled handkerchief from his back pocket and mopped the dampness from his forehead and cheeks. "Well, that depends," he replied curtly. "If we spend all our time chasing your dog, we'll most likely be here through Christmas."

Determined not to let my day go bad when it had barely started, I swallowed a retort. "Have you found anything else . . . out of the ordinary?"

"No more dead bodies," he barked. "Course, we still need to do the yard next door and the one behind you."

Poor Milton. All the care he put into his yard, and now it'd most likely look like a colony of gophers had invaded. And Bart; it served him right for dumping his dog on me.

The man's face faded to a pastel pink. He looked somewhat sheepish when he glanced past me and asked, "You got any coffee in there?"

"I wish," I told him. "The local law confiscated my Brewmaster and my coffee stash.

Truth be told, at the moment, there wasn't much I wouldn't do for a caffeine fix myself. In fact, if I wasn't standing at my back door clutching Bart's obnoxious dog in my arms, I'd now be on my way to Milton's kitchen and, hopefully, a cup of strong, hot coffee.

Evidently already in the clutches of caffeine withdrawal, the guy moaned, pinched the loose skin between his brows, and sighed resignedly before he wandered off.

"I'll see what I can do," I offered.

He glanced back. "Appreciate it."

Stonewall wiggled and whined, determined to return to his game of chase. "No way, little guy," I told him. "You're going home." I tightened my arms around him and stepped back to close and lock the door, then paused to consider my options. Sans makeup and shoes, I could feel my hair drying into a mass of riotous curls around my face. Should I take the time to traipse upstairs and make myself presentable before confronting Bart?

"Oh, what the heck!" I muttered as I grabbed my keys, Stonewall clasped in my arms.

Since the storm, it had remained in the high seventies, a perfect temperature from my perspective. Vegetation was transformed, now green and lush, preening with its newfound satiation. Blossoms were brighter, and birds were more chipper, filling the morning with a chirping cantata, flitting here and there. I breathed deeply and thanked the good Lord that I was still able to breathe as I perused the vehicle-infested street.

Annabelle sauntered through the open gate, prompting Stonewall to return to whining and wiggling. His fur was slick, his claws sharp. I set my jaw, hugged him close, and strode, as resolutely as was possible in bare feet, to the gray house next door. By maneuvering a bit, I rang the doorbell with my elbow.

On the third ring, when I was seriously considering breaking a window, Bart opened the door. Shocked, I stepped back, speechless. My eyes slid down his leather-clad body to the knee-high fringed moccasins on his feet. Cripes! What was with this guy?

"Playing dress-up?" I blurted before I took note of the glower and set jaw.

"You might say that," he uttered tersely.

"That's a whole lot of leather."

"It's buckskin."

"Oh," I whispered, caught up in throes of wonder. It wasn't everyday that a six foot plus male answered the door in full blown mountain man garb.

"Bart?" It was a sexy female voice, and it came from

somewhere behind the icon.

"I'll be right there," Bart hissed through clenched teeth.

Oh, God! I'd interrupted something. Heat radiated from my face. "Here's your dog," I muttered, shoving Stonewall into his buckskin-clad arms.

I couldn't get away from him fast enough. But at the bottom of the steps, I happened to glance down and notice the grime on my yellow tee-shirt. My head jerked around. "Keep your dog inside. They're working in my backyard," I snapped before I hustled back inside the relative safety of my home, Annabelle waddling at my feet.

Fifteen minutes later, my hair firmly trussed and my poise somewhat restored, I exited the house and locked the front door. Grasping the platter holding Milton's cake, I walked cautiously to the sidewalk and peeked next door. *Don't go there,* I told myself. Cripes! This was the man who'd seen me naked. Just how depraved was he?

"K-it! K-it!" shrieked Sophie from across the street.

I shook off thoughts of the carnal goings-on next door and turned to her. She strode briskly towards me—woman in pink on a mission. "Good morning," I greeted her.

"Mornin'. I'm glad I caught you." She eyed the chocolate cake suspiciously. "What ya doing with that?"

"I made it for Milton," I murmured.

Evidently, that was *not* okay. "You got a thing for Milton?" she demanded, glaring at me so hard that her blue eyes were completely hidden beneath a pair of seriously long fake eyelashes. "He's *mine*, you know."

The absurdity of this whole morning was too much. To suppress my laughter, I bit my lower lip so hard it hurt. My gaze wandered to the gray house next door, and I quickly reined in my snooping thoughts. Bart's predilections were none of my business.

"*Well?*" Sophie huffed.

I eyed her. Was she daft? A super stud next door who didn't even pique my interest, and she thought I was hitting on Milton! "No, Sophie," I assured her. "It's just my way to thank Milton for all of the work he's done in my yard . . . and for watching after Annabelle."

The daggers in her eyes dulled a fraction. "Well, you never know. Some young chicks prefer older men, especially hot guys like Milton. You ask me, they need to stick with men their own age. It's a rule of nature, so to speak; takes us more experienced women to keep an older man satisfied."

Which made me think of Meg. Which brought to mind Bob. "Sophie, do you know Bob Crosely?" I probed.

The daggers sharpened. "What about him?"

"Just curious," I told her, now more curious than before. "I met him at the store. He seems like a nice man."

"If you like his kind," she snapped.

"His kind?"

She sniffed in disgust. "Thinks he's hot stuff. Only been here a year, and he's already outstayed his welcome. The locals would like to see him move on."

That wasn't the impression he'd given me. "He and Levina seemed to be friends."

Her eyes narrowed "That's hogwash."

"What do you mean?"

"Levina was local folk, too." She studied me closely, her face scrunched up like a dried apricot. "Mind you, if you're looking for a man, you'd best skip right on past Bob Crosely. And Milton, too; he's already taken."

"All I want from Milton is a cup of high-test coffee," I assured her. "Cal took mine . . . and yours. I'm hoping Milton has a pot brewed."

The determined look returned to her eyes. "I heard Bart's dog dug up a skeleton in your backyard yesterday."

I nodded.

"If that don't beat all! I leave for a few hours to visit with Geraldine—she's a second cousin once removed on my mother's side—and I miss out on all the excitement." She perused the vehicles that lined the street. "The ladies in my Bunco group are counting on me to give them the latest scoop on the goings-on here, what with me living right across the street from you and being in the thick of things and all.

"Mind you, Mavis Hornsby's green with envy. She's used to being the center of attention, and now she's not; I am. Course, I do a better job than Mavis. Soon as I have a juicy tidbit, I'm on the phone."

I stared at her, speechless. Just what was Sophie telling her friends about me? "Sophie . . . did you tell your friends that . . . I'm allergic to strawberries?" I stammered.

"You're darn tootin' I did. It was the best way to get the word out. Didn't want someone giving you something that'd kill you."

So, pretty much the whole town had been aware of my strawberry allergy days before my coffee was spiked. Cripes! How would Cal ever narrow down the suspect pool?

She shook her head. "I shouldn't have gone to Geraldine's. I should've kept watch over you." Her focus turned to the crime scene tape surrounding my house. I could almost see the cogs turning beneath her kinky do. "Maybe I'll just take a gander into your backyard. I don't suppose they'll mind as long as I don't touch anything."

She was talking more to herself than to me. I'd just opened

my mouth to dissuade her when a bright flash of color next door caught my attention. A woman in a short, form-fitting sundress flounced down the front steps, her smooth blonde tresses bouncing beguilingly. Bart trailed behind her—man in fringed buckskin toting a massive black suitcase by its handle, a study in contradiction. He pushed the case into the back of a red minivan and walked around to the front of the vehicle, then glanced up into my eyes.

Aware that I was staring, I turned back to Sophie. She was looking next door, too, eyes squinting, mouth gaping. "Hmmm," she hummed. "Sometimes I wonder if that man hasn't lost touch with reality. You ask me, he spends too much time in la-la land."

Though some nosy part of me begged to hear all about Bart's *la-la land*, it seemed prudent to change the subject. "I tell you what, Sophie. The guys in back want coffee. Why don't you take a pot to them? Use my key and go through the house to the back porch. You'll be able to see what's going on from there."

Sophie's face blossomed. "Good idea. Maybe they'll find some more bodies. Could be your house was built on a sacred Indian burial ground. Wouldn't that beat all?" Now totally immersed in her new mission, she made her way back across the street.

Remembering Cal's warning, I yelled after her, "Be sure to lock my doors!" before I peeked at the red minivan and continued on my cake journey.

Milton's front door sported a beautiful brass knocker. He answered on the second knock, pleasure sparkling in his watery eyes when they dropped to the cake. "Kit. What a nice surprise," he said.

"Hi, Milton. I baked you a cake, a little something to say *thank you* for all you've done to help me out—the yard work, taking Annabelle in . . . and numerous other things."

He ogled the cake, his mouth slack, nearly drooling. When he spoke, it was a euphoric sigh. "Chocolate is my favorite."

Somehow, I'd known that. "That's good because this one is chocolaty to the point of being decadent," I told him. "I got the recipe from an elderly woman in Georgia. And believe me, people in the South do know their way around sinfully delicious food."

"So Bart's told me," he chuckled, a mischievous twinkle in his eyes. "I've always said, 'What's the harm in a little sin amongst friends?'"

This was a side of Milton I'd never before encountered. I studied his thick, neatly combed silver hair and his softened but still attractive features. Perhaps Sophie's depiction of him as a *hot guy* wasn't off the mark. In the senior crowd, he must be quite a catch.

"I've always thought a *little* sin can't hurt," I agreed, "the earlier in the day, the better. Just point me to the kitchen. And please tell me I'll find a pot of coffee when I get there."

He chucked softly. "You may not look like Levina but I hear her voice in yours. You share her spirit."

A tiny lump settled in my throat. "Thank you, Milton. I consider it an honor to share something with Levina . . . anything."

Milton's house smelled old, like the antique shop where I should be spending more of my time. I sloughed off the guilt by assuring myself that after a short visit with Milton, I'd head there. Then I followed him down a long hall that felt vaguely familiar.

When I entered the kitchen, it hit me: Milton's house appeared to have the same layout as mine. I gazed around the large room, noting the few inconsistencies. Whereas Levina had done some fairly recent remodeling, the interior of Milton's house could've been plucked from one of those mid twentieth century picture-perfect family television shows. It was clean and tidy, homey. Instead of a massive oak mantle, red bricks framed Milton's fireplace. I sniffed and felt a rush of delight. Surely, that was chicory I smelled.

"You noticed, huh?" Milton asked.

"That there's coffee in the air?"

He chuckled. "That, too. I was talking about the house. Although there've been several minor changes over the years, basically, we—you and I—have the same house."

"I thought so." I set the cake on the cluttered kitchen table and walked into the living area. Except for the floral rug, the room had a manly feel, all shades of brown and olive green and lacking the brightness of its counterpart. A picture of a woman holding a young child caught my attention. I was sure I'd seen them somewhere before.

My focus returned to Milton. "It seems kind of strange that our houses are so similar. Bart said James Wallace built my house in the eighteen- seventies."

Milton appeared to mull that over. "That sounds right. I suppose this house was built around that time, too. I'm not sure of the exact date or who built it. Somehow, my ancestors ended up living here. That's my great-grandmother and my grandfather in that picture."

That's why I recognized them. They were the same two people as those in the painting in Meg's coffee shop. Only this one had to have been painted a few years earlier. I stepped closer and noted Wallace's bold signature in the lower right corner.

Swathed in a long, lacy gown, his head covered with silky-looking dark curls, it was difficult to believe that the child in the painting was a boy. His mother held him ramrod straight, her delicate, tapered fingers wrapped around his sides. If a smile had even touched her lips, she would've been a stunning woman. Instead, her face spoke of disappointment, longing, and more perseverance than a woman her age should've had to endure. The only bright spots in the painting were the young boy's cherubic, yet stoic, face and the massive brooch adorning the woman's high-necked collar.

Great-great-granddaddy must've delighted in his use of bright colors to stun his audience. In this case, he'd painted the brooch to visually pop from the painting, an impressive ruby stone surrounded by a sea of what could only be honest-to-God genuine diamonds. The unusual setting was undoubtedly pure gold — a series of intertwining loops that brought to mind bagpipes and tartan kilts.

It was curious that the painting in the coffee shop was set where grass thrived, yet the backdrop for this portrait was as dull and desolate as its subjects: endless acres of faded dirt and sagebrush. "Where was this painted?" I asked, strangely unsettled by the silent plea in the young woman's eyes.

"Don't know," Milton replied. "All I know is that the two of them—my grandfather and his mother—lived in this house."

"Well, James Wallace must've painted this before they settled here."

"Why's that?"

"The background." I gestured towards the painting. "Supposedly, Wallace spent a lot of time over in eastern Oregon. Maybe that's where this was painted?"

Milton studied the painting, then shrugged. "Could be."

"The portrait of the two of them in Meg's coffee shop is different," I said, thinking aloud. "For one thing, they're sitting in front of a sapling, and there's plenty of vegetation, like around here. But there's something else. It's what you see in their eyes. In Meg's painting, they're sad, but there's also a sense of hope. The bleakness and utter despair in this painting is enough to send a healthy person into depression." I tore my eyes from the painting to gaze at Milton. "How can you stand to look at it every day?"

Milton smiled. "Levina used to ask me that very question. She was forever telling me to take it down and put it back in the basement where I found it. 'Hang something bright and cheery,' she'd say."

Ever so slowly, the smile on his face faded into well-worn lines of concern. Sadness wiped the sparkle from his eyes. He seemed perplexed. "You know, that last night, Levina questioned me about that painting," he murmured. "She never had before, but that night she couldn't take her eyes off it." Almost to himself, he whispered, "I forgot about that."

My pulse switched gears, accelerating. "What kinds of questions?" I probed.

Clearly upset, he rubbed at the wrinkles above his brows before he answered. "Oh, where they came from and when they moved here, who my great-grandmother's husband was: those kinds of things." Shaking his head contritely, he continued. "I told her the same thing I told you: I don't know. She wanted to know if I had any old family records. I don't. Then she asked if I had the brooch in the picture."

"Do you?" I didn't mean to blurt it so demandingly, but the prospect of touching something that had belonged to the woman in the portrait was compelling.

He sighed and slowly shook his head. "No."

"What happened after Levina questioned you about the painting?" I pressed.

He shrugged. "We ate dinner together . . . for the last time." A glassy sheen lit up his eyes, and when he spoke, his voice was choked with emotion. "Something else was on her mind though, something to do with that picture. She'd seen it hundreds of times before. Still, that night—just like you are today—she couldn't take her eyes off of it."

Funny, Meg had said the same thing about the paintings in her shop. I turned back to the picture to examine each minute detail. What was my distant ancestor seeing as he painted his depiction of these two now long dead people? Deep down inside me was an unsettling awareness that he knew them well, at least well enough to understand their pain and longing and to feel compelled to capture those feelings on canvass.

And Levina? Why her sudden interest that evening in a picture in which she'd never before shown an interest? Could a hundred-and-fifty-year-old painting have anything at all to do with her death mere hours later that same night?

☼☼☼

It was as if they spoke to me, those two pairs of eyes, transfixed in a permanent gaze that had been preserved for more than a century. No errant twinkle. No tears. Only a profound melancholy . . . and a touch of something else. Maybe hope? What had happened to etch that sorrow into their countenances?

They were dressed from head to toe in black—a young boy of about five years and his mother—sitting in matching wooden chairs, hands folded neatly in their laps and backs unnaturally erect. An oak sapling rose behind them, its green leaves grayed by an overcast sky. In the background, tall grass stretched down the hill to a murky river. James Wallace hadn't stroked his trademark splotch of vibrant color into this painting. Here, all was lifeless.

"Do you think this is about someone's death?" I asked Meg.

She shrugged. Clearly, she found my interest in the portrait on her cafe wall an enigma. "Beats me. You should see the picture of the two of them at Uncle Milton's. Nothing could be that depressing. You ask me, they could both use some Prozac. I hope it's not a genetic thing. If I ever get that down in the dumps, please put me out of my misery."

I studied the glow of cheerfulness that seemed a part of Meg. "I don't think you have to worry about that." My eyes slid back to the painting. "It's the way Wallace painted them, like he was conveying a message. They're dressed completely in black, as if in mourning. Even the trees and grass have a sorrowful quality."

"Like I said, 'Depressing as hell.' The only reason I keep it is because it's important to my mother. She gifted it to me when she moved to Phoenix. So I guess I'm the official keeper of it until I can dump it on the next generation . . . if there is a next generation."

She sighed deeply, her lips twisted. "I'm not having much luck with that. For awhile, I was seeing your cousin Roy. Thought it might work out, too. We played together when we were kids. Turns out we're more friends than lovers."

"Roy mentioned that you'd dated," I murmured.

Meg nodded and gave me a meaningful look. "I thought Cal and I might hook up, but he seemed to lose interest about the time you inherited Levina's house."

"It's not me," I informed her. "Cal and a friend of mine hooked up several weeks ago. They seem very fond of each other."

"Bummer," she muttered resignedly. "He's so gentlemanly that I was hoping it'd turn into something. I seem to attract jerks."

Which brought to mind my visit with Walker. Levina knew him; maybe Meg did, too. "Do you know a man named Ronny Walker?" I asked.

She took a step back and slid her snugly clad derrière onto a table, a strange look on her face. For several long, uncomfortable moments, we eyeballed each other. When she spoke, her voice had a curious edge to it. "Yeah, I know Ronny. He thinks he's pretty hot stuff." She made a face that clearly said she thought otherwise, then shrugged. "But if I get desperate, he's always good for a night out."

Reflexively, my hand rubbed my stomach. "How did you meet him?"

Meg picked up a napkin and began to fold it, her long fingernails crimson against the white tissue. "He came in here a couple of years ago with Levina. I remembered him from when I was a kid. We'd visit my grandparents, and sometimes Ronny'd be around annoying the hell out of everyone. What a brat!"

He still is, I wanted to inform her. Instead, I delicately probed. "Did Levina seem very close to him?"

"No." Meg's nimble fingers paused, and her features

scrunched up into a dubious frown before she returned to napkin folding. "Levina handled his aunt's estate sale. I think that's how she knew him."

Tiny tingles of anticipation simmered within me. "There wasn't anything else?"

She shook her head. "I doubt it. Levina seemed to think he was a total flake. And she wasn't too happy about me dating him."

"Did she say why?" I asked, wondering why Meg *had* dated him.

"She said Ronny was just using me, and I deserved better—another jerk." Meg wadded the napkin into a ball and squished it in her hand. "But what's a woman to do when the local eligible man pool is severely depleted?"

Why Meg didn't have a pack of panting men trailing after her was beyond my understanding. "What about Bob?" I asked, studying her closely.

Color drained from her face. "Bob?" she breathed.

"Over at the train depot. He seems nice and he's younger than Cal."

The squeak of a door gave me a quick shot of adrenaline. I jerked around as two stout, middle-aged women strolled into the cafe, arms loaded with a jumble of purses and bulging shopping bags, faces aglow.

"I told you we'd beat the noon rush," the larger of the two chirped.

"Sit wherever you'd like," Meg told them.

I turned back to her. "Well, what about Bob?"

She threw the napkin onto the table. "My advice to you is stay away from Bob."

From across the room, the scraping of chairs and shuffling of paper bags reached us. Meg glanced at the women, sighed, stood, and made her way to the back of the shop.

"Were Bob and Levina close friends?" I yelled after her.

She turned, her elegant brows curved into a puzzled frown. "No. Why?"

"He claimed they were; said she'd shown him pictures of me."

"Sounds like Bob," she uttered, her lip curled in disgust, before she turned away.

Will you please tell me about Bob I wanted to scream. Why did both Sophie and Meg refuse to talk about him? And why would he claim to be Levina's friend if he wasn't?

My eyes slid to the two paintings on the wall, the larger one a drab landscape with a vibrant blue river and the other surely a portrayal of grief. There was something similar about the two paintings—not just the style, the brush strokes, and other little idiosyncrasies that define a talented artist. Something else was tugging at me.

I stepped back several steps and squinted, trying to focus only on the two now blurry pictures. Except for the winding blue river, both canvasses were covered with shapes in various shades of dark. The only other exceptions were the stark white faces of the woman and her son and the lighter-hued river behind them in the smaller painting and a blob of stones that formed a well in the larger painting.

Then it hit me, and tiny tingles of excitement spurred me to step forward and study the paintings more closely. Sure enough, peeking from behind the woman's voluminous black skirt was the hint of stone masonry. Was this what Levina had noticed when she'd studied these same two pictures that last day of her life?

In my mind, I traveled back to the night of the storm. By light from Bart's flashlight, I saw Milton tripping. "That dang blasted well! Someday I'm gonna dig the damn thing up," he'd said.

If I was right, and I was pretty sure I was, both of these paintings had been painted at the same location—my backyard.

✵✵✵

The stillness of late night closed in around me, unsettling. Standing in the shadows created by the streetlight on the corner, I dug in my purse for my extra house key and made a mental note to get the one I'd leant to Sophie that morning back from her. Exhausted, I sighed with satisfaction at all that I'd accomplished that day. Levina's antique shop might not be up to her high standards, but everything was neat and orderly and organized into displays that I hoped wouldn't humiliate me in front of the seasoned antique connoisseur.

Which brought to mind Bob. Following my futile conversation with Meg, I'd trekked across the street to take another shot at getting to know him. But according to the sign in the depot window, Bob was traveling the state on a five-day shopping spree; planned or spur-of-the-moment? My bet was on the latter.

Distracted by my thoughts, I tried to turn the key in the deadbolt, then froze when the hard click of it disengaging didn't register. I turned the key to the right, and the bolt clunked into place. Spasms of alarm slammed through me. I eyed the doorknob, then reached out to hesitantly turn it. Sophie had left my house wide open! Once more, I turned the key to the left, heard the deadbolt's solid *thunk,* and cautiously pushed the door open several inches.

Dark and ominous, the threshold was an abyss. I stood as still as the flock of plastic flamingoes gracing Sophie's front yard, ear pressed into the dark slit. Except for the pounding of my heart, it was quiet. Then wisps of sound filtered out, as if someone were brushing up against something. A loud thumping noise followed.

I flinched and slid deeper into the shadows. Thought slogged in my brain, mired down. It seemed that I stood there for an eternity, my body shaking uncontrollably, my teeth clamped painfully together to keep them from chattering.

Finally, I dragged my eyes from the open door and glanced around. Though snippets of yellow tape streamed in the more well lit areas of the yard, all other signs of the crime squad had vanished. From across the street, suffused light filtered through Sophie's front windows. But, God forbid, what if I forced my quivering legs to carry me across the street and she wasn't home? I'd be stuck on *her* front porch, alone, defenseless.

My eyes shifted to the gray house next door—a dark, brooding shape floating in a murky sea of deep shadows. Perhaps it was only wishful thinking but a few wandering rays of light seemed to reach out from the back portion of the house. He'd said to phone him.

Ever so slowly, I slid my cell phone from my purse. It felt cool and solid in my trembling hand, my lifeline. I pushed back farther into the darkened corner of the porch and struggled to access Bart's number. Seconds later, I heard his deep voice. "Bart here."

Relief flowed through me, yet my body shook more forcefully—out of control. I pressed the phone hard against my ear. "This is Kit," I whispered shakily. "I need you."

"Where are you?"

Tears tickled my cheeks. "My front porch."

"I'll be right there."

A click, then silence. I shrank, becoming one with the shadows.

The slamming of a door, then the soft tread of running feet and Bart appeared in the meager light cast by the streetlight, tall and hulking, a pillar of strength. I swiped at tears and watched him ascend the steps in two long strides. His eyes focused on the open front door.

"Over here," I whispered.

Four quick strides and he was so close that I felt the heat from his recent exertion and swam in the woodsy scent oozing from his body. It muddled my brain even further.

"What's going on?" he asked.

"I . . . I. . . ." I was having a complete meltdown; that's what was going on.

His arms slid around me and drew me close against his solid frame—damp cotton against my cheek, a pungent smell, and the security of strong arms. At that moment, I didn't give a rip whose arms they were. I wound my arms around him and held on for dear life.

"Someone's inside my house," I spluttered.

His body stiffened. "What makes you think that?"

"I heard noises. And the door was unlocked."

"You didn't lock it?" His words were warm puffs of air caressing my ear, igniting prickles along my neck.

"Sophie was taking coffee to the workers. I asked her to lock it."

"The alarm wasn't on?" Annoyance tinged his voice now.

I hesitated, remorse gnawing at me. "No," I sighed.

He muttered something under his breath, and his arm shifted. I glanced up as a cell phone lit up his scowling features. Steeling myself, I untangled my body from his and stepped back to put some distance between us.

When he spoke, his soft-spoken words had an edge to them. "Yeah, Cal. Bart here. I'm with Kit on her front porch. She just got home. Her front door was unlocked, and she heard someone inside her house."

For several long moments, the only sounds were the drone of frogs, the distant hum of passing cars, and the tinny sound of Cal's anger. The fragrance of roses and newly mown grass permeated the night air, so familiar now that I felt new tears sting my eyes. I tried to shake off the bolt of melancholy, to reclaim the mind-numbing fear. Rather it than the feelings of deep loss I knew would claim me if I had to leave Aurora.

Bart's voice broke through my struggles. "Uh-huh. Yeah. That's right. And the alarm, too." There was a brief pause, then, "You need to take that up with Kit, not me."

It didn't take psychic powers to figure out what Cal was saying.

"Yeah. Okay. We'll wait here for you."

His hand on my back guided me to the metal glider. I sank down into it, and he sat beside me, his hard body pressed firmly against mine, one arm draped around my shoulders, invading my space. I tried to pull away but it was futile on the narrow seat.

Darkness engulfed us, making me acutely aware of the tickle of his hairy legs and arms and the deep, musky scent and heat radiating from his damp body. "You're wet," I muttered, disturbed by his overwhelming male presence.

"I was lifting weights. Next time don't call until I've showered."

Thoughts of Bart showering stirred my insides. A tight ball of panic clenched in my stomach. "It's just that you're sweaty and you're too close."

He chuckled softly and tightened his hold on my shoulder, drawing me nearer to whisper in my ear. "Too close, huh? Lady, I could teach you things about being close—and sweaty—that would make this seem like a Mennonite worship service."

Visions of Bart in his mountain man garb with his beautiful blond companion, lips and limbs locked, invaded my mind. I shoved them and him aside and stood up just as Cal's car ground to a stop in front of my house.

Bart stood, too. "The mood Cal's in, you might want to hide back here until he calms down a bit. I think you interrupted his . . . homey evening with your friend Patty."

"I deserve it," I muttered. "I keep messing up."

Actually, Cal's scolding was the least of my fears. When he stepped from his car, reality punched me in the gut. Someone had been inside my house tonight, someone who had probably intended to murder me. Terror spiraled inside me with that knowledge.

Even in the dim light, I could see that Cal was a thunderhead ready to burst. He stomped up the steps in his baggy shorts and wrinkled polo, a gun-toting holster slung over his shoulder, his dark hair standing in tufts on his head. There, he stopped to glare at the open door, then at me. I braced for his tirade.

"Dammit, Kit!" he hissed. "What the hell were you thinkin'? I told you those doors were to stay locked, didn't I?"

"Yes, you did. And I'm sorry." I hoped I sounded as contrite as I felt. "With all of those law enforcement people working in the backyard, I thought it'd be okay if Sophie locked up the house for me. Then I stayed at the store much later than I. . . ."

"No excuses! You need to do what you're told!" he stormed. He worked his mouth a bit, his shaggy mustache twitching. "Otherwise, you're gonna be dead."

Bart squeezed my shoulder reassuringly. "I understand; no excuses," I murmured.

Cal chewed on his mustache forever, his eyes narrowed and threatening. "I'm holdin' you to that." His eyes darted to the open front door and he shrugged. "If someone was in there, they're long gone now. It'll keep 'til Josh gets here. Tell me what happened."

Well," I began, thinking back to that morning. "I gave Sophie my house key, so she could take coffee to the people working in my backyard. Since she couldn't go past the crime scene tape, she took it through my house.

"She wanted to take them sandwiches for lunch, and I needed to get to the antique shop, so I asked her to keep the doors locked. She assured me she would. I planned to be home by late afternoon, but I got busy and didn't realize how dark it was getting outside."

Like a thunderbolt, it hit me and left me reeling: I'd enjoyed working in that antique shop. Surrounded by Levina's loot, I'd put my worries and fears aside to speculate on the lives of those who'd once owned her loot. Caught up in my own ruminations, I'd completely lost track of time. I filed the alarming realization away. It was bad enough that this house was fast becoming my home; I couldn't allow myself to get attached to that store, too.

Blinking hard, I pulled myself back to Cal, who was looking at me strangely. "I'm sorry; did you ask me a question?"

He frowned. "The alarm; did you show Sophie how to use it?"

"No, I planned to be home before the team in the backyard left. And . . . besides, Sophie seems to have difficulty keeping things to herself. She has this group of ladies that she calls whenever she has any new gossip. When she learned I was allergic to strawberries, she encouraged them to spread the word. Did you know that?"

"Doesn't surprise me." Cal rubbed his forehead with one hand as if it might erase both Sophie and me from his life. "Everyone I chat with knows more about your strawberry allergy than me. Milton has a whole book on it. Bet you didn't know that strawberries are part of the rose family, did you? They're not even really a fruit.

"By the way, the berries in your coffee were TriStar, same as the juice in Levina's sherry. Not that it helps much. Evidently, they're a popular berry around these parts 'cause they produce all summer long. So as far as leads go, it's another big fat zero."

A cruiser pulled in next to Cal's car, its bright lights drawing our attention. The man in uniform who stepped out of it was carrying a large black case by its handle.

"Evenin', Josh," Cal greeted him.

Josh nodded. "Chief. Bart." When he got to me, he was silent.

"Kit," I said. "Nice to meet you."

"You, too," he muttered.

"Kit here thinks someone was inside her house when she got home," Cal stated matter-of-factly. He drew his gun from its holster and added, "Go around to the back door and wait there. I'll go in the front."

He motioned to Bart, who pulled me back into the darkened corner. Josh dropped the case and became one with the shadows. Shivers tingled up my spine. If the interloper was gone, as Cal had claimed, why couldn't we just walk into the house and turn on all of the lights? Why all of this furtiveness?

Standing to the side of the door, Cal slowly pushed it open—the squeal of squeaky hinges alerting any intruder—and disappeared inside.

This time Bart pressed me down into the glider, but he remained standing, planted like a massive Redwood in front of me. I sat stiff as the washboards I'd discovered at the store that day, my hands twisting in my lap until they ached. Time crept, agonizing in its slowness. Every so often, a squeak or a thump could be heard from inside the house, and I'd freeze, holding my breath until I was woozy.

After what seemed like an eternity, light radiated out through the front door, then lit up the porch. I blinked and stared at Bart's solid butt mere inches from my nose. The man needed a lesson in personal space.

"Come on in," Cal said from the doorway. His gun lounged in its holster, his hair now slicked flat. Annabelle was stationed at his feet. She didn't look happy either.

"Don't touch anything," Cal growled before he stepped back to let me precede him into the house. "And tell me if you notice somethin's missin'."

Cool, stale air pressed in around me. My eyes scanned the narrow hall; the crowded walls looked untouched. I stepped into the dining room. It, too, appeared to be as it was that morning—piles of discarded items cluttering the space.

"That the way you left it?" Cal asked from behind me.

I nodded, feeling my shoulders relax a bit. Maybe Annabelle had made the noises. But if it had been her, she would surely have slipped outside through the crack in the door and been at my feet howling for her overdue dinner.

Which brought up another point: why wasn't she?

I turned, nearly crashing into Cal, and crossed the hall to the office. At first, my mind didn't register what it saw, and I stood paralyzed by the scene before me. Books had been dumped onto the floor, and papers were strewn across the carpet, hiding the intricate floral pattern.

Stunned, I stepped toward the desk. Its drawers hung open, their contents scattered. I sniffed. A faint anise smell clung to the stuffy air. I sniffed again. Was it my imagination, this only a flashback to when Roy had stood behind me here? My fuzzy brain struggled to make sense of it while the room heaved and swayed around me.

Strong hands grabbed my shoulders. "I take it you didn't do this," Cal muttered.

I shook my head, then couldn't seem to stop. My empty stomach heaved threateningly. I clamped my eyes shut, my world spinning out of control. "Do you smell anything?" I whispered.

Sniffing noises filled the silence. "Just old things," he finally muttered. "Take her in the back, Bart."

Strong arms encircled my shoulders, familiar arms. I grabbed my churning stomach and nestled into their comfort as they led me. Then I was laid down gently, and a pillow was stuffed beneath my head. I breathed deeply, willing myself to relax. Ever so slowly, the dizziness passed, and my stomach settled into a slow gurgle.

"I'm okay," I muttered, hoping that by stating it, I would be. I squeezed my eyes shut, shoving aside visions of a gum-chewing Roy sneaking around inside my house.

"Can I get you anything?"

I lifted one eyelid and squinted at the bright light. Bart was crouched beside me, too close, his chiseled features lined with concern.

"How about a glass of water?" I asked, more to put some distance between us than because I wanted the water. "And would you please feed Annabelle?"

He rose to his feet and disappeared. From the front of the house, the sounds of deep voices and movement filtered back to me, reminding me that someone—perhaps a cold-blooded killer—had been inside my house tonight. What if I hadn't noticed the unlocked door? Would Cal now be photographing my dead body?

I shuddered and pushed myself up into a sitting position, searching for a distraction—anything—from my terror-inducing thoughts. My eyes lit on the intricately carved mantle, and I felt its silent pull. Why was I so drawn to my distant ancestor's works of art? A passing interest might make sense, but this persistent drive went much deeper. And it was growing stronger. It was as if someone was reaching out to me, pulling me toward some elusive understanding. Good grief. Was I losing my mind?

In the kitchen, Bart was slamming cupboard doors. I rose shakily and tottered to the mantle. It seemed that every light in the room was lit, which created shadows and exposed minute details in the carvings. I eyed the covered wagons and the ferry Jack had claimed was run by descendants of Daniel Boone.

Hesitantly, I reached out a finger to trace the meandering Willamette River. Several smaller rivers snaked from it. I followed one that ran towards the floor with my eyes until several intriguing shapes caught my attention. Curious, I crouched down to investigate. The overhead light highlighted the detail: the covered front porches and two-storied façades of the two identical houses. And carved into an open stretch of land between them, beside what appeared to be a masonry well, was something that set my heart to racing.

"Annabelle's not hungry," Bart murmured. "And you better have a good reason for being down there."

I shot up, bumping his arm and spilling water down his front. Cripes! Why couldn't the guy give me some space? "Sorry," I muttered. "I was looking at the carvings."

He was too close again, his gaze too intense. Should I share my suspicions with him? I slid down and pointed to what I'd just discovered. "What do you see?"

Bart set the glass on the mantle and squatted beside me. He ran a finger lingeringly over the carvings of the two houses. "I'll be damned. Levina spent a good deal of her life in this house, and I'm pretty sure she never noticed this. How did you find it?"

"It's that light up there." I pointed at the bulb that shone onto the fireplace. "What do you think it means?"

He shrugged. "I haven't a clue. Who knows why Wallace did some of the wacky things he did. But I'd bet my buckskin leggings that those two houses are yours and Milton's. And that's definitely a cross sitting there, about where that body was buried.

"It's curious, though." He ran the edge of a fingernail around the outside of the elaborate cross. "This isn't actually carved into the wood, so it might've been added at a later date."

I leaned forward to get a closer look. Bart was right; the cross was a separate piece of wood. Had James put it there or had someone else attached it? And why?

James Wallace had painted the picture in Meg's coffee shop, the one in which the woman and young boy appeared to be in mourning. If my suspicions were correct, that picture was set right about where the cross was carved on the mantle. So who was buried there? It had to be someone important enough to Wallace that he felt the need to document it. Yet why no casket? Nor headstone? Just a young sapling to mark the location?

My mind swam with piecemeal snippets of information and too many conjectures and dead bodies. If I didn't discover what was going on soon, I might be one of the deceased myself.

I shuddered. It was time to swallow my pride, don some armor, and initiate a visit with my dear Aunt Bernice.

CHAPTER 13

The house before me was, like its owner, overly elaborate, bejeweled—I counted at least six different paint hues—and about as welcoming as a viper's den. Someone had taken a perfectly functional farmhouse and attempted to turn it into a Victorian mini mansion.

Somewhere inside that travesty was my Aunt Bernice, a woman who detested me, perhaps enough to want me dead. I studied the ornate leaded-glass door through my rain-splotched windshield and struggled to calm my edginess with deep breaths. My mind flashed back to the night before, to Cal's irate warnings. He'd probably put me under house arrest if he knew what I was up to now.

But if anyone had insights into my family history, it would be Bernice. According to Jack, she'd been here when my mother was killed. Surely, she'd been privy to handed-down tales concerning James Wallace, too. If I was ever going to figure out what was going on in my life, I needed to work up the courage to walk through that door and confront her.

"So put your *big girl* panties on and get to it," I muttered. Frustrated by my own spinelessness, I shoved the door open and geared up to sprint down the front walkway. Though dark clouds were threatening when I'd left home, I'd thought it a bluff. Now fat raindrops pelted from the sky, slathering everything with a glossy sheen.

By the time I reached the front door, my cotton sundress was plastered to me, my leather sandals squishing. I patted the tight ball of hair at the nape of my neck, then rang the doorbell. Mammoth moths fluttered inside me, begging me to turn and run.

She answered in a heartbeat, and if looks could kill, hers would have. "I see your rudeness allows you to show up at my house *uninvited*," she asserted.

Reflexively, I stepped back, then caught myself and determinedly stiffened my spine while I rummaged for words. The murmur of rain filled the gap, prattling on the porch roof and babbling in the rain gutters. "It's my understanding that my grandparents left this farm to their children, my mother included. That ownership would pass on to her heirs, right?" It was drivel. I had no idea if what I said was correct or not, but I was hoping it would shut Bernice up long enough for me to be settled in her living room.

Her penciled eyebrows peaked; her chin dropped. "Oh, you're not satisfied with stealing just one family home. Now you want this one, too?"

The remark was caustic. Still, an intriguing glint of fear sparked in her frosty pupils. Forced though it was, I smiled. "All I want are answers to a few questions."

"Here's your answer: you don't belong here," she snapped.

Her words stung. If I didn't belong here, where did I belong? I shivered, not only because of the goose bumps dotting my arms, then swallowed the burning knot in my throat and pushed forward. "I just want some information about my mother . . . and several other family members."

She planted her fists on her narrow hips. "Oh, is that all? Dredge up the past. Did it occur to you that I might not want to relive those days?"

For the first time, Bernice looked like she might harbor some human feelings. I studied her—a crumbling pillar—as prickles of apprehension slithered through me. Whatever had happened, it was bad enough to crack Bernice's determined façade.

"I'm sorry. But surely I have the right to know about my mother and her family?"

She chewed her upper lip, her intense eyes probing mine, then stepped back for me to pass into the house.

It was as I'd expected, overdone—crammed with ornate and gaudy reproductions in various shades of gold, blue, and white. The enticing aroma of something baking wafted around me, contradicting the faux elegant setting. I kicked off my wet sandals, and my damp toes curled into the plush carpet as I followed her into a blatantly formal living area. There, I froze in mid stride.

Directly in front of me, hanging in all its regal glory, was another of James Wallace's paintings. This one was a grandiose fit with Bernice's décor, its elaborate gold frame nearly out-staging it. Of those I'd now encountered, it was by far the most striking. Painted in hues of brown and gray, a mass of twisting, twining vines snaked along a rustic wall. Razor-sharp thorns posed a serious threat to anyone who dared venture too near the shrub. Bursting from the perilous vines were clumps of delicate, bright blue roses. From across the room, I fought the urge to walk forward and touch one of the elegant blossoms. Whoever touched the real thing would walk away with wounds.

"Don't tell me you've developed an interest in Great-grandfather's paintings, too?" Bernice groused from beside me.

I pulled my eyes from the painting to her. "What do you mean—*too*?"

She rolled her eyes and shook her head without moving a single strand of her perfectly coifed hair. "Your mother, then Levy, full of far-fetched ideas, as if his paintings actually have some deep, hidden meaning."

"You don't believe that?"

Only someone totally off their rocker would, her look said. "James Wallace was an artist—a duck out of water—an adventurous Scotsman stuck in a staunchly religious German community that dictated what he could and couldn't do. No doubt, he loved his wife dearly or he wouldn't have stayed in Aurora. He didn't fit in. His paintings are his portrayal of noncompliance in a society that required conformity."

They weren't Bernice's words, for sure. "Someone told you that?" I probed.

She studied me, visibly irritated. "My father."

"What did he tell you about the Blue Bucket gold?"

With a shrug, she dismissed my query. "All poppycock: an old family legend, one blown totally out of proportion."

"Aunt Levy didn't think so," a strained voice said from behind us.

I jerked, then swiveled.

"Good lord, Janet. You're going to give me a heart attack. How many times have I told you to make it known if you're nearby?" Bernice snapped.

"Sorry," Janet said, though she didn't look the least bit repentant. Her hands were wringing, her eyes angry bullets aimed at me.

Bernice gestured towards a pristine white high-back chair, one designed to seat less ample bodies than mine. I ran my trembling hands down the back of my damp dress as I sat, hoping I wouldn't leave water marks on the plush fabric. The blue roses hung before me, beguiling.

Bernice slid into a matching chair and perched daintily on its edge, knees together and hands clasped in her lap, cold eyes turned to me. "Ask your questions," she demanded.

I clasped my hands, too, so tight they hurt. "You said it was only a legend. So James Wallace didn't actually search for gold in eastern Oregon?"

She sighed, obviously exasperated by my ignorance. "I said it was blown out of proportion. He might've searched but he didn't *find* it. James was my father's grandfather. If there'd been any gold, Daddy would've known about it. He insisted that it was a fabricated story—totally unsubstantiated."

"But Great-grandpa Jim believed in the gold," Janet interrupted, the bite in her voice now aimed at her mother. "Aunt Levy told me he did. And James Wallace was *his* father, so *he* would've known more about it than *your* father."

"And your Great-grandpa Jim's the one who put all those crazy notions in Olivia's head . . . and Levy's, too. He'd go on for hours about that gold, about how his father had found it and then hid it so he wouldn't have to turn it over to the colony." Bernice shook her head and huffed. "It was only the ramblings of a foolish old man."

"You don't know that for certain, Mother. James Wallace died before the colony fell apart. Great-grandpa Jim said his father took his secret to his grave with him."

"I *do* know it," Bernice insisted, irritation rife in her voice. "Daddy would get so upset with Olivia. She believed every word that old man uttered."

If anyone was going to have a heart attack, my bet would be on Janet. She was visibly shaking, and her face had turned an unhealthy scarlet hue. "Then where did James Wallace get the money to build that house?" she spat. "Aunt Levy said it was the grandest one in the colony, a mansion by their standards."

Bernice shook her head disgustedly. "You're being ridiculous, Janet. As you well know, over the years, paintings by James Wallace have popped up here and there. He probably sold enough of them to build that house. And who knows what he was actually doing in eastern Oregon. Maybe he was working and earning that money."

"Who'd pay money for those stupid paintings back then?" Janet asserted.

My eyes drifted to the painting. I had to agree with Janet. Still, Milton's family must've forked out some dough for their two family portraits. "Do you know of a connection between Milton's ancestors and James Wallace?" I asked.

Bernice looked surprised, then eyed me suspiciously. "No. Why do you ask?"

"Well, Milton's family has three Wallace paintings. Two of them are of Milton's grandfather and great-grandmother." Bernice glared at me as if her question had not yet been answered. "And there's his house," I added.

She frowned. "His house?"

"Yes." I glanced from Bernice to Janet, who was no longer fidgeting as if she was dealing with a full bladder. "His house is a carbon copy of Levina's."

"Hmmm, I guess I never realized that." Bernice glanced quizzically at Janet, who shook her head. She seemed lost in thought, then added, "It's odd, though . . . you asking about Milton. The day

Levy died, she called and asked me about him."

Excitement stirred in my stomach, yet instinct warned me not to appear too eager. I shifted back in my chair. "What did she want to know?" I prodded.

Bernice shrugged. "If I knew anything about Milton's ancestors. I told her I didn't." As if to validate that claim, she quickly added, "I have *no* interest in the past."

Aware of my pounding heart, I tried to relax into the uncomfortable chair and breathe evenly. "When she called, did she mention anything else?"

Bernice was wringing her delicate hands. Her eyes narrowed warningly, then bounced off her daughter's before they settled back on me. "You," she muttered resignedly.

It was the last thing I'd expected her to say. I stared at her, then at Janet, who looked like she'd swallowed a cow and wasn't sure what to do about it. "Me?" I gasped.

My aunt shifted in her chair and rubbed at the deepening furrow between her brows. "Yes," she huffed. "Levy said she was including you in her will. She wanted me to know why she was leaving the store . . . and house to you. It was only foolish prattling."

I was stunned. "So . . . in the attorney's office that day . . . you weren't surprised?"

"Of course, I was surprised," Bernice asserted, back to her regal, condescending self, her voice frosty. "Levy said it but . . . well, obviously, I didn't think she'd been able to do it. She didn't tell me she'd already changed her will to include you." She shook her head disgustedly. "She was excited, spluttering about finally finding some key and about how Olivia had been telling the truth and we should've listened to her. As usual, she didn't make any sense at all!"

"You've upset Mother enough. It's time for you to go," Janet announced in a shaky voice. She was twisting her fingers, too, her eyes darting between her mother and me.

"Go check on that pie in the oven," Bernice barked.

Janet opened her mouth, then closed it firmly and marched angrily from the room.

We sat in silence, me struggling to unravel the threads of this latest bombshell. If I wasn't mistaken, Bernice had just disclosed a motive for wanting Levina dead. But why would she tell me about it if she *had* murdered Levina? I replayed her words in my mind.

"Do you know what Levina meant when she said my mother was telling the truth?" I finally asked.

Her sharp eyes studied me. "What do you know about your mother's death?"

"My father told me she was killed in an automobile accident. Other than that, he wouldn't tell me anything about my mother or their lives here."

"And you didn't ever pursue it?"

The churning in my stomach began, a familiar sensation I'd reconciled with long ago. "No," I admitted, shame eating away at me. "I wanted to . . . so many times. I even moved to the Portland area because I knew I was born here. But I didn't do any searching. My father told me that if I did, I'd regret it.

"I'd dreamed up this wonderful fantasy about my mother and was afraid I might be forced to face some brutal reality—like my mother was actually a drug addict or she'd deserted my father and me." Feeling the sting of impending tears, I blinked hard to swallow the ache in my throat. "Please tell me my mother loved me," I begged.

Bernice's features softened. Given other circumstances, I realized I might possibly like and respect this woman. "She did love you . . . very much," she assured me. "Her whole life revolved around you and your father . . . and the notions Grandpa Jim planted in her head when she was a child."

"The ones about the gold?"

Bernice rose from her chair and walked to the painting. She reached out a finger to touch a blue petal. When she turned back, her eyes had a faraway look, and her voice was a dull monotone. "Olivia was convinced that James Wallace found the gold and hid it somewhere on the family property. None of us could convince her otherwise. Grandma Kitty lived in the house well into her nineties. When she died, Momma and Daddy were no longer living, so she left the house to the four of us—Levy, Jack, Olivia, and me."

I thought back to what Jack had told me. "And you wanted to sell it?"

She draped an arm on the white marble mantle, a picture of color-coordinated elegance in her creased white slacks and blue silk blouse. "Jack and I did. Levy was hesitant but she needed the money. Olivia wouldn't hear of it. Vowed she wouldn't sign the papers. If she'd had the means, she would've bought the house, but she and David had already borrowed heavily from us on their interest in the farm."

"This farm?" The words were a gut reaction, one I should've checked.

Sparks flashed in Bernice's dark eyes. "Yes, my parents left it to their four children. Levy sold her share to my husband and me." She huffed disgustedly. "Then she used that as an excuse to not help with the cost of running it, even when she had the money. Jack was in the service at that time, but he lives here now, in the smaller house out back."

It didn't seem the right time to question my holdings in the family farm. "So what happened on the day my mother died?" I pressed, weak with apprehension.

As if I'd kicked her in the stomach, Bernice closed her eyes and clutched her middle. Though pale by nature, her skin became even more sallow. I waited.

When she opened her eyes, there was a pained determination in them. "We were here, in the kitchen— Levy, Olivia, your dad, and me—in another heated argument about selling the house in Aurora." She shook her head slowly, as if trying to understand what had transpired. "Olivia stormed out of here. She yelled something to us about knowing where the key was and that she was going to go and find it to prove once and for all that the gold really did exist. She said if we sold the house, we'd be selling the family's gold, too. Then she sped off down the driveway in her shiny red Mustang.

"That's the last time we saw her . . . alive. She pulled out onto the main road without stopping. A truck plowed into her. She died on impact."

"Tell her who her mother killed," Janet demanded from behind me.

Her words paralyzed me. My stomach clenched threateningly. Was that why my father was so mum, because my mother was responsible for someone else's death?

"Go keep an eye on the pie, Janet!" Bernice ordered.

"Tell her! If she's so damn curious, she can sure as hell know that her mom was a murderer."

"Go!"

"A murderer?" I whispered, willing myself to stay seated and not to make a beeline for the front door and the safety of ignorance.

"It was an accident. Still . . . I had another son—Charlie," Bernice said, her voice cracking with the boy's name. "He and Janet were in the truck with their dad that day. The windows were down. No seatbelts. Charlie flew out the open window." She took a deep breath, then added, "They said he died instantly."

Waves of nausea curled inside me. What does one say to someone who has lost a precious son? And Janet had been there to witness the death of her brother. Clearly, she was still dealing with that trauma. "I'm sorry," I managed to whisper.

She looked at me—not angry, not accusatory, but sad and helpless. Without a doubt, there wasn't a day that went by that she didn't mourn the loss of her child.

As if struggling for warmth, she clutched her arms and rubbed them, then shook her head resignedly. "I've always held your mother responsible for Charlie's death and Janet's—well, problems— and your father for not stopping Olivia from tearing out of here when she was so angry. It seemed to help, to have someone to blame. To hate.

"Perhaps Levy and I *were* as much at fault as Olivia. I think that's what Levy was trying to tell me that last time we spoke."

It was all so sad and unnecessary. One rephrased remark. A few seconds difference in timing. A single subtle change in the goings-on that day, and we would all have led very different lives. Overwhelmed with the need to find a quiet corner, I stood up. "I've taken enough of your time," I said.

She stood at the mantle, a softer more vulnerable person. "I have something for you."

With that, she walked away and returned with two thick leather-bound books in her arms. "Take these photo albums. I took them from the house before you moved in. Maybe they'll answer some of your questions and help you to get to know your mother."

She'd removed them from my house? Along with what else? Of course, that would mean that she'd had a key and, most likely, the security code, too. I gazed into her troubled, murky eyes as I grasped the albums. She was a thief; was she also a murderer?

After one last, lingering glance at the spellbinding, thorn-riddled roses, I strode to the front door and slipped my feet into my damp sandals. Bernice held the door open. Outside, the air was refreshing yet sultry, the bright morning rays creating a mist as they sucked up the raindrops that had recently fallen. I eyed my wrinkled dress and thought it fitting that I look as disheveled as I felt.

"Thank you," I said to Bernice, my voice shaky.

A brief nod was her only response. But as I walked away, she called out, "Kit."

I paused to turn. "Chief Preston stopped by yesterday to talk about the skeleton in your yard and the attempt on your life. I admit that I'm upset about the changes Levy made in her will but not upset enough to harm you."

Was that why she'd shown me her softer side, so I'd put in a good word to Cal on her behalf? "Any idea who the skeleton might be?" I asked.

She shook her head. "That was Levy and Olivia's area of expertise."

This time I nodded. As I turned towards my car, my eyes grazed one of the smaller side windows and paused as they caught a sudden movement. Peeking from behind the drawn blinds was Janet. The blatant hostility evident on her face sent icy shivers through me. Bernice might be warming up to me, but her daughter definitely was not.

Janet certainly had her reasons for wishing me dead. Had she eavesdropped on that phone conversation between her mother and Levina? If so, she'd know about Levina's plans to change her will.

And Janet would have access to the key to Levina's house if, indeed, Bernice did have one. Maybe the security code, too.

Yes, my dear cousin Janet with her jittery nerves and glaring eyes was definitely a possible suspect.

✿✿✿

"*Good grief!*" I spat at the disheveled piles of discarded junk and cardboard boxes surrounding the large framed painting I'd finally managed to unearth. The picture was even more disturbing than I'd remembered. Was it any wonder I hadn't known it existed until after my father's death? No one in their right mind would hang this horrific image on their wall. Why in the world my father had held onto it, hiding it away from my inquisitive eyes with each move we'd made, was beyond my understanding.

My eyes lit on the now familiar signature in the corner— *James Wallace*. Levina had her oxen yoke. Jack had his robin's eggs. Meg's family had the muddy Pudding River. Bernice had thorny blue roses. And my mother had possessed this monstrosity.

I studied the nightmarish scene Wallace had depicted on canvas. Set in the black of night, the house and farmyard had been painted in ashy shades—dreary and foreboding, tragic. Two figures, a woman and a small child, stood in the foreground, shoulders slumped hopelessly. They were facing the house—dark silhouettes against the wall of vibrant blue flames that consumed the two-story building.

Though the metal-encased storage space in which I now stood was a furnace, the air heavy and hot in my lungs, I felt the prickle of goose bumps on my bare arms. Instinctively, I shuddered and sank down onto a wooden chest, the two photo albums Bernice had given me clutched to my chest.

My visit with Bernice had left me thoroughly wilted, a bud striving to blossom but slowly succumbing to circumstances beyond its control. Grief, fear, and an overwhelming sadness were eating away at my soul. The ethereal scene depicted on the canvas wasn't helping. Nor was the sorrowful voice of Martina McBride lamenting life's tragedies from several units down where a man was working on an old car.

I hadn't intended to end up here, but somewhere between leaving Bernice's farm and my impending arrival back in Aurora, I'd taken this eighty-some-mile detour. Whether it was because I dreaded returning to my recently ransacked, empty house or because of a deep-rooted need to be surrounded by familiar items, I wasn't sure. Whatever the case, it seemed as good a place as any to do some serious soul searching.

My gaze dropped to the dusty albums clutched in my arms, and ripples of anticipation mingled with an anxious churning in my stomach. At last, I had a front-row viewing of my mother's life. But why did life have to throw a couple of bitter lemons and a handful of rancid nuts into what was supposed to be a delicious, sweet treat.

My conversation with Bernice had certainly proven that my father had good reason to pack his few belongings, including this ghastly painting, and leave Oregon for good. By her own admission, Bernice hated my mother and blamed her for Charlie's death and Janet's instability. In her grief, I could well imagine what she, and most likely the rest of her family, had said to my father.

Thus began the story of my life—an endless series of new settings and new faces. After my mother's death, my father had never again trusted another human being. He'd lived on the fringes of life, never a participant. In time, I'd learned to live my life from inside a shell, too. It was a means of survival that proved effective, especially after my lying, cheating, coldhearted fiancé introduced me to his new wife.

I paused, surprised that thoughts of the sleazy rodent—my ex—were no longer accompanied by pangs of regret or longing or even the deep pain of betrayal. In fact, if I wasn't mistaken, what I *was* feeling was relief—*interesting*. I shoved thoughts of the rat aside to focus on my current situation.

Today the prospect of a real home lay before me, one in which I was surrounded by people to whom I *had* grown attached. The experience was like indulging in a whole box of expensive chocolate-covered caramels—sweet and warm and deeply satisfying yet laced with the unsettling knowledge that there would be repercussions.

Were Bernice and her offspring right? Did I have no ethical right to Levina's belongings? Was it time for me to pack my bags and move on? With that thought, a knot of intense agony twisted inside me, and a plaintive whine escaped through my lips.

I studied the, as yet, unopened photo albums. They were tattered and scarred from decades of preserving family memories. I'd never been a part of that family. Was I destined to follow in my father's footsteps, sideswiping any emotional involvement?

A loud clanging, iron against iron, blasted my reverie. My body tensed, and melancholy thoughts slipped away momentarily, replaced by a rhythmic throbbing in my skull. It sounded more like the man was demolishing his car than repairing it.

"So what's it gonna be, Kitty?" I muttered, angry with the knowledge that I'd placed myself in this gut-wrenching situation. "Are you gonna dangle your tail between your legs and sneak away with this room full of crap strapped to your back once again? Or are you gonna stiffen your spine and fight for what you want?"

The room closed in around me, making it difficult to breathe. I wanted to scream. I wanted to throw every item in the room onto the pavement outside and walk away.

Instead, I eyed the top album. It was black with the word *photographs* printed on it in elaborate gold lettering. My heart pounded, irritatingly out of sync with the hammering from outside. I tentatively flipped the first page. A collection of small black and white photos greeted me, each one held in place by four tiny black corner pockets. There was printing below each photo, fancy white letters stark against the heavy black paper.

Curiosity overcame trepidation, and I shifted towards the sunlight streaming in through the open door to get a clearer view. Tiny particles drifted in the intense rays. The first picture was of three young children—blonde hair and radiant smiles—perched on the hood of an older model automobile, the kind you see in old black and white movies. Beneath the photo, someone had penned *Bernice, Levy, and Jack—July 1940*. No Olivia.

The next photo was also of them only a handsome man had joined them, and they appeared to be on the front porch of my current home. The name *Walt* had been added to the other three. I studied the image, hoping to experience a connection to these strangers, but all I felt was an overwhelming sadness. They looked so happy, so content and assured in what they had together, a concept as alien to me as real, honest-to-God Russian caviar.

My eyes scanned the layers of junk surrounding me. My father, my schooling, and this mess had been my constants throughout my childhood. I gripped the sides of the albums, fighting an overwhelming urge to rip it to shreds.

An upbeat tune replaced the hammering, something about some guy's babe magnet truck. I trailed my eyes along the remaining photos, then slowly turned the pages and continued to do the same. The images were mostly of the three children, often accompanied by one or more adults. The man named Walt was clearly their father, and a woman named Nora their mother—my grandparents. It was also clear that I didn't resemble any of them.

A few pages into the album, my mother finally appeared, a tiny baby, her round head peaking out from a white blanket. *Olivia— Oct 1946* was written below the picture. I pulled the album close to study the picture in detail, then the one after that and the one after that. My eyes flew over the photos, racing nearly as fast as my heart.

When I reached a picture of my mother on her tenth birthday, I noticed the similarities of which Jack had spoken. He was right; I did resemble her—the set of our mouths, the intent look in our eyes, and the way we held our bodies.

Inside me, a warm orb glowed. A smile touched my lips. Ever

so slowly, frozen lumps of me melted away. I didn't know what they were but I could feel them loosening and fading.

I hummed along with a series of country western crooners while I perused the remaining photos in the album. The ones of my mother with an older man intrigued me—one in front of the carved mantle, several beside James Wallace paintings and in various outdoor locations, and the last next to a huge portrait.

Intuitively, I knew who the man was. Bernice had called him Grandpa Jim, the man crazy enough to believe the improbable Blue Bucket tales. Clearly, the two of them, my mother and her Grandpa Jim, were close. In each pose, the composure of their bodies and their expressions spoke of an easiness with each other that was rare in two people generations apart.

I studied the picture of my mother and her grandfather standing next to a painting of a man, woman, and young boy who were all garbed in nineteenth-century clothing. My eyes slid down to the caption: *Jim and Olivia, Canyon City—Aug 1955*. Finally, I'd found a relative whose genes I could claim. Great-grandpa Jim was tall and large-boned, his limbs long and his intense eyes more light than dark. Though his hair was nearly white, shaggy eyebrows spoke of a once thick mop of dark hair.

Intrigued, I lifted the album closer to study his features—much like my own. My eyes slid sideways to the painting in the photo and stilled. Something about it triggered feelings of déjà vu.

The man in the painting was tall, clothed in a dark suit, a wide-brimmed hat pulled low over his forehead, nearly shading his eyes. What I did see in his eyes sent a shiver down my spine. They were hard, sinister. And his smile was cold as an Arctic snowstorm.

I squinted, forcing the woman and boy into focus, my labored breathing loud against the distant nasal twang of some country oldie. The photo was grainy and slightly blurred. The woman was small, barely reaching to the man's shoulders. She wore a high-necked white blouse and a black skirt, and the boy was in her arms, more in front of her than to the side. With her son in her arms and what was most likely her husband at her side, the woman should have radiated well-being. Instead, she appeared somber.

Perhaps it was her countenance that brought to mind the two paintings of Milton's ancestors. "It's only a coincidence," I mumbled. "Your over-stimulated imagination is concocting answers where there are none."

I closed the album, then rubbed at the dull ache in my forehead and relished the silence. No music. No loud banging. Just silence.

Nervous twitters came to life inside me, and I rose and crept to the open doorway to peek out. The beat-up van that had been parked several units away was now gone, the door to that storage area closed. My Hyundai sat baking in the midday sun, a safe retreat from what now seemed like an unsafe place to be.

What was I thinking? Someone was trying to kill me, and here I was, alone, in an isolated storage facility that only I knew I rented—the perfect murder site!

I shuddered, then walked quickly to James' painting and attempted to lift it with one hand. It was too heavy. I turned to drop the album onto the trunk, then froze. Slowly, I flipped the pages until I found the photo of my mother and great-grandfather standing next to the portrait. What if James Wallace had painted it, too?

My eyes darted between the two paintings—the slightly blurred image in the photo and the upsetting depiction on canvas in front of me. There were certainly similarities. For one thing, both included a woman and a small child.

But it was difficult to compare what I was beginning to think of as James' blue paintings with his renderings of people. In the first, his brushstrokes were bold, more impressionistic. The detail in the latter would be difficult to emulate. I squinted at the photo, trying to force it into focus. One of my mother's legs covered the lower right corner of the painting and any signature that might be there.

It was then that a tiny seed sprouted somewhere inside my brain to slowly blossom into a plan of action. What if the painting in the photo still existed? Even after fifty years, it might hang in some musty museum in eastern Oregon.

If I really wanted to get to the bottom of what was going on in my life, and Levina's before mine, perhaps it was time I took a road trip.

Chapter 14

Like the annoying buzz of a pesky blowfly, Harv's voice droned on. Though it was gibberish to me, those around me seemed able to decipher auction lingo. The air was electric—arms shooting up, heads jerking, and sweaty men hustling to keep items flowing at a coronary-provoking pace. For these people, this was serious business. If I wasn't vigilant, I'd miss out on the one item I was determined to purchase— Jack's painting.

I sank back into the creaking folding chair. A plump, white-haired lady nested on my right, juggling a Styrofoam cup of steaming coffee, a monstrous straw handbag, her program, and a bejeweled jumbo pen. She jotted dollar amounts after each of the auctioned items. On my left, a distinguished-looking gentleman with salt-and-pepper hair fanned himself with his bidding number when he wasn't flashing it above his head.

The room was packed with items for sale and perspiring bidders, too many of them, too ripe. Overhead, whiny ceiling fans fought a losing battle with sluggish, humid air.

"Item number twenty-one," Harv announced from his highchair on the stage. "Up for bid next is a lot of eight daguerreotypes. Hold those up, boys, so they can get a good look at 'em," he said to two red-faced men assisting him who looked to be a good decade older than Harv. "These are a real find for you Civil War buffs. Who'll give me a. . . ."

I dropped my eyes to my program as he launched into another mind-boggling spiel.

The painting by James Wallace was number fifty-two, far enough away that I could shift my thoughts from nineteenth century photographs to more recent ones in the second album Bernice had given me—a lovingly preserved collection of precious family moments. The images were mostly of my mother, my father, and me doing all of the things one would expect a normal, happy family to do. It had been sweet torture to see the anticipation on those faces and to know their hopes and dreams would never come to fruition.

The album had obviously belonged to my mother. The fact that my father had left it behind was testament to how upset he must've been when he walked away from his life here in Oregon. So why in the world had he carted that haunting painting along with him?

I pictured my mother standing up to her two much older sisters, refusing to back down. Admittedly, it had led to her death. But she must've had good reason to believe that Wallace had found the Blue Bucket gold and hidden it on his property in Aurora. Was it now my destiny to finish what my mother had started?

A sharp flash caught my attention. I blinked hard, hauling myself back to the hum of Harv's voice. The man next to me was a coiled rattler, tense, eyes focused on the stage. The only thing moving was his bidding number, which flicked up and down erratically.

My eyes darted to the stage and landed on a lovely glass lamp in the hands of one of Harv's *boys*, then dropped to search my program. The only lamp listed was one labeled *Galle*—number forty-seven.

I sighed and relaxed, my mind wandering back to the previous day. I'd spent most of it cleaning up the mess my night visitor had left in my office. Cal was convinced the intruder had been searching for something and that I'd arrived home just as he'd begun to dig through the file drawers. I'd examined the contents of those files, hoping something might jump out at me and scream, *"This is why Levina was killed and why someone is trying to kill you, too!"* No such luck.

"Item number fifty-one."

Harv's voice sliced through my thoughts, and my fingers automatically gripped my number more firmly. Since my stint in the storage facility, I'd developed an unflinching determination to uncover the truth behind Levina's death. Irrational as I knew it to be, the procurement of Jack's picture now seemed imperative in helping me to reach that goal.

From his throne, Harv was touting an ornate mirror that had *Bernice* written all over it. He claimed it was beveled and straight from the Victorian era. The crowd went wild. I silently prodded them on, hoping they'd be ready for a break when Jack's picture hit the stage. The two red-faced men stood ready, the painting of bright blue eggs propped between them. Once Harv had sealed the deal on the gaudy mirror, they lifted it forward.

A murmur hummed around me—not a good sign.

I inched forward in my protesting chair, nervous energy buzzing through me, perspiration sticky beneath my clothing. Harv mopped at his forehead and beard with a red handkerchief he'd pulled from the pocket of his wilting white dress shirt. "Folks, our next item's one you might never again see up here on the auction block," he announced.

I swallowed the urge to climb over the rows of people between him and me and throttle him. Surely, no one else would have any interest in Jack's weird painting. That is, unless Harv kept yammering on about it.

Which he did: "Many of you know the Wallace family. Our own Levy Johnson who recently passed away—God rest her soul—was a Wallace. Well, this here picture was painted by her great-grandfather James Wallace in the mid eighteen-hundreds. Jack Wallace, Levy's brother, claims this picture was painted right here in Aurora. So now's your chance to own a little piece of Aurora history." With that, he launched into auctioneer lingo.

I gripped my number with slick fingers and lifted it into the air. From the corners of my eyes, I caught numbers and arms popping up around me. Harv nodded at me and managed a half-smile, his lips moving miles-per-minute, his voice droning like an over-worked chain saw, and his eyes flicking back-and-forth across the crowd. Every so often, one of his helpers pointed a finger at someone and barked a loud guttural sound.

Eons passed before things slowed down. By then, my heart was battering my ribs, and the program on my lap was bouncing as if I was driving over a stretch of speed bumps doing sixty. I had no idea what the bid was up to. That painting would be *mine*.

But someone was still bidding against me. Curious, I stretched tall, turned around, and scanned the rows of faces. No numbers or hands flashed in the air.

Then two hands shot up at the back of the room, waving frantically. I did a double-take. Grace and Patty stood together, obviously trying to get my attention. A hefty man in an orange OSU muscle shirt said something to them, and their hands streaked down. They eyed each other guiltily. I felt my lips twitch, then noticed who was standing not far from them.

It was Bart, engaged in some form of silent communiqué with Harv.

Anger surged through my veins. "You rat," I whispered, patting my hair. "No way are you going to get *my* great-great-granddaddy's painting."

"You tell 'em, sweetie," the white-haired woman chirped from beside me.

I nodded to her in sisterly gratitude. That painting would leave my family only if over my dead body. I cringed—the expression hit way to close to home—then forced my focus back to Bart and, with a hair-singeing glower, raised my number even higher.

At last, the determined set to his steely eyes lessened, and a smile softened his mouth. Then, glory be, he shook his head at Harv's prodding.

Like a deflating balloon, air seeped through my lips, leaving me as wilted as steamed spinach. Noticing that I still held my number in the air, I jerked it into my lap. Harv's voice rattled on, an indecipherable murmur.

I breathed deeply. The painting was now mine. But how much had I paid for it?

My eyes crept down to the program clutched in the hand next to mine, then inched down the page until they came to rest on item number fifty-two. The numbers were painstakingly penned next to the listing—*nearly fourteen thousand dollars!* If I hadn't been clutching it, my stomach would've dropped to the dusty cement floor.

Woozy from sticker shock, I waited for a lull between bidding, then pressed my way between scrunched legs and chair backs, sliding sideways to the aisle. Willing the blood to return to my numb limbs and brain, I paused to focus on Patty and Grace.

Patty glanced my way, a worried frown clouding her features, and I hustled towards her, determined not to look at Bart. After a round of hugs, Patty studied me long and hard. "You do know what you paid for that painting, don't you?"

I nodded and looked to Grace. Her eyes were brimming with wary concern, too. "You're both looking at me as if I'd just finished a raunchy striptease on Harv's stage instead of merely purchasing a family heirloom," I accused.

The guy in the muscle shirt eyed me speculatively. I drilled him with my *you are so fried* teacher look. He turned as red as Patty's freshly painted fingernails and looked away.

The painting isn't exactly *you*," Grace informed me. "Is it?"

I checked for eavesdroppers before I leaned in close to whisper, "No, but I have this feeling in my gut that it's tied to what happened to Levina and to what's happening to me now. And to the skull Danny and Davy found."

Grace's eyes bulged. "The skull? Patty said Cal doesn't have any information back on it." She shivered and hugged herself.

My eyes shifted to Patty, questioning.

She shook her head. "Not yet. Cal has one of his deputies doing research. He says we might never know whose body it is." Her eyes narrowed. "You didn't find any old photos of a guy flashing a seriously silver-toothed smile floating around your house, did you?"

My prospective Visa bill was forgotten as I considered Patty's question. I'd spent hours sifting through items in the office and bedrooms, but had found no old photos. "No," I told her. "Does Cal have any news on who might've broken into my house?"

She pursed her lips and shrugged. "He seems to think it's hopeless. He ran all of the fingerprints they lifted but didn't come up with anything suspicious."

Trepidation twisted inside me. "Cripes," I snapped. "We have two dead bodies. Someone tried to kill me and then broke into my house and rifled my office. And we have absolutely no leads as to who might've done even *one* of those things."

It seemed hopeless. Here I was paying thousands of dollars for a painting I didn't particularly like, hoping it would provide a clue. If Cal and modern technology couldn't produce answers, what chance did nineteenth century brushstrokes have of doing so?

Clearly upset by my mini tirade, Patty gnawed on her lower lip, a frown darkening her usually bright features. Obviously more interested in our conversation than Harv's perpetual yammering, orange shirt inched closer to Grace, leaning at an awkward angle.

"I'm not blaming Cal," I assured Patty. "I know he's doing everything he can. I'm just frustrated . . . and to be truthful, I'm pretty darned scared."

Patty attempted a smile. "Cal's frustrated, too. He can't seem to get a break." Her eyes drilled into mine. "Be careful. I don't want to lose you, girlfriend."

I felt a stinging in my eyes, a quiver in my lips.

"And *there's* someone else who doesn't want to lose you," she added, jerking her head back and to the right.

My eyes automatically followed the movement and landed on Bart's brooding stare, then darted quickly away only to be drawn to another familiar figure, an annoying reminder of unfinished business. "Walker's here," I hissed, pressure building inside me.

I sensed that both Grace and Patty had turned to him, too. For long moments, we were silent, studying Walker. He was facing the front of the room, laughing.

"He's *so* hot," Grace's voice whispered into the relative silence.

"What?" I snapped, jerking around to face Grace. *Walker* and *hot* didn't even belong in the same sentence unless it was in reference to where he would spend eternity.

"Bart." Her dark eyes had a dreamy look when she said his name. "Isn't he that tall guy with the X-man body, the ponytail, and the sexy goatee?"

I turned to study him. As usual, he was shaggy and rumpled. Cripes. I could actually smell him and feel his bulk. It was too unsettling. "He's all yours," I informed Grace and the nosy man in the orange shirt who was no longer even making an attempt at subtlety.

"Nah, Patty says he's got the hots for you."

"Only because Patty's too hot herself to think straight." I looked to Patty for support.

She arched her eyebrows and flashed an all-knowing grin.

"You're not paying attention to his signals. And quit playing with your hair. It looks fine."

I was playing with my hair. Bart's presence always made me acutely aware of my many imperfections. So why did I care?

I don't care, I told myself adamantly before I jerked my hands up away from my hair and pledged never again to be unsettled by Bart's presence. I let my gaze drift towards Walker—ugh—then looked more closely. Surely, that wasn't Meg standing beside him? It was! Suddenly, Walker turned and his beady stare fixed on me. I shivered, then noticed that his weren't the only eyes watching me. In fact, everyone seemed to be looking at me.

"Your number," a gruff voice said.

I looked up into orange shirt's startlingly green eyes. "Huh?"

"Harv needs to see your number," he informed me.

"My number? Why?"

"My God, Kit, are you *on* something? If not, maybe you should be," Patty muttered through clenched teeth, the concern in her eyes softening her harsh words. "Hold up your damn number so everyone will quit staring at you."

I dug in my leather handbag, searching for my number. Where was the *damn* thing? Finally, my fingers closed around it, and I flashed it in the air.

"That's it," Harv announced. "Those old ranching tools go to number one-seven-six. Got to admit I'm wonderin' why you want that particular box, Kit." He chuckled and shook his head. "You might want to step lightly around the little lady, boys. She now owns that pair of castrating shears. They might be rusty, but I'm thinkin' they'd still get the job done."

Pretty much everyone in the room found Harv's remark hilarious.

Cripes! Could this night get any worse? My face was radiating more heat than one of Patty's hot flashes. I had to get out of here.

Evidently, Patty and I were sharing brainwaves. "Let's escape while you still have some dignity—and some credit—left," she murmured as she grabbed my arm and pulled me towards the side door. I glanced back, halfway expecting orange shirt to join us.

Outside, the heavy night air settled in around us, damp and balmy. Two smokers stood in the shadows, glowing cigarettes dangling between fingers and smoke curling around them like bog fog. Soft wisps of russet dusk streaked the darkening sky. Crickets buzzed in harmony with the monotonous drone from inside the building. I breathed deeply and felt tension seep from me. I was bone weary.

"I didn't want that box of tools," I whispered, unsure as to how I'd acquired it.

"Then you should've kept your hand down," Patty scolded.

Good grief! Maybe I did need some serious medication. "I'm so tired I could sleep through the next three days," I murmured.

At that moment, Walker stepped outside. He pulled a packet from his pocket, shook a cigarette out, and stuck it between his lips, then cupped his hands around it and lit it. Just as the tip glowed red, he glanced up and into my eyes. I stared; I had no idea that Walker smoked. I couldn't help but wonder how many other things I didn't know about him.

"Talk about ruining a nice evening," Grace muttered from beside me.

I eyed Grace and Patty, who were eyeing Walker, who was eyeing me. What kind of etiquette practices were an absolute must in a situation such as this?

"Just ignore him," Patty muttered. "S&M probably sent him to do her dirty work."

"Geez, Kit, you're not gonna cave, are you?" Grace asked.

"Of course, she's not; why would you even think that, Grace?" Patty snapped. It was nice to have her stand up for me but there was doubt in her face, too.

"Well, she hasn't talked with the investigator yet."

Grace had a point; I'd concocted every excuse imaginable to avoid that phone call. "I'll do it," I promised. "In case you haven't noticed, I've had a lot going on lately."

Grace slid an arm around my shoulder and squeezed. "Sorry, Kit. I know you will. I just don't want Doreen to get away free and clear this time."

Neither did I. But I was the one out on the limb here, not Grace, and not Patty. Though, to her credit, Patty was often clinging to some brittle twig.

I studied Walker. Why *was* he here? He puffed on his cig and made the first move, ignoring Patty and Grace completely when he approached and said, "I need to talk with you."

So Doreen *had* sent him. I shrugged away my friends' concerned looks to walk into the parking lot, where I stopped beneath a bright overhead light and checked to make sure my two friends were keeping watch over me. Walker followed.

The smoking cigarette dangled from his fingers. He drew it to his lips to take a long drag, then dropped it on the gravel and ground it out with a sandal-clad foot. A stream of smelly smoke spewed from his mouth. "Thanks to you, the school district placed Doreen on leave," he uttered tersely.

My reaction to his words was a plethora of emotions: relief, guilt, sadness, and even a touch of fear. They swept through me and left me too drained to comment.

"Of course, the rumblings are that I'll be named as the new principal."

And I'll be an Olympic ice dancer, I wanted to say. But I was too stunned. Realizing my mouth was gaping, I clamped it shut.

"You got what you wanted. There's no reason Doreen has to lose her license, too. Or that you have to lie about my part in it. You know you haven't been exactly truthful about what happened," he whined. "It's time to do the right thing."

Huh? Did he and Doreen really believe this whole harrowing mess was intentional, to get rid of a couple of lousy administrators? I glanced away and noticed that Bart had joined Patty and Grace, a powder horn dangling from his left shoulder. The two cigarette-toting ladies ogled him while they sucked smoke.

I studied Walker. His beady eyes probed mine, seeking my acquiescence. In the warm evening air, I shivered. "We've already had this discussion," I informed him before I turned away and strode resolutely back to Patty and Grace.

When I approached, Grace was still drooling. Bart was, too. Grace had that effect on people; even in grimy sweats, her hair greasy and sans make-up, she was gorgeous. "The boys who found the skull are yours?" Bart asked her.

"Yes, Danny and Davy," Grace crooned. "It's all they talk about, nonstop—their treasure."

Bart eyed me and chuckled softly. "And Kit bought herself a treasure tonight, a very imposing one, huh, Kit? Wouldn't want to get on your bad side now."

"For your information, you're already on my bad side. And I have plans for . . . some of the tools in that box," I snapped.

"Oh." He raised his dark brows, toying with me and enjoying it. "Thinking about going into the cattle business?"

From the corner of my eye, I watched Walker climb into his flashy car and struggled to formulate an answer. "Not in the near future, no. But I do have an antique business . . . and customers to consider . . . who have unique needs."

"Uh-huh," he uttered. "And I'm thinking that you might want to get that business up and running soon. You just bought yourself a very expensive painting, my dear."

"So that's why you're being such an ass; you're ticked because I got the painting and you didn't."

"I hadn't planned to buy the painting. I was only making sure Jack got what it's worth. He's lived a rough life. If he didn't need the money, I doubt he would've sold the painting. You inherited a treasure chest; doesn't hurt to share some of it." With that, he dipped his head and strode off murmuring, "Have a nice evening, ladies."

Dumbfounded, I stared at his retreating back. Yet again, he'd lectured me and left me feeling like an incompetent, self-centered child. He seemed to think Levina's family deserved more than they were getting of her inheritance. Was he right?

Roy had implied that Jack and Bernice were so busy fighting that they weren't making enough money to support their farm. Levina hadn't been willing to bail them out of their debt, and Roy was through doling out dough to keep the farm in the family. And Jack hadn't hidden the fact that he was strapped for cash. According to Roy, Janet was also broke.

I couldn't help but wonder what the four of them would be willing to do to get their hands on the funds they'd been so certain they'd inherit once Levina had passed on.

CHAPTER 15

What in blue blazes was Sophie wearing? She floated across the street toward me, a confectionary pink birthday cake doll with a lacy parasol clutched in one hand, a wicker picnic basket in the other. Perched atop her head was what might be a hat—a wild assemblage of magenta and white flowers and ribbons. Dangling from the bottom of the bonnet were a profusion of bouncing ash blonde ringlets.

I clamped my gaping mouth shut and glanced around to see if I'd stepped from my house into the right century. Yep! There sat my Hyundai waiting for me to load it with my Rubbermaid ice chest. Cripes! Her jumbo hoop skirt seemed to have a life of its own, undulating around her with each step she took, swallowing her tiny torso.

"Good morning, Sophie," I said warily as I labored towards her.

"Good mornin', Kit." She sounded normal, as if she appeared every morning looking like she'd stepped off the silver screen during a viewing of *Gone With the Wind*.

I tried not to gawk at the collection of flashy jewelry adorning her obviously enhanced bosom. "I thought we were going on a picnic?"

"That's right," she chirped, "the Fourth of July happenings at Willamette Mission Park. I go every year. Always dress up for it."

My eyes slid down to my rather skimpy cotton sundress. Nine-thirty, and the sun's hot rays already beat down from a cloudless sky. Come afternoon, we'd be at a slow simmer.

"Am I dressed okay?" I inquired.

She eyed me fleetingly. "It'll do. Just stay out of camp. That's harlot getup there."

Harlot? And why would I hang out in a campground? "They do have a picnic area, don't they?" I asked hopefully as I stuffed the ice chest into the back of the vehicle.

Sophie leaned forward to set her basket next to it, her massive skirt skyrocketing behind her. "Oh yeah, there's plenty of picnic tables."

I dropped the hatch into place, then turned to study her

outfit.

"Millie Swank made it for me before she passed on," she informed me, closing her parasol. "This year I added four new petticoats. They really make the skirt pop, don't you think? And makes my waist look tiny. Men like that, you know."

I sucked in my gut. "You look . . . nice. But I'm not sure you'll fit inside my car."

She opened a rear door. "No problem. You just push the dress in." With that, Sophie's upper half disappeared inside the car, and I was staring at a billowy mass of white fabric and lace. A pair of tiny black laced-up boots appeared, stamens midst fluttering petals.

I dropped my purse and set to work twisting and stuffing the metal and fabric through the doorframe. By the time I finished, Sophie's legs were flaying, and some unladylike grunting noises were filtering from inside the car. Her feet disappeared midst a churning sea of pink, and a few seconds later, her head popped out of the milieu, hat askew. I reached in and struggled to arrange her garment, so she wouldn't suffocate in its folds. A giant hoop rose before her, blocking her view.

From somewhere, she had procured a rose-covered fan and was now fanning at her flushed face. "Whew!" she gasped. "I'm a bit overheated. You got air conditioning?"

"You bet," I assured her before I pushed the door closed and trekked to the driver's door. Seated inside, I eyed the wall of fabric staring at me in my rear-view mirror. "How do we get there?"

"Head south. Take the back way down Boones Ferry," was Sophie's muffled reply. "There's a stand about a mile down it that sells honey. I need some for my cornbread."

"Boones Ferry?" An image on James Wallace's detailed carving flashed before me. But that Boones Ferry was on the Willamette River in Wilsonville, not this far south. "Are there two Boones Ferries?" I asked Sophie.

"Just the one Daniel's brood ran. The old ferry road runs north and south from it. Cross the bridge northwest of town and stay on that road. You'll see the sign for it."

So the road from the ferry came out this way. As I drove, I tried to picture what that road would look like carved into the mantle. Ever so slowly, my mind traveled along winding rivers and snaked towards the floor to where two houses were carved.

Since conversation with a concealed Sophie was difficult, I let my mind wander on the drive to the park, my thoughts always returning to James Wallace. Had he concealed the key to his secret in his art—his paintings and carvings? Is that what both my mother and Levina had discovered—the answer to where he'd hidden his gold? If so, would I be putting myself in more danger by following in their footsteps? After all, both of them had died shortly after announcing that they'd discovered that key. Prickles of fear tingled inside me.

"Well, you don't have to stay," I muttered as I dragged myself back to the present and our allotted parking space in a rutty, dusty field. I braved the sun's unrelenting rays and trekked around the car. "Please, Sophie, come out easier than you went in," I pleaded.

She did. Popped right out through the open door like those colorful party streamers that pop out of a can, and with a few shakes and some tweaking, her voluminous outfit fell into place. She adjusted her hat and parasol and fanned furtively at her perspiring face. "We'll get the food later," she announced. "I don't want to miss the first show."

So there would be entertainment. A gorgeous day and a friend with whom to share it. Good food and good music. What could possibly go wrong?

Sophie was chomping at the bit. While I slathered a healthy coat of SPF seventy on my limbs and face, she fidgeted nervously with her arsenal of accessories. "It wouldn't hurt you to get a little color on your skin," she snapped impatiently.

I eyed her. She seemed overly anxious today. What was causing her fretfulness? Wrinkled though it was, Sophie's skin was milky white. I held the tube out to her. "It looks like we're going to get a lot of sun today. Why don't you put some on your face?"

"That's what my parasol's for."

Cripes! Was she going to hold that frilly thing over her head all day? I threw the sunscreen into my purse, shoved a wide-brimmed straw hat onto my head, and Sophie and I set off, her taking three steps to every one of mine. Still, I had to hustle to keep up.

Finally, we rounded a corner into the park, and I froze, awestruck, trying to make sense of the huddle of Civil War era soldiers at the snack shack. "What is this?" I breathed.

"What do you mean?"

"*This*," I said with the sweep of a hand. "Gun-toting soldiers and women in gowns from two centuries back." I eyed the canvas tents that stretched down one side of the road. They appeared to be shops, their entrances enticing customers with racks of clothing, food supplies, and cookware—all from another time. Off in the distance, were clusters of white tents. "And what's with all the tents?"

Obviously running thin on patience, Sophie eyeballed me. She huffed a couple of times, which seemed to calm her down some. "*This* is the Fourth of July celebration. Now can we get a seat before all the good ones are gone?" With that, she bustled off.

I huffed, too, to calm myself. Off to my right, a scruffy man in a Confederate uniform was fiddling with his rifle, and two Union guys were fondling a couple of nasty-looking swords at a nearby booth. There were too many weapons around here for my comfort. "It's not like any Fourth of July celebration I've ever been to," I informed Sophie once I'd caught up with her.

"It's a re-enactment."

Maybe so. But still. . . . "I think they've got their wars confused," I muttered as I scurried after Sophie. Nestled midst trees, white tents littered the landscape to my right and left. Ahead was a huge open field sporting a couple of cannons.

Good grief! Was I really going to be a part of grownups playing at dress-up *and* shooting big guns?

A statuesque woman in a voluminous floral skirt and high-necked white blouse floated across the grass in front of us. She glanced at Sophie, did a double take, then halted, her eyes sliding over Sophie's outfit. "Hello, Sophie," she chirped.

Sophie stopped in her tracks. "Bobbi Jean." She gazed at some nearby bleachers and twirled her parasol nervously, then turned to me. "This here's Kit O'Maley. Kit's Levina's niece. Kit, this is Bobbi Jean Driscoll."

"Nice to meet you," I murmured.

"Likewise," she responded. "I was so sorry to hear about Levina's passing. We're going to miss her in the Civilian Camp. Milton seems especially lost. . . ."

"*Milton!* You know where he is?" Sophie demanded.

"He's camped next to us. I'm headed there now if you'd like to join me."

Sophie eyed the bleachers longingly. "Well . . . I did want to let him know that I brought lunch for him—his favorites. Milton and I are a couple now, you know."

"Go ahead, Sophie. I'll get us some seats," I assured her. Maybe Milton was the reason she was wound so tight. Hopefully, seeing him would calm her down.

"Well . . . okay. But front row, mind you. I can't be climbing in this getup."

The two women glided off toward a grouping of tents. I watched them, mesmerized by their elegant, flowing movements in the long gowns. Then I turned and nearly crashed into a tall, bulky man in a knee-length brown coat and felt hat. I blinked twice to bring Bob Crosley's eye-stopping features into focus. He had to be cooking beneath the layers of wool he wore. "I'm sorry," I murmured. "My mind was elsewhere."

"Someplace exciting, I hope." The twinkle in his eyes made my neck hairs prickle. Sophie had warned me to stay away from him.

"Not . . . really. Uh . . . if you'll excuse me . . . Bob," I stammered.

"Well, maybe I can find you some excitement. How about a tour of the camps, Kit?"

Sophie had also warned me to stay out of the camps. "Uh . . . I have to save some seats," I muttered, attempting to step around him.

"After the battle then?"

Battle! These people were purposefully going to fight a battle? I forced my thoughts from bloody soldiers and studied Bob. He did have a couple of adorable dimples, and I did want to find out the truth about his alleged relationship with Levina. Still, I'd promised Sophie a front row seat. "It's nice of you to offer but I'm with a . . . friend," I explained.

"Lucky man." He tipped his hat and sauntered off.

I watched him until he disappeared behind a tent, my mind replaying what had just transpired. "What a strange day," I whispered as I headed towards the bleachers.

Sophie had fretted needlessly. Except for a senior couple and three middle-aged men with monster-lens-enhanced cameras, the entire front row was empty. I chose a spot in the center section and settled gingerly onto a sun-seared metal bench to wait.

On the field in front of me, several young boys tore around, shooting cap guns and stick sword fighting. Which brought to mind my latest brouhaha with Walker and Doreen. A dreary, disquieting fog settled over me. It was now July. I had three weeks to decide if I would return to teach at Hazelnut Grove Primary School during the next school year. What if Walker was the new principal? Crazier things had happened. As the seats around me filled, I wrestled with the pros and cons—mostly cons—inherent in employment under Walker.

Soon, retaining Sophie's seat became my own heated battle. I rested my right leg along the bench while I listened with half an ear to a man who was speaking into a microphone. He claimed it was 1863 and rambled on at length about worms and swabs and thumbs. I strained to see through the thick crowds that now stretched out from the bleachers, seeking a bright pink frock among the less conspicuous versions flitting about.

My gaze skimmed a group of people, spectator variety, who were seated in chairs, then froze. Was that my dear Aunt Bernice and her two lovely children? Good grief! It was. My stomach flipped, and a dull ache sprouted behind my right eye. I squinted to get a clearer view just as Janet leaned back, exposing Roy, whose eyes locked with mine.

He scowled, then smiled and flipped a perfunctory wave. Janet's head shot around. Hostility flashed on her face. I clutched my stomach and dropped my eyelids. When I lifted them, the whole family was ogling me. I raised a hand and wiggled a couple of fingers at them, then turned away to look up into Bart's stern glower.

He was not twelve feet from me on the other side of the fence, ramrod straight astride a brown horse. From where I sat, he looked as huge as his steed—and as intimidating. Two men were mounted on horses on each side of him, all of them sporting a lot of gray wool and gold buttons and trim, their wide-brimmed hats shading their faces. Bart's eyes trailed down the leg I'd slung along the bench, and a corner of his mouth lifted.

Suddenly, I saw pink and breathed pink. For several breathless moments, Sophie's voluminous gown enfolded me. I managed to snatch my leg away before she sank down beside me, a cloud of fabric puffing up around her. We both stretched our arms out over the unruly skirt to contain it. When I could see again, Bart and his cronies were gone.

"I found Milton," Sophie said. "And oh boy, does he look spiffy in his duds. The two of us together are gonna knock your eyes out, just like Gable and Leigh." She turned and pointed off to the right. "See him over there . . . next to your Uncle Jack."

Jack was here, too? I looked to where Sophie pointed. Sure enough, there stood Milton, directly behind my kinfolk, Jack towering over him. Sophie rose and waved her arms frantically, drawing everyone's attention except Jack and Milton's. Not wanting to deal with Janet's hostility yet again, I hid behind Sophie's skirt.

"That's okay, Sophie. I'll say *hi* to him later," I assured her.

"You sure will. We're gonna eat lunch at Milton's tent." She plopped down onto the bench just as a gunshot blasted from somewhere nearby. I bounced about a foot, and my heart surged into overdrive. Automatically, my eyes dropped to search for blood seeping from my body. The beating of drums from somewhere echoed the pounding in my head.

Three more shots rang out. Then, after a short silence, all hell broke loose.

I gasped. Like an infestation of giant killer ants, soldiers swarmed onto the field, gray from my left and blue from my right. They stood in lines and fired guns at each other. Puffs of acrid smoke rose into the air, settling over the field in a foggy haze.

Off to my left, a rousing rendition of "Dixie" battled for air space. Seven rag-muffin soldiers stood in a tight group playing drums and piccolos. And up on the knoll behind them sat Bart and his buddies on their horses, gazing down onto the carnage.

My eyes fastened on Bart. There definitely was something about a man in uniform.

A sonic *boom* blasted through the park, vibrating the molecules of air, pulsating through my eardrums. For an instant, I turned to ice, my mind and body frozen by the sheer power of the explosion. Through the ringing, I heard the excited hum around me and tried to swallow the pain from my ears. Not fifteen feet from me, a cannon sat smoking.

I stared at the bloodbath and counted my blessing: at least, no one was shooting at me.

☼☼☼

As the day progressed, my Fourth of July with Sophie evolved from strange to downright bizarre. Once a serious quota of soldiers lay dead on the battlefield, the North surrendered. Weapons were discharged, and I trudged, with Sophie floating beside me, to Milton's tent, which actually resembled more the inside of a Victorian era home.

We—Sophie, Milton, and I—sat around a lace-draped, elegantly set table and feasted on the lunch Sophie had prepared: ham, cole slaw, and cornbread, minus the honey since Sophie's farm stand was closed for the holiday. As if unaware of the endless stream of gaping spectators meandering past, Sophie refilled Milton's plate and chattered incessantly, an over-excited mother chickadee. I had to hand it to Milton; clothed in his wool outfit, he managed to keep his game face on and not succumb to the heat. Feeling like a mannequin from Victoria's Secret who'd climbed into a display at the Smithsonian, I pushed my hat lower and slouched, hoping to become inconspicuous.

"Rhubarb pie, Kit?" Milton asked from beside me.

I inspected the concoction he held out to me. The filling reminded me of the mess I'd cleaned up off the hardwood floor the previous morning—minus the hairball, of course. My eyes met Sophie's. She stood transfixed, a dripping knife clutched in one hand and a scowl twisting her brows and lips. "I'd love a piece, thank you," I murmured.

"Levina used to bake me rhubarb pie," Milton informed me, a catch in his voice. "Truth be told, she had many talents, but cooking wasn't one of them." He forked a bite of pie into his mouth, chewed thoughtfully, then hummed.

Her rouged cheeks growing even rosier, Sophie beamed.

If Milton was truly that enraptured, it must not taste as bad as it looked. I slid a pinkish mound between my lips. It was tart and slimy against my tongue with a sweet kick to it, not delicious but not bad either. I flashed Sophie a reassuring smile, then turned to Milton. "Did you spend much time in Aurora before you moved there?"

He swallowed and seemed to ponder a bit before answering. "Now and then, to visit my grandparents and then my sister Flo after they died. I grew up in the Seattle area and lived there until I moved to Aurora about eleven years ago. Flo moved to Arizona on account of her rheumatism, and I'd retired and was ready for a move."

I scooped up a second bite of pie and watched a group of silent onlookers shuffle on to Bobbi Jean's gathering next door. Trickles of voyeurs continued to meander past, though for the moment, they seemed more interested in gawking than eavesdropping.

I lowered my voice and leaned closer to Milton. "Did you ever hear talk of someone being buried behind your house . . . from Levina or anyone else?"

Milton paused, his loaded fork poised in midair. "No, can't say as I did. As far as I know, most everyone was buried in the cemetery, even going way back. I know my great-grandmother's buried there—the lady in the painting. I remember visiting her grave when I was a kid." His gaze turned to Sophie. "How about you, Sophie; you ever hear mention of someone buried in Levina's backyard?"

"Nope! Not ever," Sophie blurted. She raised her fork to her mouth, but it didn't quite get there. "Especially some guy with a crack in his skull and a silver tooth. Mind you, if there'd been talk of it, you can bet some kid would've dug him up and stole his tooth."

Some bratty kid like Walker. I pictured him sneaking around in what was now my backyard just for a couple of ounces of silver. "Do you know Ronny Walker?" I asked Milton.

He frowned, thinking. "The name sounds familiar."

"Levina handled Millie Swank's estate sale for Ronny," Sophie reminded him.

"Oh, yes. I remember now," Milton muttered.

Aha! So Milton might know details about Levina's dealings with Walker? I rolled a bite of rhubarb pie around in my mouth, searching for words. "Was there something else going on between them?" I finally prodded.

He looked taken aback, as if I'd asked if he and my Aunt Levina had enjoyed an active sex life. "I doubt that," he spluttered. "He was a lot younger than her."

My face flamed. I leaned in close to Milton to murmur, "I'm sorry, Milton; I didn't phrase that well. Ronny Walker is the vice principal at the school where I teach."

"Honest to God, what's this world coming to?" Sophie screeched. "Little Ronny Walker was one huge pain in the patooty. And now he's a vice principal. Someone's sure got noodles for brains."

I pulled my hat lower over my face and eyed the parade of people filing past, then lowered my voice even further. "It seems quite a coincidence that Levina also knew him and had business dealings with him. I've been wondering if she might've had a hand in me landing my teaching position."

Milton patted his stomach as if to tamp down what was already in there. "I don't remember her ever mentioning anything about that. She did tell me about you, that you were teaching in the area and she'd like to get to know you. That's about it."

I considered Milton's words while I forked a bite of rhubarb into my mouth and savored it. Evidently it was an acquired taste. Milton worked on a second slice and Sophie preened. Next door, Bobbi Jean was serving chocolate cake from an ornate glass pedestal. I considered stepping over for a short visit, my empty dish in hand, then sighed and settled back to ruminate on the likelihood of coincidence.

According to Sophie, Millie Swank's sale was in the spring a little over two years ago. Several months later, in August, Walker hired me. It was Walker who'd sent me the recruitment package. It was Walker who'd interviewed me. It was Walker who'd offered me the teaching position. In retrospect, there was way too much Walker in the whole transaction. So what role had Levina played in it . . . if, indeed, she had?

Sophie stepped over to Bobbi Jean's tent to serve rhubarb pie, and I pulled my hat off to swipe at the perspiration tickling my cheeks. My mind was brimming with questions, but at the moment, Milton appeared to be melting, his face slack and glowing rosily and his damp hair clinging to his forehead. Still perky, Sophie was in her element. Milton might appreciate a break from her exuberance, but even the rag tail squad of Union guys marching past couldn't drag her away from his side.

I eyed Milton; maybe one more question. "Milton, do you know Bob Crosely?"

There was only a slight deepening of the weary lines on his face. "Crosely? Yeah, I've talked with him a few times. Why do you ask?"

"He introduced himself to me, and he seemed to know Levina quite well."

Milton shook his head. "I don't remember her saying much about him except that he ran the place across from her shop." He sighed and wiped the trickles of sweat off his cheeks with his napkin. "That reminds me, I keep forgetting to give you the book Levina recorded her transactions in."

My jaw dropped. "You have it?" I gasped.

"Levina asked if she could keep it at my house."

"Why?" It was more a whisper of air than a question.

He shook his head, clearly troubled. "Along about February,

she noticed things were disappearing from her house. Seemed really upset about the whole thing. I told her to tell Cal but she refused. Said she'd take care of it herself, that it was a personal matter and I should stay out of it. So, other than holding onto the book, I did."

She refused to go to the police? It didn't make sense. Unless, of course, the thief was someone she loved and trusted. "Does Cal know now?" I asked.

"Nope. I wanted to honor Levina's wishes," he murmured in a choked voice.

So did I, but I also didn't want to protect a murderer. If someone Levina cared about was money hungry enough to steal from her, mightn't that person also kill for money? I tried to rub the thought from my mind but couldn't get past the fact that not long after she'd become suspicious of the thefts, she'd changed her will.

Milton was leaning back in his uncomfortable chair, his eyelids drooping. "I'm gonna walk around a bit," I told him. "Why don't you take off that jacket and lie down awhile?"

We both eyed the canvas tent longingly. One flap was draped open, displaying a colorful quilt-covered bed with an iron headboard. "Think I will," he sighed.

I took that as my cue to step back through the time warp. There, I joined the flow of spectator traffic past the makeshift living spaces that made up what Bobbi Jean had called the Civilian Camp. They were all similar—tidy displays of people enjoying an upbeat mid nineteenth century life, minus the grime and suffering and hard work inherent in day-to-day life back then. Images of the woman and child in Milton's and Meg's paintings flashed before me; they'd lived during this era, and they certainly didn't appear to have much to smile about.

Dry grass tickled the sides of my feet and clammy sweat clung to my body as I made my way through the park, past clusters of men sitting around campfires, cooking in their wool uniforms, and the medic tent with its disturbing saws and knives. Teenage girls in bright, ballooning gowns sashayed past, giggling and eyeing young faux soldiers. A group of men in blue pounded out a plodding rendition of "Oh, When the Saints Go Marching In." Everyone looked wilted.

I spied a gathering of people clustered beneath several large leafy trees and headed in that direction. It was the right thing to do at the wrong time.

Claiming my little piece of shady heaven, I leaned against a tree trunk. A woman garbed in what had to be widow's weeds spoke into a microphone, looking rather like a giant blackberry—round and plump and glossy. Fanned out beside her were several children bedecked in an assortment of nineteenth century garments.

She spoke with a voice of authority. "Until the age of five, boys and girls dressed in the same kinds of clothing. You could tell their gender by checking their hair; boys' was parted on the side, girls' in the middle." She paused to wiggle a finger at a young boy who looked about as happy as a pig at a pig roast, then continued. "Todd here is six years old, so he's graduated into knickers with high socks and shoes."

Todd shuffled forward, stiff as a board, face flaming. Widow woman gabbed on at length about his attire while I listened with half an ear, my attention more on Bart, who was striding past the crowd of spectators. He seemed unfazed by the heat in his buttoned-to-the-neck gray jacket. There was something different about him today. Perhaps the neat and spiffy uniform? I watched until he disappeared behind a canvas snack shack, then turned my attention back to the fashion show.

". . . got longer as they got older. When they reached their teens, it was required that their clothing cover their *limbs*." Widow woman turned to the group of young women in front of her. "Thank you, girls. You all look absolutely beautiful in your outfits."

Like a swarm of colorful butterflies, the girls floated off, and Bobbi Jean materialized, carrying a cardboard box. She set the box down next to the widow, and the two of them held a brief tête-à-tête.

"And now you're in for a special treat. First, I need a warm body. Let's see," the widow said, scanning the crowd from behind her veil. "I think *yours* will be perfect."

Oh, God! She was pointing her black-gloved finger at me. The heat in my face kicked up several notches. Sophie's rhubarb pie gyrated in my belly. I glanced around at the sea of flushed faces and knew what that poor little fox must feel like at the end of a hunt. I shook my head, but the black widow had already grabbed my arm and was pulling me front and center. She snatched my hat and purse and handed them to Bobbi Jean.

"Okay, Kit. Is that right?" she probed.

I nodded, muttered a tentative, "Uh-huh," and flashed a desperate look at Bobbi Jean, who smiled reassuringly. My eyes dropped to the box.

"For all of you who knew our dear friend Levina Johnson—who we miss so very much—this is her niece Kit," the widow continued. "Thank you for helping us, Kit."

My face burning, I ground my lips into a smile and stared straight ahead. Only Bart was right there ogling me, his tongue stroking a chocolate ice cream cone.

"We'll start with under garments. Next to her body, a woman wore drawers and a chemise. As you can see, the drawers have a large opening to facilitate . . . bodily needs."

I glanced back to see Bobbi Jean push her fist through a foot-long opening in the crotch of a white garment. Cripes! Could I fake a faint well enough to make it look real?

Bobbi Jean held the drawers open at my feet, and I reached down to pull them up over the skirt of my dress. They ballooned out below my waist and fell to just below my knees.

Widow woman moved on to explain the role of the transparent chemise Bobbi Jean had dug from the box, but my mind was fastened on Bart. If I wasn't mistaken, he was snickering. I clenched my fists tight; I *so* wanted to flash him a certain finger.

The next fifteen minutes seemed like the longest of my life. By the time I was laced snuggly into the dreaded corset and covered with several voluminous petticoats and a steel contraption called a caged crinoline, fainting had become a legitimate possibility. Bart licked on his ice cream and stared at me, his gaze growing darker and more heated than amused.

"Women stretched their wardrobes by layering," the widow explained as Bobbi Jean slipped a cream-colored blouse onto my arms. "One outfit might have two different bodices, and often sleeves could be removed. Of course, it was necessary that cuffs and collars could be changed since they were easily soiled."

She rambled on while I struggled to button the blouse. Hoping to avoid Bart's disturbing gaze, I looked to my left. Bernice and her two offspring sat at a picnic table several yards from me, Bernice with displeasure curling her upper lip and Janet's eyes shooting lazars at me.

Clothed in Union blue, Roy smiled and raised his eyebrows in mock wickedness.

While the widow continued her monologue and Bobbi Jean pulled a striped skirt from her box and added it to the layers already cocooning me, my mind flashed back to my visit with Bernice. I pictured her standing at her front door, claiming that she didn't dislike me enough to harm me. She'd appeared to have made some semblance of peace with the idea that I was Levina's legal heir, yet the look on her face today was no more friendly than an irate mama grizzly.

Faces and voices faded to a background murmur as I squeezed my arms into a snug teal jacket and considered the fact that unless Levina opened the door to her murderer, that person would've needed a key to her house *and* the security code. Bernice had admitted to taking the albums from Levina's home, so she would fit the bill.

I bounced a glance off my cousins. It made sense that if Bernice had access to Levina's house, they did, too. And Jack, did he also have access?

But then wouldn't Levina invite a close relative into her home, even in the middle of the night? Maybe not if she knew that person was stealing from her.

Bobbi Jean pushed a hat down onto my head. Automatically, my hand reached up to secure my bun while my mind continued its ruminations. According to Bernice, Levina had phoned her on the day she died. During that conversation, Levina had mentioned her plan to include me in her will. Would that have been motive enough for one of Levina's own family members to murder her that very night—to stop her from changing her will?

And what if Levina had confronted the thief; would that be motive enough?

The jarring sound of clapping sliced through my ponderings. I mentally shook myself, and my eyes landed on Bart, his lips curled into a rakish grin. He dipped his head and touched the brim of his hat before he strode off towards an area I'd yet to explore.

A bit off kilter, I gazed down at the bold stripes that ballooned out below me. Cripes! I must've looked like an idiot up here, so caught up in my speculations that I'd completely lost track of what was going on around me.

"Don't forget there's another battle over at the field in thirty minutes!" the widow shrieked as her audience began to mill about and meander away.

Another battle? Wasn't one enough? If Milton was through with his nap, maybe I could have a turn. I felt so sleep-deprived that I could sleep through even the cannon's deafening boom.

"I'll be right back to help you get out of those things," Bobbi Jean muttered from behind me. "I need to make a run to the restroom."

My eyes fastened on Bernice. I nodded, grabbed my purse, and waddled toward my kinfolk, dragging what felt like a hundred pounds of baggage along with me.

"Let it go, Mother. Whether he's off his rocker or not, it was Uncle Jack's painting. He can do what he wants with it," I heard Roy say. "He's selling off stuff to help pay the bills, which is more than you're willing to do?" He huffed, a picture of exasperation.

"I won't let it go," Bernice spit. Her eyes were spitting, too—fire. "It's not right. Now that greedy little slut has *that*, too."

Perhaps Bernice should be thanking her lucky stars that this *greedy little slut* hadn't gotten her avaricious hands on the ruby ring and emerald necklace she was wearing. I coughed, partly to get their attention but mostly to dislodge the lump of hurt her words had planted inside me.

Three pairs of eyes darted up to me. At least, Roy looked embarrassed. Bernice narrowed her eyes further and set her face in a wrinkly grimace. Janet, looking especially edgy today, chewed her lips and clawed her legs through her walking shorts.

"I put myself out to be nice to you and how do you repay my kindness? You steal another family heirloom," Bernice accused.

"I paid quite an extraordinary amount of money for that family heirloom."

Coiled tight like a rattler, she struck. "Levy's money! Jack deserves it more than you do. Why didn't you give the money to him? Then the painting would still be in the family."

Her words were acid, eating away at my tenuous sense of belonging, stinging. I glanced at Janet and Roy. Evidently, they weren't moved to set their mother straight.

"Thanks to me, the painting *is* still in the family," I reminded her.

Bernice harrumphed, clearly disgusted by my claim. "That's Jack's painting, not yours!"

"Jack doesn't want it," I informed her.

"Just like he doesn't want the tool chest I suppose?" She huffed and shot Roy a beseeching look that turned deadly. Roy seemed more interested in a curvy redhead in Daisy Dukes who was folding up a blanket than the fate of the family tools.

Janet chimed in, her voice shaky and her eyes unfocused and darting faster than a hummingbird in flight. "How did you persuade Uncle Jack to leave his tools with *you*?"

I watched the slow migration of weary-looking bodies trudging toward what had to be sizzling hot bleachers. No way was I going to go from this hot seat to that one I promised myself while I considered how to respond to Janet's question. "He said they were used to carve the mantle, so they should stay with it," I explained.

"And how much whiskey did it take to get him to agree to that?" Bernice snapped.

This time, I snapped. The yards of too-tight fabric I was bound in tugged at me, dragging me down, suffocating me. And Bernice's words were poking holes in my inner fabric. "I think—no, I know—that I've listened to enough of your insults. If you'll answer a couple of quick questions, I'll get out of your way so you can enjoy *your* family outing."

Bernice worked her lips, clearly miffed. "Questions? I thought I took care of that when you showed up at my house *uninvited*?"

"You did. And I appreciate your candor . . . and the albums . . . very much." I paused, my brain scurrying to form syntax that wouldn't make me sound greedy. "I was wondering if perhaps there are some old photos.

"I gave you two albums full of old photos."

"Yes." I took another deep breath, fighting an overwhelming

desire to pounce on her, steel hoops and all. "But they begin when you were a small child. Evidently, things have disappeared from the house. I haven't found any photos so, since you took the albums, I thought you might've taken photos from before that, from the eighteen-hundreds?"

She looked like she'd bit into an unripe prune. "All I took were the albums—family mementos. That's not stealing."

I turned to Janet and Roy. Janet was wringing her hands so vigorously that I feared she'd snap a finger off. Roy's right eye was twitching and not from ogling the redhead; she was nowhere in sight. They both shook their heads.

"In the albums you gave me, I noticed that my mother seemed to be close to her grandfather, that they did a lot together," I probed.

"Olivia was Grandpa's favorite. He spoiled her. I blame him for a lot of what happened . . . back then."

Why did she always feel the need to blame someone? I wiped the sweat from my cheeks with my lace-clad fingers and studied my aunt. Whoever coined the slang term *bitch* had to have had her in mind. "There were some pictures of Olivia and him in eastern Oregon. Did they go there often?"

Her expression darkened. "They were always heading off on their hunts, just the two of them, hunting for clues to that Blue Bucket gold. Stupid fools!"

"Do you know where, exactly, they went? Burns? John Day? Vale?"

She harrumphed disgustedly. "Good lord! Don't tell me you believe that crap?"

Janet shot forward, nearly standing, quivery. Cripes. The lady was seriously in need of some sedatives. "Aunt Levy was convinced it was true!" she screeched.

"Be quiet, Janet," Bernice barked. Her eyes slid to Roy. "This whole Blue Bucket rubbish has got to stop . . . *now*. I lost a son and a sister because of it. Enough is *enough*!"

Her reaction seemed a bit over the top. But then, so did Janet's. Roy was searching his pockets and didn't appear to give a flip about the whole thing. Still, maybe it was only a laid-back façade, his means of coping with two neurotic females. He had to have spent his boyhood years on a high wire. I squinted at the stick of gum he'd salvaged from somewhere—Black Jack—before I flashed back to Bernice and Janet. Though Janet still looked as if bedbugs were chewing on her, it appeared she'd said enough about the gold.

Well, I hadn't. "What if that gold was also the reason for Levina's death? Wouldn't you want to know?" I challenged.

Bernice eyeballed me as if I'd just disclosed my secret plot to knock off the rest of *her* family. She leaned forward. "That's absurd," she hissed.

"Is it?" This time I leaned towards her and nearly toppled as the pounds of fabric shifted forward. I tottered and struggled to remain upright, then pushed on. "On the day she was murdered, Levina told several people, including you, that she'd found the key to the Blue Bucket gold. What if someone wanted to get to that gold before she did?"

Her answer was a condescending storm: "That's crap! That gold doesn't exist and it never has. You go ahead and chase all over the state looking for it, just like Levy and Olivia did, but it'll be a waste of your time the same as it was theirs." She paused long enough to level a vicious glare at me. "Maybe you'll end up *dead*, too!"

Several moments of dead silence followed that last heated remark. Talk about a slug in the gut. I struggled to get some blood back into my brain and breathe as deeply as I could with a corset squeezing my lungs, studying Janet. She'd sat here like a flea on speed during the whole conversation. Yet now she resembled more a turtle curled inside its shell, her head down and her shoulders rounded, her arms clutching herself tightly.

Roy's voice finally filled the void. "I think you just stepped over the line, Mother. *None* of us want to see Kit harmed in any way." His right eye was twitching again.

"Well, of course, not. I simply meant that if Levy died because of that gold—as Kit seems to think—then it might be dangerous for her to pursue it." Bernice sounded flustered, even somewhat apologetic. I wasn't buying it. She might be sorry she'd voiced the words; that didn't mean she wasn't silently wishing them.

Roy checked his watch and pushed himself up from the table. "I've gotta get my gear and meet Uncle Jack over at the field."

Bernice pursed her lips and threw him an exasperated look. "Why you have to go out there with all of those men shooting guns at each other is beyond me." she muttered. "Someday, someone's gonna get killed."

"We don't use real ammo, Mother," Roy assured her, his focus more on me than her. "How about helping me off the field?" he asked.

My eyes flicked and held. "Huh?"

Bernice and Janet stood up. Janet was fumbling with her cell phone, and Bernice gaped at Roy as if he'd admitted to being a left-wing liberal *and* gay.

"At the end of the battle, they'll ask family and friends to help injured soldiers off the field," Roy explained. "It's what the women did at the end of a real battle."

Was he asking me to take part in that gruesome charade? Though steaming in the heat, I shivered at the mere thought. He looked serious, even beseeching. Ironically, some inner part of me was touched, a warm glow that blossomed with the knowledge that a member of my new-found family was including me.

"Janet and Mother refuse to do it so I'm counting on you," he pleaded.

Being third choice was better than not being chosen at all . . . wasn't it? "Uh . . . I don't. . . ." Bernice's *over my dead body* stance convinced me. "Why not?"

"Great. Stand under the trees on the Union side. It's shady there, and you won't have to crawl through people to get to the field."

"I'm sorry to interrupt, but I need to get those clothes off you before the battle starts."

Bobbi Jean's voice made me flinch and twist around. When I turned back, my kinfolk were heading toward the battlefield. Bernice was trucking to keep up with Roy. No doubt, her lips were moving as furiously as her feet. Janet was trailing, cell phone to her ear.

Twenty minutes later, feeling like a well-beaten meringue— light and sticky—I trudged to the far end of the bleachers, to where only a few stragglers stood. In the trees to my right, Union soldiers clustered in small groups firing their guns. I stood in the shade of a leafy Filbert tree and squinted across the smoky field up to the top of the hill where Bart straddled his horse, erect and still, like a toy soldier.

My eyes scoured the mass of spectators until they landed on Sophie and Milton sitting in a pair of wooden folding chairs. Sophie's parasol was up, blocking the view of those behind her. Like a proud pink parrot, she sat erect, her lavish hat bobbing as she chatted with those around her. Milton had the look of someone who'd rather still be napping.

"Well, beautiful lady, this is my lucky day."

I whirled around, my heart sprinting, and looked up into a pair of twinkling hazel eyes. Bob stood beside me, his cute dimples highlighting a contagious smile. Though he still wore the felt hat, he'd wisely shed the heavy coat he'd been wearing. Beneath his loose-fitting white shirt, his arms and shoulders looked huge—muscular— as if he bench-pressed Ford trucks for fun. Beside him, I felt petite.

He leaned close. "So has your day been exciting?" he asked, his voice barely loud enough to hear over the gunfire.

Exciting wasn't the word I'd choose to describe it. More like peculiar. Or embarrassing. At times, downright uncomfortable. And of course, my encounter with Bernice had been upsetting. Maybe it *was* time for some excitement.

"Not yet," I said, curling my lips into what felt like a sexy smile.

His dark eyebrows shot up a couple of inches. "You're not with your . . . friend?"

"At the moment, *she's* with a gentleman friend," I assured him. Heat raged in my cheeks. Cripes! I'd never come on to a guy like this before in my life. I took a step back to put some distance between us.

"Oh," he breathed just as something zinged past my chest. A loud crackling snap followed. Instinctively, I whirled toward the sound, and prickly bits of something blasted me, stinging my arms and face. I froze, dazed.

"What the hell?"

His words jarred me. My eyes darted up to meet his gaping-mouthed frown. From nearby, my ears registered a high-pitched whine nanoseconds before something else zipped by my forehead. Again, a cracking sound sent shards flying. Automatically, my hand rose to the stinging pain that blossomed above my right ear.

Then a wall of steel hit me, knocking the wind from me, propelling me backwards. My head snapped. Some hazy, distant part of me registered pain as my right shoulder hit a solid object before the wall landed on top of me and pounded me into the hard ground.

My body numb and my head exploding with pain, I fought to get a breath of air into my lungs. The world around me swirled—blurry and otherworldly—as if I were dreaming. From far off, I heard yelling and gunshots, but they gradually faded. I grew heavy—cement heavy—and sank into the scratchy warmth beneath me.

✿✿✿

Violins whined a languid lament, distant yet evocative, triggering with its sorrowful notes a rush of feelings. A shroud of fear settled over me and burrowed to my core, a quivering ache, nauseating in its intensity. Still woozy from the sedative I'd slept off, I grabbed my stomach and winced as pain shot through my shoulder and radiated down my arm to tingle in my clenched fingers.

I stared into a smoky amber world as disjointed images flashed before me: a ten-ton boulder pounding me into the ground. Me, bouncing on a stretcher carried by a cluster of young men in gray. Gazing up at the giant who walks beside me, his twin dimples replaced by a grim look. He's bent over, pressing something against a burning pain in my forehead, scarlet splotches vivid against the white of his shirt. Shiny knives and saws on the table behind him. The doctor in the grungy gray uniform touching and prodding, asking too many questions.

My muscles clenched and I fought to take slow, shallow

breaths. The air was heavy and stifling, suffocating. I shook my head. A blinding pain stilled it. "I didn't dream it, did I? Those were real bullets?" I whispered, more to clarify it to myself than to get an answer from Bart, a hulking dark shape, his chair rocking in time to the music.

"Real enough to chew up the tree you were standing in front of and graze your right temple," he drawled before he gnawed a hunk from the chocolate bar in his hands.

Again I felt sharp prickles sprinkle my face—splinters from the tree. If I hadn't stepped back from Bob, I'd be the one who was chewed up . . . and, quite possibly, dead. Oh, God! Like too many Long Island iced teas on a hot day, it hit me.

"They were aimed at me?" I asked, hoping he would tell me it was all a big mistake. Some guy had forgotten to take live ammo out of his hunting rifle. A couple of real bullets got mixed in with the fake ones. Whatever.

He swallowed, then sighed a stream of warm chocolate. "Cal seems to think so."

"Cal?" Oh, God. Cal would be furious.

"Yeah, he's here nosing around. He said he'd be by later to talk with you." The dark streaks above his eyes slashed into a frown. "You might want to take another of those pain pills the doctor left and put it off until morning. I've seen him happier on a bad day."

"Morning! No way. Where's Sophie? I'm going home!"

"She's at the dance." His teeth flashed white against his dark features. "Probably plotting how she's going to seduce Milton when you're lying in his bed." He chuckled. "You're not gonna drag Sophie away from Milton tonight. I'm afraid you're stuck."

Cripes! Someone had tried to shoot me, and here I lay, sweat-drenched and shaky, in Milton's cloth tent, which would definitely not stop a bullet. The need to get inside my safe, secure home was overwhelming—obsessive. And Bart was laughing!

"Then I'll come back and pick her up tomorrow," I muttered angrily as I levered myself into a sitting position and inched my legs over the side of the bed. I gritted my teeth against the pain and held my roiling stomach, ordering the gyrating shadows to stand still.

Bart grabbed my left bicep firmly. "Uh-uh. You're not driving anywhere."

"Sorry. You're gonna have to find someone else to boss around." I pushed myself to my feet and managed to stand there for three seconds before my wobbly legs gave out.

"I'll call Patty. She'll come get me," I informed him once the storm in my head had calmed down some. "Where's my purse?"

Clearly irritated, he huffed. "According to Cal, your friend Patty has the flu. Are you gonna drag her out of her sick bed?"

"Of course, not," I murmured, suddenly more focused on Bart than getting home. In the soft light, he looked perturbed . . . and disturbingly different. His black eyes were flinty, his jaw steely. His gray jacket hung open, revealing a loose-fitting white shirt that was tucked into wool pants. Black boots covered his feet.

The notes of a languid waltz seeped in through the canvas, insipid in the sluggish heat. And somewhere inside me, butterflies awakened, fluttering alarmingly. It had to be the uniform.

My eyes dropped to my bare feet and blood-and-dirt-streaked dress. "How can you stand to wear those heavy clothes? Don't they itch?" I asked.

Still pensive, he nodded. "Uh-huh."

"So why don't you take them off then?"

The rocking ceased. "You want me naked, just say so."

My body temperature rose about twenty degrees. Alarmingly heavy, my jaw dropped and hung there as I clamored for words. "I *don't*," I uttered. "Unlike you, I'm not into kinky . . . games. I'm sweltering so you have to be, too. I thought you might be more comfortable in something else . . . like shorts and a tee-shirt."

He leaned forward, his probing eyes inches from mine. "*Kinky games*?"

Though instinct screamed to scoot to the other side of the bed, I was too wiped out to move an inch. "You know . . . your . . . dress-up games."

"What exactly are . . . dress-up games?" He actually looked somewhat puzzled.

I stared into his unsettling eyes, my heart pounding loud enough that he had to hear it. "I don't know," I mumbled, then thought to add, "And I *don't* want to know."

One eyebrow lifted sardonically.

"Whatever you and your girlfriend do when you're in your . . . costumes." That was as explicit as I was going to get.

He nailed me with his questionable IQ stare. "Lady, are you for real? First of all, I don't have a girlfriend. And second, I don't play dress-up games. Unlike you, my aunt didn't die and leave me a treasure chest, which means that I have to earn my own money.

"I write historically-significant manuscripts—documentaries and screenplays for public broadcasting and the History Channel, brochures for museums and historical landmarks, biographies, you name it. And *yes*, occasionally I wear a costume when I depict a character in a film or photo. I'd hardly call what I do a game. And it is most assuredly not *kinky*."

"Oh." It was more a whimper than a whisper. Apart from the murder thing, the moment couldn't get much worse—except for the fact that for a few very brief seconds, I'd found the idea of Bart a la nude intriguing. It had to be the medication playing mind games.

I closed my eyes. Cal would be here soon. He'd chew on me worse than those bullets had chewed up that tree, but he might finally know who'd killed Levina and who was now trying to off me. Then Cal would drive me home and deposit me safely in my house.

Right! And Annabelle would sleep until eight o'clock every morning.

Bart's hands on my knees brought my focus back to him. "Are you okay?" he asked

"I'm sorry," I murmured. And I was. Then I noticed, maybe because he was so close that my eyes darted everywhere other than directly into his. "You cut your hair," I blurted as if he didn't already know.

"Uh-huh." He smiled half of a hunky smile. "And glad to be rid of it. I'm going to be doing a series on the Civil War for the History Channel, so the tail had to go."

Just like that, his focus was on me, head tilted, eyes squinting. "So what's the story with you? All that gorgeous hair and it's always tied up in a tidy knot."

My left hand shot up. "Oh God," slipped from my lips, a frantic moan. Like Shirley Temple hair on steroids, a plethora of coiled tendrils sprang from my head and spiraled chaotically down to just below my shoulders. I gritted my teeth and gingerly raised my other hand, determined to restore order to the out-of-control mess.

Bart's large hands closed over mine. "Leave it," he murmured in a deep, silky voice, the beguiling fragrance of chocolate breathing over me. I couldn't help but stare into his eyes since they were about an inch from mine. Inside me, butterflies reawakened, flapping their wings wildly, sending heavy, pulsating tendrils through my limbs. My weakened hands went limp in Bart's, and the hair escaped.

Pressure on the back of my head drew me forward. Silently, I screamed *no,* but my traitorous body had something else in mind.

His lips touched mine—warm velvet—whispery sensations that set every nerve in my body to dancing. Humming like the violin whose notes purred languorously in the still air, my insides melted into a swirling ball of heat that started in my chest and rolled south.

Cripes! I was in serious trouble. He was chastely nuzzling my lips, and I'd already moved on to fantasizing my hands slipping under his shirt. It was my own fault. Self-enforced abstinence had placed me in this position—that and the darned uniform.

Just like that, he pulled away. I whimpered and opened my eyes to stare into his. "Now's not the time for this," he murmured in a husky voice.

Not the time? Couldn't he hear my insides screaming that now was the perfect time? I leaned forward to run my lips along his, then turned to nuzzling them with soft caresses. His body stiffened and he inched back. I followed.

Ever so slowly, our lips heated, less cuddle and more fervent pressure. I was too mesmerized by the swirls of pleasure radiating through me to care if I was now leading or following. His tongue flicked my lips and slid along them, probing. Hot lava oozed, turning my bones to goo. My lips parted. He tasted like sinfully rich, dark chocolate!

At last, he released my hands and his slipped down to my shoulders. I winced with the sudden pain. His hands moved lower, nearly to my waist, drawing me closer. Balanced on the edge of the bed, my fingers landed on the sweat-dampened fabric covering his chest—not quite skin but I could feel its warmth and firmness beneath the cotton.

Our tongues glided to the *andante* violin notes, languorously slow and sensual. Beneath my palm, his heart beat *allegro vivace*. My hand trembling, I tugged at the bottom of his shirt. In one smooth motion, he was on his knees, and I felt the prickle of wool on my inner thighs. I was pressed up against his potent body—heat and energy and hard muscle.

A harsh barking sound suddenly broke through my Bart-drugged consciousness. My eyes opened and drifted toward the sound, closed dreamily, then darted open again. Cal hovered in the doorway, looking more irritated than embarrassed. I didn't know whether to thank him or stick my tongue out at him, hoping he would take the hint and leave.

Then it hit me; at the moment, my tongue was engaged in a rather risqué tango with Bart's. I managed to untangle it and cough halfheartedly as I pushed against his chest. I refused to be mortified. After all, Cal was the one who'd barged into this private moment.

Bart's brooding eyes probed mine, questioning. I glanced at Cal and felt Bart's flesh turn to granite beneath my palms. "Dammit, Cal. Can you give us a moment?" he hissed as he dropped his hands and shifted back into the rocker. He looked like a kid who'd had his Halloween candy confiscated, all glowers and disappointment, his costume mussed.

Panic grabbed me by the throat. How could I have been such a ninny? It wasn't enough that I was being physically threatened. Now my shaky emotional well-being would most likely end up more snarled than my hair. For sure, commitment was *not* Bart's thing, and a short-lived, tumultuous fling wasn't mine. If I had the energy to kick myself, I would.

"I don't have a moment. I gotta get back to Aurora and a shit-load of illegal fireworks and party-happy people who aren't smart enough to know when they're drunk," Cal growled. He turned and nailed me with his glare. "Dammit to hell, Kit. Why can't you just stay home, locked inside that nice big house Levina gave you?"

I wanted to say, *because, thanks to you and your lack of even one solid lead, I'd be stuck there for the rest of my life, which, at this rate, won't be very long.* "Sophie invited me to come with her today. She needed a ride," I muttered meekly.

"Sophie can dog Milton without draggin' you along. Next time say *no*. And stay home!" Cal glanced around the interior of the tent, pulled a chair forward, and dropped into it. He slid a small notebook from his pocket. Hopefully, it was now lined with insightful clues and incriminating evidence that would nail a demented murderer—preferably, tonight.

Reality hit me hard. I cradled my throbbing arm and felt the sting of tears in my eyes and throat. How I wanted this mess to be gone. Every time I let my guard down, something awful happened. Cal and his doom and gloom attitude weren't helping.

"So tell me what happened . . . *this time*," Cal said, clicking his pen.

"I already told the police everything I remember," I told him. And I had, lying woozy and trembling on a rickety cot that had surely served the south during the real Civil War.

"Well, since I was in Aurora doin' my job *then*, perhaps you can go through it again for me?" It was definitely a demand, not a question.

My eyes flicked off Bart. "After I do, will you take me home?" I begged.

Cal chewed on my request and his mustache. "I will if, and only if, you promise to stay there," he grumbled. "But I think you'll be safer here with Bart to watch over you."

Bart—brooding, rumpled, and hot—looked anything but safe. Decadent butterflies awakened inside me every time I glanced his way. I needed to put some distance between us—soon. "What makes you think I'm safe with Bart?" I asked Cal.

Throwing Bart a guy-to-guy look, Cal's lips curled into a knowing smile. "Well, damn, Kit, I'm not gonna guarantee your virtue's safe with him, but I'm ninety-nine percent sure he wasn't the one shootin' at you. He was sittin' on his horse in front of a slew of witnesses without a weapon in his hand."

I eyeballed Bart, whose eyes were smoldering, then turned back to Cal. "I need to take care of Annabelle," I told him. He raised his bushy eyebrows and nodded, then pulled his notebook into the lantern's hazy glow, pencil ready.

My mind wound back to the battlefield and my brief visit with Bob. Bart had been at the top of the hill. Even if he had fired a gun at me, the angle would've been wrong.

"Sophie and Milton were sitting in chairs not too far from me, so it wasn't one of them," I said. "Do you have any idea who it could've been?"

Mustache twitching, Cal shook his head. "Nope. The sheriff and his men talked to nearly everyone in the park. No one claims to have seen or heard anything unusual. Course, with a full flown battle goin' on, some guy shootin' a gun wouldn't be unusual now, would it? With all the commotion and noise and smoke on the field, the shooter could've easily snuck away and switched his weapon . . . or left the park."

An image of Roy in Union blue flashed before me. "My Uncle Jack and Bernice's son Roy were supposed to be out on the field. Did anyone check them out?"

"They were with the sixty-ninth New Yorkers," Bart informed them, "to the back of the field, still in the trees when the two shots were fired."

Cal frowned, then squinted hard and jotted something in his notebook before he spoke. "That's where the shots came from. The state guys questioned them and searched their vehicles. No smoking gun. At least, not the one we're lookin' for. Searched all the Union and Confederate tents, too. Nothin'. Like I said, with all that was goin' on, it wouldn't have been difficult to stash a rifle somewhere."

"How about my Aunt Bernice and her daughter Janet?" I prodded. "I spoke with them earlier. They must've still been around." Thoughts of either of them toting a rifle around in their designer bags were almost laughable. Still, crazier things had happened.

"Bernice claims she was at the restroom, but we haven't found anyone to corroborate that yet," Cal said. "Janet was standin' a few yards to the left of you, near the Civilian camp, talkin' on her cell. A couple of people confirmed that. When did you last see Bernice?"

I thought back to our little heart-to-heart. Bernice had marched off with Roy in her white linen slacks ensemble and high-heeled, slip-on sandals. Trekking through underbrush in those shoes would've been next to impossible. And to get a shot at me, she would've had to hike through the bushes and then hide in the trees. Her whites would've been soiled.

"Not more than twenty minutes before the battle began," I told Cal. "Over at the fashion show. She and Janet left with Roy, heading toward the Union camp."

Cal squinted at his notepad and scrawled. "What'd you do after that?"

"I removed the clothes they put on me and went into the restroom near the food tents. After that, I walked to the battlefield. Roy asked me to help him off the field—some kind of family thing he said. He told me to stand on the Union side under the trees."

Like a colossal hailstone, it hit me: Roy had asked me to stand *there*, an easy target.

Cal and I must've been sharing a brainwave; he was scribbling madly. "And there was a man with you?" he asked.

"Bob Crosely." Heat burned in my cheeks with the memory of my botched flirtations. "We happened to be at the same place at the same time and were chatting."

"Crosely, huh? From what I hear, he probably saved your life." Cal studied the bandage above my left eye. "That first shot was close. The second nicked you. The third might've hit its target."

Chills ran up my spine, icing the back of my neck. I shuddered with the knowledge that I'd barely eluded death once again.

My eyes were drawn to Bart's. Luck had placed him in my kitchen when I'd taken my first sip of strawberry-laced coffee that morning. And now a near stranger had kept me from being gunned down. But I couldn't keep relying on others to keep me alive. Even Cal, with his gun and many law enforcement resources, couldn't protect me.

It was up to me to figure out how to keep myself alive. And I had a good idea what my next step would be.

CHAPTER 16

Storm clouds churned before us like lurking dark shadows—gloomy, hulking, looming. Before we reached the town of John Day and our next sleuthing stint, we'd be immersed in torrents of driving rain. Ominous shivers sprinted across my shoulders. When I turned to Bart, butterfly wings fluttered in my innards. "How much farther do you think it is?" I asked.

He was stretched out, his seat in a semi-reclining position, head pillowed on his palms, listening to Willie Nelson lament all the girls he'd loved and dumped. With his height, the eight hours he'd spent in my relatively small car had to be an uncomfortable ordeal. "Not far. Maybe twenty miles or so," he replied, his voice betraying his boredom.

Well, let him be bored. I hadn't asked him to ride shotgun. He'd plopped into my passenger seat before dawn that morning, uninvited *and* without asking permission to do so. "Uh-uh. No way. Get out," I'd hissed. And he'd called me Miss Marple and threatened to phone Cal and report my latest insubordination. My only choice was to surrender. If Cal knew what I was up to, he'd confiscate my car and drivers' license.

But someone had to take action. Cal was flat on his back with a bug, Nurse Patty fussing over him. Since the latest attempt on my life, I'd hidden in my house—from a murderer and from Bart—for two days, searching the internet and gathering information on the Blue Bucket gold and eastern Oregon. Now I was here, perhaps walking in James Wallace's now obscure footsteps. By the end of this day, I hoped to have answers to some of my questions concerning James' time away from Aurora, ones that I hoped connected to Levina's death and what would be mine, too, if I didn't do something to circumvent it.

The killer was lucky. Sure, he hadn't left his smoking gun on the battlefield, but one would think a botched murder in front of hundreds of spectators would elicit at least one itty bitty clue. According to Cal, it hadn't. Three—perhaps four—attempts on my life and not one lead. Cripes. It had to be some kind of record. Well, I was through being the bunny trapped in the rabbit hole. I was now on the road to tracking down a killer.

On the day she died, Levina had become excited about something she'd seen in the paintings on the wall in Meg's diner. And she'd told Bernice and Meg that she'd found the *key* to some secret. Then she'd quizzed Milton about his ancestors. A persistent voice inside me insisted that these events were connected to Levina's death in some way.

My eyes slid over to Bart. Surely, it was safe to be here. Milton was the only other person who knew where I was.

I glanced out at the pine-covered hills. Here, the sun's late afternoon rays filtered through the dense needles on the trees, creating patterns on the dry dirt floor beneath them. Since we'd left Burns behind over an hour ago, much of the land we'd traveled through had been rough and desolate—canyons chiseled through red rock and jutting ragged hills. I thought about that long ago wagon train that had wandered through this area and commiserated with its occupants. Their journey hadn't been an easy one, especially if they were faced with a thunderstorm like the one facing us.

From what I'd learned through the wonders of Google, it was clear that the exact location of the Blue Bucket gold was an enigma. In fact, there were heated debates about whether it had ever existed. Of course, there were also numerous stories pertaining to who'd found the gold and exactly what they'd found. Those stories were rarely in agreement.

However, some facts were indisputable. It seemed that in the summer of 1845, the pioneers on the lost wagon train were roaming in eastern and central Oregon, badly in need of water. At Fort Boise, they'd joined Stephen Meek, a trapper who'd assured them that he knew of a route to the Willamette Valley that was two hundred miles shorter than the old trail. Once on their way, it became clear that Meek had no idea how to get the pioneers to where they wanted to be. Wagon train members were so upset that they talked of hanging Meek. He got wind of their plans and took off, leaving them to wander on their own.

The problem was that they were doing exactly that—wandering, with no idea where they were. The land was dry and treacherous, with rocky gorges, steep cliffs, hills, and vast, open spaces. Looking out on that land now, with air conditioning and a quart of bottled water, I had a vague understanding of the fear and hopelessness those early pioneers must have felt.

If family tales were correct, my great-great-grandfather and his family were on that wagon train. But was Wallace really one of those who were sent out with blue buckets clutched in their hands to search for water? Legend claimed they had found water. And gold. "So why did they leave all of that gold behind?"

"What?" Bart asked from beside me.

My eyes drifted sideways. He was rubbing his eyes. "You said something."

Had I really voiced my thoughts? "It was nothing; just thinking about that lost wagon train," I mumbled. "Why didn't they recognize it for what it was—gold?"

In one smooth motion, he flipped the seat forward, sat up, and clicked off Willie's whining. "Well, for one thing, the people in those wagons had water on their minds, not gold. Probably just looked like some shiny rocks to them. There was no reason to think it might be gold since gold wasn't discovered out here in the west until three years later.

"Evidently, someone was intrigued enough to pick up one of the chunks and hold onto it. Once gold fever hit California, he put two and two together and came up with the notion of a stream loaded with gold nuggets. Guess Wallace was one of those people who believed the stories. Your Aunt Levina did, too. And she'd certainly done her research."

I pulled my eyes from the endless stretch of asphalt to meet his. "You know, I've looked through her whole house and haven't found any information on the Blue Bucket or James Wallace." I thought back to my futile searches during the last two days. With Levina's notebook in hand—Milton had turned it over to me the previous day—I'd painstakingly searched for items she'd listed in it. "Did you ever see the research she did?" I asked.

"Well, yeah. She had several file drawers full, and she was always adding to them. She'd get an idea in her head and off she'd go to pursue it. And I know she had several books on the subject because I read them. You sure they're not there?"

"If they are, they're well hidden." My bet was on them being gone.

"Hmmm . . ." He sighed deeply. "You might ask Janet about it?"

"Janet?" My gaze shot from the highway to him. "Why her?"

"She seemed to have more than a passing interest in the Blue Bucket. Several times, I was over at Levina's, and Janet was in the office digging through her files. Levina didn't seem to mind. She claimed that a new set of eyes might help find the missing key."

There was that word again—key. "So you think Janet might have taken the files?"

He shrugged. "Don't know. She was definitely interested in them. And if they're not there, they have to have gone somewhere."

But Janet? Personally, I couldn't see Janet buttering toast without her mother there to support her. Still, she had asserted herself when Bernice had pooh-poohed the idea that Wallace might have found the cache of Blue Bucket gold.

I sighed and stared at the ribbon of highway and the churning sea of darkness obliterating the blue sky directly ahead. "I should've skipped Burns," I muttered.

Burns had been a disappointment, one that had wasted valuable time. If the weather turned bad, it might be prudent to spend the night in John Day, something I'd planned to do before I left Aurora that morning but now didn't want to contemplate. With Bart riding shotgun, there would be no overnighter, even if I had to drive through the night.

"And deprive me of that Brahma burger. Uh-uh. I'd drive all the way back out here just to get my mouth around another one of those," Bart crooned. "Real, honest-to-goodness french fries. And that milkshake. Mmmm. . . . Good grub!"

My eyes darted from the burgeoning mass of gray to Bart. After a fruitless search through the Harney County Historical Museum and the city library in Burns, I'd dashed through a fast food drive-in for a quick lunch. Little did I know that Bart was a grease junky. "Maybe you should listen to your heart. I'm sure I hear it screaming," I told him.

"Only because you won't listen to yours," he murmured with a quirky smile. "Fortunately, your eyes speak volumes."

Warmth flooded me, melting my insides. "Look, if you feel the need to be my knight in shining armor, fine. Just leave my heart out of it. And keep in mind that I didn't invite you on this trip. You're here and I'm stuck with that. But I *don't* like it."

"Why? Because we kissed? And it was obvious you *did* like that, so don't even think about denying it." His voice was low, husky. "Fact is, we'd have been doing a whole lot more than that if Cal hadn't barged in on us."

Cripes! My face was a red hot jalapeno. I kept a death grip on the steering wheel, trying to ignore the flutterings his words had ignited. "I can't deal with this right now," I uttered. "In case you haven't noticed, someone's trying to kill me."

He sighed. "I know. It's not the right time. We'll put what's going on between us aside for now. But when the time comes, we *are* going to deal with it."

Deal with what? Except for a case of mind-boggling lust, nothing was going on between us. Choosing to ignore his words, I took a deep breath, instead. The air felt damp and cool in my chest, charged by more than Bart's comment. Tiny goose bumps sprouted on my arms and legs, sending tingles jetting through my body. The air pressure was dropping faster than Bart's chance of reaching fifty if he kept consuming fat like he had today.

Bart reached out and turned off the air conditioner. "You

might want to slow down. We're coming to a steep grade."

Even without the warning sign, it would've been hard to miss it. The highway appeared to drop off into a massive hole in the earth. Roiling dark clouds shrouded what lay beyond. Off to our left, crows rose into the sky and careened like a swarm of monster killer bees. The chills running through me weren't all due to the drop in temperature.

"Spooky," Bart muttered.

So I wasn't the only one with the willies. I eased my foot up on the gas as I headed into the downward incline, then glanced in my rearview mirror. A white pickup truck was charging towards us—a tailgate hugger. I searched for a wide shoulder on the side of the road. There were none, just a sheer drop-off to whatever lay far below. Sighing, I pressed on the brake and crept as far to the right as I dared.

"I'm gonna let that truck pass," I muttered. "I don't need him riding my tail."

Bart glanced over his shoulder, then studied me speculatively.

"Okay. So he's not riding my tail," I snapped. In fact, the truck had slowed to a crawl and was keeping its distance.

When I pulled back into the lane, I heard Bart's sigh. We rounded a corner, and the car wobbled as a strong gust hit it. Fat raindrops pelted the windshield, popping like popcorn and splattering the window like a barrage of mini water balloons. Dreary, dim dankness engulfed us. I turned the defogger and the windshield wipers to high and leaned forward, straining to see through the watery film just as the rumble of thunder pounded my eardrums.

Winding its way down the steep slope, the road was a series of tight twists and turns. I steered through another corner, then crawled forward to a sharp outer curve.

Just as I was heading into it, something bumped my rear bumper. The car surged forward. I jerked the steering wheel to the left. The tires slipped on the wet pavement. Miraculously—and most likely due to all-wheel drive—the car clung to the road.

"What the hell was that?"

I heard Bart's words, but my body had solidified into a mass of quivering flesh, and the blood churning in my head made it impossible to formulate a coherent thought. Somehow, I managed to shift my leaden foot to the brake. Then a harder wallop from behind jolted us forward. Fortunately, the car stuck to the slick asphalt.

Emerging through the terror that numbed me was the realization that this was being done intentionally . . . to harm *me*. "Oh, God. He's here," I moaned.

Finally, we were meeting face-to-face—or vehicle-to-vehicle as it were. My eyes darted to the rearview mirror only to see a wall of water reflected in it. I shifted my gaze to the outside mirror. A mottled blob of white was rolling up beside me. "Oh, shit!" I gasped.

"Speed up," Bart said in an amazingly calm voice.

Speed up? Was he crazy? We were negotiating a veritable obstacle course, one in which there was no room for failure. The loud boom of thunder blasted through the air, causing my already hyper-stiff muscles to contract into steel balls.

"Step on the gas!" Bart barked.

I did. The car surged forward to the next curve. I stomped on the brake and wrenched the steering wheel to the right. Squealing like a rusty roller coaster, the tires slid sideways into the other lane. I braced for the crash of metal hitting metal.

"Don't let him get beside us."

Bart's voice pulled me back into the fray. I steered the car to the center of the road, straddling the yellow line, and stepped hard on the accelerator. A slash of lightning streaked across the dark sky, highlighting the road. Cripes! It seemed to drop off the face of the earth. "Maybe we should stop?" I offered, my voice more squeak than human.

"What if he has a gun?" His voice was nearly drowned by the grumble of thunder.

He did have a point. Struggling to see through the stream of rainwater blasting the windshield, my eyes, mere inches from the glass, refused to move. "Where is he?" I screeched just as a loud wallop hurled the car forward. My head crashed back against the headrest, and glittery stars flashed before me. But through those stars came a vision of my Santa Fe, with Bart and I tucked inside, in a never-ending freefall.

I lurched forward, and my entire body dissolved into a numb blob of terror. Ahead, was a gravel turnout. Beyond it, air. I ground the steering wheel to the left. The entire car slithered sideways towards the edge. I closed my eyes and braced for the inevitable.

"Step on the gas!"

Instead of Bart's voice, I heard God's. I shifted my foot to the accelerator and jammed it to the floor. The grind of tires churning in loose gravel was deafening. Incredibly, the front tires clung, the rear portion of the car fanning around them. Suddenly, the car shot forward. My eyes popped open. The muddy face of the slope loomed before us.

As if by divine intervention, the steering wheel rotated beneath my immobile hands and the car landed on the pavement, then wobbled drunkenly down the highway. My eyes froze on the still-moving wheel, then dropped to where Bart's hand grasped it.

"You can stop now," he said.

Stop? Was he crazy? What if my killer had a gun? I let up on the gas a bit and pulled my eyes from the road to search the nearly useless rearview mirrors. No milky blobs of white stared back at me.

We were approaching another corner and my quaking body clenched, prepared for battle. I steered cautiously through the turn. Lightning flashed in jagged slashes, close enough to tickle my arms. I strained to search the lit-up highway ahead. No white truck there either. The loud pounding boom of thunder reverberated through the car.

"*Where is he*?" I wailed.

"*Kit,* stop the car. He's gone."

"Gone?" I stared at him. My killer was here and now he was gone? I was that close to the truth, and it had slipped through my fingers. I bounced forward, my face nearly on the glass.

Suddenly, two blurry headlights pierced the watery curtain, heading straight toward us. "Oh, no!" I groaned. Every muscle in my body clenched, prepared for the shattering impact. I fell back into the seat and closed my eyes.

Nothing happened. No bone-crushing crash. No ear-splitting, crunching metal sounds. No sprays of broken glass. No pain.

Ever so slowly, my eyelids opened. Bart's strong fingers were twined around the steering wheel, swinging it jerkily back and forth. Rain plastered the still-intact windshield. We continued our journey down the highway from hell.

"Take your foot off the gas!" Bart ordered.

My eyes dropped. Yes, my foot was still pressed firmly on the accelerator.

All of a sudden, I was slammed against the door. The screech of tires whined painfully in my ears. Instinctively, I righted myself and stomped on the brake, grasped the steering wheel firmly in my trembling hands, and finished steering through the curve.

Lightning crackled and split the sky with shards of static electricity. I breathed in the charged air deeply and let it out slowly, feeling an odd, tingling sensation in my scalp. Thunder grumbled, vibrating my numbed body. I sat forward, determined. There couldn't be that many hairpin turns left in this miserable grade. Unless a flash flood wiped me off the hill, I *would* make it safely to the bottom.

"You can stop the car," Bart said from beside me.

I heard him . . . but I didn't. I eased up on the gas and crawled forward at a snail's pace, my hands in a deadlock on the steering wheel and my eyes glued to the water-glazed pavement barely visible through the glass. I was vaguely aware of noises—the ping of numbers being punched into a cell phone and words being spoken— but I was so focused on reaching the bottom of the hill in one piece that it was a disconnected awareness.

After what seemed like an eternity, I rounded a turn to the sight of a blessedly flat stretch of highway. I inched the car onto a gravel turnout, pressed my foot on the brake, and switched the key to *off*.

Then I hauled my ass out of that car as quickly as a terror-frozen, quivering, finally reached the breaking point human body can haul herself out of a car. My legs crumbled, and I slid to the ground, barely aware of the splash of cold water chilling my butt and thighs or the obese raindrops pelting me.

Strong arms lifted me to my feet. One would think that I would curl into the comfort of Bart's arms. But no. I wailed on him. I fisted my hands and went at it, hammering his chest and keening as if I'd gone totally berserk.

Gradually, it occurred to me that Bart was standing quietly and allowing me to pummel him mercilessly. Water streamed into my eyes when I looked up, distorting his face into a garbled blob, but the concern in his eyes was clear. To still my flaying arms, I grabbed hold of his wet shirt and clung to it. The chatter of my teeth nearly drowned the sound of pounding rain. "I'm sorry," I mouthed.

Comforting hands rubbed up and down my back, soothing in their rhythm. "It's okay. The truck's gone," Bart murmured into my ear, his breath warm against my icy skin. "I called the county sheriff. He'll be here soon."

"Gone?" I squeaked, my eyes darting in search of a white truck. "Are you sure?"

He grabbed my chin and turned my face to his. Water dripped from the hair plastered to his scalp and ran in rivulets down his cheeks. "That car coming up the hill must've scared him off."

But what if it hadn't? A swarm of painful pinpricks buzzed through me, from the tips of my toes to the roots of my hair. I'd come within an inch or two of losing my life—Bart's too. My killer was getting desperate.

CHAPTER 17

From across the table, Bart's penetrating gaze melded with mine—pleading. I shook my head resolutely, my fingers tracing the cattle brands burned into the heavily lacquered tabletop.

When he spoke, it was without conviction. "She's not feeling all that well, Cal. We'll be home this evening. You can talk with her then."

Cal's voice reached me, terse and tinny, and my insides clenched into tighter knots. I knew I should grab the phone and take on the tongue-lashing myself. I couldn't. It had taken all of my reserve inner drive to talk myself out of bed that morning. Though I knew Cal's fury was fueled by concern for my safety, at the moment, I couldn't deal with his irate scolding.

Finally, Bart rubbed his forehead and sighed, an annoyed expression pinching his features. "Look, Cal. Yelling at me isn't gonna help. Besides, if you feel as bad as you sound, you need to be using your energy to get well."

A young woman in a dangerously short denim skirt and purple cowboy boots set two brand-emblazoned mugs of steaming coffee on the table. I dragged one closer and wrapped my hands around it to soak up the heat. Though the sun's early morning rays shone in through the windows, my body felt like a frozen rump roast that refuses to thaw.

"Yeah. Uh-huh. We spent several hours at the sheriff's office last evening. You could talk with him or have him send you a copy of the report." Bart poured half a pitcher of heavy cream into his coffee, then stirred it. "We're eating breakfast. I expect we'll hear from the sheriff soon. Then we'll take off. Should be home before dark."

He took a fat-laden gulp from his mug. I eyed my coffee, my stomach churning. The air, infused with breakfast smells and the up-close whiff of caffeine, was unsettling. The previous night, I'd taken one of the pills left over from the Fourth of July fiasco. Thanks to it, I'd slept deeply through the night. But this morning I'd awakened to a murky brain and a body that felt like it'd sprinted to the top of Mt. Hood in lead boots.

"They're still going over her car. It's going to need quite a bit of work before it'll be drivable, so we have a rental."

I touched the band-aid covering the bullet graze on my forehead and studied Bart. I had to admit that he was being a real peach, all gentlemanly kindness—annoyingly so.

My mind slid back to the previous night, to the motel room we'd shared. I'd dragged myself through a quick, hot shower and emerged shivering, barely able to plod the few feet to my bed.

Bart's eyes had left the weather report to study me. "You have any of those pills with you?" he'd asked.

The sight of his masculine body stretched out on the other bed, remote in hand, had awakened those persistent butterflies. Evidently, sleep and the weather were the only things on his mind. "Enough for both of us," I'd informed him.

"I'm fine. It's you I'm worried about. You need a good night's sleep," he'd said with fatherly concern before his focus had returned to the sleek redhead posed in front of a map smattered with smiling balls of sunshine.

Rather than lie awake tormenting myself with the many reasons I'd rather be sharing Bart's bed, I'd swallowed the happy pill and slipped into a dreamless sleep.

I blinked hard, drawing myself back to the diner and the quandary posed by the too-intriguing man who sat across from me. *You asked for it,* I told myself. So why this painful longing that stabbed me every time I looked across the table?

As if he read my thoughts, our eyes met. "No, neither of us saw who was driving the truck," he told Cal. "It was raining so hard it was difficult to see out the windows."

His eyes suddenly narrowed and focused on me with an intensity that made me shudder. "Yeah . . . hmmm . . . you're sure?" Then he was silent, watchful.

A mountain of food materialized in front of Bart—biscuits slathered with creamy gravy, two sunny-side-up eggs, hash browns, and a stack of heavily buttered toast. The odor of grease drifted across the table, and my stomach heaved.

"Yeah, I'll do it. Gotta go. Food's here." Bart had the look of Annabelle when she sighted a tuna can. "Yeah. Okay. Bye." He dropped his phone and sighed deeply.

The waitress set a bowl of tri-colored melon in front of me. "I need to look through the museum before we head back," I informed Bart. Since the previous day's bumper car episode, the need to discover what was going on had become an all-consuming fire that burned within me. This trip and the risk that it entailed would *not* be a lost cause.

"Are you sure you're feeling up to that?" he asked before he forked an ample bite of hash browns into his mouth and chewed.

I nodded slowly. "It's why I'm here. There has to be a reason my mother and her Grandpa Jim and then Levina kept coming over here to eastern Oregon. I know there's a clue here somewhere."

His eyebrows rose, but he didn't press me to elaborate. Instead, he enthusiastically shoveled food into his mouth while I nibbled indifferently on my melon.

"So you told Milton you planned to drive over here. Anyone else?" he asked during a shoveling break.

"No. Who told you?"

"Sophie." He paused, surely contemplating the faint possibility that Sophie might harbor a morsel of information and not pass it on through her gossip network, before he added, "When did you tell Milton?"

"Day before yesterday, early evening. He was working in my roses. I asked him to watch after Annabelle. I should've asked him to keep it to himself."

Bart gulped coffee, thinking. "We need to figure out who followed us over here. Cal sounds like hell, but he's gonna try to do some detective work from home and check out alibis. Hopefully, we'll soon know who doesn't have one."

I forked a morsel of cantaloupe into my mouth and considered the two remaining suspects after the Fourth of July shootout—Jack and Roy. There had been a Bernice sighting in the restroom, so she was off the hook. Neither Jack nor Roy seemed to be very likely murderers. I had to be missing something; what?

Before I could pose the question to Bart, he tossed a grenade my way. "They arrested your cousin Roy this morning."

"Roy!" I gasped, nearly choking on my melon. "Why?"

"Looks like he stole those missing books. I gave the titles to Cal, and a couple of them came up for sale recently on Craig's List in New Mexico. Seems Roy had a school chum down there selling them for him. It's our good luck that some cop in Taos is also a Civil War nut. He recognized the titles and notified Cal."

I laid my fork on the table. "Really?" Had Roy resorted to stealing to save the family farm? Was that why Levina hadn't wanted to go to Cal, because she knew Roy was the thief? What if Levina had confronted him? Surely, that wouldn't incite him to murder her, would it?

My mind bounced back to the Civil War reenactment. It was Roy who'd told me where to stand and Roy who'd been shooting from the back of the field, hidden in the trees. Had he rifled my office, too? And taken the missing clock and lamp and only God knew what else? And the desk set he'd been willed, did he pilfer that, too?

"But why steal a bunch of old, worthless books?" I wondered aloud.

Bart blinked several times and snorted. "Those *old books* are worth tens of thousands of dollars."

I felt my eyes pop. "You've got to be. . . ."

A hefty fiftyish man wearing a patch-laden khaki shirt plopped down at our table, drawing our attention. He pulled the cap from his head and dropped it into his lap.

A cup of steaming coffee landed in front of him. "You want breakfast, too, Sheriff?" the waitress asked.

"Just coffee. Thanks, Kelly." He eyed Bart and me and murmured, "Mornin'," before he chugged a healthy slug of steaming java.

We returned his greeting while Kelly topped off Bart's coffee. I hadn't yet touched mine. Still, I could feel my heart racing as if I'd main-lined a couple of gallons of caffeine.

His focus turned to me. "How're you doin' this mornin'?"

My eyes drifted around the dining room while I mulled over his question. A small group of leather-clad men, most likely bikers, was clustered around two corner tables. A cotton-head couple lingered over their coffee. At the table next to them, three scruffy cowboys devoured stacks of flapjacks and bacon. A rainbow assortment of hunched backs clung like over-sized lichens to the counter that stretched along one wall.

They all looked so content and carefree. A deep ache filled me, an intense desire to join them. I pressed on my abdomen, a futile attempt to ease the pain, then met Sheriff Mullin's aloof gaze and shrugged. "Is there any new information?" I asked, determined to move on to solving my problems.

He shook his head. "Not much. We found the truck and are processin' it. An employee reported it stolen yesterday afternoon from the Safeway parkin' lot over in Burns. It was ditched up off Canyon Creek Lane, not far from the bottom of that hill where you were nearly ran off the road. The front of it's pretty beat up. No blood inside that we could see."

My heart did a fluttering flip-flop. "So there are two of them," I murmured, mostly to move my own mind over to that new train of thought.

"Two of them?" Sheriff Mullin looked puzzled.

"Yes, someone had to pick up the person driving the truck." Surely, the sheriff had already considered that glaring detail. Evidently, he was considering it now, his mug poised midair and a pensive look on his face. "Right?" I prodded.

"I suppose so," he mumbled. "Unless he hitched a ride back to Burns. If he did, he's a stupid son-of-a-bitch."

"He's been too careful to blow it now. There has to be two of them," I assured him and myself as I rubbed at the pain above my right eye and added suspects back onto my list. Just like that, I was back at home plate. Unless, of course, Roy was a thief *and* a murderer.

Bart's voice broke into my thoughts. "Any news on that car that passed us?"

Sheriff Mullin shook his head. "Not yet. With luck, someone going up the grade will remember passin' you and will call in. There's a chance someone might've seen the driver in the Safeway parkin' lot or ditchin' the truck, too." He gulped some coffee. "It's early. We'll probably know more later today. You gonna stick around?"

"No," Bart informed him. "Kit wants to take a run through the museum in Canyon City. Then we'll take off."

The sheriff nodded. "I'll give you a call if. . . ." Musical notes blasted from the folds of his clothing—some honky-tonk, twangy tune. I nearly bounced out of my chair, my heart banging away in my chest.

He eyed the face of his phone and flicked the noise off. "I gotta take this," he muttered, pushing himself to his feet. "Let me know if you remember anything else." With that, he moseyed off, cell smashed to his ear.

"Interesting guy," Bart muttered before he turned his attention to his dwindling mound of cholesterol.

Interesting wasn't quite the word I'd have used to describe him. The prospect of Sheriff Mullin, or Cal, unearthing my would-be murderer had dwindled to a nearly imperceptible blip on my confidence meter. If it was going to happen, it was definitely up to me.

I sighed deeply. "Are you nearly through torturing your body? We have a murder to solve, hopefully, before it happens."

☼☼☼

Elsie's white-capped head emerged from a file drawer at the Grant County Historical Museum. "Found it!" she announced. She held up a bulging file and marched toward me as if she'd just won the pie bake-off at the local county fair.

My heart quickened. Would that file clutched in Elsie's frail arms provide some answers? If not it, then surely we would come across a clue or two somewhere in this museum. After all, back in its heyday, Canyon City had been a mining hub. Clinging to the banks of Canyon Creek and the steep slopes that bordered the stream, what was left of the once-thriving town now appeared to be struggling to hold on.

Elsie plopped the file onto the counter, her hand resting on top of it as if it contained a secret map to the cache of gold. "You're welcome to look through it right here. I can make copies of whatever you're interested in—ten cents a page."

"Thank you," I murmured as she slid the file across the worn oak surface. I opened it and flipped through several newspaper articles, a series of Xeroxed articles from books and magazines, and a lengthy hand-scrawled document written by a man named Lawrence Roba, all related to the long lost Blue Bucket nuggets. It would have to wait. "I'd like a copy of the whole file, please," I told her.

Her mouth twitched a bit, then settled into a forced smile. "It'll take awhile."

"That's fine. We're going to look through the museum," I assured her. My eyes strayed over to where Bart was perusing a display of rocks and minerals, then returned to Elsie. "Do you have any other information on the Blue Bucket?"

She took some time to mull over my request. "Not that I can think of. It's mentioned here and there in the museum and in many of our books and pamphlets but nothing that speaks specifically about it. You might try searching for a copy of *The Terrible Trail*. It's one of the best sources of information on it. Even has a list of the people who were on the wagon train." A puzzled expression creased her already wrinkled features. "If you don't mind me asking, why are you so interested in the Blue Bucket?"

I sighed. If I gave her the full explanation, Bart and I would never get out of here. "It's my great-great-grandfather James Wallace," I told her. "Family legend claims he was one of the young men on the wagon train who found the gold."

"James Wallace, you say?" Sparks of interest glittered in her eyes. "Are you any relation to Levina Johnson?"

Fearful that my legs would crumble, I grabbed the counter. "She's my aunt."

"Oh, good. Could you get a message to her? The phone number she gave me's been disconnected. She requested some testing on one of our paintings, and I have the results." She paused and worked her lips a bit, her face taking on a rosy glow. "It's a matter of payment . . . to cover the cost. I can't mail her the information until that's taken care of."

I swallowed through the steel fingers circling my neck and hoped I appeared much calmer than I felt. "I'm afraid Aunt Levina has passed on." Hopefully, she would think my strangled voice was grief speaking.

"Oh, I'm *so* sorry," she murmured, patting my hand. "It must've been recent?"

"Yes . . . and sudden," I informed her. No need to delve into details. "Uh . . . do you by any chance remember the date of her request?"

"No, but we record all our correspondence. I'll take a look-see." She made her way to a massive oak desk, then pulled a spiral-bound notebook from between two brass bookends and thumbed through it page-by-page.

"Unfenced is much more earth friendly. All of those prickly wire fences chopping up the land. It's just not right," a nearby female voice claimed.

I turned to see a young couple emerge from the museum innards, hands entwined. He was cowboy down to the wide-brimmed hat and saucer-sized silver belt buckle. She, more go-green-metro than country.

"If you want to look through the museum, we should probably get started," Bart murmured in my ear.

I glanced up at him. "I'm almost ready. Elsie's checking on something for me."

In fact, Elsie was shuffling toward us. "Thank you for visiting us," she yelled to the young couple as the door shut behind them. "April twenty-sixth," she announced triumphantly, sticking a yellow note with that date to the counter.

April twenty-sixth—the day Levina was murdered! There had to be a connection. I mentally sloughed through a quagmire of times, names, and events. "Do you know what time she called in the request?" I spluttered.

"Oh, yes. I took her call. It was late afternoon, probably around four."

Which would've been after she'd rushed out of Meg's coffee shop and, most likely, after she'd spoken on the phone with Bernice. But before she'd questioned Milton about his ancestors. "She wanted you to do something with a painting?" I probed.

Elsie sighed deeply, her white brows furled. "I suppose it's okay to tell you. I mean, she is dead. And someone's going to have to pay the balance on the expenses."

Bart's questioning eyes searched mine. "I'll cover the costs," I assured Elsie.

"Well, okay then," she murmured hesitantly. "It was the Brenning painting . . . of Lukas Brenning and his wife and son. It's our most famous painting, but not so much because of the painting itself. It's the story that goes with it."

I nodded, too excited to speak.

She stared at Bart as if he might already know the legendary tale. Frowning, he shook his head slowly, then prodded, "Sounds like a story worth telling."

"Movie worthy," Elsie proudly claimed. "The Brenning ranch was one of the first in this area. It was northwest of here, on the John Day River. Lukas Brenning was one of the wealthiest men around even after gold mining was in full steam. But he was not a very nice person—downright mean at times. As it turned out, he was also a crook."

She paused, her brows arched high, and studied us closely. "Well, he had a wife and rumor had it he didn't treat her very well. She was a little mouse of a woman—pretty but meek. One day she and their son just disappeared. Lukas didn't seem upset about it, which made people wonder if he'd gotten rid of them. Then he disappeared, too . . . along with a fortune in gold."

"What gold?" Bart asked before I got the words out.

"The bank's gold." Elsie turned abruptly to two middle-aged women who stood behind us. I'd been so engrossed in her story that I hadn't heard them enter. "If you'd like to look through the museum, we suggest a donation of three dollars. You can stick it in that box and sign your names in the register," she told them, barely missing a beat.

In the next second, her focus had returned to us. "Well, technically, it was the miners' gold. In those days, it was so wild here in Canyon City that the local bank wasn't a safe place to keep anything valuable. In the fall of 1871, Lukas took a bunch of his cattle over to sell in Oregon City. He had several of his men with him to help drive the herd, so some to the miners hired him to transport their gold to the bank there."

I scrambled to piece a mental timeline together. *Later,* I told myself. "And his wife and son disappeared before that trip?"

"Oh, yes, that happened several weeks before Lukas disappeared." Elsie stared hard at us as if to confirm that we understood the implications in those words. "One night, while he was *supposedly* away, the ranch house burned. Everyone assumed his wife and child were killed in the fire, but they didn't find any human remains in the ashes."

A vision formed before me of a woman and small child standing in front of a burning house, vibrant blue flames curling into the night sky. I rested my forearms on the counter for support and struggled to breathe evenly. "Did they ever figure out what happened to them?"

"No. Then Lukas disappeared, too, with all that gold *and* the money from the sale of his cattle. Well, they figured he'd planned the whole thing out ahead of time and escaped free and clear." Elsie shrugged her bowed shoulders. "Whether he got rid of his wife and son the night of the fire or met up with them later is still a hot topic for debate."

I was fairly certain his wife and child hadn't been killed in the fire, and I had a painting in storage to prove it. Had James Wallace actually been there that night?

Bart's voice broke into my frantic deliberations. "You said you have a painting of Brenning with his wife and child?"

"Oh, yes," Elsie chirped. "Let's go in the back and you can have a look-see." She grabbed the Blue Bucket file and dropped it onto the desktop before she turned to lead the way.

Though anticipation buzzed through me like a hot wire, my body felt like a flopped soufflé—weak and sagging. Fortunately, Elsie wasn't all that spry. I pushed myself up off the counter and trudged past an extensive exhibit on gold mining and another that dealt with cattle ranching. A display of barbed wire fencing caught my eye, most likely the instigator of the earlier exchange between the two young people.

Finally, we entered a smaller room. Elsie stepped to the side, and I came to a standstill, barely aware that Bart bumped into me from behind and clasped my shoulders in his hands to keep me from toppling forward. Thankfully, his hands remained there, supporting me.

"Who painted it?" I whispered, mesmerized by the lifelike images before me. In the photo of my mother and her Grandpa Jim, they had appeared grainy and out of focus. In reality, the three people depicted took on a life of their own. And the woman and young boy were all too familiar—Milton's great-grandmother and grandfather.

"Well, that's rather interesting." Elsie pointed to the lower right corner. "As you can see, the painting isn't signed. But your aunt was convinced that this James Wallace, her ancestor, painted it. She thought someone had painted over his signature."

I had to agree with Levina. Though not one of his *blue* paintings, it had to have been painted by Wallace. Why were this woman and boy so important to him, important enough to merit three separate portraits, perhaps four?

"To be quite truthful, I thought your aunt was a bit off her rocker," Elsie admitted. "But she was willing to pay quite a sum of money to have it checked out. The Board agreed, so we sent it off to be examined by a professional. Got it back last week."

Elsie scrutinized the painting. "Well, it turned out that several things in the original painting were painted out. And your aunt was right; it was signed by James Wallace."

"What else was painted over?" I asked.

Elsie touched a shaky finger to the neck of the woman in the portrait. "Right here, Lukas' wife wore a lovely brooch. As you can see, a cameo is there now."

I stepped forward to get a closer look, and Bart's fingers drifted down my back. The woman in the picture—certainly, Milton's great-grandmother—was as somber as in her other two portraits.

Elsie was right; she was beautiful, even with that hopeless aura. If, indeed, she did suffer mistreatment at the hands of her husband, the woman surely had cause to be disillusioned. Still, she had the darling little boy to provide daily blessings in a life otherwise riddled by abuse and despair. His mother wore a glossy black skirt and a high-necked white blouse. A large tan cameo clung to the lace at her neck.

An image of another brooch formed before me, this one on that same neck but decidedly different—dazzling diamonds and gold Celtic loops clustered around a large lustrous ruby. Was it the brooch that had been erased from this painting? If so, why?

With a sweep of her hand, Elsie indicated the man. "And one of Lukas' front teeth was silver. You can't. . . ."

"Oh, my God!" I gasped as I stared at the image of the evil-looking man in front of me. His eyes were so hard. His smile, so cold, yet originally made even colder by the glint of a *silver* tooth.

"Are you okay, dear?"

Elsie's voice pulled me around to meet her worried eyes. "I'm fine," I assured her. "Just . . . surprised . . . uh." I paused, fumbling for words. "The brooch; what did it look like?"

"Oh, it was stunning. I don't know why someone would want to cover it up. It had a large red stone in the middle and a bunch of little white stones surrounding it. I'm not sure if they were the real thing or not. And the setting was very unique, Irish or Scottish maybe."

Time seemed to stop as I considered what to do next. Should I tell her that I knew the fate of Lukas Brenning and his wife and child? That they had once lived in Aurora in a house very near and very similar to mine? That someone had crushed Lukas' skull and buried him beneath an oak sapling in my backyard?

Elsie's lips were still moving. All I heard were the pounding of my heart and the question that echoed through my mind: *if Davy and Danny dug up Lukas' body, what happened to the missing gold?*

CHAPTER 18

Cal clutched his stomach as if he were contemplating another dash from the deck.

I scooted my patio chair back as far from his germs as I could get. Any farther and I would be crashing through the cedar rail to roll downhill and splash into the dirty Pudding River. I eyed Bart. He didn't seem enamored by the prospect of a bout of stomach flu either. Fortunately, we were outside in the cool evening air where hostile micro bugs could drift off. Crickets droned, frogs crooned, and darkness pressed into the flickering glow provided by a couple of pungent citronella candles.

"You okay, hon?" Patty, all waxy skin and bed hair, asked from her chair beside Cal.

Cal rubbed his pale forehead and swallowed hard. "Yeah, I should've skipped the soup. This goddamn bug! It couldn't have picked a worse time to bite me." Sighing deeply, he focused his frustration on me. "If you'd do what you're supposed to, none of this would've happened!"

I wanted to say that if he did what he was supposed to, I wouldn't be putting my life in danger trying to save it. But I was too darned exhausted. All I wanted was my bed. As soon as I was through debriefing Cal, that's where I'd be.

That morning Bart and I had hung out with Elsie for a couple of hours. What a gem! She'd helped us search for information on Lukas Brenning and his wife and son and had made us copies of that material and the Blue Bucket file. She'd also given us photos of the work done on the James Wallace painting, ones that revealed the artist's signature, the silver tooth, and the Celtic brooch. Nearly floored by the price tag attached to a few x-rays, I'd steeled myself and written a hefty check to cover the unpaid expenses.

Now those photographs sat on the glass-topped patio table that kept me a safe distance from Cal's wrath. And Patty? She was doing weird things with her eyes and mouth, begging me to be understanding of her man's petulance. I felt my eyes roll up and drift off towards the buzz of an insect hovering in the darkness.

"You're convinced this Lukas Brenning is the man we dug up

in your backyard?"

Cal's voice pulled me back. I sighed. Bart and I had hashed this out so many times on the long drive home from Canyon City that afternoon that I was ready to click it into my mental trashcan, then empty the garbage. "Yes, the woman and boy in Milton's *and* Meg's paintings are definitely the same as those in the painting in the museum. Besides, the presence of that brooch and the fact that James Wallace painted all three pictures solidifies that fact. And both Lukas Brenning and the skull Danny and Davy found had a silver tooth in exactly the same place."

I didn't mention my blue painting of the fire. If Cal couldn't piece together something blatantly obvious, sharing my suspicions that James Wallace had also painted Milton's ancestors standing in front of their burning house would only complicate things. *Later*, I promised myself, *when he could view my painting first-hand.*

I took a sustaining breath and plodded on. "I'd bet a good night's sleep that Wallace painted out that brooch, the silver tooth, and his signature to get rid of some of the connections between the woman and child living near him and Lukas' wife and child. And if someone did discover Lukas' body years later, it wouldn't be tied to the man who'd absconded with the Canyon City miners' gold."

Cal gnawed on his mustache, then huffed. "Well, it'll be up to the experts to sort it out. I doubt they'll get any DNA off that skeleton. And we still don't know why someone whacked him on the head and split his skull open. Given the time frame, the fact that he's buried in your backyard might not be a big deal. But no coffin stinks of murder."

I nodded and glanced toward Bart with what I hoped looked like a plea for reinforcements. The hazy light accentuated the dark smudges under his eyes and the worry lining his face. Clearly, he was as wasted as I.

"Lukas Brenning and his wife and child disappeared in the fall of 1871," he began, his voice deep and smooth as warm chocolate, an invitation to settle in and listen. "Two weeks before Lukas vanished, his house on the John Day River burned to the ground. His wife and child were never seen again. Rumor had it that Lukas was *not* a loving husband and, in fact, could be quite a mean son-of-a-bitch. He claimed to be away on business the night of the fire.

"Keep in mind that this is a passed-down tale, most likely, based on facts, but we don't know how much of it is the honest-to-God truth." He leaned forward to rest his elbows on his thighs. "As the story goes, Lukas and several of his cowhands were driving cattle over here to Oregon City to sell them. Some Canyon City miners recruited him to take a hefty amount of their gold along to deposit it in the bank. After he sold his cattle, he disappeared with the gold and the money from the livestock sale and was never seen again."

Noises from the river below reached up to grab our attention momentarily—the excited garble of kids' voices and the splash of rocks hitting the water.

Cal turned back to Bart. "Is that it?"

Bart glanced at me and his face softened. "Kit thinks Lukas' wife burned down their house while Lukas was away to escape from him. Wallace painted several pictures of her with her son, so he obviously knew them and was aware of Lukas' rumored abuse. It would make sense that he might harbor them here in Aurora. Lukas must've figured out where they were and come after them. There was probably an altercation and Lukas ended up dead."

"And the gold?" Patty asked.

"Maybe it paid for the house Wallace built, the one Kit lives in now," Bart told her.

"And Milton's," I interjected.

"What d'ya mean, *Milton's*?" Cal snapped. Deep furrows burrowed into his forehead. In the candlelight, they looked like someone had penned them on with a thick black Sharpie.

I sighed in resignation and dove back into the conversation. "His floor plan is the same as mine. Milton's great-grandmother— Lukas' wife—lived in Milton's house. James Wallace lived in mine until he died in 1875." I gave him time to think it through, children's laughter wafting into the silence. He still looked puzzled. "James Wallace built *two* houses."

"Huh. I'd never noticed that . . . about Milton's house," Cal mused.

"And the miners' gold is how he paid for them, not the Blue Bucket gold," I added.

Silence settled in around us as kid sounds became an indistinct blip in the distance. Bart sank back into his chair, stretching his muscular legs out in front of him and sidetracking my attention momentarily. Cal rubbed his stomach distractedly while Patty gazed at him, concern oozing from her pasty face. I studied them, the teacher in me wishing I had a whiteboard and multi-colored dry erase pens to web the whole scenario.

The tinny whine of a renegade mosquito invaded our Citronella zone, drawing our searching eyes. Four tense seconds later, Bart nailed the beastie with a quick slap on his forearm. "You've got to admit it, Cal. In some screwball way, it all makes sense," he said.

At the moment, Cal looked more interested in holding onto his soup than sorting through a pile of clues. Still, my life was on the line here so I pressed on. "Yes, it does. And I think Levina figured it out, too, on the day she was killed."

Patty glanced at Cal, then frowned and asked, "What makes you think that?"

I sent her a silent *thank you* and proceeded to verbally map Levina's last day. "Because that's the day she called the museum and requested that they have the Brenning painting examined. Elsie claims she spoke with Levina around four o'clock."

Before I continued, I gave them time to cement that fact firmly in their minds. "Remember what Meg told us, Cal?" I prodded, hoping to distract him from his churning innards. "About how earlier that day, Levina had seemed distracted and had stared at the paintings on the coffee shop wall. Then Levina took off without paying her bill."

Cal pursed his lips and nodded.

"Well, later that afternoon, Levina spoke with Bernice on the phone. She quizzed Bernice about Milton's ancestors, and she told Bernice that she'd found the *key* to the gold."

Okay. I'd gotten through the second important item in a string of events, all of them connected to a motive for Levina's murder . . . and perhaps mine, too. Even Cal seemed to be processing the information.

"Then that evening, Levina had dinner with Milton. Milton said she seemed overly excited and that she'd grilled him about his ancestors."

"And that night she was murdered?" Cal voiced though it seemed more like he was mulling it over than wanting an answer.

"Yes," I confirmed. "And there's something else that might play into this: when Levina spoke with Bernice that day, she told Bernice she was planning to leave the house and store to me in a new will."

A flicker sparked in Cal's drooping eyes. "How do you know that?" he asked.

"Bernice told me."

He leaned forward, his forearms on the table. "So Bernice knew all along you were Levina's heir?" he growled.

I shrugged. "Evidently, Levina didn't mention that she'd already changed her will. Bernice claims she didn't think Levina would follow through and actually do it. Still, it could be a motive for her murder. That or greed for something else."

"Like what?" Cal snapped.

Cripes! Did I have to do a dot-to-dot for him? I turned to Bart for support. He was examining his arm. How many times had I gone over this with him in the museum and the car, even over a second greasy burger-and-fries chow-down? And now he was too busy itching an insect bite to assist me.

I scrambled to piece it together in my mind. "Let's say they—

and I say *they* because there had to be at least two people involved in the latest attempt on my life—believed that Levina had found the Blue Bucket gold or, at least, the key to it." Personally, I'd reached the conclusion that James Wallace hadn't found the Blue Bucket gold—perhaps hadn't even searched for it—but that was beside the point.

After a fortifying breath, I continued. "So they confronted Levina and tried to get information about that key from her. Maybe they cleared the EpiPens from her house, then spiked her sherry with strawberries and refused to give her any relief until she told them where the gold was. Maybe she led them to her office, hoping the EpiPen was still in the desk drawer. Though, most likely, they planned to kill her all along." I paused, then thought to add. "Whatever the case, they didn't get what they were after."

Cal nodded slowly, munching on his mustache, lost in thought. Finally, he sighed. "No, they're still after somethin'."

So he *was* with me. "Right. If they want my inheritance, then the murderers are those who will inherit it once I'm dead. And if they want the gold, they're probably whoever will inherit the house once I'm dead. Or, at least, whoever will have access to it." Whichever was the case, guilt pointed its ugly finger at my newfound relatives. I rubbed the prickly shivers from my arms and trudged toward the finish line. "Someone broke into my house to search it so whatever they're looking for must still be there."

Silence settled into our intimate sphere of light. As my eyes crept from face-to-face, I could almost hear the neurons synapsing.

Patty spoke first. "Any idea what they might be looking for?"

I'd given that question a lot of thought. "Maybe the gold but most likely, that key Levina—and my mother—mentioned. And no, I don't know what, or where, exactly it is." But I did have an idea of where I might look for answers. "I can't get my mind off those strange James Wallace paintings. I have a feeling he left some kind of clue in them."

Cal's mind was plodding down a different trail. "I guess we better find out what happens to Levina's stuff if you die, huh?" he posed.

I felt my mouth drop. He didn't know? "Bernice and her two kids and Jack all inherit if I die. The estate will be divided evenly between the four of them." Cripes! Did I have to do everything for him?

He must've read my mind. When he spoke, it seemed more to conciliate than to inform. "I've had Josh out talkin' with your relatives to see who has alibis for yesterday and who doesn't. He hasn't checked back in; probably will in the mornin'.

"My money's on your cousin Roy. He wasn't arrested until

this mornin', and his actions on the Fourth are kind of fishy. Could be, Levina caught him stealin' things from her house, so he killed her. If he stole from his aunt for money, he might be willin' to kill for it, too. By the way, he made bail this afternoon, so steer clear of him.

"Accordin' to Milton, Sophie spent the day harassin' him. Sophie's take on it was somethin' I'd rather forget than discuss. Whatever the case, those two are off the hook."

No surprise there. I couldn't picture either Sophie or Milton plotting a successful murder. Besides, except for the obvious fact that Sophie wanted Levina's man, she had no motive. As for Milton, it was to his advantage to keep Levina alive and Sophie at a lustful distance. And Roy; he might be a thief, but I was secretly hoping he wasn't a killer.

"Oh, by the way, Sophie lived up to her reputation; she made sure the whole town—except for me, of course—knew you were headin' over to eastern Oregon." Cal's eyes turned into two piercing metal bullets before he continued. "Please tell me you're gonna stay the hell locked in your house now."

"That's it!" Patty interjected. "I remember." She looked like she was about to pop, her eyes sparkling. "It was all of the talk about keys and locks. Finally, my well-aged brain coughed up an answer."

Which was about as clear as sludge. "What are you talking about?" I prodded.

"You remember when I told you I'd seen your cousin Janet somewhere before?"

My stomach muscles contracted. "Yeah."

"Well, you're not gonna believe where; it was at Hazelnut Grove."

My limbs melted. A zillion thoughts zinged through my mind—a brain jam.

"It gets even better," she promised. I waited; Patty loved drama. "It was late. Even Louise had gone home, so I was surprised when I found the office door unlocked. I went inside and nearly peed my undies.

"Your cousin Janet walked out of Ronny's office carrying that ridiculous green and yellow jacket he wears. I was geared up to give her the third degree as soon as she finished locking *his* door. But she gave me a condescending glare and strode out of there like she was Ms. Doreen S&M herself."

Deep within, unsettling alarms sounded. That didn't sound like the shaky demeanor I'd witnessed in my dear cousin. "Are you sure it was Janet? In Walker's office?"

"Positive. But she was more confident, not the crumbling cracker she is now."

"When was that?" I prodded.

She sighed. "Early last school year. Ronny was wearing that ridiculous jacket, so it had to be football season."

My world shifted even more off-kilter, and something slimy slithered around in my belly. Janet and Walker had known each other months before Levina's death, evidently well enough that he'd given her access to his highly revered office and his tacky Duck jacket. Weird, that's what it was.

"Quite a coincidence, don't you think?" Patty prodded, her eyes shifting to Cal.

"Seems a stretch . . . just like a lotta things involvin' Kit," Cal grumbled. "But a lotta folks around here know Ronny Walker, includin' Levina. He and Janet both spent time here as kids, so it makes sense they might know each other."

His steely gaze fastened on me. "Until I check it out, you keep the two of them out of your life. Go home, get some sleep, lock your doors, and don't open them for anyone."

Slivers of fear sliced through me. "I will . . . er. I won't. Whatever. I promise to stay safely locked inside my house," I assured him.

But would locked doors and windows and a security system be enough to stop a desperate murderer? In Levina's case, it hadn't.

☼☼☼

Cerulean flames licked high into the night sky, illuminating the woman and young child, stark silhouettes against the vibrant blaze consuming their home. Enthralled, I stepped forward to examine the picture more closely. It only confirmed my earlier suspicions: the woman and child had to be Lukas Brenning's wife and son, which would mean that James Wallace must've been madly painting somewhere outside the scene portrayed in his brushstrokes.

It didn't make sense, though. Why depict the incident on canvas? Not only would it tie him to the fire, but it would also document his relationship with Lukas' wife and child—who also happened to be Milton's ancestors? And why the bright blue flames?

My eyes slid to the second painting in the dining room—Jack's painting of the nest filled with robin eggs. Or what I assumed were robin eggs. But if the eggs didn't belong to a robin, why paint them blue?

The rapid clomp of heavy feet hitting wooden steps pounded into the stillness, and I placed my hand over my pounding heart. "Cripes. It's only Bart," I whispered in an effort to calm my hypersensitive nerves. Evidently, he'd reached the basement.

I'd been back in my house less than twenty minutes, and already I was jumping at every squeak and creak, most of which were caused by Bart's meticulous search. He'd insisted on a rummage through the entire house.

I breathed deeply as I plodded across the hall to the office. From the wall, a covered wagon pulled by blue-yoke-toting oxen posed on a sagebrush backdrop. Weathered gray buckets hung from its sides. If the passed-down stories were true, those buckets were actually blue. So why paint the wooden yoke blue but not the buckets?

There were five paintings, with one blue item in each of them, at least four of which would've been more realistic painted in another color—not blue: Bernice's roses, Meg's muddy Pudding River, Levina's oxen yoke, my mother's flames, and Jack's eggs. So why that brilliant shade of blue? Was it to represent the blue buckets the young people had carried when they found the gold?

An image of the ornate mantle formed before me—another puzzle. Carved meticulously and beautifully, it was blatantly out of place in a house the size of this one.

"What were you trying to tell us, Great-great-granddaddy?" I murmured as I struggled to piece dates together in my mind. Bart had said that Wallace died suddenly in 1875, probably somewhere close to age forty-five. Lukas Brenning and his wife and child had disappeared in the fall of 1871. That left James Wallace four years before his death to build both my house and the house Milton now lived in and to create the mantle.

I turned from the painting and ambled to where the massive fireplace stood in all its majestic glory. Dark shadows created deep crevices and knolls in the mantle's wooden surface, magnifying the graphic reminders of Oregon's past: wagons crossing the flat, dry stretches in the central and eastern portion of the state, an area from which I'd returned only hours ago. Log rafts on the mighty Columbia maneuvering their way through a deep gorge. Makeshift towns sprouting up along the meandering Willamette River.

My eyes locked on the ferry owned by Boone descendants and traced a route southeast to Aurora. There were the two houses— Milton's and mine—and the cross that was most likely a later addition. No stone had marked Lukas Brenning's grave. Was that why Wallace had added that tiny cross to the mantle, to memorialize Lukas' murder and final resting place?

I thought of the painting on Meg's wall, the one of Milton's great-grandmother and grandfather sitting in front of a newly planted sapling in what was now my backyard. I'd commented to Meg that dressed from head to toe in black and with faces filled with grief, they appeared to be mourning the loss of a loved one. Was that why they'd planted the sapling, to hide Lukas' grave? Of course, that same sapling had grown into the mighty oak that had finally fallen to disclose his remains. Mesmerized by the tiny cross, I dropped my cell phone on the mantle shelf and leaned down to get a closer look.

"Damn, Kit, you might want to consider spending some time down in your basement reclaiming it from all the six and eight-legged-wonders. Careful though; I don't think they'll give it up without a fight."

An adrenalin rush shot through me, and I twirled on one leg, nearly losing my balance. Bart brushed at his face and Hawaiian print shirt, frowning.

"I hate creepy-crawlies," I informed him. "I haven't ventured down there yet."

He raked fingers through his goatee, then ruffled his hair into an appealingly disheveled mess. When he spoke, his eyes were brimming with concern. "Well, I've checked the whole house. Now I'm gonna pull a Cal and make you promise me you'll keep your doors and windows locked and the alarm on."

With those words, tendrils of fear slithered along my bones and nested in my stomach. Bart was going to leave, and I would be here alone, just Annabelle and me. Only Annabelle wasn't here. Milton must've taken her in for the night. I shivered and rubbed at the goose bumps on my arms. "No problem. I'm so tired I could sleep through an earthquake."

"Yeah. Me, too. But I'm gonna lie awake all night worrying about you. I'd feel a whole lot better if you'd let me stay here?'

The look in his eyes spoke of things other than sleep. No doubt about it, if he stayed, we'd end up in the same bed, and I'd definitely be unable to focus on hunting a killer. No, I needed a clear head and some time alone to examine what I'd learned during the last two days. I was close to an answer; like an annoying itch between my shoulder blades, I could feel its pestering.

I also needed some time to think through what was going on between Bart and me before I made a decision to step from the pot into what was sure to be a sizzling hot fire.

"I appreciate your concern," I told him. "But it's not your job to keep me safe. It's mine. And Cal's . . . whatever that's worth." Before he could retort, I turned away and hustled down the hall toward the front door.

His hand reached out and pushed the door shut before I got it completely open. Pressed between his warm body and the cool wood, I closed my eyes and fought an overwhelming desire to turn and burrow into the comfort he offered.

Wisps of air tickled my right ear. "I don't want anything to happen to you," he murmured, his voice warm velvet.

His hands on my shoulders, he turned me and drew me in. I wrapped my arms around him and snuggled close against soft cotton, conscious of the hardness beneath it. Gentle kisses ruffled the hair on top of my head. A slow, languorous meltdown flowed through my limbs and into my center. Bart's arms kept me from slithering to the floor.

He loosened his hold, lifted my chin and studied me with an intensity that sent spirals of pleasure twirling through me. "I want to be with you," he sighed before his lips caressed mine with whispery kisses.

For long moments, I savored the feelings that claimed my body. I savored Bart's comforting strength and the thrill that came with believing he cared about me. I savored my warm, dreamy state—the tingles skittering along my nerve endings and the blood pounding through my veins. And I savored the joy of life.

Only I *wouldn't* be enjoying life if I didn't track down a killer, and soon. That little brainwave jolted me back to the reality of my present situation. At the moment, savoring anything except the fact that I was still alive was a luxury I couldn't afford.

I filled my lungs, braced myself, and pushed away from him before I looked into his concerned eyes. "I'm sorry but I can't do this right now. I need to be able to think clearly. I can't do that when I'm with you."

"Let me help you."

His beseeching look nearly crumbled my resolve. "You have helped me . . . a lot. Good grief, you've saved my life at least twice." I steeled myself, slid my hands from his, and opened the door. "And right now the best way you can help me is to leave. I know the answers to what's going on are whirling around in my brain, but when I'm this exhausted, it's a struggle to formulate a coherent thought, let alone sort this mess out. I need a clear head. I need *sleep.*"

He stood like a sentinel, not budging.

"Alone," I added.

A scowl transformed him into the Bart I'd first met. "Glue your cell phone to you, and if anything seems unusual, call me," he ordered.

"I will," I assured him

With a long sigh, Bart passed by me, then turned and said sternly, "Set the alarm and don't open the door for anything . . . or anyone."

I nodded. But as I shut the door, I had an overwhelming feeling that shooing Bart away might have been a fatal mistake.

CHAPTER 19

"*Kitty! Kitty! Kitty!*" My call chirped into the cool darkness, mingling with the not-too-far-off drone of voices and the whisper of Milton's sprinklers. I eyed his house and struggled to squelch the coils of fear twisting in my gut. His back porch light cast a faint amber glow, but not enough to make the shadowed trek across my yard and into his an inviting prospect.

I breathed deeply. The heavy, cloying scent of jasmine and roses enticed me one step farther from my back door. "*Annabelle! Kitty! Kitty!*" I'd given Milton my house key and security code, so Annabelle would have access to her home. Maybe he'd taken her in for the night, so he wouldn't have to mess with the alarm. After all, it'd been after ten o'clock when Bart and I had finally left Cal's house and arrived here.

"*Kitty! Kitty! Kitty!*" I examined the shades of murkiness beyond my back porch one last time. No way was I venturing into that heavily shadowed booby-trap tonight. "Annabelle's with Milton," I told myself firmly. Still, maybe I'd call him to make certain.

My eyes scanned the yard as I shuffled backwards to the door. "*Kitty! Kitty! Ki. . . .*"

A vise encircled my neck. It slammed me back against a rigid shape. Automatically, my hands struggled to pry it loose. I gasped for air. None reached my lungs; an iron clamp gripped my throat. My head swam in a sea of stars. A bitter taste burned in my mouth. I twisted, trying to wiggle free. A steel band circled my waist and held me securely.

"*Kitty, Kitty, Kitty*; you calling yourself?" a mocking voice murmured in my ear.

It stilled my movements, the familiarity triggering recollections. But with the kettle drum pounding in my head, it was difficult to think. A dark cloud closed in around me.

The lock on my neck loosened slightly. A wheezing sound erupted from my mouth. Air filled my lungs. I breathed deeply, savoring the luxury of oxygen. And there was something else—a smell, one that triggered memories.

"You are so predictable, *Kitty*," the derision continued. "And foolish."

With oxygen, came the awareness that I was secured against a man's body, one near my own height. A soft belly pressed into the small of my back. I fought the urge to sneeze.

Walker!

"I knew you'd search for that stupid cat," he hissed. "You and that old man. And he left your door wide open when he went looking, so I guess it was worth messing with the damn beast."

"Annabelle!" It came out a hoarse whimper. A heavy ache settled around my heart. "What did you do with her?"

"She can rot in hell. I've had to deal with her twice now—two times too many."

Twice? "Levina?" I rasped over the throbbing pain in my throat. "It was *you*?"

The muscles in his arms flexed momentarily, pulling me closer. Their strength surprised me. "Damned right."

"Why?" And even more puzzling: why me?

When he spoke, his voice was caustic, a vial of acid spilling into my ear. "That old biddy thought she could take it all away from me. No way in hell I was gonna let that happen. Since I was a kid, I've dreamed of it." He tightened his hold and dragged me backwards several steps. The door clicked. "Damned easy to get rid of her, too. If it wasn't for her nosy neighbors, no one would've known what we did to her."

My mind fastened onto the word *we*. His arm dropped from my waist, and I leaned forward, fighting to get footing, my neck clamped in an iron lock. Patty's recollections drifted through my oxygen-deprived brain. "You and Janet?" I wheezed.

His body stilled, more alert. "What makes you think she's involved?"

"She was in your office . . . at school."

"That useless bitch!" Spit sprayed my cheek, and my stomach roiled. "Can't she do anything right? Well, we're married now, so it doesn't matter who knows. Once I get rid of you, everything's finally gonna fall into place."

"Married? To Janet?" I spluttered. Why would Walker marry my batty cousin?

"Yeah, thanks to you I'm saddled with a screwball. Won't be for long, though." Something sharp pressed into my back. A gun? Icy prickles streaked up my spine to where he kept a leaden grip on my neck. "Now move," he barked before he pushed me ahead of him down the hall.

A few feet from the front door, he paused, flipped on a light, and shoved me inside the dining room. I stumbled over a box bulging with cast iron. "Sit down," he uttered tersely as he jerked my head back and down.

I landed in an oak dining chair. He removed his hand from my neck and yanked at my ponytail. Sharp pain was replaced by cold metal against the back of my skull. Finally able to breathe freely, my mind grasped several alarming thoughts at once: Walker was not just a creep; he was a cold-blooded killer! He'd killed Levina. Getting rid of Janet was also a part of his plan. And I was next on his hit list. But why?

Shivering with the chilling knowledge, I scurried to formulate a way out of my prospective death. "You know . . . you don't need to kill anyone else. Just tell me what you want. I'll help you," I stammered.

His laugh was sinister. "This is all *your* fault. If you'd done what you were supposed to, I wouldn't have had to kill anyone. Instead, you looked down your snooty nose at me like I was a pile of shit you couldn't get off your lily white feet fast enough."

My skin crawled with memories of his grimy touches and disgusting innuendos. "My fault; you're blaming me for the fact that you're a murderer?"

"Sure am, *Kitty*. I did my part; you didn't do yours." The gun barrel slid down to my neck, trailing icy heat. "Levina kept a file on you, you know. When I saw it on her desk, I knew it was meant to be—a niece who wasn't wacko. Her will was there, too, so I knew you'd get her house once Janet was out of the picture—not a problem with someone as whacked out as she is. It was almost too easy, luring you out here with that teaching job. When the old bat figured out what I'd done, she actually thanked me.

"Then she turned on me. Tried to get to the gold before me. I knew she had to go when Janet told me the old biddy'd found the key. Had to get that key first, though."

"You have the key?" I blurted. Was I finally going to find out what, exactly, it was?

He appeared in front of me, the gun barrel staring me in the eyes. Though lacking the false good-guy facade, he was the same old Walker—comb-over now slightly askew, beady snake eyes, over-baked tube tan, and thin lips set in a contemptuous smile.

"You think I'd still be looking for it if I had it?" He gaped at me as if I were a total idiot, what appeared to be a remarkably hefty gun clutched tightly in his right hand, which I noticed was sheathed in a plastic glove and trembling. Leave it to Walker to go overboard on the size of his weapon.

"You know," he continued, "the loony gene must run in your family 'cause there she is facing death if she doesn't cough up some answers, and all she does is ramble on about some dead guy and a fairy. As if some fairy's gonna save her. Damn crazy woman!"

A dead guy and a fairy? The dead guy might be Lukas Brenning. But a fairy? I pictured Levina lying dead at her desk and shivered uncontrollably. If I didn't do something soon, I'd be dead, too.

I studied Walker. He was studying me, too, his chilling eyes narrowed to black pinpricks. Beads of perspiration created a sheen on his carroty face and arms. Although he was huskier and more muscular, we were about the same height. My eyes slid from his shaking gun to the hands clenching in my lap and on down to my bare feet. He was close enough to touch. If I surprised him, could I knock that monster from his hands and escape?

As if he'd read my thoughts, he took a step back. "Uh-uh, Kitty. You don't want to do that. There'd be a lot of blood and it's a bitch to clean up." He smiled his sleazy smile and chortled. "Besides, you're leaving with me. I have plans for the two of us—for later."

Bitter bile rose in my throat at the thought of him touching me. "I'd rather be dead."

"Oh, you will be, soon enough." He chuckled gutturally. "Do you really believe I still want you? Stupid girl. You blew that. You can't treat me like shit and get away with it. First I'm gonna find that key and maybe the gold. *Then* we'll finish what your meddling boyfriend interrupted. Voila! No more Kitty. They'll think the stress was too much for you, and you took off.

"You know, it was fate, you and Levina both being allergic to strawberries. Too easy, actually. There's that canister sitting right there on the counter with *coffee* in big black letters calling to me. Lucky for me: Sophie ringing your doorbell."

A dam had opened; words were flowing from Walker's mouth like water through a floodgate—rushing and surging, fighting to be freed. Eyes wild, gun jabbing erratically, and his voice a high-pitched wail, agitation swelled within him. I stared at him and felt needles prick my skin and the fiery ball of fear inside me burn hotter. Walker wasn't only a murderer; he was honestly and truly insane.

"You were supposed to die, just like your aunt," he fumed, jabbing the gun barrel to within an inch of my forehead. "Well, actually, you were supposed to die before that—run down in the parking lot by an unknown driver. It was dark. Couldn't see you through the rain . . . blah, blah, blah. Poor Kitty."

I pictured those relentless twin orbs, blinding in the darkness and driving rain, hurrying towards me—a foretelling if I'd only listened. So that had been Walker, too.

"Damn bad luck, you getting invited to the reading of that old bat's will. When I saw that letter on Louise's desk, I knew you had to die, too. Killing Levina was supposed to take care of everything. No new will. The house goes to the loony niece. The loony niece belongs to me. Soon she's out of the picture, and who gets the gold? Me. Even if I have to tear down the whole blasted house and dig up the yard to find it."

At last, he paused and breathed deeply as if he was sucking it all back into his body—his words, his movements, his emotions. He shuddered and placed two hands on the gun, then glared at me, his eyes twin slits.

"And you ruined it all, *Kitty*. I planned it so carefully. When I met you, I knew it'd work. I'd use you to get to the gold. Then we'd be set for the rest of our lives—you and me." His voice had a whiny, everyone-picks-on-me twang, like fingernails running lingeringly down a chalkboard.

He took a deep breath, then continued his poor-me tirade. "But *no*, you didn't even give me a chance. So I had to resort to my backup plan—the *crazy* niece. Now you'll suffer, just like I am. I'm gonna enjoy watching you die, struggling to get air into your lungs, slowly suffocating, like Levina.

"She thought she was so clever. Told me the key was in her office. What she was really looking for was that medicine." His face twisted with anger before he snarled, "You'd think Janet could do something right. All she had to do was get that stuff out of the house and learn the security code. And she botched it. Damn nutcase!"

"You chose to get involved with her," I informed him, fed up with his martyrdom.

His eyes narrowed. "No, not my choice; *yours*. I *have* to find that gold. I grew up hearing stories about it. Searched the whole town looking for it when I was a kid and read every book there is on it. I knew it'd be mine someday.

"I'd pretty much given up on it. Then Janet spilled the beans at Aunt Millie's funeral. Said Levina was close to finding it. No way was that old lady gonna take *my* gold." He stabbed the gun at me. "That's when I came up with my plan. Of course, I didn't know about you then, so I was gonna make do with the lunatic niece."

He stopped talking and stood transfixed, his ear cocked towards the entry. Light from a passing car filtered through the blinds. Melding with the car noises was another sound, one barely audible and for once, not so annoying. Annabelle? I swallowed the lump of joy in my throat and prayed that Walker wouldn't hear the yowling.

He shook his head, blinked several times, and seemed to refocus. "Crazy Janet." He leaned close, in my face, the gun barrel pressed into my chest. "You see, unlike you, she recognizes a man of quality when she sees one. Adores me. Can't live without me."

Thoughts of Annabelle evaporated as I stared at the trembling gun. The cold metal was an icicle piercing my skin and slicing on through my body. I squelched a shudder, fearful that it would trigger a deadly reaction from Walker.

I had to get his focus off me and onto searching for that elusive key or whatever the heck it actually was. Maybe then I'd find an opportunity to escape. "You didn't need me; you had Janet," I prodded.

"It was supposed to be you, dammit!" The gun was a battering ram stabbing me with each word he spoke. Walker was growing more agitated and I, more petrified. "I was just stringing her along in case I needed her. You and I getting married would've sent her off the deep end and turned the house over to us. But you went and ruined it."

He raised the gun and pressed it to my forehead. "Then that bitch changed her will and left everything to you," he seethed through clenched teeth. "You blew to hell the whole thing up into something it didn't need to be!"

Fear jolted through my body. His eyes were cold and hard. Rage leeched from him and ignited the air between us. Would his fury cause him to pull the trigger?

He blinked hard and stepped back, his gun hand clenching and unclenching. His free hand dug in the pocket of his shorts and withdrew a roll of silver duct tape. "Now shut up and put your hands behind your back."

Panic engulfed me, heavy and foreboding. Instinct took over, and I surged forward and plowed into him. Something pounded into my stomach and knocked the air out of me. I doubled over, clutching my middle and struggling to swallow the vomit rising in my throat. The burning in my gut was unbearable.

"You try that again and you're dead. Now *sit down!*" he hissed.

Fighting dizziness, I forced myself to breathe slowly and deeply as I sank back into the chair. He moved behind me, the gun digging into my head.

"Give me your hands!" he barked.

I eyed my trembling hands, still clutching my stomach. They refused to move.

"*Now!*" he roared.

Slowly, I snaked them around the chair back, steeling against the pain in my right shoulder. My eyes scanned the room in search of a sharp object. There were cabinets full of glass and china and even some tarnished silver items, all safely ensconced behind closed doors. Colorful floral pictures lined the walls, and the two Wallace paintings taunted me from across the room. The floor was littered with boxes of items I'd yet to discard—more pictures, gaudy wooden frames, the stuff Harv had called graniteware, and a stash of cast iron. No knives or sharp scissors were lying around in wait of a moment such as this.

The gun barrel moved to my left ear. I felt the sticky pressure of tape on my right wrist and heard the grating sound of it unwinding from the roll. Instinctively, I clenched my fists and pressed them inward to loosen the binding. He drew my wrists together and wrapped layer after layer of the unyielding stuff around them.

A ripping sound and he appeared in front of me. "You try to kick me, and you'll never walk again," he warned as he fell to his knees, the gun pressed into my right kneecap. Which was a totally ludicrous threat since I would soon be dead.

One-handed, he secured my ankles to the front chair rails. When he was done, except for my head and my throbbing innards, I was alarmingly immobile. Though it might've been only wishful thinking, I swore I heard Annabelle's plaintive wails. I said a silent prayer that she had access to a secret passage into the house. Then she would materialize to nibble her way through my bindings.

Whom was I kidding? Annabelle was as dead as I soon would be.

Walker stepped back and eyed his handiwork, a smug look on his repulsive face, the gun now dangling at his side. He chuckled. "Ah, just the way I like my women—bound and submissive. Now tell me what you know about that damn key."

"Why should I?" I challenged. I knew I shouldn't push my luck, but that key was the one ace I had up my sleeve, and I planned to milk it for all it was worth. If Walker was set on possessing it, I hoped I could convince him that I actually did know something about it.

Anger flared in his eyes. "Because I'll kill you if you don't," he fumed, wagging his monstrous weapon threateningly at me.

"Whether I do or don't tell you, I die." Something had snapped inside me. I felt it unwinding like a tightly coiled slinky that is suddenly released. "So if you're gonna kill me, do it. Then you'll always wonder if I knew where the gold is," I taunted.

It wasn't what he expected. I saw it in his eyes—surprise and hate. He slammed the gun down, then ripped a healthy slab of duct tape from the roll and slapped it over my mouth, his gloved fingers digging into my cheeks. I slipped my tongue between my captive lips and pushed against the tape, a plastic taste invading my mouth. The tape didn't budge.

"You'd be amazed at what I can do when I set my mind to it, *Kitty*. Oh, and by the way, thanks for getting rid of Doreen. Thanks to you, until the time is right to reveal my fortune, I can now play principal without having to kiss that bitch's fat ass.

"But back to business; I've gotta find that key before Janet's greedy mother or your snoopy boyfriend get their hands on it, which just might happen before I have control of this house." He squinted, studying me closely. "I know you've been looking for it. Close, too, aren't you? All of those questions you've been asking. And you bought that painting and drove to hell and gone looking for answers. Yeah, that was me in that truck. Almost got you, too, didn't I?"

He chuckled and reached out a hand to stroke my cheek as if he were petting an adoring puppy. "Yeah, you're close. But you haven't found it yet, have you?"

I held myself still, refusing to give him the satisfaction of seeing me recoil from his touch. He moved closer, his smoker's breath hot on my face, and grasped my chin firmly in his hand. "No need to worry, Kitty. We have all night here, just you and me. I need to finish in the office and search the basement. Then I'll find out what you know before I kill you.

"You sit here and think about that. I'll be back."

☼☼☼

Walker's footsteps grew fainter as he made his way down into the basement. For about an hour, I'd heard him shuffling through drawers and papers in the office across the hall. Every so often, there'd been a thump that sounded as if his fist had hit something hard followed by a string of expletives. Several times, he'd peeked in to check on me.

Now, except for pools of light filtering in through the closed blinds from the streetlights, all was dark and unnervingly silent. I'd sat quietly while he rifled the office, my mind frenetic, searching for a way out of my predicament. My think time was over; if I was going to act, it had to be now.

I surveyed the dimly lit room. The two James Wallace paintings reached out to me: bright blue flames and eggs bursting from their dark settings. Flames, eggs, a yoke, roses, and a river, all painted in brilliant blue in five different paintings. Was it a message or merely the work of a man who viewed the world through a pair of unique eyes?

Whatever the case, those ponderings would have to wait. A few short hours and it would be daylight . . . and my death. An escape plan was my priority at the moment.

Again, I heard a faint yowling. I froze, straining to hear more clearly, then told myself to focus on my getaway. My eyes traveled on around the room to dark shapes scattered on the floor: boxes bulging with discards. In the right hands, cast iron would be a formidable weapon. Unfortunately, my hands were tied. Ditto the enamelware. Unless there was a protruding nail on one of the frames, they, too, were useless.

For the umpteenth time, I tried to wedge my tongue beneath

the duct tape. The sticky fabric held.

Perhaps I could maneuver my way into the office. I gripped the hardwood floor with my bare toes, gritted my teeth against the pain in my gut, and leaned forward, then tried to tug the chair forward. It didn't budge.

Maybe backwards. I glanced over my left shoulder, then my right. My eyes landed on a black blob tucked under a small table a couple of feet back, a box I'd placed there after an evening at Harv's auction. At the time, I hadn't taken more than a cursory glance at its contents. Now my mind slid back to replay Harv's words. He'd called them ranching tools.

I'd been embarrassed when he'd needled me about one specific tool—a pair of castrating shearers. I pictured them flashing in the air accompanied by a roomful of snickers. They'd looked like a mammoth pair of scissors!

I pressed my toes into the floor and pushed. The chair inched back, its legs squeaking painfully loud on the polished wood beneath them. I sat still and listened for footsteps on the basement stairs, afraid to even swallow the lump of fear in my throat. Except for the mysterious wailing sound, all I heard was the pounding of my blood. I pushed back several more inches and listened.

Two pushes later I gazed down into the box and tried to visualize its contents: a tangled mass of rust-splotched tools—hammers and pliers and screwdrivers and only God knew what else. The shears had lain on top of the pile, a humiliating reminder of what can happen when one doesn't pay attention.

I leveraged with my toes to work the chair sideways. Then I leaned back as far as I could and tugged on the cardboard. The box didn't budge. Pushing firmly with my toes, I prayed that the small table would grab the back of the chair and hold it in place.

Balancing carefully, I gritted against the pain radiating from my sore shoulder and ran my fingertips along the roughened metal, searching for those giant scissors. My knuckles touched smooth wood, and I traced the familiar shape of a hammer, then what felt like oversized pliers. My pinkie slid sideways, and a stinging pain shot through it when it skimmed the prickly points on a saw blade.

'Bingo," I breathed as I examined the tool. It was small, rather like one used by butchers to saw through bone. Excitement tingled inside me. It might work! I slid an index finger beneath the blade and gripped it firmly.

Then I heard it: the harsh squeak of a floorboard. I froze, my mind concocting scenarios I didn't want to contemplate. Walker? Had I been so caught up in my prospective escape that I'd missed his tread on the stairs?

Another telltale squeak screamed that my life was about to

end. My jaw clenched so tight it quivered. Sweat pooled, clammy, on my skin. A presence lurked outside the dining room entrance. I felt it deep in my bones, a weakening, throbbing sensation. As if it might save me, I kept a one-finger death grip on the saw.

"Kit?" It was barely audible, a mere breath of air.

I stared at the entry, afraid to move lest the chair shift and make a sudden noise.

"Meee . . . owww!" The screech pierced the silence. A dark form streaked across the table and disappeared in the darkness beyond. Startled, I jerked back and the chair legs slid forward, grating on the hardwood floors. My upper body wrenched forward. The chair rocked upright, then sideways to balance on one back leg for several long seconds before it swiveled towards the door and landed on all four with a loud, vibrating knock.

Bright light lit up the room. Blinded, I blinked hard and stared up into Sophie's startled blue eyes. They were huge, popping from their sockets. I tried to tell her to turn off the light, but all that came out were some strange warbling sounds. I stared at the ornate crystal fixture over the table and shook my head firmly. The room went dark.

"Holy Moses, Kit?" she muttered, drawing closer, a silhouette in the dimness. "Are you really taped to that chair?"

I nodded, then realized that Sophie couldn't see me. "Uh-huh," I voiced. I tried to add, "Shhh," but it came out as a hiss. Instead, I made guttural noises that sounded more like a painful, lingering death than a plea for help.

"You'll have to speak up. I can't understand a word you're saying."

She was close enough to touch me—a dark form with vague features. Something feather-soft stroked my calf. I recoiled, then remembered the cat that had shot across the room. Annabelle! Was it she who had lured Sophie here?

And Walker? If he'd heard the racket, my life wouldn't be the only one in danger. I had to get free from this chair. Then Sophie, Annabelle, and I had to get out of here. Pronto!

I took a deep breath and made what I hoped resembled pleading noises. It sounded remarkably like one of Stonewall's anxiety fits.

"Honest to God, Kit, did you snap a few wires? Someone's taped you to a chair, and you're sitting there making strange noises." Her hands were like parchment as they ran down my calves and tugged at the tape circling my ankles. She worked at the tape a bit, then sighed, clearly frustrated. "I'm gonna have to get a knife."

"I don't think so," a deep voice said from the doorway.

As if a jolt of electricity streaked through me, my whole body stiffened. Light showcased Sophie and me, blinding with its intensity. Walker stood glaring at us, trimmed with dirt and cobweb wisps, his massive gun clutched in two trembling hands and pointed at us. One shaky finger curled around the trigger.

"Ronny Walker, what the dickens are you up to now? If your Aunt Millie knew about this, she'd rise plum up out of her grave and give you the what for," Sophie fumed. In one fluid motion, she rose and stepped in front of me, a gauzy cloud in her pink peignoir, hands firmly planted on her tiny hips. "Now put that cannon down, and help me get Kit out of that chair."

"You couldn't keep your nose out of this, could you, Sophie? Always prying into other people's business. Well, you're gonna wish you'd stayed home tonight." Walker's voice was derisive, spitting venom.

Thanking Sophie mentally, I formulated a new plan, one that, at least, would save *her*. The saw still dangled from my index finger. If I could grasp the handle, I might be able to angle it so I could saw through the tape circling my wrists. As long as Sophie didn't move, the upper part of me was semi-concealed behind her gauzy nightwear. Perspiration dripped down my cheeks and underarms. I gripped the saw with both hands and began to inch my fingers along the blade. My right shoulder screamed.

"You don't scare me, Ronny," Sophie retorted. "You were a sneaky little kid, and now you're a sneaky, rotten adult—and a murderer, to boot."

I had to hand it to Sophie; she had spunk. Staring at her pink-clad back, I clasped the saw handle in one hand and worked the blade between my wrists as my heart clamored and Sophie's alarmingly shrill voice fumed. "It was you, wasn't it, sneaking around Kit's house in the middle of the night? And shooting at her during that battle? Like a low-life Reb coward, hiding in the trees. Mind you, it's a wonder you didn't kill someone."

Mentally urging Sophie on, I worked the tines back and forth against the tape, my hand trembling with the effort. Faint rasping noises reached up to me to become lost in Sophie's screeching.

"And trying to run her off the road. You almost killed Bart, too. But you don't care, do you? As long as you get what you want, that's all that matters to you. Ain't that right?"

The tape was loosening. I wiggled my wrists and felt it give, then willed Sophie to stay put until I was free.

"Well, your luck just ran out, mister, 'cause you're not getting away with this. You killed my best friend, and I don't put up with crap like that from anyone, especially a little rat like you. Cal's coming, and he's gonna lock you away for the rest of your lousy life."

My heart surged; Cal was coming to our rescue. Sophie and I

were *not* going to die—not tonight, anyway.

Except that *we* knew Walker had killed Levina! Oh, God. We were both as good as dead.

"You really expect me to believe you called the cops before you nosed around in here yourself?" Walker growled. "Come on; we're going to the basement."

Sophie's back stiffened like a soldier on parade. "No way. I'm staying right here with Kit."

"Well then, I'll kill you here, instead."

It was deathly silent, a face-off. I held the saw still.

"You wouldn't dare, you dirty, rotten vermin!" Sophie finally hissed.

"Try me, you old bat! I was just trying to save myself from hauling your body down those stairs." A heart-stopping *click* followed Walker's words. I froze, steeling myself for the bullet that would pass through Sophie and into me.

Instead, Sophie took several hesitant steps, glanced back at me and shuffled out the door ahead of Walker.

Oh, no! He was going to kill Sophie and hide her body in my filthy basement. I wiggled my hands free. Sophie's minutes were numbered. I had to save her.

I wrenched the tape from my mouth, then licked at the stinging burn while I sawed at the tape around my ankles. The plodding of feet on the steps to the basement spurred me on.

One leg pulled free. "Please, Sophie, be a huge pain in the butt," I begged as I set to work on the other.

Surely Cal should be here by now . . . if Sophie had called him. Oh, God! Was she lying, trying to scare Walker? I sawed harder.

Finally, I was free. I dropped the saw and made a mad dash for the mantle, where I grabbed my cell phone. No sounds filtered up from the basement—no thumps, no screams, no gunshots. That had to be a good sign.

I punched Bart's name. He answered on the second ring. Tears pooled in my eyes. "Help!" It was a quiet shriek but a shriek, nonetheless.

"I'm on my way." His words were clipped. The pounding of his feet thumped in my ear in time to my shrieking pulse. "Where are you?"

"The back door," I murmured as I strode towards it. "And bring a gun."

"A gun?" I heard as I clicked off the connection.

My hand trembling as if I'd curled fifty-pound weights for a couple of hours, I swiped at my eyes and managed to punch in 9-1-1 before I inched the door open and slipped outside. When I heard the click, I exploded. "I'm at the corner of Fourth and Main. Ronny

Walker's here with a gun, and he's got Sophie in the basement. He's gonna kill her. Call Chief Preston. Tell him Kit called. And *hurry!*"

Bart sprinted up the steps in shorts, shirtless, his feet bare. My heart did a couple of cartwheels, and for the first time that night, I felt like I might have a future. And Sophie would, too, if we worked quickly. Disregarding the chatter leaking from my cell, I snapped it shut.

"It's Walker—Ronny Walker," I murmured, words coming so quickly that my tongue tangled in them. "He's got Sophie in the basement. He has a gun and he's going to kill her. I called the cops." My eyes dropped to what he cradled in his hand. "What in the hell is that?" I asked, hope deserting me.

He held the weapon up, the long brass barrel pointing into the darkness. "You said to bring a gun."

I studied the odd-shaped gadget. Cripes! Was he serious? It looked like a prop from a pirate movie. "A *real* gun," I snapped as I slid back into the house.

"It is a real gun . . . and it's very reliable. It's a rare flintlock blunderbuss pistol, and it's fully cocked," he whispered. "But we only have one shot, so it needs to be a good one."

One shot! My hope was that no shots would be fired. But Walker would take one look at Bart's *gun* and have himself a good laugh. Our only hope was to overpower him. Or—please, God—for Cal and his posse to come to our rescue.

I closed my eyes and strained my ears, hoping to hear a shrill siren screaming. No such luck! We couldn't wait any longer; we had to distract Walker before he killed Sophie.

Bart grabbed my arm. "I'm going down. You stay here and wait for Cal."

"Not gonna happen!" I whispered as I jerked away and crept slowly down the stairs.

I could feel him breathing down my neck, fuming. Old, musty air assaulted my nostrils, an annoying burning sensation. Dim light from a lone dust-coated ceiling light didn't hide the dirt and webs that had taken over.

Muted voices drifted from a far corner, one of them Sophie's. Relief flowed through me. I swiped at bugs on my face and arms and told myself that the crawling sensations were a figment of my imagination. Bart cut in front of me and slid towards the darkened shadows, motioning me to follow and stay behind a wall of old furniture and boxes.

"I did, too, call Cal," I heard Sophie insist, her voice shaky.

"Shut your trap, you old slut!" Walker growled. "I saw you sneaking around in that ridiculous outfit. What happened? That old guy turn you down, so you stopped by here to whine to Kit about it?"

"If you think I'm gonna chitchat about what Milton and I do behind closed doors, you can just forget about it. I'm a lady and ladies don't. . . ."

A ripping sound, then a slap followed by some garbled noises urged me to sneak a peek around Bart's broad back. Walker was on his knees next to Sophie, facing away from us. Sophie looked like a trussed up flamingo, her ankles and feet tethered and a swatch of tape hiding half of her face. Still, she was wiggling and warbling and her blue eyes were spitting fire.

A flash of gold from on top of an old chest caught my attention. In the dim light, I could barely make out Annabelle's feline form, her tail twitching erratically.

Walker dropped a roll of duct tape next to his gun and stood up. "Well, whether you're lovers or only wish you were, I'm thinking I can use that to make it look like *you* killed Levina . . . and Kit, too. So shut up and let me think this through."

I blinked hard. Was I seeing correctly? Yes! Walker's mammoth gun was on the floor a good yard from his feet.

"Don't move!" Bart ordered as he stepped out from our fortress, me on his shirttails.

Walker froze. Slowly he turned towards us, eyeing first Bart and then his gun.

"Don't do it," Bart warned. "This pistol might be old, but I guarantee it'll do more damage than yours."

Above us, all hell broke loose—crashing and yelling and the deafening pound of footsteps. My eyes jigged to the stairs, then jagged back when a blood-curdling yowl screamed through my ears.

Walker turned as if to dive for his gun. A ball of flying fluff flew through the air and attached itself to his chest.

He howled, grabbed handfuls of fur, and tugged, trying to disconnect the cat's sharp claws. "Let go, you worthless piece of shit!" he bawled.

The thunder of running feet on the steps echoed through the dank chamber. Annabelle screeched, dropped to the floor, leaped through a mass of spider webs, and disappeared into the dark recesses of the basement.

"Stay where you are, Ronny!"

I turned and my eyes grazed Cal's hard stare. He wore boxers, flip-flops, and one of Patty's bumblebee tee-shirts, and his hair was standing at odd angles as if he'd meticulously jelled it there—bed hair. Fortunately, he had a normal-looking gun in his hands, and it was aimed at Walker. Behind him, his backup stood frozen, legs apart, faces stern, and guns clutched in front of them.

"You okay?" Cal asked, his steely gaze affixed to Walker, his face deathly pale.

"I think so," I sighed and felt myself deflate as several weeks of pent-up tension spewed from me.

Then I remembered. "It's Sophie who needs your help. She saved my life."

Sophie was stretched out on her side on the floor. Walker towered over her, glaring at me with eyes full of hate. Most likely, he would blame me for this, too.

"Cuff him," Cal ordered. Two men stepped forward. One of them grabbed Walker's left arm and pulled it behind him while the other recited some familiar legal verbiage.

Bart made his way towards Sophie, where he set his blunderbuss on the floor and began to work at Sophie's bindings.

A sinking feeling settled over me, of something found, then lost. I turned to Cal and muttered, "You need to arrest my cousin Janet, too. She was helping him. They think the Blue Bucket gold is somewhere on this property. They killed Levina to get to it and were going to kill me, too." Sadness engulfed me. If not for me, my Aunt Levina might still be alive. "They did it to get this house," I finally added.

Cal shook his head and made a disgusted sound, clutching his stomach like he was afraid it was going somewhere.

I watched the two officers usher Walker towards the steps. He glanced back over his shoulder and made one last parting shot, an angry snarl: "This isn't over, *Kitty.*"

It was for me. I shrugged it off and knelt beside Bart. He was working on Sophie's feet. I pulled her into a sitting position and curled her into a lengthy hug. She might be tough as nails, but she felt tiny and vulnerable in my arms.

"Thank you, Sophie," I murmured before I pulled back and began to cautiously peel the tape from her wrinkled face.

"What the hell's that?" I heard Cal say. When I glanced up, he was staring at the ancient pistol, an astounded smirk lighting his face.

"My words, exactly," I informed him. A smile twitched at the corners of my lips. "Bart claims it's reliable. He had it cocked and ready to shoot . . . *one* shot. So he. . . ."

"Well, I hope he remembered to uncock it," Sophie spluttered.

My gaze drifted to Bart's blunderbuss. It lay innocently on the grimy floor, its barrel pointed to the wall. Sitting a couple of inches from it, directly in its line of fire, was Annabelle, her fur coated with a layer of russet soot. Mangled webs dangled from her whiskers and tail.

She bent over as if to sniff the pistol just as Bart's hand closed around the stock. He picked it up, pointed it to an unoccupied corner, and fiddled with it. Annabelle cast him an annoyed look and sauntered off.

I covered my eyes and rubbed at my forehead willing my heart to slow down. "No more guns," I announced. "No more locked doors and illusive secret keys. No more worrying about gold that doesn't exist. And no more dead bodies!"

CHAPTER 20

Life can be so sweet, especially when no one is trying to kill you. I might not have blood relatives gathered around me but even better, I had a family of friends. And I was feeling their love—a warm glow that permeated my entire being.

I breathed deeply, savoring the dusky sweet scent of roses and freshly mown grass in the sultry mid afternoon air, and gazed down the lounge chair to my neglected feet. Tomorrow I'd paint my toenails. Not today. Today I wanted to enjoy this special moment in my life.

"So it was all because of that gold?" Patty asked. She—who had always claimed to dislike beer—chugged on Cal's Mirror Pond. Snuggled up to him on the matching wicker lounge, she looked as content as Annabelle had after she'd finally consumed her dinner well past midnight. The two of them, Cal and Patty, were like chocolate and caramel—great on their own, but put them together and they become sinfully sweet and gooey.

Cal took a long swig of ale before he answered. "Yep. Ronny's mad as hell; refuses to talk to us. But when Janet was brought in, she was like water behind a cracked dam. At first, the words trickled. Then they spilled out so fast it was hard to keep up with her.

"Course, she thinks the house and store are hers, and everything in them. She and Roy have been takin' things from them for over a year and sellin' them to keep the farm out of hock. Seems Levina figured it out. Probably why she changed her will. After her death, they figured the stuff was theirs, so they kept sellin' it. Roy was the one searchin' your office that night. Heard you say somethin' about that record book of Levina's. Wanted to find it before you did."

Cal gulped from his bottle, then continued. "Anyway, Janet claims Ronny killed Levina so he could find that gold. Ronny grew up hearin' about James Wallace and the Blue Bucket and believed the stories. Got it in his head the gold belongs to him." Cal harrumphed and shook his head. "Thought it was his *destiny* to find it."

Patty's eyebrows arched. "I knew Ronny had a few loose

screws, but he's actually certifiably crazy."

"Could be," Cal muttered, running his fingers up and down Patty's bare arm. "One thing's for sure: he can manipulate a situation to get what he wants. Hired Levina to take on Millie's estate sale, so he could cozy up to her. He played her like a well-tuned Gibson.

"Got in tight with her niece—Janet—who, by the way, is about a hair and a half from being a total wacko. Wired as hell. When her mom found out we'd arrested her, she was spittin' mad. Brought in the family lawyer, so we're not gettin' much out of her now. She'll probably end up in some psychiatric ward somewhere."

I was surprised at the relief I felt at his words. Evidently, blood was pretty darned thick. The idea of Janet spending time in prison didn't sit well, maybe because I knew what an ass Walker was. He'd taken my borderline crazy cousin and used her mental illness to manipulate her.

"How involved was she?" I asked, not sure that I really wanted to know.

Cal finished off the ale. "Seemed to be more of an informant than anything. She wasn't here with Ronny the night Levina died. That day at Willamette Park she was trackin' you most of the afternoon and relayin' the information to Ronny. Course, she was the one who picked him up in Canyon City, too."

"It was Walker who tried to run me down in the school parking lot," I added.

"Yep," he agreed. "Janet heard her mother talkin' on the phone with Levina. She was afraid her aunt was gonna change her will and leave everything to you."

"Which she'd already done," I clarified.

He nodded. "They thought they had the money—or rather, gold—in the bag."

"Then Walker found out I was invited to the reading of Levina's will. He saw the letter on Louise's desk." I thought back to that fateful morning and pictured Walker in his BMW, eyes searching through the pounding rain, waiting for me to appear in the school parking lot. He'd known that I planned to arrive at work in the wee morning hours. I'd told him that when he'd questioned me about my early departure the previous day.

"The next morning he tried to kill me," I told Patty.

Her eyes sad, Patty nodded. "You looked like you'd been mugged and left for dead. I thought it was odd that he didn't notice what a train wreck you were in the hall that morning, but I chalked it up to him being a self-absorbed jerk."

"If only Levina hadn't decided to change her will." Those words had run through my mind so many times that they slipped out on their own.

"She'd probably still be dead," Cal asserted. "Janet told Ronny Levina'd found a key to the gold. She claims he went ballistic. Couldn't have someone else takin' *his* gold."

His gold; there was absolutely no proof the gold even existed, and if it did, the chance that it was hidden on this property was infinitesimal. Yet Walker had committed murder based on that minuscule chance.

"And that night he killed Levina," I said, more a sigh than a statement.

"Maybe he didn't mean for her to actually die?" Patty asked.

"Oh yes, he did." I was adamant about that one fact. Patty hadn't been there to witness the hatred in Walker when he spoke of it; I had. "He had Janet clear all of the EpiPens from the house. The one that was left in the desk drawer was a mistake. He wanted her dead. And he wants me dead, too."

My eyes met Patty's. She and I were channeling on the same brainwave. Walker blamed me for his demise. He'd do everything within his power to exact retribution. At this very moment, he was probably plotting my slow, painful death.

"They won't let him out on bail, will they?" Patty pleaded.

Cold shivers pricked my spine. What if Walker was released? Something twisted in my gut—an agonizing ache. I'd found my home; I wouldn't leave it.

Cal shrugged. "A judge'll decide that. But don't worry. If he gets out on bail, we'll keep you safe," Cal assured me.

Hopefully, I managed a semblance of a grateful smile when I nodded. Cal had good intentions; the problem was with his follow-through.

"What about Roy?" I asked. The thought of Roy spending time in prison for something he'd felt forced to do for his family— also my family—was unsettling.

"That's probably up to you," Cal informed me.

"Me?" Was he serious?

He eyed me intently. "You gonna press charges? It's your stuff he stole."

"Family stuff," I mumbled, a gut reaction. I truly believed that Roy's heart was in the right place; it was his reasoning and actions that weren't. "I have to think about it," I admitted.

My gaze traveled out to the rose garden where Sophie trailed Milton. Her mouth was shaded beneath a wide-brimmed straw hat, but I knew her lips were moving. Not that Milton was paying her much attention. He was busy snipping at my roses—some kind of healing process he seemed to be going through. With the hat and her short, gathered sundress and stick-thin milky legs, Sophie resembled one of her pink flamingoes.

What a woman—my heroine! If I could choose to be more like any one person, it would be Sophie—brave, headstrong, feisty Sophie. Most likely, she'd saved my life the previous night. On her way home from a late night tryst with Milton, she'd cut through my backyard, where she'd heard Annabelle's squawking and had stopped to investigate. Fortunately, Walker hadn't locked the door. Sophie had suspected something was amiss but in true Sophie style, had forged ahead anyway to search the darkened house with Annabelle squirming in her arms.

I pulled my mind's meanderings back to Cal and Patty, who were whispering secret something's-that-I-didn't-want-to-know to each other. Cal was nibbling on Patty's impeccably manicured fingertips.

"Stonewall, sit!" a deep voice growled. I turned back to the senior lovebirds spooning midst my rosebushes. At their feet, a compact, russet dog bounced like a four-legged pogo stick, his runty tail wagging.

Bart stepped through the broken fence toting several bulging bags. Stonewall sank onto his rump and panted at his master, who paused to speak with Milton and Sophie.

Those annoying butterfly wings sprouted inside me, unsettling my stomach, causing my heart to flutter. Snippets of Bart's vibrant voice wafting across the yard turned me warm and mushy. Cripes! I was worse off than Patty and Sophie combined—not that it was going anywhere. "You have yourself to blame for that," I muttered under my breath.

Bart strode across the lawn toward us, Stonewall dancing at his heels. The Colonel's familiar face was stamped on the bags in his arms. Of course, he would have to bring something calorie oozing and fried. I pushed myself up out of the recliner and winced at the pain from various body parts, residue from my close calls with death.

"Bart's here with chicken and all the fixin's, enough for a small army," I announced.

"Which is fortunate for you since your friend Grace just pulled up out front with two boys who look like they could consume a bucket of drumsticks on their own," Bart challenged, taking the steps in two long strides. Stonewall pranced over to Cal, his nails clicking like typewriter keys. Cal reached out a hand and scratched him behind his ears.

The aroma of fried chicken melted into the air, sinfully tantalizing but no more so than the man who stood before me. Bart's eyes met mine and clung. My belly did flip-flops.

A knowing smile curled his lips. "Nice hair," he whispered.

I fought the urge to touch it. He'd said he liked it loose.

"Oh, my God! That smells good. The lady who's been off food

for days says it's eatin' time," Patty said. She pecked Cal on his lips and started to stand.

"You and Cal save your strength. We'll take care of the food," Bart told her as he unloaded the bags onto the patio table.

The doorbell clanged. I flinched, then remembered. "Grace!"

I bolted for the front door. When I opened it, Grace attacked. She hugged me close, then pushed back and stared into my eyes. "Why the hell didn't you call me? Walker is *not* someone you mess with. That asshole would've killed you." Tears glistened in her eyes.

I swallowed over the ache in my throat. "But he didn't."

"Potty mouth!" a young boy's voice announced from somewhere behind Grace.

Another voice took up the chant. "Potty mouth! Potty mouth! Potty mouth!"

"Okay, all right!" Grace said sternly, backing up to let Danny and Davy into the house. "Mommy shouldn't have used bad words. Now Kit needs a big hug from you boys."

The two scowling boys reached their arms around me, one glued to each hip, and clung tightly for several seconds.

"Mommy said you don't feel good," Danny said when he let go.

"You look okay," Davy added.

I knelt down beside them. "And thanks to your hugs, I'm feeling much better."

They studied me as only young children can—all earnest intent and knowing eyes. Finally, smiles replaced the frowns on first Danny's face, then Davy's.

"We went on a ferry," Danny told me.

Not to be outdone, Davy added, "On the river."

Confused, I glanced up at Grace.

"The Willamette River," Grace said. "We crossed it on the Canby Ferry. I thought the boys would get a kick out of it. And they did."

"Wow! I wish I'd been there," I told the boys. "Now, I happen to know that Stonewall's in the backyard waiting for you. Why don't you head out there and play with him while I get some food ready for you two hungry munchkins?"

"Stonewall!" Danny screamed. "I'm gonna dig for treasures!" He took off down the hall at breakneck speed.

Davy watched him, blinked several times, then chased after him. "Me, too!"

"No digging!" Grace yelled as she strode off in pursuit.

I rose gingerly to my feet and followed. "It's all right. Patty's out there . . . and Sophie. Osama bin Laden himself couldn't weasel his way around those two."

"Sophie, huh?" A panicked look was on her face. "Geez! I better get out there."

She probably had a point. "Go ahead. I'll get some drinks and be out in a few minutes." Grace disappeared out the door and I turned towards the kitchen.

Bart's face was in the fridge. "She have a problem with Sophie?" he asked.

I grabbed some paper plates from a cupboard. "Sophie's not overly fond of children, and those two boys are as feisty as she is. Put them together and things get . . . tense."

He chuckled and set a carton of milk and several bottles of Mirror Pond on the counter. "Sounds like they enjoyed the ferry?"

I froze. "Fairy?" I squeaked, my mind replaying Walker's words: *all she does is ramble on about some dead guy and a fairy.*

Bart paused to study me. "Yes, on their way here. Didn't I hear Grace say they rode the Canby Ferry?"

Snippets of memory snapped into place in my cluttered brain—paintings and bright blue objects, keys and carvings. "That's what she meant!" I gasped, jittery with the knowledge. "Not fairy. *Ferry!*"

I plopped the plates down and strode to the mantle.

Bart followed. "What are you talking about?"

My finger landed on the meandering Willamette River and traced it downstream. "The ferry—Boones Ferry. Right here." I squinted and ran my fingertip over the heavily carved oak, searching. "There had to be other ferries, but this is the one Wallace put on here."

"It's nearby and was on the main route north. He probably crossed the Willamette on it many times," Bart informed me.

He was looking at me as if I had a few chips that had jiggled loose. "It's the *key*," I told him, "The one Levina claimed she'd found. And my mother, too."

Clearly, he wasn't getting it. My fingers continued their probing as I searched for words. "James Wallace painted five special pictures, and he put a blue object in each of them—flames, eggs, roses, a river, and a yoke. Take the beginning letter from each of those words and you can spell the word *ferry.*

"Walker told me that the night she died, Levina kept talking about a dead man and a ferry. Only, he thought she was talking about a fairy . . . like the tooth fairy. She had to be talking about this ferry. It's right. . . ."

Hidden beneath a swollen horse's belly, I felt it—a small hole. I sank to my knees and searched the spot my finger touched. Sure enough, there was a tiny rectangular opening.

"Bring me that letter opener on the kitchen counter, would

you, please?" I muttered as I examined the small, carved beast. A barely discernible crack outlined it.

"Here," Bart said, handing me the opener.

I pressed the tip up into the hole and attempted to pry the horse from the mantle. With a little added force, it popped out and landed in my free hand.

"*Damn!*" Bart's whispered exclamation voiced my thoughts exactly. He dropped to his knees beside me. We both stared at what appeared to be a rather crude keyhole.

"Do you think there's really a cache of gold hidden in your mantle?" Bart asked.

Our eyes met. "I don't know. But I'll bet something's in there."

My mind scrambled through tidbits of information, searching and sorting. The paintings; the key had to be in them. Levina had been looking at Meg's painting of Lukas Brenning's wife and son. Then, excited about some discovery, she'd phoned Bernice and told her she'd found the key. And she'd spoken with Elsie concerning the painting of Lukas' family in Canyon City. That evening, she'd questioned Milton about his ancestors. Finally, that night, she'd rambled on about a dead man to Walker.

I turned back to the carvings, searched downward, and paused at the two houses, Milton's and mine. Between them, at the spot where Danny and Davy had found their treasured skull, was the Celtic-fashioned cross.

"Dear God, I think I've got it," I uttered as I slipped the letter opener beneath the cross and pried it from the slab of wood. Lying in my hand, it actually looked like a key.

As I stabbed at the keyhole, my hands shook so hard the key vibrated. After several attempts at getting it into the slot, it finally slid neatly into place.

"*Damn!*" Bart whispered again.

I could feel his excitement—jangled nerves and anticipation; it matched my own. I took a deep breath and turned the key. Something clicked, and the ferry the horse had been standing on popped out a fraction of an inch.

"*Damn!*" This time I whispered it, tension bubbling within me.

I handed the letter opener to Bart and pulled out the small section of wood. The ferry slid free to disclose an opening large enough to insert a hand. I peered inside.

"Cripes! There *is* something in there. It looks like leather."

Excitement hummed between us. My nose twitched from a musty, stagnant odor. Was this the legendary Blue Bucket gold? If so, it would mean that the passed-down tales of my great-great-grandfather's exploits were true.

I reached a trembling hand into the hole. The aged leather was stiff and rough against my fingertips. It barely budged when I tugged on it. I handed the ferry to Bart.

Using my left hand for leverage, I fisted my right hand around the edge of the bag and hauled it forward to the opening, its rigid edges grating against the wooden walls of the chamber. A couple more hard yanks and it scraped free. I grasped it in both hands and lowered it to the floor. The brown bag—powdery in spots and cracked with age—held its boxed shape.

"You open it." I whispered, my heart threatening to burst from my chest.

He set to work on the tie that held the bag closed. After some concerted effort, the thongs fell free, and he folded the rigid flap up, the aged leather crackling its complaint.

Then he peered inside and whispered, "*Wow!*" with even more enthusiasm.

Vibrating like a tuning fork, I leaned forward, my head nearly touching Bart's, to examine the contents. "*Oh . . . my . . . God!*" I wheezed. "It's not the gold."

"Oh, it's gold all right. Not Blue Bucket gold. This is even better."

Puzzled, I glanced into his intense eyes. What could be better than discovering a cache of missing gold and substantiating a legend that had begun a century and a half ago?

"It's nineteenth century gold coin—the real thing, solid gold pieces." He reached in and selected a coin. "See," he said, holding it in the palm of his hand. "Today, this one ten pennyweight piece is worth three thousand, maybe four thousand, dollars. And that's not counting their historical value. You have a whole bag of them."

Did Bart think the gold was mine? I reached into the bag and dug deep into the metal pieces. They felt cold and hard as they sifted through my fingers. "It must be what remained of Lukas Brenning's money," I surmised.

He frowned. "Or James Wallace *did* find the Blue Bucket gold and traded it for gold currency. Whatever the case, it'll take a lot of research to sort it out. I'd say it's a safe bet that Wallace hid this here, though. And I don't think it's been touched since then, even by Levina. So she must've been still searching for the actual key."

A bright flash drew my attention. Sunrays streaming through a window seemed to bounce off something deep inside the opening. I leaned forward to examine the interior. An ornate blackened box sat against the back wall, a round gold sphere topping its lid.

My insides did handsprings. The discovery of the coins was exciting, but this box might actually hold some answers—a journal or some letters, idle doodles or jottings.

"There's something else in here," I gasped as I pressed a hand into the opening. The box was cool against my fingertips, riddled with bumps and crevices. I slid it forward.

"It's covered with more than a century of tarnish, but it looks like sterling," Bart murmured. Our eyes met. His were glittery with excitement.

I took a deep breath and lifted the lid, then gasped. Inside, nestled in a blanket of aged black satin, was a stunning Celtic brooch. Intertwining gold ribbons snaked midst clusters of sparkling diamonds. A multi-faceted, glossy ruby gleamed from the center of the setting.

I picked up the brooch to examine it more closely. For its size, it felt amazingly heavy in my hands. "It's Lukas' wife's brooch," I murmured, handing the brooch to him. "But why's it in here? It should be with Milton's family."

Bart shrugged and turned his focus to the brooch's clasp before he offered his two cents. "Maybe it was how she paid Wallace to help her get away from her husband?"

It made sense. I fingered the silky-smooth, faded satin and lifted it from the box. Tucked beneath it was a folded piece of paper, yellow with age, its edges stained brown.

My fingers shaking, I carefully unfolded the fragile sheet and cupped it in my hands. The writing was faded and difficult to decipher—all tiny letters with curls and flourishes—but it appeared to be written in English. It was dated July 23, 1874, and a signature graced its lower edge—*Margaret Brenning.*

"What is it?" Bart asked.

"I think it's a letter written by Lukas' wife. I can't make out what it says."

He set the brooch back in the box. "I live with my nose in old documents. Why don't you let me give it a try?"

I dropped the letter into his waiting hands and watched his eyes scan the lines. Every so often, he made a guttural noise or hummed. Finally, he looked up. "You were right about the person who wrote it. She wasn't only Lukas' wife and Milton's great-grandmother. She was also James Wallace's sister, which would make her one of your kinfolk, too."

Tingles of excitement buzzed through me to settle somewhere near my heart. Milton and I shared genes. I actually had a blood relative who liked me. Make that two—Meg. "So he built the house for his sister, to have her nearby." It all made so much sense.

"Yes, she says in her letter that her house in Canyon City burned to the ground. She took advantage of the opportunity to escape from her husband and live with Wallace and his family. She thought it would be assumed that she and her son had perished in the fire." Bart paused and seemed to consider his words carefully before he continued. "Then one night Brenning showed up and demanded that she leave with him. There was a scuffle and Brenning ended up dead. She claims it was an accident."

As if I'd been there, I pictured it: her abusive husband hurling insults, furious and violent, his silver tooth gleaming in the firelight. I sighed. "But who would believe her, right? So they buried him in the backyard."

"Yes." Bart stared at the gold coin still in his palm. "Margaret says that Brenning's saddlebags were filled with gold pieces. To keep his death a secret, Wallace hid the gold, which she justifies by saying that she thought the coins were her husband's. It was only later, after the two houses were built, that she heard rumors of the Canyon City miners' missing gold and realized that some of the coins might belong to them."

Poor Margaret; the predicament she'd put herself into must have tormented her until she died. "But she was stuck. If she stepped forward, she'd most likely be tried for murder."

"Her hands were tied, all right. So she wrote this letter, probably to ease her conscience to future generations or hoping they'd return the gold to its owners. Whatever the case, Wallace died. And evidently he didn't tell anyone where he'd hidden the. . . ."

"What's a man gotta do to get fed around here? What the hell?"

My eyes locked with Cal's. He stepped toward us, glowering, as his eyes slid from the leather bag to the gold coin and letter in Bart's hand and on to the hole in the mantle.

His steely gaze met mine and held for several seconds before he spoke, his voice harsh, scolding. "You just can't stay out of trouble, can you?"

✿✿✿

Annabelle and Stonewall lay curled up together on the couch, a portent even I couldn't ignore. I peeked at Bart, who was loading the dishes into the dishwasher.

He winked. "Looks like Stonewall's settled in for the night," he murmured, a suggestive smile curling one corner of his lips. "Lucky dog!"

Heat scorched my cheeks. I returned to stuffing leftover chicken into a zip-lock bag. The previous night had been a long one and, with the discovery of Great-great-granddaddy's hidden treasure, today seemed endless. The prospect of a good night's sleep was tantalizing.

Still? My gaze skimmed Bart. He was darned tantalizing,

too—all dark streaks, hard muscle, and what I'd come to discover was a soft center. I sighed. With all the fluttering going on inside me, it was difficult to think rationally.

Bart looked up and smiled as if he knew my mind's wanderings.

And his smile? It would melt a bar of bitter chocolate on a frosty day.

I stuffed the chicken into the refrigerator and closed the door. "Cal's really ticked at me," I said, mostly to change the subject to something safer.

He clicked the dishwasher shut. "He'll get over it. He's just frustrated with you being naughty and all the added work it's causing him."

Automatically, my gaze darted to the bag of coins on the kitchen table. Since no one knew what to do with our find, they were here for, at least, one more night. There was no doubt that those coins were going to bed with me.

And Bart? Well, so far, it'd been my lucky day.

"He won't have to worry about me any longer," I told him.

"Why's that?" A pained look twisted his features. "You're not leaving, are you?"

Leave here—my home? I had an antique shop to run. And Annabelle to serve. And family. Besides, whom would Sophie watch over if I left?

Bart stood still, eyeing me intently.

And I had an unbelievable man who found me attractive, one who liked me enough to save my life twice and even load my dishwasher. One who liked me a bit out of control.

Tiny sunbeams blossomed and grew in my chest. I smiled. "I'm not going anywhere," I murmured as I stepped towards him.

His arms slid around me, drawing me close. He lowered his head and pressed his lips to mine softly before he drew back. "Good," he whispered. "It'll be easier for me to keep an eye on you. Besides, we have things to do."

"Things to do?" My insides turned gooey with the thought.

"Uh-huh." He nodded slowly, studying me. "Research."

"Oh, the coins." Disappointment crept into my voice.

"Uh-huh. I'm thinking we might collaborate. Maybe write a book."

"You and me?"

"Uh-huh. You seem to have a talent for digging up dirt and piecing it together into something plausible."

Yes, as stressful as the past few weeks had been, I'd been invigorated by the challenge of gathering tidbits of information and solving puzzles. "What about the antique store?" I reminded him.

"Well, I was thinking that Patty might help with that. She seems to know quite a bit about antiques, and I have a feeling she'll be living here in Aurora very soon."

He was right, of course. Like me, Patty planned to turn in her leave request to the school district. Plus, she'd be the perfect person to manage the antique shop.

Which would leave me free to partner with Bart. "You're enticing me," I told him.

He kissed me again. This time his lips lingered, caressing mine lovingly. "Am I still enticing you?" he finally asked.

His heart hammered against my chest, competing with the racing rhythm of mine. I was warm and mushy inside, my limbs sluggish. "Uh-huh," I sighed, "Enticing me to do naughty things. Cal would not be happy."

"Cal's not here; I am. And, unlike Cal, I find your naughtiness downright fascinating." He ran his hands around my neck and lifted my hair from my shoulders. "That and your beautiful hair. And your beautiful eyes," he murmured before he placed a kiss above each of them. "Mmmm . . . your beautiful mouth." His lips covered mine, at first lightly but then the kiss deepened. I held onto his shoulders for support while I floated in a mist of pleasure—all weak knees and melting, aching insides.

He nibbled on my lower lip and whispered, "And your beautiful body, which I've had the pleasure of viewing up close and personal. I'm fascinated with that, too."

Long fingers caressed my cheek. "I think you're perfect," he murmured.

This time, I slid my arms around his neck and pulled his lips down to meet mine. He thought I was perfect. Which was about as perfect as it could get.

Several minutes later, he withdrew his lips and cuddled me against his chest. When he spoke, his voice was deep, husky. "How about we take this upstairs?"

Upstairs? I searched for my legs. They had to be down there somewhere. I sighed. "At the moment, I don't think I can walk."

Before I finished the sentence, he scooped me up into his arms. Mortified, I locked my arms around his neck and tried to wiggle free.

He held tight and bounced me a couple of times, then shook his head. "We're gonna have to get some meat back on your bones. I'm thinking milkshakes and fries. Maybe pizza. Mac and cheese. Biscuits with gravy."

"Cripes! Now *you're* trying to kill me," I muttered as I settled into his very capable arms.

CHAPTER 21

Through the browsing antique hounds outside *Levy's Loot*, Meg strode purposefully toward me, tanned limbs and blonde mane flashing. "Nice brooch," I said when she plopped into the folding chair next to mine. "Way to accessorize shorts and a tank top."

She handed me a drink topped with swirls of whipped cream and chocolate sprinkles. "Thanks. It's a family heirloom—a gift from my favorite cousin."

"Thanks to you, too, for the drink." I sipped the frozen concoction and nearly swooned when the icy sweetness hit my tongue. "Wow! A caramel frappe. You read my mind. Must be the cousin thing."

"No doubt about it. Thanks to you, I escaped from that mob inside the coffee shop." She slipped four-inch wedgies off her feet and wiggled her toes. "We haven't hit the noon rush yet, and my pigs are squealin'. Sophie runs a tight ship—no *dilly-dallying* or *socializing*. She put Uncle Milton in charge of drinks, and she's making all the customers stand in a straight line at the counter to order and pick up their food. No talking. Lord help me if she ever convinces Uncle Milton to marry her."

I glanced at people loitering outside the *Coffee Counter*, then on up the hill. Multi-colored canopies lined both sides of the street, tables covered with odds and ends, furniture, and a plethora of do-dads—the one rule was that it had to be old—spilling from their shaded interiors. Swarms of warm bodies were milling, foraging, and hopefully, buying.

It was *Colony Days* in Aurora, the annual street fest that, according to Harv, drew the bottom feeders, dabblers, connoisseurs, and a whole lot of lookers to town. He didn't explain what a *looker* was, but after observing the goings-on for a couple of hours, I'd pretty much figured it out. They were doing only that: looking.

Meg tittered softly. "It's bad now, but once Sophie gets her new neighbors, she's really gonna put the screws on Uncle Milton. It ain't gonna be pretty. Have you seen her running around in that pink see-through thing?"

I turned back to Meg and laughed. "Oh, yeah. Enough that I

don't cringe when she's strutting around the neighborhood in it anymore. The truth is it's probably what saved my life."

Five weeks had passed since that night Sophie had come to my rescue in her transparent pink peignoir. A lot had happened in those five weeks. My path had changed; so had others'. So far, no one had worked up the courage to tell Sophie about one big change—her new next-door neighbors.

"Grace and the boys are moving in next week." A warm glow settled over me with my words. "She starts her new teaching job at North Marion the last week of August. I'm thinking it might be best for Sophie to discover it herself and just let the fur fly."

Meg nodded, her focus more on a nice-looking man in snug Wranglers and cowboy boots who was pawing through the clutter on the porch. "Just let me know which day so I can avoid that part of town."

My mind turned to Grace's two energetic, strong-willed sons. Even if Sophie lived with Milton, there'd be turbulent moments, with me planted smack dab between the two households. Of course, if things got too stormy, there was always Bart's house next door. He'd welcome me with open arms and lingering hugs and passionate kisses and. . . .

"Whew! It's hot out here," I said, rubbing the icy container against my cheek.

"Thinking about Bart, huh?" She pulled her eyes from tight jeans to peruse the crowded street. "Where is he? I thought he'd be here scavenging with the masses."

"Inside, helping Patty," I told her. "They sent me out here where I can't do any damage. 'Just sit there quietly, and if anyone asks a question about one of those *valuable* items on the porch, send them inside,' is how Bart put it."

Meg returned to her drooling and mumbled, "Have you started on the book yet?"

"Nope."

We watched the nice-looking man move on up the street. I sipped on my frappe while Meg mourned his passing. Finally, he walked into a shop, out of sight.

"Thanks to Roy and Uncle Jack's prodding, Bernice, kicking and screaming, of course, finally coughed up the Blue Bucket materials Janet had pilfered," I told her. "There are a lot of interesting old photos in the files that stretch back into the eighteen hundreds—our kinfolk. "

Meg sighed dejectedly. "And the gold?"

I huffed and rolled my eyes, exasperated with the workings of government. "It's a mess. No one can say for sure exactly where the coins came from or where they should go. Do they belong to me? Or you and Milton? Or to descendants of those miners? I wouldn't be surprised if it drags on and never gets closure.

"Once the book is completed, the Oregon Historical Society wants to do an exhibit on Great-great-granddaddy—his art, the Blue Bucket story, and all the trimmings. They've asked to use the coins in the display. Fortunately Bart is familiar with how it all works."

A perspiring, middle-aged woman examined the underside of a metal watering can, then dropped her glasses to dangle by a strap and stepped toward me. I smiled and did my job. "You can pay inside," I told her and pointed toward the air-conditioned shop. She returned my smile and disappeared through the door.

From somewhere, the aroma of barbeque permeated the warm, still air, whetting my appetite. I sighed contentedly, stretched, and searched for the source. My gaze landed on Bob over at the train depot. He was visiting with a buxom brunette. Since he'd flattened me with his massive body, he'd avoided me as if I were a barrel of Nitroglycerin.

My pulse quickened. "What's with Bob?" I asked Meg.

"Bob?" The look on her face said she didn't have a clue who I was asking about.

"Bob Crosely." I nodded at him and her eyes followed. "Every time I ask about him, I hit a brick wall and people act strange. Is there something I should know?"

She scrunched up her face and made a disgusting guttural noise. "Bob's a player. That's all you need to know. That and the farther you are from him, the better. He could charm the slime off a slug." She paused, then added, "Oh, and he'll say pretty much anything to get into your pants."

We both turned to study Bob. He was still chatting with the brunette, albeit a few inches closer. "So Levina didn't really show him pictures of me?" I asked.

"Fat chance!" she exploded. "After what he did to me, Levina detested the guy."

My eyes darted around to meet hers. "What'd he do to you?"

"Took me for quite a ride, then dumped me. *Jerk*! I really thought he was the one. Turns out that's what he does for fun." She frowned. "When I saw Bob going after you that day, I was livid. Told him I'd cut off his pathetic little you-know-what and its two playmates if he didn't stay the hell away from you. Cousins watch out for each other, you know."

I laughed. "You didn't know we were related then, Meg."

"It's the cousin thing. Can't explain it." She smiled and I felt warm and tingly all over. "And speaking of cousins, isn't that Roy?" Meg exclaimed.

Sure enough, Roy stood not eight feet from Bob, blonde hair

shimmering in the mid morning sunrays, a mammoth blue vase clutched in one arm and several loaded bags in the other.

"And Bernice," I moaned as my dear aunt stepped from the shadows and draped another bag over Roy's hand.

Meg moaned, too. "Looks like she's spreading the family wealth."

Looks can be deceiving I wanted to tell Meg. Bernice might appear to be wealthy, but she'd managed to get herself in debt up to her expensively adorned limbs, dragging her family and the farm along with her. On top of that, there were spiraling attorney expenses and psychiatric care for her daughter to pile on debt mountain. I ground my teeth together, anger threatening to ruin my peaceful morning. It appeared she was still spending money like her supply was endless. Was it any wonder Levina had refused to support her habit?

"Yes, Bernice likes to shop," was all I said.

We watched Bernice and Roy slowly weave their way across the teeming street. Several heads turned as they passed by. No doubt, Janet and her family were still a hot topic in the local gossip mill.

Meg was first to break the silence. "I knew there had to be a reason Roy and I didn't date well. I mean, look at him; he's gorgeous."

Yes, Roy definitely epitomized the word *handsome*. He was also thoroughly devastated that he'd stolen from his aunt. But property taxes and loans had to be paid or the family would lose the farm. Jack and Bernice weren't willing to cough up the dough, so Roy had felt that he had no other recourse but to sell a few of Levina's treasures. After all, one day he and Janet would possess all of those treasures.

In the past few weeks, Roy and I had spent time together, and I'd come to know him as a thoughtful, caring person. He didn't deserve a prison sentence.

"Thank God he takes after his daddy," Meg muttered. "Uncle Milton says we need to treat others the way we want to be treated, and they'll come around. He's probably right. Bernice is the exception . . . and maybe Bob. Oh, and Ronny Walker."

Dread dropped over me like a truckload of gravel, poking at my newfound sense of security and weighing me down with what wasn't finished. Walker was at the top of that list. For now, he was housed in the county jail. Hopefully, he wouldn't be joining Janet in the mental health ward at the Oregon State Hospital. I wanted him locked behind bars permanently.

And Doreen's hearing with TSPC was scheduled for mid September. I'd be there. The investigator had taken both my statement and Walker's. Lord knows what he'd said. If it was the truth, it would certainly make my life easier. Someday I might want to return to teaching. For now, I was taking a reprieve, which was just fine with me.

"Mornin' Cousin Roy," Meg said, interrupting my ponderings.

I glanced up and couldn't help but feel pity for him, loaded as he was with Bernice's purchases. The vase was a gaudy mess of scrolls and cupids, a Bernice pleaser, for sure.

Roy's face lit up. "Morning to you, too, cousins."

Shaking my demons aside, I returned his smile. "Hi, Roy. Lovely vase," I teased.

He threw us an exasperated eye-roll, his mouth chewing away on what was sure to be a wad of Black Jack. "Mother's," he muttered.

"And where is your charming mother?" Meg asked.

A twinkle sparkled in Roy's eyes, and his lips twitched before he turned to search the browsing throngs. Several seconds later, he walked off.

"Was it something I said?" Meg mumbled.

At that moment, Bart exited *Levy's Loot*, trailed by an older gentleman. My heart set to pitter-pattering as I watched him hand a fishing pole to the man. While Bart talked, the man ran his fingers up and down the pole and examined it closely. I examined Bart and wished my fingers were running up and down him. As if he sensed my thoughts, he turned and smiled.

"I don't know why you're making me do this?" Bernice's shrill voice was a splash of icy water. Roy was prodding her, not an easy task with his arms loaded.

"Because for once in your life, you're gonna put your feelings aside and do the right thing." I was surprised at how stern his voice was.

"I'm your mother; you can't tell me what to do," Bernice groused. She reached up to pat her hair, as if it would dare to become mussed, and looked everywhere but at me.

"Oh? Seems that's exactly what I *am* doing" he retorted, pushing her in front of me. "Now tell her!"

I gazed up at my only living aunt, at her set scowl and the hate in her eyes, and something inside me twisted painfully. The first thing that popped into my mind popped out of my mouth. "Hi, Bernice. Spending money?"

She recoiled, then snapped, "You don't have to be a bitch about it."

Cripes. The ultimate bitch was calling me a bitch? Actually, my remark had been kind of bitchy. "I'm sorry; that was uncalled for," I told her truthfully. "Is there something you wanted to say?"

She glanced at Roy, then back at me, though her eyes still didn't meet mine. "Thank you for paying Janet's attorney fees," she muttered more under her breath than to me.

"And. . . ." Roy prompted sternly.

"And the bills for her care."

"And. . . ."

"And for not filing charges against her . . . and Roy."

As for Janet, I couldn't shake empathy for where she'd ended up. Because of my mother's impulsive actions, she'd watched her brother die a violent death, which had surely left her more susceptible to Walker's machinations. Paying her bills was the least I could do.

"You're welcome," I told Bernice, hoping this was a step toward resolving our differences.

"Well, actually I don't see why I have to thank you since it was Levy's money you used. Technically, it's more mine than yours anyway," she complained.

Before I could respond, Roy barked, "*Mother!*"

With Bernice, I traveled in circles, pushing but never moving forward, always ending up back where I started. I knew I shouldn't do it, but Bernice was going to get a lecture—from me.

"If that's how you want to see it, go ahead," I told her. "Just don't expect me to bail you out again. And remember the agreement we made: Uncle Jack gets to run the farm as he wants to *and* handle the money generated by the farm. No more interference from you and no more running to Roy for money." I paused to eye Roy's loaded arms. "If I remember right, you're now on a strict allowance."

Bernice was a volcano about to pop, her eyes simmering, her mouth undulating.

I wasn't through. "Roy says Uncle Jack has some sound ideas that could very well turn the farm around. And he's using his money from the sale of the painting to get the farm running again. Give him a chance."

I didn't add that now that Jack was in charge of the farm, the changes in him were startling. No more drinking. As far as I knew, no more gambling. There was a sparkle in his eyes and a kick in his step that hadn't been there before. In no time, he'd be back on Sophie's list of most eligible senior hotties.

Mouth set and penciled brows furled, she looked like I'd just told her she had to sell off her gaudy stuff and expensive jewelry to help out, something she'd already refused to do. "Jack'll blow it; he blows everything," she stormed. "Then it'll be back on my shoulders, only in worse shape than before. Besides, it's none of your business."

"Technically, that's not true, Mother," Roy calmly reminded her.

Bernice glared at him, working her lips, fuming. Roy was right; once the dust settled, I'd discovered that I still owned a small interest in the family farm. Not that I was going to push the matter. I definitely had my fair share of the family inheritance.

"You and Uncle Jack make the farm work, and I'll sign my portion of it over to the two of you," I offered.

Her eyes lit up. "Then I need to be in charge," she insisted.

Roy sighed and rubbed his forehead. "You need to be there for Janet, Mother."

Bernice's whole body drooped; a lost look settled over her.

Somewhere deep inside me, something tugged. "I'm sorry about Janet," I said.

"Well, you should be! If it weren't for you, she'd be home with me instead of in . . . that *place*. You sh. . . ."

"Time for us to take our leave," Roy blurted. He took a couple of steps, looked back and gave her a firm look."

Bernice froze, speechless, mouth open and eyes spitting.

"Come on, Mother. Kit and Meg have work to do," Roy pleaded.

Bernice eyed me, then turned to Bart, who was staring at her, a warning gleam in his eyes. Just like that, air spewed from her mouth in a long sigh and her spunk fizzled. She blinked several times and shuffled towards Roy. As they walked away, Roy threw an *I'm sorry* look over his shoulder.

"Wow," Meg uttered. "And that's all I'm gonna say about that." She shook her head in disbelief, then sighed and stood up. "Roy's right; I gotta get back to the sweat shop before Sophie hauls her tiny ass out here and finds out I'm *socializing*." With that, she slipped into her wedgies and wiggled off.

"Thanks again for the drink . . . and the visit," I yelled after her.

"You bet. Catch you later."

I lodged the rest of my drink between my thighs and rubbed at the pressure above my right eye, then checked my watch—eleven o'clock. Six more hours of looking at people look at old things. And cripes! The smell of that barbecue had my stomach rumbling.

The man who'd been checking out the fishing pole was now digging through a pile of old *Field and Stream*s. Bart left him to plop into the vacant chair. "You okay?" he asked, wrapping a hand around mine, rubbing my thumb with his. It made me feel warm and safe.

"Yeah," I lied, staring into his concerned eyes. "Bernice was just being . . . Bernice. You suppose she and I'll ever be able to sit down to a holiday dinner together?"

"If not, it won't be because you haven't tried."

I had tried. And I'd also tried to understand her bitterness. "I do feel sorry for her, you know. She lost her son Charlie, and now Janet's pretty much lost to her, too. It has to be devastating."

He dropped his forehead forward, his gaze intense. "Bernice chooses to be miserable. From what you've told me about your father, he chose that, too.

"You could've done that. But you stepped out of your safe place and took a chance." His lips softened into a seductive smile. "And because of that, look at what you've got—me. And I'm one very lucky man to have you."

Forever; that's how long I could've sat there with Bart, sharing tender looks.

Unfortunately, the man with the fishing pole was fidgeting and sneaking glances our way. Bart sighed and pushed himself up. "I'd better get back to work. My boss is a tyrant." He stood and eyed my frappe. "You gonna drink that?"

I shook my head. "You can have it."

Before he grabbed the drink and rejoined the angler, he leaned down and gave me a lengthy kiss.

I watched him while I thought about what he'd said. Bart was right; we all make our choices. Lately, I *had* chosen the less safe routes. Where would I be if I hadn't?

For sure, I wouldn't have realized my dreams of having a home of my own, with family and friends who love me and care about me. I wouldn't have a place where belonging is a deep down part of who I am. I wouldn't have a cat who urges me to rise early every morning and enjoy the sunrise. And I wouldn't have Bart, a man I'm learning to love and trust a little more each day.

"Yep, Kit. If you really want it, you gotta go for it," I whispered.

I hoped those words would be with me the next time I doubted my ability to make things happen.

If you enjoyed *Blue Bucket* you might also find *Tattered Lace*, of interest. Set on Central Oregon's High Desert, it is a riveting mystery laced with memorable characters, romance, numerous twists and turns, and a touch of history:

A mysterious letter brings Lizzy Stewart back to her childhood home, one that was written twenty-five years ago. It's a call for help from John Craig, a close childhood friend. All these years she's believed he took his own life, but the letter tells a different story. In her search for the truth, Lizzy packs up the secrets she's clung to far too long and returns to her grandparents' deserted, ramshackle farm. But life on the farm challenges her emotional and physical wellbeing. As she attempts to pull together the remnants of her tattered life and solve the puzzle of John's death, she's plagued by bittersweet memories and unsettling threats. And by Sam Craig, John's older brother and her closest neighbor.

Sam Craig has his own problems, all of them sparked by Lizzy's return. From the moment Lizzy rises out of the dark corner in the dreary farmhouse, he's hounded by unsettling memories he's tried hard to forget and by the all too familiar hold she has on him. He wants Lizzy gone and his humdrum life back. As he tries to figure out why she's returned and finagle a way to keep his cattle on her land, he slowly realizes that he's the only person who's not privy to the frayed web of life-altering secrets and lies lurking about. There are strange goings-on around the Stewart farm, and Sam is determined to get to the bottom of them. Soon it becomes apparent that he has a bigger problem: if Lizzy doesn't leave the farm, she just might end up dead.

Suzanne Grant, who spent her growing-up years in Central Oregon, is enamored of her state's beauty, its people, and its historical mysteries. Prevalent in her writing is her fascination with the ways in which the past reaches out to influence who we are today. She enjoys weaving mystery-driven tales that transport readers into unique times and places.

Made in the USA
Charleston, SC
23 January 2013